HOPE BYTHEWAY

Wandering Strong

Book One of the Coeur Legacy

With love and gratitude...
For my mother, Edith Robina Hope Williams,
whose strength lives on in every word.

For Amber, Jade, Alex, and Reuben,
my greatest joys and reason to keep going.

For Cal,
who reminded me I could do this.

And for Tom Hollander,
whose screen presence became a voice on the page
and reminded me how to feel deeply.

Preface

At the Hay Festival, some years ago, actor Tom Hollander was asked what character he would most like to play.

He answered without hesitation: *an Elizabethan jester.*

That moment was a spark, quick as flint striking steel, and it caught in my imagination. From it grew a tale of jest and shadow, of love and loss, and of a jester who bears his name.

In shaping him, I drew on the adaptability I've seen in Tom Hollander's work — the way he moves between comedy and gravity, wit and stillness, each role carrying a different shade. These nuances became threads woven into my Tom's soul.

Though he did not know it, a single answer set this story on its path.

Prologue

Visions and dreams swept through her, a gathering storm,
    Past and present collided, a truth began to form.
    Friends and foes contended to claim
    A life, a love, and a name.
    Now travel with me to a Mistress true,
    To future dreams of hazy hue.
    Will she ever find a true home of her own?

* * *

Farran lived on an ordinary street, no drama, just peace. It was a place she had known for years; people came and went, but she remained. Nothing in her life was untoward, nothing exciting, just steadfast friends and a steady job she loved.

Yet her life was about to change into something unrecognisable, intangible. To find the truth, she would have to encounter the unbelievable. Become the unbelievable. But could she?

1

Restless Dawn (2018)

A face blurred in the gold-framed mirror that hung crookedly on the plain wall. At first, it was only a shadow... then it began to beckon, slowly, deliberately. Its features flickered into focus: eyes wide with warning, or was it an invitation? It was hard to tell. Then, just as suddenly as it had formed, the image shattered into a jumble of pixels, as if the mirror itself had glitched.

Beckoning again, the face reformed, but this time it wasn't a face at all. The glass rippled, melted, and resolved into a garden scene: a place long lost to time. Spring flowers bloomed in neat beds. Deftly clipped bushes lined a path that curled through a perfectly mown lawn. At its centre, a fountain danced, scattering sunlight like a spray of gems. Somewhere, birds were singing. Somewhere... the garden still lived.

Home.

Farran's eyes blinked open, adjusting slowly to the dark. A fog of unfinished business and restless longing clung to her mind. The bedside clock glared: **3:04 a.m.**, its red digits vivid against black.

She groaned softly, turned onto her side, and tugged the duvet to her chin, willing sleep to return. It didn't.

The dream returned instead, insistent, twisting, images churning in her head like a storm. Each restless toss only fed them, the pressure building, pounding behind her eyes. It pressed down like a weight, aching through her nerves.

Finally, she gave in. With a frustrated toss, she threw off the duvet and swung her legs over the bed. Her feet sank into the rough carpet; cool air kissed her skin. The hem of her cotton nightdress slipped to her knees. She shivered.

Dragging unwilling limbs across the dark room, she reached for her fleecy dressing gown. She didn't turn on the light. That would make it real, admitting the dream had followed her into the waking.

So she moved through the shadows instead, letting them cling to her like mist. Down the stairs, one careful step at a time. Into the kitchen. Each footfall muffled, each breath a quiet rebellion. She moved in a dull haze, willing the images away, clinging to the stillness before dawn.

Her bare feet tapped the cold linoleum as she crossed to the silver fridge freezer. She opened the door. A harsh stream of white light spilt out, slicing the dark. She blinked, eyes slow to adjust, and reached for the milk.

Setting it on the grey worktop beside the microwave, she reached into the cupboard above. Her hand knocked against a mug. It clinked loudly against another, a bright chime that shattered the silence. Farran jumped, her heart thudding. She muttered under her breath. *What was wrong with me?*

The images had been haunting her sleep for weeks, vivid, insistent. But now they came harder, faster, tangled with a sense of urgency she couldn't explain; A warning written in a language just beyond understanding.

She picked a mug with an owl curling across its side, poured in the milk, and slid it into the microwave. The door clicked shut; she stabbed at the buttons. The machine hummed, low and steady, comfortingly ordinary, though it barely dented the unease coiling in her gut.

As the microwave hummed, Farran leaned against the counter, arms folded tight. Her thoughts drifted back to fragments of the dream.

It had been too serene, unnaturally so. A vast grassy expanse stretched before her like an emerald quilt, its scent sweet and hauntingly familiar. Along the edges, flowers bloomed in vivid bursts, swaying in a spring breeze she could still feel on her skin.

In the centre, a fountain rose from an ornate pond, flinging glittering arcs of water skyward. Droplets twisted and fell in a rhythm that felt endless.

Behind her, though she had never turned, she somehow knew a gravel path led to a towering building. Hedges lined the pathway, shaped into spiralling columns with obsessive care.
But how could she know that? She'd never seen it.

Still, every detail clung to her memory like a scar. She could hear the hedges rustle, feel sunlight warming her face, and smell flowers mingled with damp stone.
These weren't just dreams.
They were visits.
And that was what unsettled her most. They felt real.
More real, even, than the sleepy Shropshire town she'd known all her life.

Her temples throbbed. The pressure returned, tight, creeping, wrapping around her skull. She squeezed her eyes shut, but the images only burned brighter.

The microwave pinged, snapping her back to the present. She opened the door and took out the owl mug, its warmth seeping into her hands as steam curled gently into the air.

Without turning on the light, she padded to the living room. Her favourite chair, an old wing-back upholstered in faded green velvet, waited in its usual corner. Next to it sat a small wooden table, just big enough for a mug, a remote, and the half-read books she never quite finished.

She set the mug down and curled into the seat, pulling her dressing gown close, feet tucked beneath her like a child warding off a storm. Reaching forward, she clicked on the radio. The soft strains of '*Flow My Tears, Fall from Your Springs*' drifted into the room, candlelight woven into sound. She exhaled.

This was what she needed. Dowland's music always grounded her, a balm for sleepless nights. It stirred something long buried, a sense of safety she couldn't place. Lately, her thoughts had turned strange, foreign, even. It was as though they didn't belong to her.

The music swelled, then faded.

She reached for her mug, grateful for its warmth, as silence folded around her once more.

"*That was 'Flow My Tears, Fall from Your Springs*' by John Dowland," came the radio voice, smooth, low, intimate against the hush of morning. "We'll be celebrating the work of this astounding composer until four. I hope you'll stay with me."

There was a wry warmth to his tone, as if he knew she was his only listener.

"Next, *Gloria Tibi Trinitas*, another piece steeped in quiet power. Let it carry you somewhere old and still."

Music returned, soft and enveloping. Farran leaned back, letting it wrap around her like a familiar blanket. She sipped her drink slowly. She'd heard this show before. That voice, gentle, steady, had a way of curling around words like it knew their weight. What was his name? It hovered just beyond reach, like a tune half-remembered. She could have listened to him for hours, lost in that voice, dreaming of... What, exactly? A garden blooming beyond time? A face she almost knew, always turning away? A love she hadn't met ... or had forgotten? A darkness just out of reach? She shook her head. Why did her mind keep circling back to these half-formed visions?

Gripping the anchor of the announcer's voice, she nudged the thoughts aside and took another slow sip of milk. And then, as if summoned by the music, drowsiness returned, gentler this time. She let it take her.

She woke with a jolt, briefly disoriented. The radio was still on, but the music had gone, replaced by a clipped, unfamiliar voice.

6:29. The square wall clock confirmed it.

"...Easter Monday," the announcer said, voice brisk. "Time for the morning news."

Farran sat still, letting the date settle strangely in her mind. Then she stretched, limbs stiff but less sore than usual. Rising, she padded into the kitchen. The faint scent of milk and sleep lingered. Pale daylight pressed against the closed blinds. She drew them open, blinking as the brightness spilt across the walls.

Outside, her eyes drifted over the enclosed backyard, her garden, though it barely earned the name. A tall brick wall enclosed it, stealing the warmth of the sun. The wooden gate, high and solid, stood guard like a sentinel.

No grass grew beneath her window, only cold, grey slabs of concrete. A lone plant pot clung to the edge, its rosemary tuft the sole spark of life. In the far corner, a small brick shed leaned against the wall. Once an outdoor toilet, it sheltered dusty crates, forgotten relics hiding silent secrets.

The back door, streaked brown, held two frosted glass panes split by a slender wooden beam carved into twin arches. Sunlight struggled past the heavy wall, casting shadows that felt like more than just stone; barriers both seen and unseen. Her mind flickered to the garden from her dreams, wild, vast, bursting with colour, and she blinked, letting the vision slip away with a slow, wistful sigh.

Farran moved through the kitchen, preparing breakfast. She filled the silver kettle from the matching taps, set it on its black base, and switched it on. Crossing the room, she opened a cupboard and took down a white ceramic bowl. From below the counter, she scooped muesli into it, then fetched milk from the fridge and poured a splash over the cereal.

The kettle bubbled loudly, then clicked off. A mug sat ready with a teabag; she poured in the boiling water, added a splash of milk, and stirred absent-mindedly. Fishing out the teabag, she flicked it into the food caddy by the sink.

Back in the living room, the radio played a soft selection of tunes. She set down her mug and sank into her chair, eyes drifting around the room. Heavy dark green curtains hung over the bay windows, blocking much of the morning light and tinting the room with a muted emerald glow.

To the left of the window, a television hung above a small shelf holding a DVD player, the radio, and a modest collection of DVDs. Farran's laptop usually rested there too, but today it was tucked beneath the table.

On the adjacent wall, a clock ticked steadily beneath a portrait of a stern Elizabethan man. His hard gaze seemed to follow her wherever she went. Farran often wondered why she kept the painting, yet it gave her a strange comfort. She never thought to move it, and it sparked curiosity among guests, though she had little to say about it.

Rising, she pulled back the curtains, flooding the room with daylight. Outside paving slabs led from the front door to the tarmac, a solitary pot of rue standing amid a barren stretch of concrete. Across the way, rows of Edwardian houses stood tightly joined, stretching as far as she could see. Farran had lived here as long as she could remember, watching neighbours come and go. Leaving had never crossed her mind.

Back at her seat, she began breakfast, forcing herself not to dwell on the restless night. Slowly, tension eased, muscles unwinding with each breath. Finally, she relaxed.

Her phone flashed softly, chiming a simple tune. Elwyna's name lit the screen. A smile spread across Farran's face. Best friends forever, never tired of each other's company. She eagerly accepted the call.

"Hi, Farr, how are you?" Elwyna's voice was bright and warm. "I haven't heard from you all Easter. Just wanted to check you're okay." The excitement made Farran chuckle softly.

"Hi, Elv, I'm good, ta," Farran replied, matching her cheer. "Quiet time before work. You?"

A pang of guilt pricked her; she hadn't been truthful, but she didn't want to worry Elwyna. There was nothing to fret over.

"Daryll and I went to Paris for our anniversary," Elwyna exclaimed. "So romantic! Can you believe we've been married 30 years and he still surprises me?"

"Oh wow, Elv. That's lovely," Farran said. "We must meet for a cuppa so you can tell me all about it."

"What are you doing today?" Elwyna asked. "Bank holiday, you have the day off, right?"

"I'm going in," Farran said carefully. "It'll be quiet. There's a lot to do with the new exhibition starting soon." Several items still needed to be catalogued for the Stevens family, a Cotswold line with ties to Shrewsbury.

Secretly, Farran relished the museum's stillness when it was empty. Being surrounded by the past gave her a satisfaction that nowhere else could.

"Farr, you work too hard," Elwyna's voice held playful disappointment. "How about tonight? That Italian restaurant in the square always serves a decent meal. Bet you haven't eaten properly!" Mischief laced her tone.

"Okay, that sounds great," Farran laughed, giving in. "I finish around four, meet you there just after?"

"Great!" Elwyna said. "Table booked for 4:30."

"Perfect. See you later."

"See you," Elwyna said.

Farran smiled as the call ended. She took her breakfast things and the mug she'd used overnight to the kitchen, quickly washing up and wiping surfaces. Then she headed upstairs to get ready.

Farran stepped into bright sunshine, closing the blue wooden door behind her and turning the key with a satisfying click. She slipped the key into her bag and walked down the short path of slabs to the pavement. Her eyes lingered on the grey concrete garden. She decided to get a few pots and flowers to brighten the space, wondering why she hadn't before.

The morning sun warmed her as she walked, glad for light trousers and a flowing top. Her jacket hung over one arm, and deck shoes padded softly. A cool breeze tousled her hair. She loved mornings like this, walking to work, clearing the clutter swirling in her mind.

Minutes later, Farran left the quiet street behind, heading down the main road toward the town centre. Ahead, the red sandstone walls of the Abbey loomed, a magnificent sight in its heyday.

Built on the site of a wooden chapel in 1083 by Roger de Montgomery, the original structure once stretched across the road. The pulpit still stood in a small garden opposite, a silent witness to the past. Now, cars rumbled by, oblivious. It saddened Farran how people discarded their past, uninterested in stories that shaped them.

She glanced up as she passed the building. Not today, but soon she would stop to take in its full majesty. The clock tower bell chimed the hour: seven, eight, nine, ten. She'd hoped to be at work by now, but recalled that she needed the library first. Quickening her pace, she pressed on.

Her route took her beneath the Victorian railway bridge, past the old grammar school, and over English Bridge spanning the rushing Severn. She passed shops and a car park before beginning the steep climb up Wyle Cop, a street lined with shops and pubs curving past the Lion Hotel, then branching onto Dogpole.

At the top stood St Mary's Church, brickwork darkened by years of petrol fumes. Turning the corner, she reached Castle Street, walking past larger shops toward the library, once Shrewsbury School, where Charles Darwin had studied.

She reached the library steps, slightly breathless but pressing on. Climbing stone steps, she followed the path past Darwin's statue, seated thoughtfully in his chair. The path curved beneath a stone archway to the building's rear. There, she unlocked the staff door and stepped into a long corridor. A beeping alarm sounded, a warning of a possible intruder. Farran hurried to the control panel and entered the code. Silence returned.

Down the corridor, Farran reached the storeroom. She fumbled in her bag for the lanyard holding her badge and black fob. Pressing the fob to a small black panel, a green light flickered and a beep confirmed access. She turned the handle and pushed open the door, stepping inside as lights flickered on.

Rows of shelves stretched before her, packed with books and boxes holding centuries of history. A musty scent hung, an aroma of days past and knowledge not to be forgotten. Farran went straight to the Stephens family archive shelf and gathered a selection of books, sliding them into her bag alongside a small box. Satisfied, she left the storeroom and stepped back into the street, ready to walk the short distance to the museum.

Farran walked down the pedestrianised Pride Hill, where a few people leisurely strolled. She enjoyed these quieter moments, free from weaving through crowds. Reaching the corner at the hill's base, she followed the pavement curving into High Street.

More people gathered here, drawn by charity stalls in the town square. Farran paused opposite a weather-worn statue, overlooking the road and facing a former fire station, now a bank. After checking traffic, she crossed and headed toward the old stone market hall.

The market hall, a beautiful two-storey structure with arches opening onto the ground floor, echoed softly under her footsteps as she passed through the front arch and emerged through the rear. Bathed in sunlight ahead stood the majestic music hall, now the town's museum.

The grand white building rose in three tiers. On the ground floor, original wooden doors were replaced by automatic glass ones. Flanking them were large windows, an estate agent's office on the left and the tourist information centre on the right. Above, windows recessed behind stately pillars, topped by a subtly decorated triangular roof.

Farran stepped inside, feeling her load heavier than it was at the start. She moved through the echoing entrance hall toward the office door. Nearby, the café was buzzing softly with muffled chatter and clinking cups. She made a mental note to return later for a drink, and perhaps some cake, after unloading.

Turning left, she entered a red-carpeted area with stairs leading up. At the top, a white door on her right beckoned. She pushed it open, relieved to reach her destination, and sighed as she approached a clear desk to set down her load.

Nearby, a cluttered desk held a phone. She checked it, shaking the stiffness from her arms; no messages. Good. Now, start sorting or get that cuppa and cake? The latter won, and she headed back to the café with a small smile.

Returning to the office with goodies in hand, Farran headed straight to the desk where she'd placed the library materials. Carefully, she began organising the documents while sipping her hot drink. Gradually, she lost herself in the Stephens family history; the drama and turmoil of one family was heartbreaking.

She'd found some information online before, but now hoped to uncover much more. Why she felt such a deep connection to people long gone, she didn't know, but the feeling was real and grew stronger with each new detail.

Excitedly, Farran pieced the jigsaw together, watching stories unfold before her eyes. The family spanned back centuries, growing into an influential dynasty, until tragedy struck and changed everything.

So engrossed, time slipped away unnoticed. When her mobile phone rang suddenly, she jumped, as if flung from the past into the present. For a moment, disoriented, she reached for the phone on the desk and "Hey, Farr," came a familiar voice, teasingly giggling. "Thought I'd give you an alarm call."

"Oh! Hi, Elv," Farran said, still feeling pulled back to the present.

"Are you alright?" Concern crept into Elwyna's voice. "You sound a little out of it."

"I'm fine, really," Farran replied, shaking her head. "Caught up in the research, lost all sense of time." She glanced at the clock, nearly four o'clock. Where had the hours gone? She'd been working solidly, even forgetting to eat. Her stomach growled.

"That's why I rang," Elwyna said softly. "You'd better get ready for the restaurant. Bet you haven't eaten properly."

"I had a little," Farran admitted, thinking of the cake earlier.

"A cake's not enough," Elwyna laughed softly.

"You know me too well," Farran chuckled. "Give me ten minutes, I'll be ready."

"Okay," Elwyna replied. "See you soon."

Farran glanced at the piles of information on the desk. She'd done well so far, but the pull of history kept her lingering longer than planned.

Twenty minutes later, Farran stepped into the warm buzz of the busy Italian restaurant, the cool spring air still brushing her face. She spotted Elwyna near the back and gave a small wave. Elwyna returned a bright smile, her blue eyes sparkling; Farran eased off her bag and jacket, draping them over the empty chair before settling opposite her friend.

"Hi. How are you?" Farran bubbled, her smile brightening. "You look fabulous."

Elwyna's elf-like face lit up, framed by short chestnut hair. "I'm good. How are you?" Her eyes narrowed playfully, as if seeing past Farran's cheer.

"I'm good," Farran replied, picking up the menu.

Elwyna studied her for a moment. "Mmm... you look tired." She raised a dark eyebrow, tone gentle but probing. Farran felt vulnerability flicker. Elwyna always knew when something was wrong.

Farran forced a light laugh. "Of course. Just one of those dreams last night. I fell asleep in the chair." She tucked a loose strand behind her ear, avoiding admitting it was the third or fourth restless night recently. "Plus, Darnell's still a pain. Don't understand his problem." She shuddered slightly at the name.

"You should tell him where to get off," Elwyna said, leaning forward, eyes sparkling with mischief. "Who does he think he is?"

Farran sighed, fiddling with the neatly folded napkin, pushing back irritation. "Only a few more weeks. Then he goes back where he came from."

Elwyna smiled knowingly and shifted the subject. "Enough work talk. Tell me about your amazing husband and your weekend away."

"Okay, I'll save that for later," Elwyna grinned. "We'll catch up after we order. So, what do you want?"

Farran hesitated, then smiled. "A margarita and a small glass of wine."

Elwyna laughed softly. "Predictable."

They caught the waiter's eye, placed orders, then slipped into easy conversation.

"It sounds fantastic," Farran said as Elwyna recounted her weekend. "You're lucky to have Daryll."

Elwyna's smile softened. "You'll meet someone soon," she said warmly.

Farran looked down, a shadow crossing her smile. "I don't think so. I'm nearly fifty. Who'd want me?"

"Well, funny you say that," Elwyna teased. Farran groaned inwardly. "I met someone I think you'd like."

Farran's stomach tightened. This wasn't Elwyna's first matchmaking attempt, and none ended well.

"I don't know, Elv," she hesitated. "It's never worked before…"

"Just come meet him," Elwyna pressed gently, squeezing Farran's hand. "He's coming for drinks Thursday at seven-thirty. It'll be fun." She looked pleadingly, and Farran laughed.

"Okay, I'll come for drinks. But no promises I'll stay!"

"At least you're coming," Elwyna smiled. "Daryll said you wouldn't."

"Don't gloat yet, I might change my mind," Farran warned, raising an eyebrow. "What's his name?"

"Tom. Tom Gester."

A sharp prickle raced across Farran's skin. She was sure she'd heard the name, but where? She pushed the thought aside as they chatted and laughed.

Finishing their meal, Elwyna winked. "See you Thursday."

Farran smiled, shaking her head. "Yes."

They hugged tightly, savouring friendship's comfort, before going their separate ways into the night.

2

The Seal and the Shadows

A face blurred in the gold-framed mirror hanging on the plain wall of a long corridor. The light around it shimmered unnaturally, as if the very air were breathing. It beckoned as it flickered into focus. Grey-green eyes stared intently at her. Dark hair, threaded with silver, framed a softly rounded face with a tender mouth and a slender nose. There was a hint of stubble. A voice whispered, low, broken, desperate, but the words slipped past her understanding like water through fingers. Her heart clenched. She knew that voice. Then, just as quickly, the face disintegrated into a jumbled mash of pixels. Gone. The corridor grew darker, as if the mirror had taken its light with it.

Farran jolted awake, heart pounding, mind tangled in confusion. The clock's red digits glared back at her: **3:04**. Again.

Night had become a predictable torment, each hour a reflection of the one before. What was the point in lying there? Sleep had already fled. With a soft sigh, she threw off the covers and padded to the kitchen.

Her nightly ritual unfolded: tea brewing, radio clicking on, confusion swirling with restlessness. She settled into the quiet, letting the presenter's gentle tones wash over her. His voice was a soothing thread in the darkness, almost intimate, as if he knew exactly what she needed to hear. She half expected him to say her name. Absurd, she thought. Sleeplessness was unravelling her grip on reality. But then something he said pulled her from the haze.

"This next piece was, apparently, a favourite of Richard Stephens, an Elizabethan magistrate from 1592 in the county of Gloucester. There's an exhibition at Shrewsbury Museum over the next few weeks, exploring his life and times. It's believed he had ties here through his third wife, Anne Kery. So, if you're in the area, be sure to stop by... Now, sit back and enjoy '*Ave Verum Corpus*' by William Byrd, published in 1605, though likely composed earlier."

Farran sat transfixed as the room filled with a soft, mournful voice drifting through the airwaves. How did he know so much about Richard Stevens, someone she was still trying to understand?

Her gaze flicked to the painting on the wall. The painted eyes seemed sharper tonight, harsher. Were there more lines etched into the face? No, just her imagination playing tricks. She looked away, unable to hold its gaze. What's the matter with me? she thought. It's just a painting, for goodness' sake.

She shifted in her seat, trying to block it from view, but her breathing quickened. Panic crept in, thin, sharp, and unexpected. On impulse, she switched the channel. A thudding bass line filled the room, club music pounding through her chest like a second heartbeat, pushing the panic back. She let the beat play on, its rhythm filling the silence, and rose to make another drink.

When she returned, she changed the station again. This time, soft jazz spilt into the room, low and comforting. She left it playing and curled back into the chair. Her mind still raced, thoughts tangled and knotted, but the music wrapped around her like a blanket. Slowly, calm began to seep in. Bit by bit, she began to unwind. Finally, sleep found her, quiet and kind.

6:29. Farran jolted awake. Pale morning light slipped through the curtains, streaking across the room. She groaned and stretched, muscles stiff with the shock of waking. Skipping her usual morning drink, she shuffled upstairs to the bathroom, slow, heavy-limbed, as the day began to call.

Sunlight filtered through the frosted glass, bathing the small room in warm, golden hues. She brushed her teeth methodically, then turned on the shower. Water cascaded down, its steady rhythm like soft rain dancing in her ears. She slipped out of her nightdress, the fabric whispering to the floor, and dipped a tentative toe under the spray. Perfect.

Encouraged, she stepped in fully. The warmth embraced her skin. She let herself relax, standing still beneath the stream, simply savouring the sensation. She reached for the shampoo and massaged the cool, raspberry-scented gel into her scalp. The fragrance enveloped her like a spring breeze, as bubbles foamed, cleansing and refreshing.

Next, she lathered a rich red gel over her body. Each stroke seemed to lift away the remnants of a restless night, washing aches and tension down the drain. She lingered beneath the jets, letting the water's gentle pressure soothe her skin. Finally, she turned off the water and stepped out, reaching for the fluffy red towel on the rail. Wrapping it around herself, she felt a quiet comfort settle in as she prepared for the day.

Now dressed, Farran padded into the kitchen. Morning light spilt across the countertops, soft and familiar. She slipped into routine: a strong cup of tea, a bowl of muesli. She chuckled, quietly amused by her predictability. The same breakfast, for years.

Her mind drifted to the dreams again, growing more vivid, more insistent with each passing night. They pressed at the edges of her waking thoughts, intense and persistent, yet everything else remained stubbornly unchanged. She gave her head a small shake, as if she could dislodge the unease, banish the confusion before it took hold.

Tea in hand, she glanced out the window, then gathered her things and set off for the museum. She was grateful for yesterday's head start. A flicker of relief settled beneath the tension that still clung to her.

The moment she stepped into the office, Darnell Stenet's presence hit her like a wall. He'd joined a few weeks earlier as a temporary assistant curator, meant to support her with the Stephens exhibition. But from the first moment, she'd found him utterly disagreeable, abrasive in a way that set her nerves on edge. His sullen expression seemed to drain the light from the room. Uneasy didn't quite cover it. A flicker of apprehension twisted in her gut. Instinctively, she kept her distance. But with the exhibition looming, dodging him had become harder by the day.

She swallowed, steadying her breath. Today, like too many lately, she braced for the inevitable: the snide comments, the sneering glances, that constant sense of being watched and judged before she'd even spoken.

Darnell stood at the desk, surveying the carefully arranged piles of notes she'd left the day before. He wore his usual blue suit jacket over an open-necked white shirt, the effect undermined by the worn jeans. His brown hair was cropped short, rigid, unmoving, as if even it resisted softness.

At the sound of the door clicking shut, he glanced up. Her skin prickled. His ice-blue eyes met hers, and a chill ran down her spine. That gaze always left her uneasy. A quiet tension coiled in her stomach, tightening like a noose.

"Morning, Farran," he drawled, voice slick with something unnameable.

"Looks like you were in yesterday. Getting ahead?" He nodded toward the stacked papers.

"Yes. I had the time, so I thought I'd get started." She moved toward her desk, widening the space between them.

"Shame you didn't say." He met her eyes with a slow, unsettling stare. His lips twisted into a leering smirk. "I wasn't doing anything."

Farran's jaw tightened. "I'm sure your wife appreciated the company," she said coolly, wondering who could tolerate a man like him. Something in his voice made her skin crawl; it felt... rehearsed.

He gave a low chuckle, licking his lips as he rifled through a stack. "Yeah... come to think of it, we did enjoy the day."

Eager to break the tension, Farran glanced at her phone, pretending to scroll. She exhaled quietly, then reached for the papers she'd marked out yesterday. Her fingers trembled faintly as she flipped through the pages. She steadied herself; there was work to do. The collection was due that afternoon.

Still not looking up, she murmured, "Plenty left to sort."

"What time's the collection arriving?" Darnell asked, as if reading her mind.

"One o'clock," she replied, eyes fixed on the text.

"So what's this guy's connection to Shrewsbury? Thought he was from Gloucester," Darnell said, tone casual but probing.

"That's what I'm digging into," she replied, her voice lifting slightly. "His third wife, Anne Kery, is the link..."

"But she's from Gloucester too, isn't she?" he snapped.

The sharpness in his tone made her blink. "She was, but the link's through one of Richard's associates, Henry Bromwell... or Bromley. Something like that."

"Bromley. Henry Bromley," Darnell repeated, too quickly. Farran looked up, not just at the tone, but at the name itself. It struck a chord.

"You sound like you've heard of him," she said, studying his face.

He shook his head, slow and measured. "No. Just came up at a previous exhibition."
But her unease returned; he was hiding something.

"Maybe you could help me dig into his background," she said lightly, watching for his reaction.

"I doubt I'd be much help," he said, dry as dust. Then, with careful precision, he shrugged off his jacket and hung it over the back of his chair. Papers shuffled. Silence thickened.

Farran watched him shuffle aimlessly through the mess. Feigned busyness. She wasn't fooled. His movements were tight. Too deliberate. Something was off.
Was it nerves?

They worked in silence, heavy and taut. Farran sifted papers. Darnell tapped rhythmically at the keyboard. Minutes dragged. The air between them thickened, unspoken, unresolved, until lunchtime arrived like a breath held too long.

Finally, Farran stood and stretched, working out the stiffness in her limbs. She headed down to the café, hoping a short break might soothe the unease building inside her. Soon she returned with drinks and sandwiches, setting them down gently between them. Moments later, the sharp ring of her desk phone broke the silence.

"Farran Armstrong," she answered briskly, blinking herself back to the present.

Darnell glanced up, alert.

"Fantastic!" Farran exclaimed into the receiver. "Yes, we'll be right down."

"It's here?" Darnell asked, already rising.

She nodded. "Come on, let's take a look."

They moved quickly through the building, footsteps echoing in rhythm. Darnell seemed unusually animated, almost likeable, though Farran wasn't ready to trust it. They reached the exhibition hall.

The room was flooded with light. Spotlights framed a wide window where boxes and crates lay scattered across the floor. Plinths and display cases stood ready, waiting. Farran knelt beside one of the opened crates and gently peeled back layers of packaging.

"Do you have the sheet for this one?" she asked a staff member, who handed it over with a nod.

Darnell joined her, visibly eager.

"Shall we do this together?" he asked, his smile disarming.

She hesitated, then nodded.

They unpacked side by side, Farran describing each item while Darnell checked them off. Colleagues placed the artefacts into displays, adding handwritten labels with quiet efficiency. The room buzzed with energy, focused, collaborative, quietly thrilling.

Near the bottom of the crate, Farran's fingers closed around a small box, about the size of a watch case. She eased it into the light, her hands instinctively careful. Lifting the lid with deliberate precision, she uncovered a seal nestled within.

The handle was unusual, wooden, bulbous, and slightly worn by time. The base gleamed: silver, highly polished. She turned it over and caught her breath.

There it was: the Stephens crest.

A winged sphinx with plaited hair, enclosed within a shield. Beneath it, a single word etched in fine lettering:

Secretum.

Secret.

A tremor passed through her body. The lights around her dimmed, as if some unseen veil had fallen. A shadow, soft and steady, slipped silently to her side, unseen by others but keenly felt, an ancient presence guiding her away from the crate. Her feet moved before her mind could follow, drawn by something beyond reason.

Colours bloomed behind her eyelids, vivid, startling, like fragments of forgotten memories surfacing from deep beneath the surface. A whisper brushed through her thoughts, soft, urgent, unintelligible, but carrying the weight of secrets that had slipped through the cracks of time. A sharp ache bloomed behind her eyes, followed by a rolling wave of nausea.

"Farran! Farran!"

He crouched beside her, face etched with concern. "Are you okay? What happened?"

She blinked, struggling to focus. The room slid back into place, the fog receding. A scent drifted by: rosemary. Clean, sharp, grounding.

Her voice came out thin, a breath more than a word. A box appeared before her, silent, perfectly timed, and she reached for it just as the nausea crested. Quiet, grateful relief. Moments later, a cool glass pressed into her hands. She drank deeply, the cold water soothing her throat, steadying her nerves.

Darnell gently prised the seal from her grip. He turned it over, studying the details, eyes narrowing slightly. For a moment, something flickered across his face, recognition? Surprise? And then it was gone.

"It's an interesting design, isn't it?" Farran managed, her voice steadier now.

A flush rose to her cheeks.
    Embarrassment.
    Confusion.
    And something else, something she couldn't yet name.

Darnell nodded distractedly. "It is," he said, handing the seal to a woman nearby. "Put it straight into cabinet three."

Then he turned back to Farran, his gaze narrowing. "What happened to you?"

"I don't know," she said honestly. "I was fine, then suddenly this wave just... hit me."
    She took another sip of water, grateful for its cool, steadying calm.

"How are you feeling now?"
    His hand rested lightly on her shoulder.

She froze. The touch was soft, even caring, but her spine tightened, instinct flaring sharp beneath her skin. The urge to pull away buzzed just under the surface.

"I'm fine," she said, shifting in the chair. "Whatever it was, it's passed. Probably just the excitement."

Darnell smiled, the tension in his face easing. "Yeah, I can see that. Go get some fresh air, we'll pick up in twenty."

Farran stood, brushing her hands down the front of her skirt, grateful for the excuse to move. She stepped outside into a rush of spring air, warm sunlight washing over her like balm. The pressure in her chest loosened with each breath. She hadn't realised just how tightly wound she'd been until the threads began to slip free.

She wandered to a quiet wooden bench overlooking the town square and sank with a sigh. Around her, planter boxes overflowed with colour: pansies, tulips, trailing lobelia. A few pigeons strutted across the flagstones, pecking at invisible crumbs, unfazed by the passing feet. Stillness settled around her like a soft blanket.
  For now, at least, she could breathe.

She became aware of a shadow beside her and turned to see Darnell standing quietly by the bench.

"Would you mind if I sat with you?" he asked, voice low, almost cautious.

Farran hesitated a fraction, a flicker of warning, but then shook her head. He lowered himself onto the bench beside her. She shifted slightly, keeping a polite distance.

"Are you alright? Really?" His tone softened, carrying a note of concern, sincere, perhaps, or at least expertly practised.

Farran met his eyes briefly, searching for truth beneath the surface. Was this a rare moment of kindness, or another move to unsettle her? She chose to trust the moment, at least for now. "Yes, I'm fine. Really," she said softly...

"Simon and Daphne are checking that the labels are correct," Darnell added, falling back into his usual drawl.

She began to move, "I should go and clean up."

He watched her closely, the faintest crease of tension returning to his brow. "No, it's okay," he said, voice low, following her movement with his eyes. "Daphne's sorted it."

That small, watching look unsettled her more than any harsh word ever had.

"That was thoughtful of her. A flush crept into Farran's cheeks, embarrassment prickling at the thought of someone else tidying up after her.

"You know Daphne," he said quietly. "She just gets on with things." Then, after a pause: "She's worried about you."

He stood too, stepping closer. "We all are. You've been looking pale. Tired."

His hand reached for hers. Farran jerked back instinctively, her voice sharper than intended. "I'm fine. Just a few bad nights. Nothing to worry about."

She didn't wait for a reply. Chin lifted, pulse racing, she walked briskly toward the museum doors. The dreams. The scent. The seal.
    None of it concerned him... did it?

* * *

Darnell remained still, watching her disappear through the glass into the vaulted hush.

He had wanted to tell her he'd felt it too; that wave of nausea, the flicker of something ancient when his fingers brushed the seal. The ghost-scent of rosemary. The whisper that didn't belong in this world.

He exhaled slowly, jaw tight. The memories surged, faces, voices, the weight of choices made long ago. They weren't dreams. They were real.
And still, the same question gnawed at him:
How much damage had he already done?
A bitter laugh escaped.
Recent memories.
What a joke.

Pushing the thought aside, he shook his head and followed her path back inside.

* * *

The rest of the unpacking went without a hitch. Soon, only the paintings remained to be hung. Farran strolled between the plinths and cabinets, admiring the items on loan for the exhibition: silver buckles, lace cuffs, letters written in a tight hand, tokens of grief and ceremony. Darnell joined her.

"It looks good, doesn't it?" she said quietly.

"It does," he replied.

They strolled around the room for a moment in companionable silence.

"I'm looking forward to seeing the paintings up," Farran added. "They'll have to wait until tomorrow, though. A few more pieces are still due to arrive; some were in storage and missed the shipment."

Darnell nodded but said nothing. His gaze had drifted. He stopped in front of the cabinet housing the seal. It sat beside a set of quills, an ink pot, a selection of yellowed letters and a diary. The soft backlighting cast warm glints across the polished glass, as if the past itself were being coaxed into view.

Farran joined him, her eyes on the seal. "It's an interesting design," she murmured.

"Yes," Darnell replied, his voice distant. "A family of secrets."

There was a weight in his tone, too heavy for a casual comment. Farran turned, studying his face. His eyes were slightly hooded, unreadable.

"I get the feeling you know more about Richard Stephens than you're letting on," she said, frowning.

He gave a soft laugh, evasive, practised. "Just an educated guess. Any crest with a sphinx usually suggests there's something to hide."

"I suppose," she said, still watching him. Her fingers tingled, an odd and sudden urge rising, impulsive, insistent, to reach into the case and touch the seal again. Not now, she told herself, forcing the feeling down.

They turned as footsteps echoed across the tiled floor behind them. Daphne approached, her face alight with happiness.

"Thank you so much for earlier, that really isn't in your job description," Farran said with a laugh, though inwardly she cringed.

"No problem," Daphne beamed. "It's been quite an exciting day."

Darnell nodded. "Yes. It has."

"Have you and Simon finished for today?" Farran asked.

"Yeah," Daphne replied. "We can't hang the paintings until the hoist is in place. That'll be mid-morning tomorrow."

"Okay," Farran said. "I'm really looking forward to seeing them up. Everything's coming together beautifully. Once the paintings are hung, it'll be the icing on the cake."

"Do we know which ones they've sent?" Darnell asked casually.

"I looked through the description labels," Farran said, "but none of them were familiar. The collection's always been closely guarded; hardly any images exist online."

"Mmm," he murmured, brushing at an invisible speck on his shirt sleeve.

"We're heading to the Wheatsheaf for a quick drink if you want to join us," Daphne said, looking at them both with a hopeful smile.

Farran groaned inwardly. The last thing she wanted was to extend the day, especially with Darnell's unpredictable presence hovering nearby.

Before she could respond, Darnell's voice cut in smoothly. "Sure, we'll come.”

Heat flared up her neck. How dare he decide for me? Was this another of his power plays, or had he misread her silence?

She forced a smile. “Of course. But I won’t be able to stay long.”

Darnell’s quick grin was unsettlingly confident, like a man who’d just won a small victory. She turned toward the exit, her footsteps echoing more sharply than she intended. Irritation bristled under her skin. A presence fell into step beside her, Darnell again, silent, matching her pace. They walked in silence back to the office, gathered their coats and bags, and headed out to meet the others.

Evening had softened the light, and the pub wasn’t overly crowded. As Farran stepped through the door, her eyes swept the room. The long bar stretched along one wall, and stools occupied by quiet drinkers and murmuring groups. Tables dotted the floor, some full, some empty, voices blending into the low hum of music. A large mirror opposite the bar reflected the scene, doubling space and movement.

She spotted Daphne and Simon already seated and made her way toward them, her steps steady, though her mood still brittle. In the mirror, she caught Darnell’s reflection trailing behind, smug smile in place. Her jaw tightened. Who does he think he is, making decisions for both of us?

She draped her jacket over the back of a chair while Darnell tossed his jacket onto the leather bench beside Simon.

“What would you like to drink?” he asked, his gaze flicking to hers.

“A small Diet Coke, please. I really can’t be late home,” she said, light but firm.

He paused, then turned without a word and headed to the bar.

Farran filled the silence with small talk, chatting quietly with Daphne and Simon until he returned and set their drinks down.

"So," Darnell said, glancing around as if to smooth over what had passed, "what's been your favourite part of the collection so far?"

Daphne answered quickly. "The jewellery from his first wife, Margaret Audley. That pearl necklace... exquisite." Her eyes lit up. "I can't wait to see her portrait. I think it's arriving tomorrow?"

Simon nodded. "I was impressed by the armoury. For someone who wasn't military, Stephens had quite the collection."

Farran's thoughts drifted to the seal and diary she hadn't yet had time to explore. "The written pieces," she said quickly. "I just love seeing what people thought and said. You really get to know them."

Darnell raised an eyebrow, his voice taking on a teasing edge. "Didn't think you were that interested in people."

Farran felt the sting beneath the words. "People from the past are different," she replied, trying to keep her tone light. "What they endured, how they survived..."

"They can't answer back or ask questions. So you're safe," he cut in, his voice suddenly low and flat.

The shift punched the air out of the conversation. Daphne and Simon glanced at each other, awkwardness settling in.

Farran blinked. There it was again, one moment disarming, the next bruising. Was he trying to make up for something? Or did he enjoy keeping her off balance?

"Have I upset you, Darnell?" she asked, carefully.

He stared at her too long. Then laughed. Abrupt. Forced. "Of course not. I'm just having a bit of fun."

But the tension had already frayed the edges of the group. Farran turned her eyes to her drink, and this time she didn't meet his gaze.

When the moment felt right, she murmured her goodbyes and slipped away, relieved when Darnell didn't follow. He was deep in conversation with Simon, their voices low, drifting toward talk of the weaponry collection.

But he noticed her leave. Tracked her with his eyes. Said nothing. His thoughts spun. He had believed he could manage this, being near her without falling apart. But it was proving impossible. And still, what choice did he have?

They would take her soon. That much he knew. And once they did, she would be gone forever. That thought, losing her again, was unbearable. Did he even have the right to stop it? He doubted it.

He drained his drink, stood, and murmured a few quiet farewells. Then he stepped out into the cool spring evening, the fading light softening the town's edges. Without thinking, he turned into a narrow alleyway where the lamplight couldn't reach. And let the shadows swallow him.

3

Secretum

A face blurred in the gold-framed mirror, which hung on the plain wall in a long corridor. The air felt still, almost expectant, as the image flickered into focus. Grey-green eyes stared intently at her. Dark hair with flecks of grey became clearer. A softly rounded face, with a tender mouth and slender nose. There was a hint of stubble.

It was whispering something, soft, rhythmic. She couldn't make out the words. Her feet moved before her thoughts caught up, drawing her closer. She reached out, fingertips trembling. The mirror shimmered beneath her touch. The face smiled, slow and familiar, and nodded once.

"Come," it said, faint as a breeze.

Her heart thudded. The voice tugged at something buried deep within. Then, just as suddenly, the image shattered into a jumbled mash of pixels. Gone.

She was alone once more, the corridor stretching endlessly behind her.

3:04

"Aargh," Farran groaned into her pillow, willing this nightmare and that haunting face to end. All she wanted was one full night's sleep, free of dreams and the recurring figure shadowing her nights. Who was this figure, anyway? Why did they keep coming back?

She flung back the sheets and crept through the darkened house. Silence pressed in, thick and suffocating. She made straight for the radio and flicked it on. A familiar voice filled the room, bringing a quiet wash of comfort. Leaving the hum of words and music to anchor the space, she moved into the kitchen to make a drink, her body moving on instinct.

Mug in hand, she returned to the living room and curled into her favourite corner of the sofa. Slowly, her breathing eased. The voice on the radio was warm and hypnotic, wrapping around her like a soft embrace, coaxing her mind to quiet. She wasn't listening. She didn't want to think; too tired for that. Instead, she let the voice soothe her, stroke her thoughts into silence. At last, she slept.

The face smiled.

"Come, Anne," it whispered.

The name stirred something faint and distant within her, like a note half-remembered from a forgotten song. Her breath caught, though she didn't understand why.

Then the image shimmered and faded, replaced by a garden bursting with colour. Spring flowers bowed and swayed in a gentle breeze. Deftly shaped bushes curved along gravel paths, and a perfectly mown lawn stretched beneath a sky of soft gold. Somewhere, birds sang in layered melody. A fountain leapt in the centre, its water catching the light like falling stars. The air was sweet with blossom. The scene pulsed with warmth and peace. She didn't know this place, and yet... something about it ached.

Home, whispered the thought, unbidden.

6:29

Farran slowly opened her eyes, disoriented and unsure of where she was. Gradually, the familiar shapes of her living room furniture came into focus, sunlight timidly filtering around the edges of the curtains. She blinked a few times, then stretched. The radio softly murmured, a newsreader calmly reporting on world events. She rose, made breakfast, and got ready for work.

The morning was unusually warm as she walked into town. Despite another restless night, she felt surprisingly composed, almost ready to face Darnell. His outburst from the day before still lingered, clouded by confusion, but she resolved that whatever burden he carried, it was his alone.

Stepping into the building, the faint hum of movement and voices drifted from corridors beyond. Rather than heading straight to her office, Farran turned into the exhibition hall. The glass cabinets stood unlit and still, dim shapes in the soft morning light. She wandered between them, letting the silence settle around her. Yesterday had been too chaotic to truly absorb anything. Now, the quiet felt strangely welcome.

She moved slowly from cabinet to cabinet, pausing at each plinth to study the contents. Her gaze lingered, not just admiring, but absorbing, as if trying to read the silence they held. Each label seemed to murmur of stories untold. A subtle thrill stirred, a rising tide of anticipation, threaded with shadowy whispers of the unknown.

Then she saw it, the seal. She leaned closer, eyes tracing every detail. The sphinx crouched low, chest curled protectively around the shield. Its head tilted slightly, hair thick and braided, like serpents coiled and waiting. Beneath it, a single word: Secretum. An invitation whispered in Latin. What hidden truths lie buried in the family's history, locked behind that symbol? A chill ran through her, a warning or a promise, she couldn't tell.

Her hand rose, fingertips brushing the glass. A soft rustle behind her broke the moment. She turned. Daphne was approaching with a warm smile. The simple normalcy of her presence grounded her. Farran drew her hand back from the case.

"Morning, Daph. How are you?" Farran asked, smiling warmly.

"Good, ta," Daphne replied with her usual cheer. "I'm eager to get these paintings up," she added, glancing around the room.

"Yes, me too," Farran agreed. "Did you enjoy the rest of the evening? Sorry, I couldn't stay long."

"I did. It's nice to relax after a busy day," Daphne said. "Simon's such a laugh."

Farran smiled. "He does seem like a good chap."

"Mmm, he is," Daphne said, a subtle glow in her expression. "Darnell didn't stay long after you left."

"No?" Farran said, turning back to the cabinet. Her eyes were drawn once more to its contents. She didn't want to think about Darnell. Instead, she let the objects pull her focus, each whispering its fragment of history.

"I'd better get up to the office, see what's going on," she said, glancing back at Daphne. "Will you be down here?"

"Yes," Daphne nodded. "I was going to run a few checks. There's a copy of The Faerie Queene I want to look at, too."

"Ah, yes, an interesting piece."

"Lo, I the man, whose Muse whylome did maske,
    As time her taught, in lowly shepherd's weeds,
    Am now enforced a far more unfit task..."
    "For trumpets stern to change mine oaten reeds,
    And sing of knights and ladies' gentle deeds;
    Whose praises having slept in silence long..."

Daphne blinked. "Wow. I didn't know you knew it so well."

"Huh. Neither did I," Farran murmured, puzzled. She shook her head gently. "I'll be back down soon so we can start unwrapping the paintings."

She cast one last glance at the seal before turning and making her way out of the hall, the air shifting behind her like breath held too long.

Darnell sat at his desk, head bent over a scattering of papers. As Farran entered, he glanced up briefly, then slid a piece of parchment beneath the clutter. His eyes followed her silently as she put her things away.

"Good morning, Darnell. How are you today?" Farran asked, a flicker of unease threading her voice under his steady stare.

"Fine," he replied curtly, offering no warmth. "You're late."

The pointed remark made her pause. She met his gaze squarely. "I've been checking the exhibition and talking with Daphne, if you really want to know," she shot back, narrowing her eyes.

Darnell's gaze lingered, making her want to leave. "Fair enough," he drawled, lowering his eyes. "The hoist will be arriving soon."

"Yes, I'm heading back down to unpack the paintings with Daphne and Simon," Farran said, glancing at her phone. She wanted to be anywhere but there with *him.*

"I'll be there in a bit," Darnell muttered, already returning to his papers.

Farran walked out, frustration tightening her chest. What was his problem? Yesterday, he'd seemed almost human; now he was distant and unbearable. She didn't understand him.

In the hall, Simon and Daphne chatted and laughed as Farran arrived.

"How are you, Simon?" she asked.

"Good, thanks," he replied with a smile.

"Right, let's get started," Farran said, heading for the stack of paintings. "We'll begin with this one." She selected the largest canvas.

Simon moved to the opposite side, and together they lifted the wrapped piece with care. Daphne knelt beside them, peeling back the protective cloth gently, careful not to damage the surface.

Slowly, the image revealed itself...

A man with dark, thick hair framing a pale face. His piercing blue eyes stared out beneath a strong brow and prominent nose. Full lips, unsmiling. He wore a rich brown Elizabethan doublet, seated at a table strewn with papers. Near his right hand rested a seal and a quill. Above him, a stained-glass window cast a soft glow, its colours bleeding into the surrounding shadows.

Farran gasped, her breath caught. "*Darnell,*" she whispered.

A voice came from behind. "What?"

She turned sharply. Darnell stood just behind her, gaze fixed on the painting. His face betrayed nothing, no shock, no emotion, but his stillness told her he recognised it.

"Crikey, Darnell," Simon said, eyes wide. "The likeness between you and Richard Stephens is uncanny!"

Daphne nodded, still speechless.

"Do you think so?" Darnell said mildly, eyes never leaving the portrait. He cast a glance at Farran. "I can't see it."

"I'd say it's the spitting image of you," Simon insisted.

"I have to agree," Daphne said softly. "The resemblance is... unmistakable."

Darnell's eyes locked on Farran. "What are you thinking, Farran?"

Her head swam. Heart pounding, she looked from the portrait to Darnell. "I think... I have to agree. It's you."

Darnell sneered.

Before she could press him, two men entered the hall, pushing a hoist and carrying a ladder. The spell broke. The questions and tension were suspended for now.

"Where do you want this, love?" one of the men called.

Farran gave directions automatically, mind spinning. Behind her, Simon and Daphne resumed unwrapping paintings, checking labels, quietly murmuring to each other. When she looked up again, Darnell was gone, like a shadow swallowed by the room.

Despite her best efforts, Farran's gaze kept returning to the portrait of Richard Stephens. The uncanny resemblance to Darnell unsettled her every time. Each time she found herself drifting back to that haunting face, she forced herself to look away and focus on the next painting, hoping the distractions would steady her racing thoughts.

It was late in the day, and Darnell still hadn't reappeared. Farran was exhausted. Only one painting remained to be unwrapped and hung. She turned to Simon and Daphne, her voice tinged with weariness and a hint of pleading. "Are you two okay to handle this last one? I've got some paperwork to finish up and really need to get home at a reasonable time."

"No problem," Simon replied easily. Daphne nodded in agreement.

The first painting hadn't been mentioned again, and Farran said her goodbyes before heading up to the office. As she climbed the stairs, her mind drifted back to that portrait. The startling likeness between Darnell and Richard Stephens was unbelievable. She'd seen family resemblances before, sometimes uncanny, but this felt different, almost as if they were one and the same. It was the eyes, she decided, that same piercing look Darnell wore when annoyed. Farran had seen that look more times than she could count, often for no good reason.

Farran walked into the quiet office, closing the door behind her. Darnell looked up from his desk, sliding a piece of parchment beneath the clutter. They locked eyes before she spoke.

"I thought you'd gone."

He shook his head. "No. Had some things to finish," he said, watching her.

"Oh." She shifted uncomfortably, walking to her desk. "Just got a couple of bits to finish, then I'm heading home."

"Right." He hadn't looked away.

Farran shuffled through paperwork, but her mind wandered. Eventually, she gathered her things and moved to leave, only to find Darnell at the door.

"What are you doing?"

"I just... I don't want the day to end like this." His voice was quiet and pleading. "It really shouldn't matter that the man looked like me."

"No, I suppose it shouldn't," she said. "It was just... a shock."

He laughed softly. "Yeah. Honestly, I don't see the resemblance. But you all looked so spooked, I figured I'd give you space."

There was something rehearsed in his tone. Something too calm.

"I'll see you tomorrow," she said quickly.

"Yeah. Sleep well," he said.

She paused. The words landed oddly.

"You mentioned not sleeping," he added.

She nodded faintly. "Thanks." Then she slipped past him.

"Right," he sighed, not to himself, exactly, but to the room. Or something listening in.

He watched the door long after it closed. Her scent lingered. So did the look in her eyes, confusion wrapped in something deeper. Not fear. Not yet. Just the impossibility of what she'd seen refused to settle into sense.

She couldn't see it yet. But her bones knew. As if some long-lost part of her had recognised him first, and now waited, quietly screaming, to be heard. He let the pen fall. It skittered across the floor, a small rebellion against the calm he'd been pretending to hold. No one had told him how much it would ache. Or maybe they had, in a language he no longer understood.

He gathered the papers, useless decoys, because the weight of routine still helped. Still kept him tethered. Would going back solve anything? He looked toward the filing cabinet, where the shadows stretched long. They whispered the same thing they always did.

Not yet.

He turned off the light. Closed the door with care. And vanished into the dark.

4

In the Hollow of the Dark (1593)

The scream shattered the silence; deafening, raw.

For a moment, she didn't know where it had come from. Then the truth hit: it was her own voice. Darkness closed in, thick and suffocating. She wasn't alone. A steady breath sounded beside her. Warm fingers gently clasped her own.

A voice emerged from the shadows; soft, urgent.
   "It's alright. Not long now."

Pain throbbed through her legs, sharp and relentless. She tried to move but found herself wedged tight in a narrow space.

"You can't move," the voice said again, calm but firm. "Your legs... they're too badly damaged."

Panic surged, squeezing the air from her lungs.

"We're going to help you, but you must keep still." The voice coaxed, gentle but insistent. "Trust me. Please."

That tone calmed her, just enough. What had happened?

A fog of memory, an attack from behind... a shove... then the terrifying fall.

"I must leave you for a while," the voice whispered near her ear, breath warm. "But I'll be back. I promise."

A soft kiss brushed her forehead.

"I love you."

Footsteps echoed on stone, receding. Then silence.

She was alone again. Panic clawed at her, rising fast.

But those final words, whispered, tender, gave her something to hold.

A fragile thread in the dark.

"I love you too," she breathed, barely audible.

The pain rose, crested, and then pulled her under.

Into oblivion.

* * *

In a small, weathered cottage nestled at the edge of the dark wood, three figures gathered, their voices low but urgent in heated discussion.

"The lady can't take much more," said the first man, his bright tunic and trousers a jarring contrast to the gloom. His voice was edged with desperation. "Every day worsens her chances."

A pixie-faced woman with dark, cropped hair stood rigid beside him, wrapped in a long brown wool dress that shielded her from neck to toe.

"It won't be long now," she said, her eyes flickering with cautious hope. "He'll believe she's dead. Then we can move her to safety."

The third, a tall man with mousy-blonde hair and deep-set eyes, placed a steady hand on the younger man's shoulder, offering a faint smile.

"The lady will be fine," he said with quiet conviction. "But you know the timing must be exact."

The first man's expression twisted with anguish. He nodded slowly.

"I know. I just want this nightmare to end. None of us is safe until it's done. He will hunt us down... I should know."

"Come, sit by the fire. You look exhausted," said the taller man, his long white sleeves visible beneath a dull blue, sleeveless jacket. His voice was gentle but firm.

"I have to get back to her," the first man protested, eyes darting toward the door.

"You need to conserve your strength," the woman said sharply, though her gaze held concern. "The journey ahead will be treacherous. You'll need every ounce of your wits to see it through."

With that, she guided him toward a sturdy wooden chair beside the open hearth.

He sank, letting the warmth of the fire curl around him, the flames crackling and popping in a soothing rhythm. From a large pot suspended above the blaze came the rich aroma of stewed vegetables, mingled with the soft, calming scent of rosemary. Closing his eyes, he let the sounds and scents begin to soothe him.

"She's lucky," the second man murmured. "To have someone who loves her so deeply."

"He wasn't always like this," the woman replied with a faint smile. "Always claimed he was content alone. But since she shared her feelings these last few months... well, he's truly changed."

"Mmm. He doesn't make it easy," the man chuckled softly.

"True love rarely does." A knowing light danced in her eyes.

"Oh, I'm not so sure," he said, pulling her close for a sudden, tender kiss.

She turned away, ladling steaming broth into two rough-hewn wooden bowls, and they settled at the small, worn table.

"How long until it's over?" he asked between mouthfuls.

"A couple more nights," she replied thoughtfully. "I only hope her injuries heal enough by then. Though I believe the help that's coming... will be beyond anything we could imagine." Her voice trembled slightly with awe.

"We'll have to leave too," he said quietly. "Is there any chance we'll ever return?"

She shook her head, eyes fixed on the half-empty bowl in front of her.

"No, my sweet. And if the tyrant finds us before it's done, none of us will survive. You know he's already hunting my blood."

He reached across the table and took her hand, fingers curling gently around hers.

"I know, my love. I know."

He gave a small, reassuring smile.

"It's just… this life is all I've ever known. If I'm honest, the future scares me."

She frowned, eyes soft.

"Yes, but at least we have a future. Right now, we don't."

A heavy silence lingered as they ate, each lost in their thoughts.

5

Come to Me (2018)

A face blurred in the gold-framed mirror hanging on the plain wall of a long corridor. The corridor stretched endlessly in both directions, its stillness pressing in. Paintings lined the walls, their subjects peering down at her. She glanced to the left. One portrait stood out: a man in a gentleman's dress. His ice-blue eyes followed her, boring into her soul, accusing or warning; she couldn't tell.

The mirror shimmered again. A shape swam into view, beckoning. The face flickered into focus. Soft grey-green eyes locked onto hers, unwavering. They were kind, yet intense, as if they knew her. Thick, dark hair streaked with grey curled around a softly rounded face. A tender mouth. A slender nose. A shadow of stubble lined the jaw.

It was whispering something. She leaned in, heart thudding. The words brushed her memory but stayed just out of reach. She moved closer. Reached out. The face smiled and nodded, lips barely moving.

"Come to me," it whispered, just loud enough to stir something deep in her chest.

The image rippled. A flicker, a jumble of pixels. Then: gone.

She was alone again in the corridor.

Farran knew, without looking at the clock, what time it was: **3:04.**

She lay motionless, staring at the ceiling, her limbs too heavy to move. With a sigh, she rolled onto her side, watching the curtains ripple in the spring night air. The occasional rumble of passing cars drifted in through the open window. Who was out there at this hour? Where were they going?

Her thoughts tugged her backwards to the vision from her sleep. She shut her eyes tightly, trying to push it away, but it clung. The face emerged again, swimming behind her lids.

"Come to me," the voice whispered, soft, familiar, and impossibly near.

Pulling her toward somewhere, something, someone. She forced her eyes open. The curtains fluttered gently in the darkness, their hypnotic movement lulling her mind toward stillness, but not peace. She lay frozen in the hush. Was she losing her mind?
The dream.
The seal.
The painting.
Darnell.

She shuddered. Her mind strained to tether her to reality, but nothing made sense. Reason had lost its battle; all that remained was a tangle of jagged thoughts, scraping against the softness of her mind and one another. She closed her eyes, willing herself not to rise. Maybe if she stayed still long enough, sleep would return. The right kind of sleep. The kind untouched by shadows.

Her limbs gradually loosened, the tension ebbing as she sank deeper into the mattress. Outside, a car passed; its low growl dissolved into the quiet, a reminder that the world still turned. Then she heard him.

"Come to me."

Her body locked, every muscle taut.

"You know I love you. More than he ever could."

The words made sense, far too much sense, to her half-asleep mind. But as wakefulness crept in, the meaning frayed.

"Come to me," he whispered again.

Farran's eyes snapped open. The room was dark and still. Her heart hammered as she pushed herself upright and stumbled toward the window. Drawing back the curtain, she peered out, straining to locate the voice. The street lay deserted. A tabby cat padded across the road, tail twitching, and slipped into a shadowed garden. She scanned both ends of the road. Nothing; no one. With a sigh, she let the curtain fall. She was awake now. She might as well get up.

Downstairs, she made herself a drink and settled quietly in the living room, the soft murmur of the radio filling the background. Her gaze drifted to a painting hanging on the wall, roughly the size of an A3 sheet. Its frame was simple: dark wood with gently bevelled edges. It had always hung in her home; too old to be a replica, too obscure to be famous.

The man looked to be in his late thirties. Dark, wavy hair blended into the shadowed background. His grey-green eyes, lined with worry, were framed by fine creases at the corners. A slender nose and gently curved mouth formed a half-smile, but there was little joy in it; more a quiet concern.

He wore a dark brown tunic tied at the waist with a length of rope. His legs were clad in scarlet tights, and black leather shoes adorned his feet. He sat beneath an oak tree, one knee raised, his arm resting casually on it. To one side, a small wooden bowl held a single peach; On the other, a clump of violets pushed through their foliage, delicate petals just beginning to bloom.

Farran had always wondered who he was. There was something about him: a quiet strength, a watchful presence that felt almost guardian-like. The symbols painted around him suggested he had been seen that way in his lifetime. Still, she couldn't help but wonder what had caused the sadness in his eyes. Had he been in trouble? Had his lover been taken from him?

She frowned, surprised at herself. It was strange that she hadn't investigated it before; it should have been second nature. *Call yourself a historian*, she muttered, shaking her head.

She reached up to take the painting from the wall but froze, her hand halfway raised. Something on the radio caught her attention, tugging her focus away. It was him. His voice entered the room: rich, unmistakable. As the familiar tones filled the space, she forgot the picture. She sank into the chair, drawn in by the voice.

"I hope you're having a restful night, listening to some of the great music from the 16th century," he said, joyful, at ease. Farran felt, once again, as though he were speaking directly to her.

The room's edges softened. Tension eased from her shoulders. Gradually, she relaxed into the chair, her eyes drifting closed.

The face smiled, his eyes shining with something like love or longing.
"Come, Anne, it's time," he whispered.

She flinched at the name. It stirred something distant within her; familiar, yet foreign, like a half-forgotten song.

He stepped back, and the world beyond him unfolded. A magnificent

garden stretched out before her, bursting with spring flowers in every shade imaginable. Deftly shaped bushes lined the edges like silent guardians. A perfectly mown lawn rolled out ahead, edged with lavender whose calming scent curled through the air. Nearby, birds sang sweet, clear tones, and a fountain danced in the sunlight. Water trickled rhythmically: steady, reassuring. Home.

She stepped forward hesitantly. Gravel crunched beneath her bare feet. The path was cool beneath her, and the breeze was soft against her skin. She turned slowly, drinking in the breathtaking beauty: the kind of place one only dreamed of, or remembered.

A presence stood near. She hadn't seen him move, but she felt him: a warmth, a shift in the air, a trace of musk.
"I promised I would come back for you," he said, voice lower, nearer.

She turned, breath catching as he leaned in. He was so close now, too close, eyes searching hers, lips parting as though to kiss. Her pulse quickened. Part of her wanted to lean in, but something deeper was afraid.

Farran awoke to a sharp, pulsing pain in her head. The strange nausea from days ago had returned; stronger now, curling through her like smoke. Every inch of her body ached, as if crushed from within.

A waft of rosemary.

The clock read **6:29**.

She tried to shift, but a bolt of pain sliced through her, splitting her in two. Gritting her teeth, she clawed at the arms of the chair, dragging herself forward. The movement tore through her like fire. Her eyes locked on her phone resting on the table. She reached for it, breath ragged and shallow. Her hand trembled, twitched, and the phone slipped from her grasp, landing with a soft, devastating thud.

"No…" she whispered, voice barely audible.

Desperation surged. She leaned, stretching toward it. Her fingertips brushed the edge. Then: blackness. It crashed over her, swallowing her whole. She collapsed, limp and silent, to the floor.

* * *

Elwyna heard the phone ringing and set down the shirt she was folding. Crossing the small living room, she grabbed the buzzing device from the sideboard.

"Hi, how are you? Bit early, isn't it?" she said with a smile, expecting the caller's familiar warmth.

But the words that followed made her freeze.

"You need to get to Farran!" The voice was urgent, breathless.

"What's happened?" Elwyna's heart pounded. "Where is she?"

"She's at home. She needs help," came the anxious reply. A silence stretched too long, too still. Then, softly: "I wish I could be there."

"It's okay. We'll go to her," Elwyna said, trying to stay calm. After a beat, she added quietly: "It won't be long now."

The line went dead. She stood still for a moment, then sprang into action, grabbing her bag.

"Daryll!" she called. "Something's happened to Farr. I'm going to her."

"I'll come with you, Elv," he said, already reaching for the car keys, concern etched across his face.

Together, they stepped into the morning air, unusually dull for this time of year, as if the day itself sensed something was wrong.

Once in the car, with Daryll at the wheel, he asked, "How do you know?"

"He rang to tell me," Elwyna replied, staring out the window. "I've said it before: he's making his presence too strong."

"How can he?" Daryll frowned. "He's been keeping his distance. Tonight was supposed to be the first contact in months."

"Well then, how else does he know she needs help?" Elwyna's voice sharpened. "This could set everything back, again."

Ten tense minutes later, they pulled up outside Farran's house.

"The curtains are still closed," Elwyna noted grimly.

"That doesn't mean anything," Daryll offered gently.

"She would've left for work by now," Elwyna shot back, already striding toward the door.

She knocked once. No answer. Again, harder. Still nothing. She bent down, opened the letterbox, and peered through: just an empty hallway.

"Farran!" she called through the gap. Was that a faint groan?

"Farran!" she called louder, now certain she'd heard movement. Panic rising, she fumbled through her bag with trembling fingers, pulled out a key, and jammed it into the lock.

The door creaked open. Elwyna rushed in, leaving it wide for Daryll, and darted into the living room. There, on the floor, was Farran, groaning, curled slightly on her side, clearly in pain. Elwyna was beside her in a heartbeat.

"Farran! Can you hear me?" she said urgently, brushing hair from her friend's face. "What happened?"

Farran's lips parted, but no words came. Her eyes fluttered shut.

"We need to get help," Daryll said, pulling out his phone. "I'll ring for an ambulance."

Elwyna knelt beside Farran, gently taking her hand. "It's okay, love. Help's on the way."

Within twenty minutes, the ambulance arrived. A young paramedic crouched beside Farran, checking her vitals with calm efficiency.

"She's running a high temperature and her heart rate is elevated," he said, glancing up. "Has she been unwell recently?"

"I had dinner with her at the beginning of the week; she seemed fine," Elwyna replied. "Though she did mention trouble sleeping."

"We'll get her to the hospital," the paramedic said, already prepping equipment. "They'll run some tests. It could be an infection."

"Can I go with her?" Elwyna asked. "She doesn't have family nearby; we're all she's got."

"Of course," the paramedic nodded kindly. "We'll just get the stretcher."

He disappeared briefly, returning with a second paramedic and the trolley. In one fluid motion, they transferred Farran and wheeled her out to the ambulance.

"I'll meet you there," Daryll said, already heading toward the car.

Elwyna climbed into the back, her eyes never leaving Farran's pale face. The doors slammed shut behind her with a final thud, echoing in her chest.

6

The Fool's Promise (1592)

I saw Anne crossing the precisely trimmed lawn, and my heart leapt.

She looked magnificent in her emerald green silk gown, adorned with lace and tiny buttons that caught the light. Her cane-coloured hair was pinned high, interwoven with pearl drops that shimmered like dew. She carried the regal air of Queen Elizabeth herself. She held her head with quiet dignity and gently wafted a lace fan, seeking relief from the heat.

Her wooden soles crunched softly on the stony path as she moved with grace. Even on cloudy days, Anne brought the sun with her. Her warmth was impossible to ignore. Without thinking, I moved toward her, hoping our paths would cross.

"Good morning, fool," her voice rang like music, soft and clear. "Where are you going?"

"Good morning, Mistress," I replied, offering a low, theatrical bow and carefully shifting my lute to one side. "I'm off to the chestnut tree; it is a fine day to greet travellers."

"Well, none of your tomfoolery today," she said, a playful smile tugging at her lips. "The Master is due back, and he'll expect the place to be running smoothly."

"I cannot promise that, Mistress," I teased, stretching the moment a little longer. "Mischief is the essence of my being."

I glimpsed the edge of a handkerchief peeking from her sleeve. I plucked it free with a swift flick and stepped out of reach.

"I appear to have lost my handkerchief, fool," she laughed, and the sound sent butterflies fluttering through my chest. I danced in a circle, waving it like a flag, her laughter ringing through the air.

"Fool, give it back to me," she called, her words laced with mirth.

"Finders keepers," I grinned, twirling just beyond her reach, basking in the warmth of her attention.

"What's going on here?" A deep voice cut through the moment like a blade. "Is this how you behave?"

I turned. Richard Stephens, Master of the house, strode toward us, his face already clouded.

"Oh, Richard, you're here," Anne said, hurrying to meet her husband, forgetting her handkerchief. "Thomas was only cheering me up while we waited for you," she added with a light smile. As she reached him, Richard pulled her into a kiss, fierce and possessive. I heard her gasp.

"Thomas," he snapped, once he had released her, "get on with the tasks I pay you for and stop distracting my wife. That's my role."

With that, they turned and walked back toward the house, leaving me alone, the handkerchief still in my hand. I folded it and tucked it into my tunic, a small trophy of the moment. Then I made my way out of the grand grounds, heading for the chestnut tree that stood sentinel at the crossroads. It had become a favourite spot since I'd arrived in this quiet Cotswold village twenty years ago.

I had fled Harrogate, forced to leave in haste. My former master enjoyed my performances, but he demanded more. Darker services. Services that dealt death to his adversaries.

The Master I serve now had been passing through the village I had entertained when we first met. His previous jester had met an untimely end, an unfortunate accident, according to the whispers. And he needed a replacement. I told him my story. He seemed to believe I was exactly the kind of fool he required. And I proved him right, and more.

At the old, gnarled chestnut tree, I set my lute aside and sank against its rough bark. With one knee bent and my arm on it, I settled in. Hours would pass like this, watching and speaking with travellers as they passed through the crossroads. Those who greeted me with respect, I sent safely on their way, mostly. But not all were so courteous, nor so fortunate. The others were dealt with accordingly, as per the Master's instructions. He expected certain standards; I was determined to uphold them.

It was while I sat beneath the glorious spring sun that I espied Henry Bromley, a justice of the peace and an acquaintance of the Master. From our first meeting, I had not trusted the man. I shared my misgivings with the Master, but he paid them no heed.

"He's good to have on your side," the Master would say.

I disagreed, yet I dared not oppose him openly, for one day I might require protection from Bromley himself.

He came riding up on a brown stallion, hooves stirring the dry earth, raising a cloud of dust behind him. As he reached the crossroads, he reined in, his eyes locked with mine.

"Good morrow, Thomas," he called out, his Gloucester accent sharp and clear. "How fare you this fine morning?"

Something about him stirred in me an urge to knock his head clean off. Still, I forced my voice to remain civil.

"Good morrow, sire. I fare well, and yourself?"

"Aye, well enough, thank you," he replied smoothly. "Is the Master returned?"

"Yes, sire, he is," I answered cautiously, weighing each word. "I'm certain he would be glad to welcome you." Though I knew well his gaze would be fixed solely upon his lady wife after a week spent away.

A spark of mischief flickered through me. I scarcely fathomed how Anne endured his company. Perhaps I might offer her a moment's respite, if only for a little while.

"Thank you, Thomas," he said, flashing a courteous smile before urging his horse onward. Dust swirled in his wake as he rode toward the house.

I smiled to myself and reached for my lute, letting my fingers dance lightly across the strings. My thoughts wandered back to Anne. Foolish though it was, I could not help the way I felt. Her smile, her laughter, they sent my head spinning. I'd give all to see them once more.

Leaning back against the rough bark, I closed my eyes and let myself dream. In that dream, it was I who held her close, who kissed her softly, who felt her lean into me as we strolled back toward the house together. Something sharp tapped my cheek. I flinched, trying to ignore it, desperate to linger in the dream a moment longer. Then it came again, followed by a gruff chuckle.

"Dreaming again, are you, Tom?" came a familiar voice.

I opened my eyes to see Davy standing over me, his face bright with that silly grin of his. I sighed, overly dramatic. "You've caught me, Davy," I said, returning the grin. "And naturally, you choose the very moment when things were taking a lively turn to interrupt."

Springing to my feet, I set my lute down carefully and brushed the dust from my tunic. I had known Davy for all the years I'd been here. He and his wife, Wynn, had long served the Master, the first friends I'd made in this place.

"So?" I asked, arching an eyebrow. "What brings you here, friend? Come to spoil more of my whimsical daydreams?"

"Cook has sent me to fetch extra supplies," Davy replied, "and the Master's in foul humour because Sir Henry turned up. He'd been hoping for time alone with the Mistress."

"Ah, really?" I said, fighting to keep laughter from my voice.

"You wouldn't happen to know anything about that, would you?" Davy asked, shooting me a knowing look.

"I might have seen him pass," I said vaguely. "I suppose I should be heading back," I added, suddenly eager to return.

"Just be careful, Tom," Davy warned, his tone turning serious. "The lady is the Mistress, far beyond your reach."

"I don't know what you mean," I replied. But of course I did. Still, a man can dream.

"Mmm. See you back at the house later," Davy said with a twinkle in his eye before setting off down the path toward town. He was a good man, devoted to his wife. A junior footman to the Master, he wore the deep blue uniform of his station, though I had always thought he deserved more.

I turned back toward the house, hoping to catch some of the entertainment I had set in motion. The long dirt track stretched ahead, winding through trees that at first concealed the house from view. As I drew nearer, the white stone façade and grey-tiled roof emerged through the greenery. The chimneys stood like sentinels, poised to release smoke from the fires within.

The trees thinned, revealing the full grandeur of the house. The Master's father had begun the grand extensions years ago, and the Master himself had finished them, adding touches all his own. The building formed a capital 'E', its many windows lining the walls like watchful eyes. Ivy crept up one side, softening the stone's sharpness.

The front door stood proud at the centre, reached by a shallow flight of steps. In the circular driveway, a fountain sent jets of water arcing through the air, droplets catching the light as they danced and fell into the basin below, their ripples folding into endless patterns.

I skirted around to the rear entrance. The front door was forbidden to me for now. One day, I would cross that threshold.

Inside, the familiar kitchen chaos greeted me. Cook's voice rang out above the clatter.

"Get those vegetables peeled!" she barked at one of the younger girls. "We don't have time for standin' and gawpin'!"

The girl jumped, dropping her load of carrots and onions.

"Oh, for heaven's sake... I don't know why you're even here!" Cook snapped.

I stepped forward. "Let's get these on the table," I said, stooping to scoop up the vegetables. I juggled a few, drawing a giggle from the girl. Which, of course, only made Cook more agitated.

"Tom, I don't need you messin' about," she snapped. "Be gone. Celia, get those vegetables peeled!"

"Sorry, Cook," I said, setting the vegetables on the table. "What's all the commotion?"

"One of the Master's acquaintances has turned up unannounced," she huffed, banging a pot onto the stove. "Now he wants a full banquet put on, like we've got a feast hidden in the bloody walls! And that Davy'd better get a move on."

She heaved a pot of water onto the fire hook and began clattering pans again. I plucked an apple from the basket on the sideboard and bit into it, grinning at the string of muttered curses that followed me from the kitchen. Cook's frustration was practically a language of its own.

I wandered out into the corridor, chewing, passing several open doorways: laundry, scullery, storeroom, until I reached the servants' stairs. Taking them two at a time, I climbed to the upper floor.

Before me stretched another long corridor, running left and right. To the left lay the dining room, where the family usually took their meals. To the right, the banquet hall, and beyond that, the library and living room. I turned right. As I passed the library door, I glanced inside.

Anne sat quietly reading with the Master's twin daughters, Abigail and Sarah. He had been married twice before. First to Margaret Audley, mother of the girls and his eldest sons, Thomas and Richard, both tragically killed several years earlier. And then to Margaret St. Loe, who had passed away on New Year's Day that very year.

It had caused no small scandal when the Master married Anne just one month after his second wife's death. Still, his children accepted her, calling her "Mother" as he insisted. No one disobeyed the Master.

Anne looked up as I passed. Was that a smile? A flicker of recognition? Just my imagination again? I dared not linger. I continued toward the living room, where the Master's voice drifted softly down the corridor.

"I know he's coming to the end, so it's time."

Curiosity piqued, I slowed, pausing outside the door, taking care not to be seen.

"Yes, Richard," came Henry's reply. "No one will contest you for the position. You have our backing."

"Good," said the Master, his voice low and thoughtful.

I shifted slightly, and the traitorous floorboard beneath my foot creaked, loud as a shot. Henry's eyes flicked toward the doorway.

I stepped in at once. "Good day, Sires," I announced cheerfully, sweeping in with an exaggerated bow.

"Ah, Thomas," the Master greeted. His tone was cordial but tight. "Henry tells me he saw you by the chestnut tree earlier." His ice-blue eyes fixed on mine, a warning beneath the calm.

"Yes, Sire," I replied smoothly. "It's such a beautiful morning, it would've been a shame not to enjoy it." I smiled, as innocent as a choirboy.

"Did you greet any travellers?" His tone relaxed a touch. He even gave me a wink.

"Only Sir Henry," I said, bowing toward him, "and Davy, running an errand for Cook."

"So the roads are safe, for now," the Master chuckled. "Sir Henry will be staying for a few days. Business discussions. I'm counting on you to provide suitable entertainment."

"But of course, Master," I said, pulling juggling balls from my belt. I began to juggle, letting one drop before snatching it back with flair. The two men laughed.

"Save it for later," the Master said, waving me off. "We have matters to discuss."

"Anything I can help with?" I asked lightly, though a knot tightened in my chest.

Sir Henry smirked. "What would you know?"

"No, not for this, Thomas," the Master replied, already turning away.

I offered another bow and withdrew.

Behind me, Henry sneered, "The cheek of him."

The Master replied, dryly: "I value Thomas's input. He has alternative ideas." Their shared laughter echoed behind me as I walked the corridor alone.

* * *

It had been a chaotic few days. I was constantly called upon to entertain the Master's guest, which grew tiresome quickly. The only saving grace was catching glimpses of Anne. She always looked radiant, a soft smile playing on her lips like a secret not yet told.

I hadn't noticed these feelings until several months ago, when they hit me like a blow to the chest. She had come to Coeur House soon after the last mistress's death, unaware of the impact she would have on the household and me. Now, I found myself waiting for every chance to see her, to speak with her, just to be near her. A fool in every sense, and she, the Mistress. It could never be more than admiration. But still, I dreamed. Often, beneath the chestnut tree.

One such daydream was broken by a poor, unfortunate soul. I had a gift, or perhaps a curse, for taking a dislike to travellers at first glance. This one was more than just unlikeable. Its timing was deadly.

I heard it long before I saw it, singing a jaunty little ditty that grated on every nerve. I was already in a foul mood. Henry Bromley still loitered like an unwelcome shadow, and Anne was confined to her chambers, caught by one of her '*illnesses.*' No soft glance. No kind words. Just her absence, and this wretch's grating melody. I pried open my eyes slowly, unwilling to fully surrender the comfort of my brooding. Still singing. Still smiling. Still alive, for now.

As it came within speaking distance, I called out, "Good day to you," forcing a smile.

"Good day, sir," it replied cheerfully.

"Where are you off to?" I asked, masking my irritation behind a smile I didn't mean.

"I hope to find work," it answered, its young face shining like polished brass. "I heard there might be a position opening in the Stephens' house."

My teeth ground together. No way on this earth would that creature find work there, certainly not on my watch.

"Ah. Right."

"Would you know of the place?" it asked, innocence dripping from every word like fresh sap.

"Well, yes," I replied, feeling mischief swell inside me, threatening to spill over.

"Could you kindly give me directions, sir?" it continued, eagerness bubbling like a kettle left too long on the fire.

Before I could stop myself, or perhaps because I didn't want to, I gave it the directions.

"Can you see that oak tree yonder?" I pointed to an ancient tree standing alone in the distance, bowed with age and wisdom it did not share. It nodded.

"Head towards it, and you'll see the house. Just keep going. It's a shortcut and shall get you to *your* destination."

"Thank you, sir," it said brightly, and turned to go on its way.

A flicker of conscience stirred, but it was already singing again. I watched it walk, step by step, ever closer to its now unstoppable fate. With each footfall, death screamed louder, yet that infernal tune drowned it out.

Step.

By step.

Then I saw it. The sudden jolt of panic in its eyes as its feet vanished beneath the surface. The ground had opened its maw. It tried to move, to twist free, to shout. Its arms flailed, desperation rising, but each motion only dragged it further in.

Up to the waist now.

It thrashed, turned, and caught my eye.

Up to the chest.

It banged at the earth, pleaded with it, but the ground paid no mind.

Inch by inch, it swallowed.

And then it was gone.

The earth swallowed it whole. Nothing left but its stick, a cloth bundle now spattered in dark soil, a final pointless echo of its journey. A dark satisfaction bloomed within me. I leaned back against the chestnut tree, the bark biting into my spine like applause. The branches swayed above, whispering like voices from another time, and my eyes slid shut.

Somewhere between waking and sleep, she came.

She was there, smiling at me, her brown eyes glowing with warmth. Her cane-coloured hair was pinned high atop her head, soft wisps escaping to frame her delicate face. Freckles dusted her pale skin, lending her a quiet, human beauty.

"Thomas," she said. Her voice was music, and it made my heart dance.

"Thomas, why do you do it?"

Her tone shifted. The smile faded. Shadows swallowed the light as clouds rolled overhead.

"What?"

The light in her eyes dimmed into sorrow. Deep, unspoken sorrow that pierced me in two.

"That knave," she said, stepping away, her voice distant. "The other travellers. Margaret?"

The name struck like a thunderclap.
Margaret.
Buried, locked away, now unearthed.

"I... it was annoying," I stammered. The words felt thin, brittle. "Some were cruel. They threatened the Master," I added, grasping at justifications like driftwood in a storm. "I was protecting him."

She said nothing. Only shook her head slowly. Her eyes, deep and unbearable, held mine.
The sickness rose again.

"Margaret?" she asked once more, softly. Her delicate brow arched, accusing, heartbroken.
And I could not speak.
A searing pain shot through me, as if she had struck my very soul.
That night had been buried in shadow.

But now:
A candle flickered in the dark, and her face swam into view.
Margaret.
Her eyes were wide with surprise.

A bed.
The feel of her neck,
No.
The panic in her breath,
No.
The Master's voice, somewhere behind me: "I want it done. Now."
And me, obeying.
She had fought. She had not wanted to go.
But I had no choice.
It was the Master's will.

"That's not an excuse, Thomas," Anne's voice cut clean through the memory, slicing into Margaret's final gasp. "Her children needed her."

"I... I had to..." I stammered, heart hammering. She knew. Somehow, she knew.

Anne's expression twisted, torn and broken. I wanted to block her out, to close my ears.

"And when he tires of me?" she pressed, her voice tight with rising fury. "Will that be my fate too? Shall I become an 'it' as well?"

Her words gutted me. The very thought of my hands around her neck, as they had been around Margaret's, filled me with horror. With sickness. Not Anne. Never Anne.

"He was just as obsessed with her in the beginning," she said coldly.

"I couldn't protect her. She did not understand," I whispered.

"And you think that makes it right?" she spat.

Panic clutched at my throat. "I would never let that happen to you," I said. "I,

I love you."

She laughed.

"You? Love me?" Her voice rang with disbelief. "Thomas the fool. Murderer with painted smiles. In love with his Mistress?"

The laughter echoed inside my ears, around my head, from within and without.

"What on earth makes you think I could ever love you?" she sneered. "You're a murderer."

That word struck like a blade.

Her hatred was a storm, and I stood unguarded in its path.

I wanted to vanish. To melt into the earth like the boy I had so gleefully condemned.

"Please, Anne, no," I begged, my voice cracking. "Please... I can change. I promise."

She stepped closer, her eyes blazing.

"Thomas," she said slowly, each word sharp as flint, "thou blinking, blood-handed fool."

My stomach twisted. My whole being recoiled.

"How could I possibly love that?" she whispered.

And with a shudder, she turned away, leaving only silence behind.

"Tom!"

A voice cut through the fog. "Tom! Tom! Wake up, you fool."

A sharp shake followed, and I jolted upright, blinking into the midday sunlight. Davy's face hovered above mine, his green eyes wide with concern.

"What do you think you're doing, shouting the Mistress's name like that?" he hissed.

My head swam with images that made my stomach churn. I swallowed the bitter bile rising in my throat. "I was dreaming," I croaked.

"I could see that," Davy said, sitting back on his heels. "And the whole county could probably hear it. You need to be careful who you dream about. If the Master had heard you..." He winced and trailed off. "Well, you know how he'd take it."

"Yes," I murmured, dragging a hand across my face. "Indeed. I won't be dreaming of that again."

Not willingly, I added in silence. I pushed myself upright and stretched stiffly. The sick taste of guilt still clung to the back of my throat.

"The Master's going to Gloucester with Sir Henry," Davy said, watching me closely. "He wants you to go with him. Something about advising on a situation."

"Oh?" I blinked. "Advising?" It wasn't unheard of, but never for anything of real importance.

"That's all you have to say?" Davy raised an eyebrow. "The Master wants you at his side, and you're just sitting there like a sack of turnips."

"I'm... intrigued," I said, brushing dirt from my sleeve. "Though if I'm honest, I can't imagine what on earth he needs me for. Sir Henry looked ready to choke on his wine when it was mentioned the other evening."

A chill crept into my chest, slow and unwelcome. The promise. The dream had barely faded, and already it stirred again, rising like rot beneath the floorboards. I groaned inwardly. Whatever the Master had in mind, it wouldn't end well.

73

7

The Silent Blade (Gloucester 1592)

The room was dark.

A chink in the shutters let in a narrow slice of moonlight, illuminating a thin strip of floor, just enough to guide my steps toward the bed. A large form lay beneath the covers, motionless but breathing. The rise and fall of its chest was steady. Shallow. Air slipped through its half-open mouth in soft, rhythmic bursts.

The sooner this was done, the better.

Slowly, I withdrew the dagger from inside my tunic and stepped to the headboard.

One strike. That was all.

I hovered. The sleeper shifted slightly, adjusting position.

I didn't let myself think.

In a single, swift motion, I drew the dagger across the throat. Its eyes snapped open, bulging with pain and disbelief. Blood spurted, dark and hot, staining the sheets and soaking the nightshirt. Its hand flew to the wound, clutching, scrabbling. Useless.

A wet gurgle rose. A rasping wheeze. Panic twisted into pleading. Its face, tear-streaked and blood-smeared, looked straight at me. Its mouth opened and closed like a dying fish, silent. One hand reached out, slick and trembling, fingers curled in desperation.

I couldn't bear to watch.

I raised the dagger again.

It saw the glint of steel catching moonlight.

Its eyes widened.

Frenzied.

With a thrust, I drove the blade into its chest. The body jolted once, then fell slack. Darkness spread from the wound, soaking the fabric, the mattress. The blood carried its life with it. I stepped back. Withdrew the blade.

Melted into the shadows.

The room held its breath.

And then, only silence.

8

Beneath the Mask

The Master celebrated with Sir Henry for several days after we returned to the house. Their jovial mood only papered over the tension that lingered, like smoke clinging to the rafters. Anne and the children joined the festivities, though Anne herself seemed quieter than usual, her smiles softer, her gaze distant.

"Apparently, while we were in Gloucester," the Master said breezily, swirling wine in his goblet, "the justice of the peace from Worcester met an untimely end." He paused theatrically. "All rather unpleasant. The poor chap was asleep when some scoundrel crept into his chamber and slit his throat." He raised an eyebrow, smirking. "Then, just to be sure, stabbed him in the heart." He winked at me.

I forced a smile and played my part. I cracked jokes, juggled anything within reach, and caught the laughter in Anne's voice when I dared to listen. She sat by the unlit fire, hands folded in her lap, hair pinned up with care.

I dropped one of the apples I was juggling and watched it.

"Careful, Thomas," the Master chuckled, eyes bright with amusement.

The apple rolled across the floor, bumping gently against the hem of Anne's gown. She bent to retrieve it, her movements quiet and graceful. The neckline of her dress revealed the long, pale curve of her neck, so exposed, so fragile. It made me pause. And that's when I saw them. Marks on the back of her neck.

Scratches.

Red. Raw.

Still healing.

I stared, just for a second too long. She sat back upright, apple in hand. Our eyes met, and she smiled, a quiet, knowing smile.

"Thank you, Mistress," I said, accepting the apple, forcing brightness into my voice.

I turned back to the others and resumed juggling, but my thoughts clung to those marks like burrs. Anne watched me still, her smile soft, her eyes distant.

"They've asked me to step in," The Master boomed. His words slurred with drink. "Of course, I agreed." His laughter rumbled through the room, bouncing off the walls. He raised his glass in my direction and met my eye.

I dropped another apple, this time on purpose. The children burst into laughter, swept up in the merriment.

Miss Abigail stood and lingered shyly for a moment before turning to Anne. "Would you care to come to the library, Mother?" she asked, already moving toward the door.

Anne rose and turned to her husband. "Will you excuse us, Richard?" she said, dipping into a graceful curtsy.

As she moved, I caught sight of them again:
the scratches,
still red,
still healing.
My stomach clenched.

The Master crossed the room to her and took her hand, drawing her close.

"Of course, my love," he murmured, his voice thick with wine. His lips brushed her cheek, then her mouth, his hands following with calculated ease. Fingers lingered just a moment too long. Then, abruptly, he let her go.

She stumbled, catching herself on the edge of the door frame. But her composure snapped back with practised grace.

"Thank you, Richard. Good night, Sir Henry," Anne said, offering a curtsy.

Back straight, chin high, she followed Abigail from the room, leaving behind the last echoes of laughter and the weight of things unspoken. Their footsteps echoed against the stone.

With the ladies and children gone, the conversation turned.

"A fine Mistress you have there, Richard," Sir Henry said, his gaze lingering a moment too long on the empty doorway.

The Master grinned. "The lady is," he chuckled, "very satisfactory. Thank you for introducing us."

"I knew she would be," Henry replied, lifting his cup. "Far more appealing than your previous choice." He took a long swig. "If not for our close ties and the rather persistent Miss Elizabeth Varney, I might have claimed her myself."

"Well, I'm grateful," the Master said smoothly. "She's excellent. And speaking of Elizabeth, I'll be seeing her again next week. The deal's nearly sealed."

They laughed together. Then they turned to me.

"I'll say again," Sir Henry slurred, "excellent work the other night, Thomas. No one suspected a thing."

I gave a sweeping, theatrical bow, my smile wide and my heart hollow. God, how I hated him. How I hated myself.

"Yes, Thomas," the Master added, lifting his cup. "You did a fine job, as always. I know I can rely on you."

A flicker of contempt burned in my chest.

"Would you excuse me, sir?" I asked. "Unless, of course, you need further assistance this evening."

"Yes, you may go," the Master said, already turning back to Henry and his half-empty goblet. "I'll be retiring. Time for some well-deserved attention from my wife." He laughed.

Sir Henry joined him, raising his cup. "Don't keep her waiting, eh?"

"Good night to you, sirs," I said with another grand bow, then turned and stepped into the corridor.

My stomach churned. My head spun. I should have gone to bed and shut the door on it all for the night. But instead, my feet carried me forward. After a moment's pause, I headed down the corridor toward the library.
    Fool.

I didn't know why I was doing this. I only knew I had to see her.

Anne.

The image of those cruel marks haunted me. Driven by something I couldn't name, my steps quickened, echoing softly on the stone floor.

As I neared the library, I heard voices: Anne's low murmur and the sleepy tones of the twins replying.

"Mother, how do you endure such treatment?" Concern edged Miss Abigail's voice.

"He is our father," Miss Sarah added. "But even we can see he is not always a kind man."

"Your father has much on his mind," Anne replied gently. "Sometimes the pressures weigh heavily."

"Mother, you are far too forgiving," Sarah said.

"I am grateful to your father and to you children," Anne went on. "Had you not taken me in, on Sir Henry's suggestion, I would likely be penniless. My family might have lost even more."

But she knew the truth, and it was far more than that.

"But still, Mother," Abigail pressed, "you deserve better."

"I am quite content," Anne said firmly. "And I have you girls to keep me company."

I heard the smile in her voice, and my heart fluttered. I stepped closer to the doorway and caught sight of them glowing in the firelight. Anne looked up and smiled.

"Forgive the interruption, Mistress," I said, bowing low.

"That's quite all right, Thomas." Her smile deepened, and I fought to rein in the rush of joy. "Is something wrong?"

The scratches flashed across my mind again. I wanted to ask, to reach for her, to kiss the wounds, to promise she'd never be hurt again. But I did not.

"No, Mistress," I said, clearing my throat. "Good night to you all."

As I turned, I heard the Master's voice echo faintly down the corridor, bidding Sir Henry good night. I slipped quietly from the doorway and made my way to my room. Once inside, I lay on the bed and let the week unravel behind my eyes.
The laughter.
The blood.
The bruises.
The apple.
Her smile.
Hours passed before sleep finally came.

* * *

I know what you're going to say, Thomas," he said, exasperation in his voice. Sir Henry had returned several days before, leaving the Master restless and eager to rejoin the succession talks in London. "That I shouldn't involve myself in such matters. But I believe the man and his followers make a fair point."

"Just don't commit to anything yet, sir," I said carefully, hoping he'd hear the quiet plea beneath my words. I doubted he did.

"I shall listen to their arguments," he said, half-distracted as he adjusted the saddle. "Then I'll decide, once I've had time to consider."

I nodded respectfully as he mounted his brown horse, waiting patiently nearby. He settled into the saddle and glanced down at me again.

"You can keep an eye on things here, can't you, Thomas?" he asked. He paused. "And take care of my Anne," he added softly. "The lady hasn't been well. I worry for her. She doesn't quite understand how things work."

A trace of genuine sorrow touched his voice.

"Indeed, sir," I said, bowing. "How long do you expect to be gone?"

"A couple of weeks should suffice," he replied. "Thankfully, Miss Elizabeth is finally about to settle the deal with Henry. The lady dallied so long I feared Henry might lose interest."

"Not Sir Henry," I said dryly. "He's been besotted with Miss Elizabeth for some time, or rather with her dowry and your position."

The Master gave me a mock-stern look. "Thomas, if I didn't value you so highly, you'd be keeping company with those unfortunate travellers we turned away last winter." Then his face broke into a grin, and he laughed. "But I cannot say you're wrong."

I bowed again, accepting the jest.

"I shall be calling upon Wentworth and his associates," he said, adjusting the reins.

"May I speak freely?" I ventured, concern gnawing like a splinter beneath the skin.

He glanced at me expectantly.

"It troubles me that you're dealing with Peter Wentworth," I said. "The man may be a lawyer, but his obsession with Her Majesty's succession borders on treason."

The Master gave me a long, thoughtful look and said no more. With a flick of the reins, he turned and rode off. I watched the dust rise behind him, curling in the morning light until he vanished from sight.

I was turning back toward the house, about to step inside, when I heard children laughing. Grateful for the distraction, I followed the voices to the lawn beside the pond. Wynn sat on the grass, her skirts spread neatly, watching them. She waved as I approached. I lowered myself onto the soft earth beside her.

"Morning, Tom," she said with a smile. "Has the Master gone then?"

"Yes," I said.

"You seem a bit down," she said, eyeing me shrewdly. "That's not a good look for a jester," she added with a chuckle.

"Just feeling a bit lost," I said, lying. The truth sat heavily in my chest. I knew exactly where I wanted to be, and with whom, but I couldn't.

"I'm sure the children would enjoy your company," Wynn said, giving me a knowing look.

"Yes," I said, mustering a smile. "I shall be delighted to oblige."

It was true. I always enjoyed spending time with the children, and the sound of their laughter was already lifting the weight from my chest. We sat in companionable silence, watching the children play.

The two girls were trying to teach Nathaniel how to play Chase. At just three years old, his version involved running in circles, arms flailing, and shouting, "Did get ya!" whenever either girl came near. The girls were endlessly patient, gently encouraging his chaotic efforts. Their laughter rang across the grass. For a moment, all was well. Hester, the eldest girl, wandered over and plopped down beside us. A moment later, Johannah and Nathaniel followed, settling cross-legged in the grass beside us.

"I'm filled with pangs of hunger," Nathaniel declared solemnly, looking up at Wynn with hopeful eyes.

"You're always filled with pangs of hunger," Wynn said, laughing. "Girls, take him to Cook. See if she has any fruit left. That should keep your pangs at bay until dinner."

Hester stood, brushed grass from her skirts, and coaxed the others to their feet. Together, they ambled toward the house. Then disappeared inside, their laughter lingering in the air. Wynn's gaze lingered on the door before she turned back to me.

"She's so good with them," Wynn sighed softly. "All of them are lovely, considering all they've been through."

"They're lucky to have you," I said, smiling.

Wynn was small in stature, her short brown hair framing an elf-like face. Her blue eyes held that familiar, mischievous twinkle.

"I consider myself the lucky one," she replied. "To have met such loving souls."

"How's Davy this morning?" I asked. I hadn't seen much of him while Sir Henry was visiting. He'd been constantly busy, running errands for Cook or answering the Master's every whim.

"He's good," Wynn said. "Tired, though. He's been at the Master's beck and call these past few days, now catching up on everything else."

"Yes. It's been intense," I murmured.

For a moment, the image of that dark bedroom returned: blood, silence, the wheeze of a dying breath.

"It'll be nice to have some quiet."

"You must've had a good time in Gloucester," she said. "The Master returned in fine humour."

"Not much to tell." I didn't want to think about what had taken place. "Just business. It clearly went well."

"Such secrecy," Wynn laughed. "You'd make a fine jester."

I chuckled, though it didn't quite reach my heart.

"How is the Mistress today?" I asked, eager to change the subject.

"She's better." Wynn's smile faded. A quiet moment passed between us.

"The Master's asked me to keep an eye on her while he's away," I said, trying to hide a flicker of pride.

"Mmm. Is that such a good idea?" Her voice dipped as her eyes locked onto mine. "We both know how you feel about her."

Her blue gaze searched my face, gentle but unflinching.

"It'll be fine," I said with a sigh, though my mind screamed the lie.

"Be careful." Wynn touched my arm, offering a small, knowing smile.

I nodded just as the children came dashing back, arms full of apples.

"Apple," Nathaniel declared proudly, holding up a shiny red prize.

"That looks tasty," I said with a smile. He took a generous bite and plopped down beside me.

"Can you show us some of your tricks?" Johannah asked. She was a quiet girl, her hair fairer than her siblings', her dark eyes full of hope.

"I have a couple of tasks to do first," I said gently.

Disappointment flickered across her face.

"But I'll show you something before bed," I added.

Her face lit up, and Hester clapped in delight.

"Yay!" Nathaniel cried, unsure why but eager to be part of it.

"I'll see you all later," I said, standing and stretching. I caught Wynn's eye and gave her a wink.

I set off toward the house, intending to carry out the Master's orders. But my mind wandered, and before I knew it, my steps had turned toward the library. I knew she would be there; it was her favourite place. Feigning casualness, I stepped inside. The musty scent of old pages and leather bindings wrapped around me, welcoming and familiar. I understood why she liked it.

There she was, curled on the window seat, legs tucked beneath her, head bent over a book. Light from the tall windows spilt across her hair like burnished copper. My breath caught. Just the sight of her stirred something deep and unfamiliar, something I barely understood. She looked up at the sound of the door. When she saw me, she smiled.

"Thomas," she said, her face brightening. "What can I do for you?"

"I came to see if all was well with you," I replied, relieved my voice held steady, though her smile had sent a jolt straight through me. "The Master asked me to keep an eye on you, since you've not been well." I bowed low.

"I am well, thank you, Thomas." Her hand lifted, almost absently, brushing her neck and arm. "Still, it is good to know you are here."

Her smile lingered, soft and unguarded. I wanted to stay in that moment, to let it last. Realising I had lingered too long, I stepped forward.

"May I ask what you're reading, Mistress?"

"The Faerie Queene," she said, still smiling. "I've read it a few times, but I always find something new."

I could hardly believe it. The words leapt from my lips before I could stop them:
    "Lo, I the man, whose Muse whylome did maske,
    As time her taught, in lowly shepherd's weeds,
    Am now enforced a far more unfit task..."

"For trumpets stern to change mine oaten reeds,"

Anne finished, her voice lilting with enthusiasm:
   "And sing of knights and ladies' gentle deeds;
   Whose praises having slept in silence long…"

We laughed together.

"You have read it too," she said, eyes wide. There was real warmth in her expression.

"Yes, Mistress," I replied. "It's one of my favourites, especially as it is dedicated to our beloved Queen."

"You may use my copy, if you wish," she said. Her voice softened, with a hint of hesitation.

"Thank you, Mistress." I bowed. "I shall bear that in mind."

I lingered a moment, taking in the scene. She was the picture of perfection. The mid-morning sun streamed through the window, casting a golden halo around her. My heart beat steadily and loudly in the hush. I knew I had to leave before I said something I shouldn't.

"I should tend to my duties. The Master left me several errands, and I promised to entertain the children before bed."

"That's fine, Thomas," she said. Was that disappointment in her voice, or only wishful thinking on my part?

"I meant my offer of the book," she called after me.

I turned back. "Thank you, Mistress." I bowed again, backing out, reluctant to take my eyes off her. Her face glowed in the sunlight, and something warm unfurled in my chest. I almost danced down the corridor.

"You're in fine humour," Davy said, stepping from one of the doorways.

"Yes, Davy," I replied, the smile refusing to leave my face. "I am."

"Just be careful, Tom," he said with a laugh, though a warning edged his voice.

"It may be too late for that," I laughed, and stepped out into the bright sunshine.

9

The Dream Beneath the Chestnut Tree

The sun warmed my face as she came to sit beside me. Its warmth echoed the fire that burned within. She lowered herself in silence. She wore the green dress I favoured most. It almost rivalled her beauty.

Without a word, she lay her head on my shoulder and draped an arm across my chest. She rested there a moment while I soaked it in, letting myself ease against the tree. Gently, I wrapped an arm around her and drew her closer. Her rose perfume drifted up, intoxicating and familiar. My senses reeled. She tilted her head to look at me, and I lowered mine. Our lips met softly, unhurried, melting into one. She pulled away and smiled wistfully.

"I can scarcely believe you are here," I whispered.

I leaned in to kiss her again, but she pushed back. The smile vanished; a frown creased her brow.

"Why did you do it?" she asked, her dark gaze fixed upon me. The moment shattered.

"Why did you break your promise?"

Fear closed around my throat. I was dumbstruck.

"I did only as the Master asked," I stammered.

The words tasted hollow. Guilt seared through me.

She continued to stare as she spoke:
"Full many mischiefes follow cruell wrath;
Abhorred bloodshed, and tumultuous strife,
Unmanly murder, and unthrifty scath,
Bitter dispight, with rancour's rusty knife;
And fretting griefe, the enemy of life:
All these, and many evils moe haunt ire."

No, not those words. She could not. They cut deeper than any blade and were matched only by the disdain in her eyes. She rose to her feet and began to walk away. I called after her, begging forgiveness, knowing that if she ever learned the whole truth, she never would.

My eyes flew open. I was beneath the chestnut tree, alone. I wept, unaware of the spying eyes and listening ears.

10

The Master's Game

The weeks passed, and I went about my duties, always with a constant ache to be near Anne. The Master had returned, his mind abuzz with the ideas of Peter Wentworth and his fellow schemers.

"He makes a fair point, Thomas," he said one afternoon, pacing the drawing room, his hands slicing the air with restless energy. "If Her Grace were to die, the realm would be left without a monarch. There would be unrest."

"I understand that, sir," I replied, though in truth, I believed our beloved Queen would reign for many years yet. "But it is not for him to press such matters." I hoped my voice did not betray the frustration stirring in my chest.

"He claims to have the support of certain members of the Privy Council," the Master said, his voice rising. "He is sure of it. He believes the time is right to raise the issue."

"Our Queen knows what she is about," I said, unable to keep my tongue. "Look how far she has led us already. She sent the Spaniards packing with their tails between their forks in no time."

The Master turned and regarded me closely. A chill crept through my bones. Had I said too much? His ice-blue eyes locked on mine, as though sifting through my thoughts. Then, slowly, a grimace twisted into a strained smile. He let out a sharp laugh.

"I forget how devoted you are to the Queen," he said, his voice light but edged.

He paused. The smile deepened, growing sharper.

"Or is it to any mistress with cane-coloured hair, perhaps?"

The breath caught in my chest like a blow. I managed a short, awkward chuckle. Did he know? Surely not. I hadn't been foolish enough to show my feelings outright. But now my thoughts reeled, sifting through every glance I might have stolen, every lingering look. No, I had always been careful when he was near. Or perhaps that was the very thing that gave me away. Had someone been watching? I laughed again, forcing a casual tone.

"Our beloved Queen is quite mistress enough for me."

"Mmm." He kept staring, searching. Then, as if satisfied for now, he turned back to his original point.

"Well, we are having further discussions soon."

"Yes, sir," I replied, eager to move on. "How did things go with Mistress Elizabeth? Is the betrothal to Sir Henry arranged?"

His expression softened, content.

"Ah, yes. It is all arranged. The betrothal will take place in a few weeks."

"That is good news," I said. "I always enjoy a betrothal. Plenty of excuse for mischief and mirth."

The Master smiled.

"Yes. A good pairing. The lady has done rather well for herself."

I smiled back, teasing lightly.

"I was under the impression Sir Henry was the fortunate one."

He gave me another long, unreadable look, then laughed.

"If I didn't know better," he said, "I'd think you were going soft." His eyes narrowed. "'Tis fortunate I have another task for you."

My stomach turned to ice. In my mind, the words of The Faerie Queene returned, haunting and bitter:
>   *'Abhorred bloodshed, and tumultuous strife,*
>   *Unmanly murder, and unthrifty scath...'*

Each line struck like a tolling bell, echoing what I had done and what I might yet be asked to do again. Anne's voice accompanied the thought, along with her look of quiet, piercing disappointment.

The task turned out to be one of persuasion, though not the verbal kind. The Master hated being kept waiting for payment. This unfortunate soul had delayed for months after committing a crime serious enough to warrant prison or the gallows. He had been caught poaching in broad daylight.
   His excuse?
   He needed to feed his family and saw no other way.

Surprisingly, the Master had shown pity, a rare thing for him, and struck a deal: the man would be spared prison if he paid a penny fine. But the man hadn't paid.

Not a farthing.

Not until I went to persuade him.

By the time I left, he was a sorry sight. Blood trickled from his nose, both eyes swollen shut, and a few teeth were scattered across the dirt floor. And somehow, miraculously, he found his penny.

That evening, as I made my way back to the house, a weight lifted from my chest. I reminded myself:

At least I hadn't broken my promise again.

No lives taken.

Only bruises.

Only pain.

"How did it go, Thomas?" the Master asked as I entered the drawing room.

"Fine, sir," I said, placing the penny carefully on the Master's desk by the window. "I doubt he'll delay payment again."

"Well done."

The Master picked up the coin, turning it slowly between thumb and finger. He crossed to a large picture frame bearing the family crest, a sphinx on a black shield. With practised care, he lifted it down, revealing a safe embedded in the stone behind it.

He rifled through the keys at his belt until he found the right one. A soft click echoed as the lock turned. The door swung open, revealing papers, jewellery, and a heavy leather pouch filled with coins. He slipped the penny inside, closed the safe, and restored everything to its exact place. The crest hung straight as ever when he stepped back.

Then he moved to his writing desk, dark polished wood, everything arranged just so: papers, a quill, an ink pot, and his seal with its rounded wooden handle. He sat, opened a drawer, and pulled out a ledger. After scribbling a few lines, he leaned back in his chair and fixed his eyes on me.

"What do you think of the Mistress?"

The question landed like a stone.

"The lady is especially good with the children. Miss Sarah and Miss Abigail have grown quite fond of her," I said carefully, weighing each word.

His gaze did not waver. I felt as though he were sifting my soul, piece by piece. Something tightened in my chest. The silence thickened. The walls seemed to press in. Idly, the Master moved the quill back and forth across the desk. The soft rasp of a feather against wood was the only sound.

"Those girls miss their mother," he said at last, voice low. "As do I."

It was the first time he had spoken of his first wife in years. There was sorrow in his tone, but it was twisted, hard-edged, and unresolved.

"I remember her well," I said quietly. "She was kind. The house was different then, lighter somehow."

He laid down the quill. His voice dropped to a whisper.

"She was a fine mistress. She knew how things should be."

He stood and crossed to the sideboard, where he poured a generous glass of brandy. He took a sip and grimaced.

"The Mistress Anne does not." Another sip, longer this time.

"I have been trying to make her understand, but she just does not seem to get it." A third swallow. I did not like where this was heading.

"If I may be so bold," I began.

"Again?" he snapped, the words sharp, like flint striking steel. But then he caught himself. A slight smile softened his face. "Forgive me. Do continue. You are my voice of reason, Thomas."

I swallowed hard. "The lady is still new to the household. In time, I am sure she will come to understand."

Cold sweat slid beneath my collar.

"I thought that of Mistress Margaret," he said quietly. "Look how that ended."

For a moment, a shadow flickered across his face. Remorse? Or something darker? Pain clenched my heart. I understood now where this conversation was heading.

"Sir... Mistress Margaret was a different sort of mistress," I said, my voice sounding small and weak.

"But how long do I give her?" he muttered, pouring another measure of brandy. He began pacing again.

"She is so naïve for a woman of her years, and it is not as if she shall bear children."

He took a deeper drink, the glass trembling slightly in his hand.

"The children need a mother," I said quietly, trying to anchor us both.

"Miss Sarah and Miss Abigail do a fine job, and there is Wynn."

"It is not the same."

His voice was slurred now, frustrated and fraying at the edges.

"Sarah and Abigail will soon have families of their own," I offered gently. "They are of age now."

He paused and considered.

"True. Twenty already." Another gulp. "I must get them betrothed; Mr Wentworth can assist me."

He drained the last of the brandy and slammed the glass onto the sideboard. The crack echoed through the room like a shot. Then he turned, stumbling toward the door, calling out with growing agitation.

"Anne! Anne! Where are you?"

Then he was gone, his footsteps echoing down the corridor, his voice growing fainter. I stood alone in the dim light of the drawing room. The scent of brandy still lingered in the air. Silence pressed in, thick and breathless. I prayed the drink had dulled his edge and that Anne was safely out of reach.

From down the corridor, raised voices reached me as the Master began outlining his plan. Was it wrong to feel a flicker of relief that his attention had turned to the girls instead? As I made my way toward the library, Miss Sarah and Miss Abigail passed me, their faces drawn, eyes wet with tears. Behind them, their father's imposing shadow loomed.

"Richard, how can you suggest such a thing?" Anne's voice trembled, a quiet plea threaded with steel. "They aren't ready. Surely love should count for something?"

"What would you know?" The Master's reply cracked like a whip.

"If their mother were here, those girls would already be betrothed. The lady understood how things should be."

I reached the doorway and froze. Anne looked as though she had been struck, her pale cheeks stained with tears not yet fallen, trembling at their edges. My stomach twisted. I fought the urge to rush forward, to pull her into my arms and shield her from the storm raging around her.

"Sir," I said carefully, my voice low, "perhaps it would be best to continue this discussion tomorrow."

The Master glared at me, his gaze blurred by drink. I braced myself for an outburst, but he only gave a slow, grudging nod and turned away. At the door, he paused. "Deal with her. Make her understand."

Then he was gone, leaving the room thick with tension and Anne trembling at its centre. Fear shone starkly in her eyes as I stepped forward.

"Shh," I whispered, gently raising my hands. "I am not going to hurt you."

At last, the tears broke free, trailing down her cheeks and soaking into her dress. Without thinking, I drew her close. She stiffened at first, then slowly melted against me, her sobs muffled by my shoulder.

"It is all alright now, Mistress," I murmured. "I will look after you."

We stood in silence until her sobs began to ease. She pulled away slightly, her face streaked and searching. I lifted a hand to brush her cheek. She flinched. I stepped back at once, my heart aching. She studied me a moment longer.

In a low, steady voice, she asked, "The whispers say Mistress Margaret, Nathaniel's mother, was murdered."

The words hung between us like smoke, heavy and suffocating. Her eyes searched mine with desperate urgency. I took a step back, unsettled by the question and by the raw fear reflected in her gaze.

"It is not always wise to heed whispers, Mistress," I said at last, my voice measured but gentle, though the truth twisted in my gut.

"No, Thomas," she replied softly, her voice tinged with resignation. "You are right."

She turned away briefly, and I caught a faint glimpse of bruises hidden beneath her collar. She wiped her face with trembling hands before turning back to face me.

"I suppose you agree with the Master," she said quietly, "that the girls should be married off?"

I hesitated, weighing my words carefully. "It is the custom. They are of an age."

She exhaled a bitter breath. "You men all think the same, marry into fortune as though love were some luxury to be afforded only by the foolish."

I closed my eyes, wishing I could speak the truth aloud, that love should be at the heart of it all, the only reason.

"Love can grow later," I said instead, striving to keep my voice steady.

"Security is important, especially now."

Her glare cut through me like a blade. "I thought you were different, Thomas, a man who reveres the Queen, who recites poetry." She shook her head slowly. "I was wrong."

No, you were not. I wanted to scream it aloud. Instead, I bowed my head. "I am sorry to disappoint you, Mistress."

I had to ease her worries. "The Master will ensure they are matched with men of standing. Mr Wentworth has made some promising suggestions."

Anne looked stricken. "Those poor girls... how can he do this to them?" Her voice cracked. "To live without choice. To be owned by a man who does not even see you."

For the first time, I truly saw her loneliness and felt its weight. I stepped closer and reached for her hand.

"I am sorry," I whispered. "Please believe me, I will look after you. And Miss Sarah. And Miss Abigail."

She lifted her eyes to mine, and my heart leapt. There, a fragile glimmer of trust.

"Thank you, Thomas," she said softly, offering a smile that was too weary to reach her eyes. "I want to believe you." She paused, her eyes still on mine. "I shall retire now, the Master will be waiting, and I can tell him you made me understand."

She turned without another word and walked away with quiet grace. I remained standing there in the hush of the library. Her copy of The Faerie Queene lay open on the chair, still warm from her touch. My eyes fell upon the passage:

'Mirrour of grace and majestie divine,
Great ladie of the greatest isle, whose light,
Like Phoebus lampe throughout the world do shine,
Shed Your faire beames into my feeble eyne,
And raise my thoughts too humble and too vile...'

I set the book gently down. The words lingered like a bruise. I vowed, then and there, to protect her. And the girls. Whatever the cost.

As I walked the halls, checking doors and extinguishing candles, I passed the Master's chamber. Behind the closed door came muffled sounds, rhythmic, cruelly familiar. I stopped, hand at my side. She was safe. For now. But my heart splintered. Anne had understood all too well what was expected of her. And I shuddered.

* * *

The weeks passed. Summer melted into autumn, and Anne's relationship with the Master began to blossom. They seemed to be falling in love. I should have felt relief; she was safe, after all. Instead, jealousy coursed through me like poison.

At first, I found comfort in the time I still spent with her. The Master, in rare good humour, began including me in discussions about the gentlemen he deemed suitable for the girls. The morning after that night in the library, he pulled me aside.

"Well done, Thomas," he said, grinning. "Whatever you did with the Mistress has worked. The lady could not be more compliant."

I smiled tightly. "Glad to be of service, sir."

I hated him.

"I shall be meeting with Wentworth soon to discuss suitable husbands. There are several to choose from." He rubbed his hands together like a man preparing for a feast.

"Very good, sir." I kept my voice steady, smothering the surge of anger rising in my chest.

"I want you to come with me," he added. "The Mistress seems to hark to you. If she sees you involved, she might take the suggestions more gently."

"I'd be delighted to help," I lied, forcing a smile. I told myself that any chance to be near Anne was worth it. It was the only thread of comfort I had left.

Once the arrangements were made and the suitors agreed upon, the Master's attention shifted to Wentworth and the cause he and his companions championed.

Summer waned, giving way to the bite of late autumn. One autumn afternoon, as fallen leaves crunched beneath my boots, I returned from the chestnut tree to find the Master flushed and radiant with excitement.

"Thomas!" he called out. "I've been looking for you."

"Yes, sir," I replied cautiously. "I've been at the chestnut tree."

"Ah, how are the travellers?" He laughed.

"Few and far between," I said. That was a lie. There had been many, yet the promise endured, burning deep within me.

"They must have heard of your reputation!" he guffawed. "But enough of that. I'm going away for a few weeks. There are discussions among Wentworth's circle about the succession, and I've been invited to join."

"Are you sure that's wise?" A ripple of worry passed through me, settling in tight knots. I may have despised him, but once he had been good to me.

"We're merely discussing our next move," he said, striding across the drawing room. He gathered books and papers, stacking them into his worn leather satchel.

"I had hoped you might reconsider," I said, barely containing the tremor in my voice.

"Don't worry, Thomas," he replied without looking up. "While I'm away, I need you to keep an eye on things. Particularly Anne. Now that the girls have gone, the lady misses them."

My heart leapt. The past weeks had been chaotic. Miss Sarah and Miss Abigail had both moved to their husbands' households, and the younger children still mourned their absence. Apart from the wedding celebrations, I had hardly seen Anne. I mourned her company, too.

"Of course, sir," I said, doing my best to mask my excitement. "But... are you certain this is the right thing to do?"

The Master stopped, turned, and fixed me with a hard glare. "I appreciate your counsel, Thomas, but I know what I'm doing."

"Indeed, sir." I should have known better than to question him. He was always so bloody stubborn.

"Wentworth assures us the Privy Council is sympathetic." His glare softened into a confident smile. "You do worry so, for a jester. I shall see you on my return."

And with that, he was gone. I stood alone in the drawing room, battling the urge to seek out Anne. Instead, I turned and buried myself in my duties. But no matter how I tried to focus, my thoughts strayed back to her.

Later that day, I heard Anne, Wynn, and the children playing in the gardens. Drawn by the sound of laughter, I followed it and found them amid a game of Blind Man's Bluff. Anne wore a white cloth over her eyes, her hands stretched ahead, sweeping the air in search of her companions. The children squealed with delight each time her fingers came near, darting away at the last moment to avoid being caught.

Wynn spotted me and beckoned, pressing a finger to her lips as she motioned for the children to keep quiet. Their giggles swelled as we joined in teasing Anne. I stood, watching her move. Her fingers drifted through the air like wisps of smoke, the faint curve of a smile beneath the blindfold. Each time a noise flared behind her, she spun quickly, only to return to her slow, graceful searching. Step forward. Back. And that laugh. It could have filled a cathedral and still made me crave more.

Quietly, I crept behind her. To the children's great amusement, I tapped her shoulder and stepped away. She turned, and suddenly we were face to face. My breath caught. I could think of nothing but how much I wanted to reach for her. I had lost my focus. Her hands reached out and found me. Her fingers brushed my waistcoat. She froze, then tore off the blindfold. The blush blooming on her cheeks made her beauty glow brighter than the sun.

"Thomas," she said, eyes wide, "I didn't know you'd joined us."

"The children thought it a splendid joke to invite Tom to take part," Wynn chimed in, her eyes gleaming with mischief.

"I hope you didn't mind, Mistress," I said, bowing low, only then realising I must have looked a fool with my mouth hanging open.

As I straightened, our eyes met, and for a fleeting second, I thought I saw something there. Something more. No. Just my own foolish hope.

"No, of course not," she said lightly. "The children always light up when you're around."

"Come on, Thomas!" Hester called. "It's your turn!"

"Indeed, Miss," I said, giving a comical curtsey as their laughter erupted.

Anne stepped forward and tied the blindfold over my eyes. Her fingers brushed my skin, a light, swift touch, and a shiver raced through me.
  Darkness fell.

Without sight, the world sharpened: birdsong, distant laughter, the hush of leaves. I turned slowly, arms outstretched, the cool breeze dancing across my face. To my left, a rustle. I pivoted. My foot slipped slightly on uneven ground.

"Careful, Tom!" Wynn called.

I turned again, adjusting my stance. My hands sliced through the air, slow and steady, but still no one. Giggles circled me like playful spirits. At last, hair brushed my fingertips. I caught the figure gently and drew it close. I pulled off the blindfold. Light poured in. Johannah stood before me, her face glowing with laughter. The other children shrieked with delight, clamouring for their turn. I handed her the cloth with a mock flourish, and the game carried on.

"I must give my apologies, Mistress, Wynn," I said, brushing grass from my coat.

"Of course, Thomas," Anne replied. Her eyes lingered on mine. A smile played at her lips, soft and searching.

I bowed and turned to leave.

"Thomas!" Anne called.

I stopped. She walked toward me. "The children love your antics," she said, a flicker of something, hope perhaps, in her voice.

"Would you find time, perhaps, to entertain them again?"

"Indeed, Mistress," I said, trying and failing to suppress my elation.

I walked away with my heart full, already wishing the hours would fly until evening.

* * *

"Tom! Tom!"

I heard Davy calling just as I stepped into my room. I groaned; it was bound to be another message from the Master. Several glorious weeks with the children and Anne were drawing to a close, and the household had begun to shift in anticipation of the Master's return. An air of unease drifted through the house. Messages had been arriving almost daily: mostly mundane instructions.

"Tom... been looking for you," Davy panted, sweat beading on his forehead. "A message from the Master, urgent."

I took the paper from his outstretched hand, noting the seal pressed into the wax.

What did he want now?

I'd spent days sorting documents, ensuring everything he'd asked for was in place. I broke the seal with a sharp pop and began to read. I held my breath. No, I must have read it wrong.

I read it again.

There was no mistake.

"Anything wrong, Tom?"

I'd forgotten Davy was still there and flinched at his voice.

"You look like you've seen an apparition."

"No, it's fine, Davy," I said smoothly. "The Master wants me to join him in Gloucester. He has a task for me."

"Ah," Davy said knowingly. "Then it must be important."

I managed a smile and nodded. "Yes... I'm sure it is."

My heart sank. It had been months since I last broke my promise. I should have known it wouldn't last.

I looked at Davy. "Can you ready a horse? He wants me there by nightfall."

"Indeed."

He turned and hurried down the corridor toward the stables.

I made my way to the library; Anne would be there. Sure enough, she was seated by the window, eyes skimming the page. I paused in the doorway, watching as a faint smirk curled her lips; so small a gesture, yet it lit her face with quiet radiance.

I cleared my throat. "Good day, Mistress."

She looked up. The smirk bloomed into a full smile and seemed to consume me whole.

"Hello, Thomas," she said softly. "Come, sit." She patted the space beside her.

This had become something of a habit, one I knew must end when the Master returned. But I wasn't ready to let it go. Not yet.

I crossed the room and sat beside her. The soft scent of her perfume caught me off guard and made my head swim.

"You are reading it again, Mistress?" I asked, nodding at her worn copy of The Faerie Queene.

"Mmm," she murmured. "I can not get enough of it. Sharing it with you makes it more enjoyable. Sarah and Abigail tried, but they do not understand the humour or the tragedy, not the way you do."

"Yes, Mistress."

Her soft brown eyes gleamed as she spoke, drawing me in, feeding dreams I should have long abandoned. How many times had she given me that look? That quiet, kind look, and each time, I had to fight the urge to pull her close, confess everything, and kiss those lips that haunted my sleep. Each time, my heart broke anew with the truth: it could never be.

"You seem a little down, Thomas." Her voice was light, teasing, yet gentle. "What's wrong?"

She reached over and placed her fingers lightly on mine. Did she know what that touch did to me? Was I imagining the warmth, the tremble, the possibility she might feel the same? My heart leapt. Then sank, heavy with reality. Foolish, foolish hope.

"The Master has summoned me," I said quietly, breaking the spell.

Her hand slipped from mine.

"Oh," she breathed, the disappointment on her face cutting deeper than I expected.

She glanced down at the book resting in her lap. "The children will be sad... they have loved your little plays so much. When do you leave?"

"He wants me there tonight," I said, the knot in my stomach tightening. I already knew what I'd be asked to do.

"Ah."

She kept staring at the book, her fingers absently tracing the page. I don't know what I was thinking, but I reached out and gently lifted her chin, urging her to meet my gaze. Her eyes shimmered with unshed tears. My heart ached.

"Mistress... what is wrong?" I breathed, letting my fingers slip from her chin to softly caress her hand.

"I shall miss this," she said, glancing around the room before meeting my gaze again. "I have been so caught up playing the Master's game, I forgot what true companionship... no, what friendship feels like."

The lingering tears finally spilt down her cheeks. I moved my hand gently to wipe them away. She caught it and pressed it to her lips. The whole world stilled. Could this truly be happening? Longing surged through me... for a moment, I teetered on the edge of reason... only just pulling myself back.

"Mistress," I murmured, withdrawing my hand, "we can not."

She held my gaze a moment longer, then gave a small, understanding nod. "I know, Thomas."

Her voice was soft, her eyes still bright with tears. "I know."
    She turned to the window, hiding her face from me.

"You never gave me cause to doubt you," she whispered. "You have stood by me through the darkest days. And in another time, another life, who knows what might have been. I was wrong to say you were like him. You are a good man, Thomas."

I rose slowly, heart heavy with the truth: I was far from the good man she believed me to be.

"We shall return in a few days," I said. "Until then, Davy will ensure you have all you require."

For a moment, she said nothing. Then softly, "Thank you, Thomas. I shall wait in eager anticipation for the return of my husband, and of you."
    She didn't turn as I left.

Outside, Davy waited by the horse. I mounted, the weight of the moment heavy on my shoulders.

"We should only be gone a couple of days," I said. "Give my love to Wynn."

He nodded, brow furrowed. "Are you all right, Tom? You look troubled."

I glanced back at the house; its windows shimmered in soft golden light. Anne still sat at the library window, her gaze cast across the courtyard.

"Look after the Mistress," I said.

Then I turned the horse, spurred it on, and galloped down the gravel drive, toward Gloucester... and whatever fate awaited me there.

11

The Narrow Shut (Gloucester Again 1592)

The shut was quiet.

I heard footsteps, slow and deliberate, walking toward certain death.

I held my breath as they neared the nook where I lay concealed. With every step, the knife in my hand grew heavier, the weight of what I was about to do pressing down on me like stone.

The urge to drop the blade and flee surged within me, but that was not an option. This was kill or be killed.

It came closer, tugging a dark doublet tighter around its slender frame. Shadows clung to it, folding around each step like a shroud.

I knew the odds were against me: I was smaller, weaker, but I had the element of surprise.

It never saw the blade coming.

The knife sank into the soft flesh of its stomach, drawing a gasp before it collapsed to its knees. Before it could understand what was happening, I moved behind it, gripped a handful of dark hair, and yanked its head back, exposing the pale skin of its throat.

The blade met little resistance.

Blood spilt freely from the gash, gurgling as it tried to cry out. It slumped, trembling, still trying to push itself up.

"I'm sorry," I whispered. "I can't let you go."

The knife plunged again, deep into its back. Once. Twice. Again and again.

Until it lay still.

Tears streaked my cheeks before I realised I was crying. My stomach twisted, heaved, and emptied onto the ground.

The stench of blood and bile filled the narrow shut.

I wiped my mouth with the back of my hand and reached for the money purse on its belt.

Without looking back, I walked away, leaving the body still and crumpled in the dark.

12

Another Time, Another Place

"Here he is!" the Master shouted as I entered the establishment where he stayed. "The man that solves all our troubles." He slapped me on the back, then frowned at my clothing. "Get yourself cleaned up. You're drawing attention to us," he hissed through clenched teeth.

I wandered through the inn and out into the dark courtyard, candles lighting several windows along the gallery; ivy trailed decoratively from the balcony above. I climbed the stairs to an unlit room, pushed open the door and stepped inside. A candle sat on the table near the entrance. I tossed the purse down and struck a flint to light the wick.

The room flickered to life.

Crossing to a jug resting on the side, I picked it up and returned to the courtyard, to the pump standing in its corner like a silent sentinel. As I worked the handle, water gushed into the jug, and my thoughts snapped back to him, the body, the thing, lying motionless; blood gushed from wounds I had caused.

Jug full, I climbed the stairs again and poured the water into the waiting basin. I splashed the icy liquid over my face and began scrubbing my hands.

115

But they would not come clean.
They could never be clean.

I stripped off my clothes and used the remaining water to wash the blood from the fabric. When done, I flung the red-tinged water out of the window. It hit the stones below with a slap, loud and brutal, and the sound stabbed my ears like a knife.

I dropped to my knees, breath ragged and broken. The weight of it all pressed down until I could no longer hold up my head. I curled tightly into a ball, letting the shadows fold around me, closing over me. A low groan rose in the room, and only slowly did I realise it came from me, deep and primal, rising from somewhere I could not reach. It swelled, took hold and grew into sobs. My limbs shook as I dragged myself to the narrow bed in the corner and climbed onto it.

Sleep, when it came, brought no peace. Instead, it brought words, words I had read, now echoing in my mind like a curse:
> Full many mischiefes follow cruell wrath;
> Abhorred bloodshed, and tumultuous strife,
> Unmanly murder, and unthrifty scath,
> Bitter despight, with rancour's rusty knife...

And images of Anne: Anne turning away, Anne laughing at the very idea of loving me. Unseen eyes and ears took it all in, and so my fight to survive began.

* * *

I awoke to the sound of hammering at the door and the Master shouting,

"Thomas! Thomas! What happened to you? I came to find you! His tone was severe, impatient.

The stickiness that glued my eyes together slowly cleared as I prised them open. They were puffy and sore, and rubbing them brought no relief. I staggered from the bed and grabbed my still-damp clothes.

"Sorry, sir, I had fallen asleep. Coming!" I called through the door.

"See to the horses," the Master barked. "We are finished here."

I heard his footsteps fade into the distance. My head ached and felt loose, as though it no longer belonged to me. It took all my wits to get dressed, concealing the purse inside my tunic, and stumble out toward the stables. Damp clothes made the autumn air bite even deeper. I shivered. As I drew closer, I heard the animals inside stamping and whinnying.

I stepped into the gloom. The warm air and familiar scent enveloped me. I closed my eyes. And there it was... the turmoil, the memory. I saw him lying lifeless in that cold shut. Other shadows flickered before me, crawling through my mind. I opened my eyes to drive them away, but voices whispered around me, accusing, berating, taunting.
   Suffocating.

I clumsily readied the horses, finding relief only when I could lead them back into the open air. The Master was waiting as I crossed the courtyard.

"You look awful, Thomas," he said, clearly enjoying the moment; his tone still brisk. "Come. I want to get back to the Mistress. We have more celebrating to do."

There was a relish in his voice that made me shudder. He mounted his horse in one swift motion and was already through the arched carriageway before

I'd even fumbled onto mine.

As we journeyed back to Coeur House, the sky darkened, and a stillness surrounded us as we headed back to the house. Clouds gathered like an army falling into formation. The Master galloped a short distance ahead, the house just in sight, when a bolt of lightning split the sky. A second later, thunder cracked overhead.

My horse pressed on, unfazed; the Master's reared in fright. Though he was a skilled horseman and held control for a moment, the next thunderclap undid it: his horse bucked violently and threw him into the air. I watched as he flew backwards and landed head-first on the hard ground. The horse galloped on, kicking out with each crack and rumble.

Rain began to beat down, sharp and fast. The Master lay motionless as the downpour pelted his body. I jumped down as I reached him, just as another crack of thunder startled my horse, sending it bolting into the distance. The Master stirred, clearly disoriented, groaning faintly. Fighting to clear the water from my eyes, I reached out to lift him.

Lightning flashed again, illuminating the rawness of the moment. For a split second, I hesitated; I could leave him there, let it end. The thought pulsed through me like a jolt; hatred coursed hot and fast. The promise, once again, would be broken.

"Come, sir," I shouted above the storm, forcing my hand to stay.

He tried to stand, but his legs gave way; I caught him, slinging his arm around my shoulders and grasping his waist. "Come, sir," I urged again. "We have to go."

Thus we stumbled back together, the earth beneath us sodden, slick, dragging at our feet; Slipping, cursing, and gritting our teeth. Our soaked clothes clung to our skin, our hair plastered to our skulls.

As we neared the rear entrance, I heard Davy shouting for help. The weight of the Master lifted from me as hands pulled him away. I heard myself shouting about the commotion, explaining what had happened, my voice rasping with effort. Someone guided me into the house, into my room. They urged me to remove the wet clothes and handed me dry ones; I obeyed without thought. Exhaustion gripped every muscle, and my whole body ached with strain. But I forced myself forward.

In the Master's room, he lay in the grand four-poster bed, its heavy curtains pulled back. A makeshift bandage was tied around his head, already stained with a red patch on the left side. Anne sat on the edge of the bed, holding his hand; her face was unreadable, carved from restraint. She heard me enter and looked up. A smile hovered over her lips but dissolved before it could form. I walked further into the room and stood silently at the end of the bed.

"How is he?" I asked, my eyes fixed on the Master.

"Quiet. We are waiting for the doctor," Anne replied. "Thank you for getting him home," she added, looking at me with a soft warmth lighting her eyes.

I nodded, drinking in the way she was looking at me. If only she knew of the temptation I had fought, nearly allowing him to perish.

Davy appeared in the doorway. "Excuse me, Mistress, but Cook wants Tom; she's worried he's not taking care of himself."

"Of course," Anne said. Concern flickered across her face as she turned her gaze back to me with more scrutiny. "You must look after yourself, Thomas. You have been such a strength; we need you around. I suppose you've not eaten. Make sure he eats. And rests."

"Yes, Mistress." Davy bowed low and turned away.

I followed but turned back once more at the door. Anne had already returned her attention to the Master, who was beginning to stir restlessly. She leaned close to him, softly whispering and placed a cool cloth on his forehead.

* * *

Down in the kitchen, Cook bustled around, clattering spoons and muttering to herself. She placed a bowl of steaming broth on the heavy wooden table. A spoon clinked sharply beside it.

"Come, Tom," she bellowed. "Sit yourself down and eat."

Embarrassed by the fuss, I obeyed. The smell was rich and savoury; as I lifted the spoon, the warmth began to steady me. Cook slapped a thick chunk of bread beside the bowl. Tearing it into pieces, I dunked them into the dark broth, letting the heat draw me back to myself.

Once I'd eaten, Davy led me to the cottage he shared with Wynn. The storm that had raged just hours before had nearly passed; only a drizzle remained. We walked through the grounds, chatting idly, then headed toward the small wood bordering the estate. At its edge stood a simple wooden cottage with a thatched roof, a small window, and a sturdy door.

Davy opened it, and we stepped into a room warmed by a glowing hearth. Two chairs flanked the fire; a wooden table stood proudly in the centre, surrounded by a couple more. A doorway to the right led into a darker room where a bed waited in shadow. I dropped into a chair as Davy fetched a beer jug and two tankards. He poured the amber liquid, handed me one, then sat opposite with his own. We drank in silence. Slowly, I began to relax. I hadn't realised how tightly wound I'd been until now.

"It has been quite a morning," Davy said softly.

"Mmm..." was all I could manage. Exhaustion crept in again; my eyes closed, and I drifted into a fitful sleep.

I awoke to the sound of Davy pacing; anxiety pulsed from him like heat from the fire. I kept still, feigning sleep and giving myself a moment to gather my thoughts. The latch clicked, and the door opened. Light footsteps followed.

"Well, what a mornin'," came Wynn's voice.

"Shh," Davy hushed her. "He's been asleep almost since we got here."

"Bless him," Wynn said gently. "It must have taken a lot, getting the Master home on his own like that."

"Yes," Davy replied, but now his tone had darkened.

"What's wrong, love?" she asked.

He paused. "He was talking in his sleep," Davy said at last. "Saying all manner of things..."

A chair scraped as Wynn sat down. "What sort of things?"

"A promise to the Mistress: saying how sorry he was, that he didn't want to do it any more."

"You know how dreams are," Wynn said gently, trying to comfort him.

"But it's not the first time," Davy pressed. "I've heard him before, talking about loving the Mistress. I'm worried about what he's gotten himself involved in."

"I think you're worrying about nothin'," Wynn replied, though her voice had lost some of its certainty.

I let out a low groan and began to stir, stretching as though just waking. When I opened my eyes, Davy stood by Wynn.

"You're awake," Wynn smiled. "How are you feeling now?"

I stretched again and stood, every part of me aching. "I'm good," I said. "Is everything alright? You look worried, Davy. Is the Master well?"

"He's fine, and so is the Master," Wynn jumped in quickly. "He's just worried about you."

"Wynn!" Davy snapped, not unkindly.

"Why?" I asked, feigning confusion. "I'm just stiff. The Master is no light man."

Davy looked at me, then at his wife, who gave a small nod.

"You... you were talking in your sleep, Tom."

The room spun; I knew I couldn't lie.

"Ah, you caught me again," I joked weakly, knowing full well I wouldn't joke my way out of this. Davy would want more than a shrug; he would demand the truth.

"It wasn't just about the Mistress, Tom," he said quietly. "You were talking about murder."

Wynn gasped. Inside, my body knotted tight, twisted into a ball that would not unravel.

"Oh," I breathed.

"What? Is that all you have to say?" Wynn sat upright now, eyes bright with shock.

"I don't know what else to say," I sighed.

"How about the truth?" Her voice was clipped; her arms folded tightly across her chest.

"It clearly troubles you, Tom," Davy said more gently. "If you tell us, maybe we can help."

I gave a sad smile. "No one can help me. I am a murderer. Have been for many years." I paused, then added, "That is why the Master took me into his service. He had heard how I dealt with my last employer's troubles... those who would not be rid of. I made sure they were gone, for good."

Saying it aloud brought relief, but it was short-lived as the horror on their faces cut me like my blade.

"I don't want to do it any more," I said, voice firmer. "Last night has to be the last."

Both Davy and Wynn gasped. I saw Wynn's expression of utter distaste for me. Davy pulled out a chair and sat beside his wife, taking her hand.

"Who was it?" he asked quietly.

I drew in a long breath. "A justice of the peace, someone Sir Henry Bromley and the Master wanted removed. It clears the way for Sir Henry to take his place."

They stared at me, mouths open in stunned silence.

"I don't want to do it any more," my voice thick with desperation. I needed them to understand, to believe me.

"Did you have anything to do with that poor fellow the Master and Sir Henry were talking about a few months ago?" Wynn's voice trembled, her eyes wide. I nodded. She covered her mouth.

"I didn't want to," I said, the words tumbling now. "I promised Anne I would stop. But he made me. I had no choice."

"The Mistress knows?" Now it was Davy's turn to be shocked.

I ran my fingers through my hair. "No... in my dreams I promised her." I sounded mad. Perhaps I was.

We sat in silence for what felt like an age. My world crumbled into ash, and I sank with it. Tears slid down my face, remorse searing deep within me. Wynn rose and came to me, her arms wrapping gently around my shoulders, pulling me close. She cradled me like a child until the crying stopped. Finally, the tears dried. I wiped the rest away with my sleeve, my breath coming in ragged gasps.

"So... what happens now?" Davy asked once I'd calmed.

I looked at him, shoulders slumped, and gave a helpless shrug. "I don't know." My voice cracked. "If I refuse, I'll end up like the one before me, but I can't go on. I'm trapped, and I need to protect Anne."

"What do you mean?" Wynn asked. There was something in her voice, guarded, uncertain. It made me look up.

"I've managed to persuade the Master, once, that she's a good wife; that she will learn the ways of the household."

"Ah," Wynn exhaled. "So that is why things have changed between them. I noticed... the beatings became less." She looked away, shoulders tense.

"What?" I choked. The word burst out of me, raw. My stomach twisted. I had feared as much, but to hear it confirmed ignited a fury I could barely contain. "I should've left him this morning, let him die right there. I thought about it, God help me, I did. But I didn't want to break my promise. Not again."

I began pacing the floor, anger surging through every step. My fists clenched. I wanted to find the Master and finish what his horse had started, but before I could make it far, Davy stepped in front of me. His hands gripped my arms, steady and firm.

"Tom," he said, urgent but calm, "come to your senses. You can not go against a man like the Master; you would be hanged before anyone believed your word over his."

I knew he was right, but it didn't stop the swell of anger and hatred rising in me. The guilt of encouraging Anne to stay with him gnawed at my thoughts, tearing through me with every breath. I lashed out, kicking the empty chair Davy had vacated. It flew across the room, crashing into the door frame of the back room.

I buried my head in my hands and let out a yell, tearing from somewhere deep. When I looked up again, Wynn was at my side, silent and steady. Davy filled my tankard and handed it to me.

"Here," he said. "Drink."

I took it and drank deeply. He refilled it, and without pause, I drank again, emptying the second in one long pull and slamming the tankard onto the table.

Wynn laid a hand gently on my arm. "What are you going to do?"

I looked at her, hollow. I couldn't think straight, let alone plan. "I don't know," I said. "All I know is, I can't. I won't kill anyone else."

I turned and walked to the door.

"Where are you going?" Davy called after me.

"I don't know, but I need to get away... for a while."

I opened the door and stepped out into the cool afternoon, heading for the cover of the woods.

* * *

It took several weeks for the Master to recover from the fall. When I returned a few days later, I found Anne tending her husband. He insisted on her constant presence, refusing to let her leave his side for a moment.

"Where did you go, Thomas?" the Master demanded. He was propped against a stack of puffed pillows, wrapped in a soft blanket. His head was still bandaged, though the old bloodstained cloth had been replaced with a clean white one. "I should have you whipped for disappearing as you did."

I stood at the end of the bed as I had on the day of the accident. This time, Anne kept her eyes fixed on her husband, offering him her full attention.

"I had errands to run, sir," I lied.

"And have you finished them?" His voice was sharp, the edge setting me on edge. As he spoke, he reached out and took Anne's hand, squeezing it tightly.

"Yes, sir."

"Good. I need your full attention here," he said. "You'll be carrying messages to Mr Wentworth, and there will be other jobs for you to attend to."

My body stiffened, dreading what that might mean. "Indeed, sir," I replied obediently. "Is there anything you require at the moment?"

"No, I think you can go now." Anne gently squeezed his hand and nodded toward me.

"Ah, my *wife* reminds me I should thank you for making sure I got home the other day," he added, flashing a grin that reminded me of a snarling cat just before it pounced.

"It was nothing, sir," I said.

"Mmm..." He stared at me with sharp, calculating eyes; a familiar unease settled over me.

I bowed, giving Anne a subtle glance, hoping for a sign. She remained focused on him. I turned and left the room.

As I walked down the corridor, a sharp slap cracked through the air, followed by a gasp. His voice thundered:

"Don't you ever make such suggestions again! I shall give thanks when I decide."

I froze, fists clenched at my sides. I wanted to turn back, tear him away from her, take her and run. But the time wasn't right. I walked on, tears stinging my eyes and a fire of fury rising within me.

* * *

The weeks wore on, and I snatched time with Anne whenever she was not with the Master. Our stolen moments in the library remained treasured. But the Master seemed intent on keeping me away, sending me on arduous journeys and relaying messages to and from Mr Wentworth. It unsettled me, knowing their plans and how our beloved Queen might respond. There was no persuading the Master. He insisted Mr Wentworth had support and that there was nothing to fear. Sir Henry was now deeply involved, appearing at intervals to discuss plans behind closed doors.

In the quiet moments when I wasn't summoned, I began forming plans to get Anne to safety. But none were reliable. Each idea, tested in my mind, crumbled under scrutiny. I abandoned them all. The Master no longer hid his attacks on Anne. I feared he would go too far one day. Still, she played his game. She endured quietly, calculating perhaps.

Wynn and Davy were worried, too.

"What can we possibly do?" Davy paced the floor of their cottage one evening. Outside, darkness crept in earlier each day as the year rolled toward

Christmas and Twelfth Night. Wynn stirred a large pot hung over the fire; her brow furrowed, a quiet stiffness in her shoulders.

"We need to get Anne away," I said at last. The words hung heavy.

"Shall she even go?" Wynn asked, voice taut, eyes quietly glowing. "She still wants to make sure her family is taken care of. The Master's giving them a reasonable fortune."

I groaned, exasperated. "Does she not see? The way things are going, her life and their security are anything but safe. He's tiring of her. She'll face the same fate as Margaret." Speaking her name tightened something in my chest. I slumped into an empty chair and buried my face in my hands.

Davy lowered himself into the seat across from me. "So what can be done?" he asked, eyes usually calm but now wide and urgent.

I stared into the flames. The fire danced and flickered, pulling at the edges of my thoughts and helping my mind drift into possibility. "We need to get her far away, somewhere the Master would never think to look. If only we were in another time and place."

Davy and Wynn exchanged glances, then looked back at me.

"What are you talking about?" Davy asked.

"Anne once said to me, 'If we were in another time and place, who knows what we might have,'" I said, a wistful smile brushing my lips. "It was in the library. We have spent many an hour there, reading The Faerie Queene together when the Master was away. Blissful times."

"The lady does love that book," Wynn said softly, her voice touched with fondness. "Another time and place..." Her brow furrowed as she stood by the fire, quietly stirring the pot.

Davy turned toward her, concern tightening his features. "What are you thinking, my love?" His voice trembled, eyes pleading. Wynn met his gaze, unreadable.

"No, my love. Please don't." He shook his head, desperation rising. "You know what it might do to you."

"But if I don't?" Wynn's voice was calm but resolute. "The consequences would be far worse. I couldn't live with myself if I didn't try." She looked at him with quiet fire in her eyes.

"It could mean your death," Davy said, voice cracking. "Don't ask me to watch you risk that."

"If I don't, it'll be Anne who pays with her life," she said, with quiet firmness.

I sat frozen, heart thudding with confusion. "Please, what are you talking about?" I asked, searching both their faces.

Wynn turned away from Davy's silent plea. "I know a way, a way we could all get free of the Master's grip."

"Wynn, no," Davy said sharply, but she continued.

"A way to get you and Anne to another time, another place," she said, her eyes fixed on the bubbling pot as though it held the answer to everything.

Davy groaned, burying his face in his hands.

"I don't understand," I murmured.

"Wynn, please…" Davy's voice was taut, clinging to the last thread of control. But it was clear he had already lost.

"You need a new time and place," she said. It wasn't a question, but a certainty.

"Yes," I replied, watching as she lifted the pot from the fire and carried it to the table.

"Leave it with me," she said, ladling the steaming contents into bowls. Davy reached out and gently touched her arm as she passed. His eyes searched hers, fear etched deep into his face. She gave him a small smile. "Eat up; it'll get cold."

We ate in silence. The air was heavy with unspoken words; only the crackling fire and soft clinking of spoons broke the stillness. I was desperate to understand what Wynn was planning, what she could do, and why Davy was so afraid.

In time, I would learn.

* * *

Wynn sat beside the table, shrouded in candlelight, her eyes closed and lips moving with silent words. A sharp, clean scent of rosemary lingered in the air. Her breath caught as visions flashed before her: a darkened sky as the sun withdrew, strange bright lights, contraptions that beeped, miraculous healings, and flying vessels crossing a pale blue sky. Numbers blazed in fire – 2, 0, 1, 7.

She gasped, eyes springing open, and knew at once what she must do.

13

Fractures (2018)

Elwyna sat beside Farran's hospital bed, watching her sleep. A clear fluid flowed through a tube into her arm, and a wire clipped to her finger fed a steadily bleeping monitor. Around the pale hospital ward, visitors quietly murmured while nurses moved from bed to bed, checking charts and adjusting drips. A bell rang nearby. Elwyna glanced left as a nurse in a white tunic and grey trousers crossed the ward to press a red button on the wall, silencing it instantly. Farran stirred, brow furrowing as she blinked awake. She grimaced as she tried to sit.

"Hey, take it steady," Elwyna said gently.

Farran groaned, her voice rough. "What happened?"

"The doctors think you picked up some sort of virus," Elwyna replied, reaching for her hand. "You gave us quite a fright." She smiled, though worry lingered in her eyes.

"How long have I been here?" Farran asked, dazed.

"Since this morning," said Elwyna. "Daryll and I popped over to check you were still coming for drinks. Found you collapsed in your living room."

"Oh." Farran frowned, trying to piece things together. "Just as well you did… thanks."

Her mind felt foggy, thoughts arriving in broken fits. She tried to focus. "What about the exhibition?"

Elwyna gave a small sigh. "Don't worry about that. I spoke to that chap, Darnell. He says he's got it all under control. You've always been so hard on him, but he sounded genuinely lovely. Very concerned about you."

Farran's eyes drifted closed. "You haven't met him," she murmured. "He can be a right pain."

"Well, he sends his best and hopes you're back on your feet soon," Elwyna said, her tone overly bright. "Ah… look, here comes Daryll."

Farran opened her eyes again as Elwyna's husband approached, carrying two cups. He grinned broadly.

"Hey, good to see you awake," he said, settling into the empty chair beside Elwyna and handing her a drink. "You gave us a proper scare earlier."

He took a sip of coffee. "See?" he added with a wink. "Told you she'd bail on drinks."

Elwyna chuckled softly, shaking her head.

"Right now, I'd much prefer to be having drinks," Farran whispered, a faint smile brushing her lips.

"Tom says he's looking forward to meeting you when you're feeling better," Elwyna added.

Farran noted a glance pass between the couple, but didn't have the energy to question it.

"We'll be off in a bit," Elwyna said once they had chatted for a while.

"Okay," Farran murmured. "I'm feeling a little tired." She closed her eyes.

Elwyna and Daryll quietly left the room.

"I had awful trouble convincing him not to come," Daryll said as they walked down the corridor. "He was waiting by the car."

"He's worried," Elwyna replied, chewing her lip. "And he's waited so long. He's never been apart from her this long; this was meant to be the moment."

"I know. But he said something odd."

"What do you mean?" Elwyna looked up.

Daryll hesitated. "He said, 'He was here.'"

Elwyna stopped walking. "Who's he on about?" Her brow furrowed, then her eyes widened. "No. He couldn't be... could he?"

Daryll gave a slow nod. "He's convinced. Says he's made contact with her."

They stepped through the hospital doors into the bright car park, the sterile smell of the ward fading behind them.

"But how?" Elwyna said, disbelief creeping into her voice. "How could he have got past everything? I didn't think he even knew where we'd gone, or how."

"I don't know, Elv," Daryll said quietly. "But I don't think this is just a coincidence."

Elwyna nodded, her thoughts racing. "We need to make sure everything's still in place before she gets home."

Daryll grunted in agreement. As they reached the car, Elwyna's phone rang; she answered on speaker. A familiar voice crackled through, thick with concern.

"How is she?"

"She's fine," Elwyna said, keeping her voice calm. "It's just a virus. She'll be okay in a day or two."

He exhaled, the relief audible. "I was so worried. I thought we might have gone through everything for nothing."

"Don't worry," Elwyna said firmly. "Daryll and I will make sure everything is still in place before she gets back."

There was a pause.

"Daryll told you I think he's here?"

"Yes," Elwyna replied. "But how could he possibly know where she is? You're just being paranoid," she said with a half-laugh. "I know you miss her, but it won't be long now." Her voice softened.

"No, you've got to listen to me," the voice said with quiet determination. "At first, I just felt it. Don't ask me how, I just knew something was wrong." He hesitated. "Then I saw them together, going into the pub the other evening. It was her, Elwyna. And him. I'd recognise that bastard anywhere."

A pause followed as the realisation settled between them. They needed to act now.

Elwyna took a deep breath, her eyes alight with urgency. "We'll sort it, and you'll soon be back with her."

"Yeah..." he breathed. More quietly, he said, "Then, the really hard part starts."

"We'll be there too," Elwyna reassured him, glancing at Daryll, who gave her a soft smile. "We promised we'd be there for you both; we're not going back on that."

"I'm so grateful to have you as friends," he said, his voice catching slightly.

Silence settled between them.

"We'll let you know as soon as she's well enough," Elwyna said gently, though he couldn't see the smile that accompanied it. "And we'll reunite you. It's just going to take a little longer than we hoped."

A long sigh drifted through the line. "Okay," came the quiet reply. "I've waited this long. A couple more days is nothing." He gave a forced laugh, but Elwyna could hear the sorrow behind it. She sighed.

"I'll speak to you soon," she said, then tapped the screen and ended the call.

Turning to Daryll, her eyes alight with determination, she said, "Come on. Let's get back to Farr's house. If he's already found her, then we need to make sure she's protected."

* * *

Darnell watched as they left the car park. Of course, they were here. He should've known. He watched them leave the car park. He had been through too much to let anything stop him now. After months of not knowing where she was, he was finally with her. This was how it was meant to be.

Adjusting the cuffs of his immaculate blue suit, he strode confidently toward the hospital entrance and down the corridor. The white shirt beneath his blazer caught the sterile light. He moved with purpose, charm, and control. He reached the ward and scanned the room with sharp eyes.

She felt him before she saw him, a shift in the air, a familiar tightening in her chest. Forcing her gritty eyes open, she turned her head slowly. There he was. Darnell: white shirt, blue suit, smiling that smooth, self-assured smile that always made her stomach twist, though not, as others seemed to think, with pleasure.

If she did not feel such unease when he was near, she might have admitted he was attractive. The women on the ward certainly thought so. They glanced up, some with open curiosity, others with something closer to admiration as he passed. Disappointment followed as he walked past without acknowledgement. He went straight to her bed, his smile broadening.

"Hi, Farran," he said warmly. "How are you?"

Without waiting for an answer, he lowered himself into the empty chair beside her, still smiling.

Farran gave a weak smile. "I've been better," she joked.

She studied his face, the way that smile transformed him from the ogre he could be into something almost angelic. She laughed inwardly at herself. This virus must be playing tricks on her mind.

"Well, you have looked better," he chuckled, still smiling, but she was sure she saw a flicker of concern in his eyes.

"Daphne and Simon send their best wishes," he added.

"That's kind of them," Farran replied, her voice cracking. She licked her lips, trying to soothe the dryness. "How are the preparations going for the exhibition?"

"Good," said Darnell. "We've got all the pictures in place, just waiting on the final couple of items."

"It's so frustrating being stuck in here," she muttered, uneasiness creeping over her as his gaze lingered.

"It won't be for long." He reached out to touch her hand.
    She flinched.

He pulled back quickly. "They've given us permission to postpone the opening if needed, to make sure you're there."

Farran stared at him. Her mind began to fog again, and a dull ache started behind her eyes.

"That's... great," she stammered, shutting her eyes against the oncoming wave.

"Do you want me to get someone?" His voice held genuine concern, and she forced her eyes open. His hand was on hers again, but this time she didn't have the energy to pull away.

She looked at him, and fear surged through her. Her head pounded. She wanted to run, to scream, but all she could manage was a faint nod. She heard him call for a nurse. Footsteps approached.

"I think she's in pain," she heard him explain. She could still feel the warmth of his hand, but couldn't move.

"Farran, I'm just going to take your temperature, love," said the nurse gently. She nodded.

The cold plastic of the thermometer slid into her ear. A few short bleeps sounded, then it was gone.

"It's still slightly raised," the nurse said. "That'd explain the aches and feeling a bit foggy. I'll go get you something for the pain."

She turned to go.

"Wait. My whole body feels wrong," Farran said hoarsely. "I can't explain it."

The nurse paused, puzzled. "There was no mention of any injuries when you were admitted."

"I didn't think I had any," Farran replied. "But it hurts like I've fallen. Hard. I just don't remember doing it."

The nurse studied her. "Hmm. I'll flag the doctor for a full check. Might be worth getting you down for an X-ray."

Farran nodded weakly. Something flickered inside her: not fear, but confirmation. Of what, she didn't know yet. She could still feel his hand; the grip tightened slightly. She forced her eyes open. Darnell sat there, eyes closed, lips moving as though in silent prayer. Then suddenly his eyes snapped open and locked with hers. She couldn't look away. There was anguish in his eyes: something raw, deep. He looked as if battling himself.

"I'm sorry," he whispered. "I'm so, so sorry. I couldn't..." He trailed off.

For a breath longer, he held her gaze. Then he looked away and gently removed his hand.

The nurse returned, a small pot of tablets in hand.

"I'd better go," he said quietly. "I'll keep you updated. Daphne will likely visit soon as well."

Farran nodded, unable to process what had just happened. She watched him go.

"He's a good-looking bloke, your fella," said the nurse, passing her the paper pot.

"He's not my fella," Farran said, a faint tightening in her tone. "I just work with him."

The nurse smiled. "Well, you're lucky. I wouldn't mind working with him."

Farran snorted, the pressure in her chest easing just a little. She tipped the tablets into her mouth and swallowed.

Outside, Darnell stepped into the cool night air, the breeze brushing his face.

What had he done?

More importantly, how could he make it right before it was too late?

He walked toward town, disappearing into the darkness.

14

Rosemary and Rue

"It's not here," Elwyna whispered, tearing frantically at the rosemary plant in the terracotta pot by the front door.

"Are you sure it was that one?" Daryll asked, his face drawn with panic as he scoured the small front garden. "Could it have been swapped?"

Elwyna glanced at him and shrugged. "Maybe. Check the backyard."

As Daryll disappeared into the house, she gently pressed the disturbed earth back around the roots. The bitter scent of rosemary rose in waves, carrying her back to another life. Everything had felt simpler until danger crept in and surrounded them. She joined him in the backyard. He was crouched by another pot, soil scattered around him.

"Anything?" she asked, hopeful, but already knowing the answer.

Daryll shook his head. "Nothing," he said, his voice low with dread.

Frustration coiled in her chest. How had he undone it?
   "Do you have the shed key with you?"

Daryll froze, then nodded. "Y–Y–Yes." He reached into his coat pocket and pulled out a single key on a silver key chain. A small coin dangled from it, engraved with a full moon.

He handed it over. She murmured her thanks and turned toward the small brick shed. The lock was stiff from disuse, but after a few firm turns, it gave way with a soft click. She turned the handle. The door creaked open, and the hinges groaned in protest.

Inside, shadows pooled in the corners. She waited for her eyes to adjust, slowly making out the stacked wooden crates near the back wall. Groping forward, she found the cord and tugged at it. The bulb above flickered, then flared into a steady, pale glow. Dust swirled in the beam of light, stirred by her presence. The air was stale, thick and unmoving, only now stirred by the faint breath of her arrival.

She moved to the crates. She used the coin to pry open the top one with a reluctant rasp and set the lid aside. Reaching in, she pulled out a sealed glass jar and handed it to Daryll as he joined her. Then came a cloth pouch that jingled faintly, followed by a sturdier one that clinked. She passed them to him, too. Finally, she retrieved a bundle of dried rosemary and rue. Replacing the lid, she switched off the light and stepped into the open air, pausing to savour the clean, living breeze. Behind her, Daryll locked the door and returned to her side. For a moment, they stood in silence, exchanging a look of quiet understanding. Then, without a word, they turned and walked into the kitchen, closing the door behind them.

15

The Weight of the Past (1592)

Christmas had arrived, and with the darker days came a quiet sense of hope. Anne and I had managed to snatch more time together: reading, laughing, simply being. The Master had made a full recovery and often rode out with Peter Wentworth and Sir Henry to discuss the succession to the throne. It no longer filled me with the dread it once had, for while he was away, Anne was granted a brief reprieve. That alone was something.

Wynn, too, had been busy with her idea, though she kept the details closely guarded. "You shall see in time" was all she ever said, no matter how often I asked. Davy, on the other hand, had grown quiet and withdrawn. I feared the strain was threatening their marriage, but whenever I voiced concern, he gave a tired smile and said, "All is well, Tom. Don't you worry."

But I did worry.

My unease only deepened with the arrival of a new servant, a boy barely into his twenties. Gregory, though everyone called him Greg, had been hired shortly after the accident. He was given menial tasks, carrying messages and mucking out the stables, but something about him unsettled me. He lingered in odd places, often appearing where he had no business being. More than once, I caught him watching me.

One evening, Anne had asked for my help in decorating for the children. The Master had gone off again, not bothering to request my company, a pattern that had become familiar. *"I know you wouldn't enjoy coming, not with your loyalty to the Queen,"* he had said more than once. He wasn't wrong, but I had come to suspect it wasn't about loyalty. It felt more like banishment.

Anne and I sat together in the library, threading garlands from the evergreens Wynn and the children had gathered. Our laughter came easily, our hands were busy, and the fire crackled nearby. For a moment, it almost felt like another life. Then I saw him: Greg, slipping past the doorway, heading toward the kitchen stairs.

"Are you ready to entertain us tomorrow?" Anne asked, her eyes on her work. Her fingers moved deftly as she knotted another loop of evergreen.

"Of course, Mistress," I said, my eyes fixed on the doorway.

"The Master is not here..." she began, giving me a quizzical look.

I raised a finger to my lips and gave the faintest nod toward the door. We had grown careless in the Master's absence. She had started to call me Tom, and I had begun calling her Anne. It felt right; it was right. But it was also dangerous. And if we were caught, there would be no forgiveness.

"...it will be a good opportunity to plan a surprise for him," she continued after a brief pause.

I exhaled, grateful she had caught my meaning.

"A good idea, Mistress," I replied, casting another glance toward the doorway, where a flicker of shadow crossed the threshold. A faint creak of a floorboard followed.

"Well, I know how much he enjoys poetry," she said smoothly, slipping into the performance without effort. "How about Thomas Tusser's Good Husband and Huswife?"

"A fine Christmas choice, Mistress," I said with deliberate cheer.

"Perhaps the children could be taught a juggling dissemble too," she added, laughing lightly. "Although I'm not sure young Nathaniel will manage it."

"We shall work on it tomorrow, Mistress," I said, chuckling. "I'm sure Master Nathaniel will rise to the occasion."

We kept the conversation light and idle until soft footsteps echoed down the corridor.

"Ah, Greg," Wynn's voice called, clear and composed. "Cook's been looking for you. She needs more logs for the hearth."

"Indeed," he replied, a note of hesitation in his voice. "I'll go straight away."

I watched as he passed. The boy gave me chills. He crept about like a dram-snitch in the shadows, always present, always listening. Something about him sat wrong with me. I listened to his footsteps retreat down the corridor. A moment later, Wynn appeared in the library doorway.

"Evening, Mistress, Tom," she said with a smile. "I hope the evening finds you well."

"It does now, thank you, Wynn," Anne said warmly.

"Yes, now that our dram-snitch has slunk off," I muttered. "He creeps about like a rat," I added, unable to mask the snap in my voice.

"I am just so pleased you spotted his skulking, Tom," Anne said, her eyes shining as she spoke. I could never tire of that look. But deep down, I knew the truth of my past would reach her one day, and all of this would end.

"I am, too," I replied, reaching out to take her hand. My rough fingers closed around hers: soft and perfect.

"You are both taking far too many risks," Wynn warned, her voice troubled. "Greg is spying for the Master; I am sure of it."

"What makes you think that?" Anne asked, her brow furrowing. Though deep down she knew it to be true.

"I think Wynn may be right," I agreed. "He is always there. Watching. Waiting."

"But why would Richard suspect anything?" Anne's voice dropped to a murmur, laced with concern. "We have never given him a reason."

I shook my head slowly. "I do not know." Yet unease churned in my gut. I thought back to the morning of the Master's accident; his tone, his look. Something had shifted that day, something I had not wanted to admit. Restlessness took hold.

"I shall retire now, Anne," I said softly, lifting her hand and pressing a kiss to her fingers. Their warmth lingered on my lips.

"Yes, my love," she whispered. "I shall dream of you tonight." She raised my hand and kissed it in return, sending a joyfulness through me like I had never known.

"Go now, Tom," Wynn urged. "Greg will be back soon. Cook did not want him hanging about; what I said was only to get him out of the way."

I rose and moved toward the door. "Wynn, is Davy still at work, or has he returned home?"

"He is back now," she replied. Then, turning to Anne, she added, "Mistress, I have not had the chance to speak with you lately: how is your family?"

I paused in the corridor, listening closely to their voices.

"They are well," Anne said brightly, "though I do not receive as much news."

"That is good," Wynn said carefully. "And the Master, he is still keeping to his word?"

"I believe so. All the evidence and 'witnesses' have been disposed of," Anne replied. "Why do you ask, Wynn?"

There was a brief silence.

"Are you truly obliged to stay with the Master, then?" Wynn asked, cautious now.

"Where else have I to go? My uncle never wished for me. Now Aunt is gone, and he has Miss Elizabeth. I have no coin of mine own; they took it all to see Jasper safe," Anne said sharply. I could hear the strain in her voice. "I was given to Richard with the understanding I would never return, after the incident. What is this about?"

Another silence followed, deeper this time.

"If I could find a safe place for you and Tom, would you go?" Wynn's voice dropped to a whisper. I strained to hear more, but nothing came; only silence.

Then, at last: "I cannot tell you much now, but leave it with me."

I heard her chair scrape and stood quickly, retreating from the door. My heart ached with every echoing footstep. I stepped out into the sharp winter night and made my way to the cottage, knocking firmly when I arrived. Within moments, I heard Davy's steps cross the floor toward the door.

"Tom, come in," Davy said with a smile, walking back into the room and settling himself in front of the fire. "It is a bitterly cold night."

"It is," I agreed, taking the empty chair beside him. "How are things?" I asked, watching as his whole body sagged into the seat.

"They are good," he replied, though his tone was clipped.

"I have just seen Wynn. She is talking to Anne," I said, noting how his expression shifted to concern.

"Ah," he muttered, almost to himself. "She is determined." He gave a half-hearted chuckle. "She knows how to live dangerously."

"She said something about finding a safe place for Anne and for me," I added quietly. "What do you suppose she is planning?"

"I cannot answer that, Tom," he sighed. "You must wait until she is ready to tell you herself."

"Mmm." My mind raced. What could Wynn possibly organise?

After a pause, I shifted the conversation. "I need to speak to you about Greg."

"What about the dram-rat?" Davy snarled. "He is always lurking. Always listening. No one likes him."

"No." I hesitated. "I noticed him eavesdropping earlier," I said, a short laugh escaping with the apprehension. "It is a good thing I did."

"You need to be more careful," Davy urged, leaning forward. "If the Master finds out about you two, well, I dread to think what might happen."

"I fear he may suspect something already."

Davy turned sharply. "Why do you say that? He has been too caught up with Wentworth to notice anything."

I took a deep breath. "The night of the last murder, I had a dream. It was about Anne. You know I talk in my sleep. The Master came to find me that night to continue the celebrations, but he could not wake me."

A heavy silence fell between us as the truth sank in.

"Ah, Tom..." Davy ran his fingers through his hair and stared into the fire. Then he looked at me. "He hired Greg shortly after the accident."

I nodded. "I believe Greg has been asked to spy on us while the Master is away. He is always there, no matter what. He would have heard enough earlier if I had not spotted him and warned Anne."

Davy let out a long breath. "You and the Mistress must take heed."

"I know. I know." Frustration sharpened in those few words.

The latch on the door clicked, and Wynn stepped inside; a gust of cold air followed her in.

"Tom," she said, surprised to see me still sitting there.

Davy crossed the room quickly and wrapped his arms around her. "My love, are you well?" she asked, surprised by his unexpected welcome.

"Now you are here, I am well," he said with a smile, kissing her gently. His voice was gentle.

"It is bitterly cold out." She gave Davy a puzzled look, then turned to me. "Are you staying for something to eat, Tom?"

"No, I must be getting back," I replied. "Thank you, Davy. Pray, keep me informed of any news."

"I shall," Davy replied.

I nodded and stepped back out into the cold. As I approached the house, I noticed a faint glow in Anne's window. My heart ached with longing to be near her, but we both knew it was impossible, at least while we remained here.

Soon, I was in my room. It felt colder and emptier than I remembered. My eyes caught the painting hanging above the hearth now, moved from the Master's gallery long ago. He had commissioned it to immortalise his jester. I remembered the day it was unveiled: how proud I had stood beneath it with lute in hand, blood still fresh under my fingernails. A grinning fool, untouched by guilt. Now I could barely look at it.

The man in the painting stared out with that same smug half-smile, his scarlet tights bright against the brown tunic, his arm resting lazily on a bent knee. He looked carefree, adored. Untouchable. But I was no longer that man.

I crawled into bed, the covers barely holding off the chill. The room pressed in around me, heavy with everything I had done. My mind refused to settle. Why, if the Master knew, had he not acted already? What was he planning? Sleep came slowly: fitful, fragile.

When I woke, morning had already broken, yet I felt no more rested than the night before.

* * *

Anne sat at her dressing mirror, brush poised in hand. Her gaze was distant, her reflection swimming through long-buried memories.

"Stephens wants revenge!" her uncle's voice thundered from the past. "It's either Jasper or Anne."

"Jasper is just a boy," came her aunt's shrill reply.

"Anne is a grown woman. She can defend herself," her aunt said sharply. "She's been a parasite long enough. Let her deal with a monster of her own."

Even now, the memory made her blood run cold.

"I agree, my wife," her uncle said thoughtfully. "With Anne's inheritance, Jasper can start afresh. And I am sure if Stephens tires of her... well, his jester can see to a timely end. Just as he did with Mistress Margaret. God rest her soul."

In that moment, her fate had been sealed.

16

Sealed and Unspoken (2018)

Farran sat restlessly.

She had been kept in the hospital for observation, then sent home with strict instructions: take it easy and rest. All her test results were inconclusive; the diagnosis was vague: just an infection, they had said. Something that would run its course. Yet her body still ached. She shifted in her seat by the window, wincing. It was deeper than muscle ache; something gnawed at her bones, especially in her hip and shoulder. She remembered the doctor's frown.

"Your scans show signs of several fractures. Old ones. One in your hip, two ribs, your wrist... even your scapula. They have mostly healed, but not cleanly."

She stared at him, dazed. "I have never had an accident. I would remember that."

The doctor and nurse had exchanged glances.

"These were not minor breaks, Miss Armstrong."

Her chest tightened now at the thought. She had felt pain in her dreams. She had fallen; that terrifying vision: the crash of stone, the searing agony. Now, under the grey morning light, all she could think about was the exhibition. It had become an even more of an obsession. She was desperate to check on everything, especially the newest additions that had arrived the day she collapsed.

Outside, the street was still. The silence sharpened her frustration. Her laptop was warm against her knees. She clicked on the Coeur House website link. Nothing. Determined, she clicked again. This time, the website appeared. She looked at the different tabs: vacancies. She hesitated... Instinctively, she clicked the link.

As the page loaded, she scrolled through the listings: Assistant Archivist, Education Officer, Gallery Technician. She was about to close the tab when one title caught her eye:

Programme Curator.

Her pulse quickened. She clicked and began to read.

About the Role:

Coeur House is seeking a creative, driven and detail-oriented Programme Curator to lead the delivery of several key public-facing projects forming part of our upcoming cultural programme. This role offers a unique opportunity to shape and deliver innovative commissions, exhibitions, residencies, and events both within the house and in off-site locations.

You will play a central role in developing and delivering a dynamic and inclusive programme that reflects our mission to connect people with place, heritage and contemporary creativity. Working closely with artists, researchers, and community groups, you will ensure that Coeur House remains a vibrant and relevant cultural space.

Farran opened the supporting documents, hardly believing what she was seeing. Could this really be an opportunity meant for her? The role tugged at something deep inside her, something she hadn't felt in a long time. Without thinking twice, she downloaded the application form and began filling it in. That part was easy; she'd been at the same museum for what felt like forever.

The challenging part came next: writing her CV.

Farran Armstrong – Curriculum Vitae – 2018
  Age: Not as young as she once was.
  Home: A busy town in Shropshire.
  Occupation: Museum Curator.
  Married: Nope.

She sighed, staring at the screen. Why was she doing this again? It wasn't as though she wanted another job, but lately the lure of the idyllic Cotswold countryside had been growing stronger by the day. There was a strange sense of unfinished business. With a resigned huff, she highlighted her flippant list and pressed delete. Okay, concentrate. After a pause, just long enough to consider making tea, inspiration struck. Her fingers flew across the keys.

After completing the application, she read it through one last time. She hovered over the send button, an entire parliament debating in her head. They won't want someone like me anyway. Too little experience, too much baggage. She took a breath.
  She clicked send.

She shut the laptop and set it gently on the side table, her thoughts drifting back to the painting on the wall. Somehow, the man's expression always seemed to shift with her moods. Today, he looked caring, concerned even. His eyes were luminous, a strange colour: grey? No, green? Hard to tell.

As she gazed into his face, she realised she hadn't had a single dream since waking in the hospital. For the first time in weeks, her body felt rested; her mind almost quiet. Eyes drifting shut, she sank deeper into the chair.

Farran woke with a start as the front door slammed.

"Farr, you okay?" Elwyna's voice called from the hallway, breaking through the haze of sleep.

"I'm in here," Farran croaked, reaching for the half-empty glass of water on the table.

"Oh, sorry," Elwyna said, appearing in the doorway. "Didn't realise you were asleep." She dropped into the armchair opposite and smiled. "How are you feeling?"

"Yeah, not bad," Farran said, blinking herself awake. "Nice to sleep without being disturbed." She managed a smile.

"Glad to hear it," Elwyna said, her face softening with relief.

"Mmm." Farran shifted in her chair. "Want a cuppa?" she asked, starting to rise.

"No, I can't stay long," Elwyna said. "I've got work this afternoon and need to get a few things done first."

"Daryll still can't cook his own tea?" Farran smirked.

"He's getting better," Elwyna laughed. "He can boil an egg and cook beans on toast, so at least he wouldn't starve."

Farran giggled. Daryll had always been hopeless with anything remotely domestic. He'd joke it was women's work, which usually earned him a slap from Elwyna and a lecture about 'living' in the twenty-first century. Farran had always envied their relationship: playful, enduring, full of love. Her gaze drifted toward the painting. What kind of man had he been? Kindness showed in his face sometimes. Other times, something else: a flicker of uncertainty. There was depth to his gaze that unsettled her. A life she couldn't quite grasp. What was she thinking? Pining after a man from centuries ago?

She stifled a laugh at her absurdity.

"You okay?" Elwyna looked up from her phone, brow furrowed.

"Yeah, I'm fine," Farran said, smiling. "I was... oh, it doesn't matter."

"What?" Elwyna leaned forward. "You can't start saying something and then not finish. You know my curiosity can't take it."

Farran laughed and took a deep breath.

"You'll think I've lost the plot, but... I was looking at that portrait," she nodded toward the painting, "and wondering what kind of man he might have been. He has kind eyes sometimes, but at other times," she hesitated, "almost menacing. And he's surrounded by all these odd items that feel symbolic, like he was some sort of protector."

She glanced at Elwyna, who was staring at the picture, a small smile tugging at her lips.

"I've been trying to find out more about him, but every time I try, something gets in the way. Like earlier, I was researching, and I saw a job vacancy."

"A job?" Elwyna turned sharply, shifting in her chair. "Where?"

"At Coeur House," Farran replied.

"Oh, the place where, oh, what's his name? Richard, the man from your exhibition, lived," Elwyna said, shifting again.

"That's it," Farran said, her voice lifting with excitement. "I know it sounds mad, but I applied for the position. It just felt like more than a coincidence: I'm curating the exhibition, and this pops up. I probably don't have enough experience, but I had to try."

Elwyna stared at her, fingers fidgeting with the phone in her lap.

"Wow. That's... extraordinary," she said softly. "But you wouldn't really want to move away from here, would you?"

"As I said, it's unlikely I'll even get an interview," Farran replied, brushing it off. "But I think I will visit. I've read so much about the place and the family. I feel like I should know it, like I've already been there somehow."

She looked at Elwyna, who gave her a weak smile.

"Don't look so worried," Farran chuckled. "You'd think I was walking into a lion's den, the way you're looking at me."

"Sorry, Farr," Elwyna murmured. "I guess I'm just surprised. I didn't expect you to think about moving, that's all. Plus, I don't want you overdoing it."

"There's a good chance I won't be moving. And I'm going crazy just sitting here. I feel so much better," Farran said with a reassuring smile. "So don't worry."

"When are you planning to go for a visit?" Elwyna asked, still fidgeting.

"Tomorrow," Farran replied. "The weather's supposed to be lovely again. Might as well make the most of it."

Elwyna glanced at her phone, lighting up the screen. A photo of her and Daryll smiled back.

"I've got to go," she said suddenly. "If I don't leave now, I won't have time to sort everything before work." She stood, crossed to Farran, and gave her a tight hug.

"I'll ring you later, okay?"

Then she swept out of the house, and a few seconds later, Farran heard the car pull away. She sat for a moment, frowning. Elwyna's reaction had taken her by surprise. She had expected teasing about the portrait or her romantic ideas, not that strange obsession with the job. Not worry.

"What do you think?" Farran murmured, glancing back at the man in the picture.

She stood and left the room.
   A faint sigh stirred the air behind her.
   "Come to me."

17

A Feast of Fear (1592)

Merriment filled the house, carried on the sounds of music and laughter. The Master had arrived early that morning, full of cheer for the festivities. Anne had been at his beck and call all day, and I had caught only fleeting glimpses of her as she hurried past.

Now the family were seated for the evening meal before the jollities began anew. Their table overflowed with dishes and bowls of meat and vegetables, its aroma drifting down the corridor. They were well into their feasting.

I sat in the warmth of the kitchen with Davy, Wynn, and young Celia. Cook was in a fine mood, bustling about and making certain that no one went without. Usually, I would be swept up in the joy these feast days brought, yet this year a shadow lingered in my thoughts.

Earlier, the household had attended service at the small chapel behind the house. It was a modest space, still stripped bare by the will of our late King Henry. Behind the altar, one stained glass window remained: the Adoration of the Magi. As the low winter sun poured through, the jewel-toned colours danced across the walls, throwing a rainbow across the priest as he spoke of joy and salvation.

Anne sat in the front pew beside the Master. For once, in what seemed an age, I could watch her freely; Greg had been sent behind the servants' screen. I gave quiet thanks for the custom that allowed the Master's advisor to sit close on feast days. Her head was bowed as the priest gave his sermon. The Master stared straight ahead, his expression unreadable. I wondered how he could sit so piously, betraying not a flicker of guilt.

Then I thought of myself. The cruelties I had committed. The faces of the innocent still haunted me. I prayed, not for favour, but for the forgiveness I could not offer even myself. The psalms echoed in my ears like a divine plea. Could the Almighty grant grace to one such as me? Could Anne?

I sighed and rose when the time came for the Holy Sacrament. I watched as the family received communion first; the priest served them reverently from the silver paten. Then it was my turn. I knelt, received the bread and wine, and murmured my thanks before rising and walking past the family pew. As I passed, Anne looked up, and I saw it. A red mark slashed across her cheek. She shook her head so slightly it might have been imagined.

My gut clenched. Fury surged in my chest. The Master had taken out his frustrations upon her once again. His wife, his property in the eyes of the law, though not in the eyes of heaven. I gripped the edge of the pew to steady myself. The incense lingered; the rainbow light from the window faded.

Knowing I could not act while within the house of God, I returned to my seat. I shifted restlessly in the pew, the words of the service melting into a haze. My mind refused stillness. The sight of that mark on Anne's cheek had ignited a fire within me; the urgency to see her safe burned brighter than ever.

I turned over every possibility in my head, but each crumbled under scrutiny. Anxiety coiled tightly in my chest as the truth became clearer: we had but one real choice, to get her as far from that tyrant of a husband as possible.

Yet even that path was fraught with flaws. Chief among them: coin. It would take months to save enough for such a flight. And where in this kingdom might we hide without one of the Master's men sniffing us out like hounds on a scent?

I exhaled sharply, only then realising the congregation had begun to stir. The service had ended. The congregation murmured blessings and gathered their cloaks as the priest passed down the aisle. I stood just in time, with a quiet bow of the head as he moved past, trailed by his attendants. The family followed, pausing to exchange pleasantries with the priest in the small narthex. I kept a respectful distance while they conversed. When they had turned to leave, I came forward.

The priest turned to me with his customary kind expression and extended his hand to mine.

"Good day, Thomas," he said in his soft voice. "How finds this fine morning treat you?"

"Well enough," I replied, attempting to gently draw back my hand from his lingering grip.

"Is that so?" he asked, lifting his thin spectacles to peer more closely. "You seem somewhat troubled."

"No, Father," I said, shifting where I stood, eager to be alone with my thoughts. "There are many tasks to tend to."

"Indeed, Thomas," he said with a knowing smile, revealing a row of yellowed, uneven teeth. "But never forget: God's house is ever open to you."

"Thank you, Father," I said, nodding once and turning away.

As I stepped past, his voice followed me:

"God keeps all His children safe... The lady shall find sanctuary."

I froze, breath catching in my throat.

But when I turned, he was already walking away, his cassock rustling softly against the chapel floor. He disappeared back into the church, vanishing into that gaping mouth like a shadow swallowed by darkness. Did he know what the Master was doing? His parting words echoed in my mind: cryptic, yet pointed. I had questions by the dozen, but no time to pursue them. I needed to find Davy and Wynn. I needed to know how far their plans had come, if there were any at all. I was still being kept in the dark, and I could bear it no longer.

It wasn't until we were gathered around Cook's table that I managed to speak with them properly. Davy shovelled food with great enthusiasm, while Wynn sat quietly, nibbling from her bowl. I sat beside Davy, my own bowl untouched before me, my expression almost mournful.

"You not eating?" Cook called, brandishing a ladle across the table.

I nodded quickly and reached for the dishes; bowls brimming with root vegetables, meat in rich gravy, even a sugared parsnip or two. I filled my bowl despite no appetite, forcing mouthfuls past the tightness in my throat. When I was sure no one was paying attention, I nudged Davy with my elbow.

"Did you see her face?" I whispered low.

"Mmm," Davy murmured through a mouthful. "T'was a good one."

I clenched my fists beneath the table. "How can you say such things?"

He looked at me, guilt flickering. "Pray pardon, Tom, I meant no harm. I did see," he said earnestly. "I did see. Wynn said the Master was foul of humour this morn."

"But why?" I asked, my voice low and strained, struggling to keep the bitterness from spilling out.

Davy glanced about to ensure our words went no further. "The Master believes the Mistress is not loyal to him," he whispered. "Claims he's heard whispers that she's been intimate with another."

The blood drained from my face. I felt cold, and yet my heart thudded violently in my chest. I knew the consequences of such a belief. Anne was in mortal danger.

"He told her," Davy continued, even quieter now, "that, owing to the Christmas festivities, she would be spared, for now. But she was to be on her guard thereafter. The slap was a warning."

I stared at him, every nerve alight. A warning, like the kind a hunter gives just before he looses the hounds. I kept forcing food into me, though each mouthful turned my stomach further. Sickness rose slowly, a weight gathering in my throat. I tried to catch Wynn's eye as the meal wore on and household chatter swelled around me, but she avoided my gaze, keeping a bright conversation with Celia at her side.

When the meal finally ended, Wynn slipped away to tend to the children. I climbed the stairs to my chamber, needing space to think. I paced back and forth; the narrow room felt both too small and endless. Each step brought fresh waves of emotion: guilt, fury, but most of all, desperation. How could I keep her safe? How could I protect her?

At last, my steps slowed. I slumped onto the edge of the bed, staring out through the frost-misted pane. Beyond, the back lawn stretched beneath a blanket of dull winter sky. I remembered summer, how we had played Blind Man's Bluff out there, sunlight spilling over the grass like honey. It felt like another lifetime. How had I been so foolish to believe we could have something, anything? I should have walked away the moment I felt the first tug on my heart. Instead, I had placed her in mortal danger.

I lay back, staring up at the cracked, grey ceiling, struggling to form a plan. But my mind a storm; every idea slipped through my fingers like water. At length, I drifted into restless sleep. Peace did not follow.

The dream returned.

Margaret lay in the great bed, wrapped in velvet and silk. At first, I thought she slept: the soft murmur of her breath rising and falling. But then she stirred at the sound of my footsteps, the name of the Master slipping from her lips in confusion. He had told me she had been given a sleeping draught. "To make the task easier," he had said, grinning like the Devil.

As I reached the bed, her eyes fluttered open. Confusion crossed her face, followed swiftly by fear. She tried to speak; the words caught in her throat. I pulled the rope from around my waist, the coarse fibres rough against my fingers. She watched while I twisted it into place. Slowly, I climbed onto the bed, straddling her, pinning her beneath the heavy covers.

Her eyes widened in terror. She began to struggle. Her movements were sluggish, the drug threading its poison through her limbs; still, she fought. I slid the rope behind her neck. She whimpered, whispered protests. Her arms flailed beneath the blankets, seeking freedom.

"Do not fight this," I whispered into her ear. "It is the Master's wish. Therefore, his will shall be done."

I began to tie the knot. She freed one hand, clawing at mine with fading strength.

Her nails tore into my skin. But the knot held. Her resistance weakened. The scratching slowed. Her eyes, still locked on mine, began to dull.

Then, her face changed: it shifted, transformed.

Anne.

She lay there, her cane-coloured hair splayed across the pillow. Her lips were parted slightly, her cheeks pale. Her eyes stared, unseeing.

"No!" I gasped, my hands flying to the rope, tearing it loose. I gathered her in my arms. "Anne, my love. Wake up. Speak to me."

But she did not move.

Tears slipped down my cheeks as I held her close, the dream becoming a nightmare I could not escape.

"Tom, the Master wants you," came Davy's voice, pulling me from sleep's clutches.

I wiped the dampness from my face and sat up, groggy. "I'm coming," I called, my voice thick with dream's residue.

As I stepped out into the corridor, Davy was waiting. His eyes scanned my face.

"Are you good now?"

"Yes," I replied, forcing a small smile. "I had not realised how tired I'd become."

Davy did not smile; instead, his brow furrowed. "I heard you dreaming again." His concern was plain. "If that maggot Greg had heard, you would be for the rope, along with the Mistress."

I gave a dry laugh. "The rope would not be harsh enough for the Master. He would find a way to make it linger, for us both."

As we made our way through the house, laughter spilt from every room, servants caught in the season's cheer. But all within me was twisted and tight. The desperation I had felt earlier still gnawed at my gut. The dreams stalked me even in waking hours. I was beginning to wonder if I was losing my mind.

"Is the plan near ready?" I asked, voice low, tension seeping through despite my best effort to still it.

"Not now, Tom," Davy hissed. "The maggot could be round any corner, waiting to hear your words."

I nodded, falling silent as we reached the drawing room. The Master sat behind his desk, a quill in hand, paused above a piece of parchment. Davy moved on down the corridor. I paused at the threshold, took a steadying breath, and stepped inside.

"You wanted to see me, Sire?"

"Ah, Thomas. Yes, indeed," he said, flashing a wide smile. His flushed cheeks and slack posture told me the festive drink had already taken hold.

I approached the desk and stood before him. He set down the quill, folded the parchment with care, pressed his seal into the wax, and then placed it aside.

"Will you take a festive drink with me?" he asked, rising and crossing to the sideboard, where several glass decanters gleamed in the candlelight. I nodded, and he poured two glasses, handing one to me.

"To the good fortune of our company," he said, lifting his glass and taking a generous swallow. I drank, though the liquid burned down my throat and drew a cough.

"Steady there, Tom," he chuckled, settling back into his seat.

A moment passed in silence, broken only by the fire's crackle and the gentle clink of swirling glass.

"I will not keep you long, Thomas," he said at last, his tone almost congenial. He toyed with the quill between his fingers, glancing at me with half-lidded eyes. "I know you are to entertain us later, and time will be needed for that. And it is Christmas, after all; work should not disturb our merriment."

He leaned back slightly.

"However," he continued, "I shall be travelling to London tomorrow with Sir Henry and Mr Wentworth, and there are certain duties I need you to see to while I am gone."

"I did not know you would be going away quite so soon again," I said, trying to keep the relief from showing. "Pray, tell me how the discussions go?"

"You may," he replied, his smile curling with satisfaction. "They are developing well. We have an audience with Her Grace and the Privy Council later in the new year. We are finalising a list of suitable successors, and are confident one or two shall be accepted."

His arrogance lingered in the air like stale perfume. Every word was steeped in self-importance, and I forced myself to nod, to keep my voice steady.

"That is heartening news, sir," I answered. "I shall do whatever you require."

"Good, Thomas." He gestured toward the parchment I had seen him seal earlier. "Your instructions lie within. Do not open it until I am gone."

My eyes lingered on the scroll. Why not simply tell me, as he always had? Unease stirred in my chest. He downed the last of his drink, then crossed the room toward the door. Pausing at the threshold, he turned.

"The Mistress tells me we are in for a treat with your entertainment later," he said, smiling.

Then he was gone. Only then did I realise I had been holding my breath.

* * *

The day's festivities dragged; the letter tucked in my tunic burned like a brand. Davy bustled about, running errands for Cook and tending the household. Wynn was absorbed with the children. And Anne... Anne played the dutiful wife. The mark on her cheek had faded, yet I had seen it. Its ghost lingered still in my thoughts. We had not spoken, nor exchanged so much as a glance. It was torment beyond bearing. Never had I known such loneliness within a house so full of life.

At last, evening came. The family and their guests dined, then gathered in the great hall for dancing and merriment. Hundreds of candles flickered along the walls and from the great chandelier overhead, their light catching glass and casting glimmers and shadows across the floor. Garlands Anne and I had crafted now hung from the beams, to the delight of the children.

The air hung heavy with the scent of Christmas spices, warm wax, and perfume. Every so often, the faint trace of Anne's scent drifted past, floral, soft, unforgettable. She moved among them with practised grace, the perfect hostess, her smile concealing all that mattered.

Sir Henry was there with his wife, Elizabeth; his voice rose above the music like a trumpet as he lumbered through the dance. Mr Wentworth had arrived, accompanied by the husbands of Miss Sarah and Miss Abigail. The two daughters were deep in conversation with their stepmother. The Master, ever radiant, danced with Mr Wentworth's wife to The Pavane for the Queen, while the children clapped along, spurred by Wynn's cheerful urging.

And I... I stood at the edges of it all, no more present than the trembling shadows upon the walls.

When the music next came to a close, the guests were invited to step aside, leaving a clear space in the centre of the hall for the evening's entertainment. By then, I had changed into my brightest tunic and tights, my lute slung across my shoulder, though the sealed letter beneath the fabric still pressed against my chest like a second heart. I stepped forward, the melody drifting into every shadowed corner of the hall, and began with:
"Upon a summer's day
Love went to swim,"

As I sang, I turned slowly, meeting each guest's gaze in turn. When my eyes reached the Master and Anne, I faltered, not in voice, but in breath. He held her waist, his smile resting on me like a challenge. And then Anne's eyes met mine. Just for a moment. A flicker. A ghost of a smile brushed her lips before she turned away.

The song ended. I wasted no time in lifting the mood. Shifting tempo, I struck up a brisker tune and clapped in rhythm, coaxing the crowd to join me. Laughter rippled through the hall. Then I began the recitation Anne had chosen; festive, clever, full of dry wit. My voice carried above the flicker of candles and the clink of goblets:
Good husband and huswife, now chiefly be glad,
Things handsome to have, as they ought to be had.
They both do provide, against Christmas do come,
To welcome their neighbours, good cheer to have some...

Chuckles rose, followed by appreciative groans and delighted applause. I bowed grandly, lacing it with theatrical flourish, and for a moment, the letter's weight lifted. The tension in my chest gave way to something brighter. The warmth of the room, the merriment, the echo of Anne's faint smile, it felt almost bearable.

"Now, fair ladies and noble gentlemen!" I cried, extending one hand with gallant exaggeration, "Master Nathaniel shall astound you with his most wondrous juggling prowess!"

I moved to the children and knelt before the boy, taking his hand. "Are you ready?" I whispered. He nodded solemnly, his cheeks flushed with excitement. I handed him the balls. He had learned quickly, if not always precisely, and tonight, by some miracle, he completed the routine. The hall erupted with cheers and laughter. He raced back to Wynn, who caught him in a hug and whispered praise in his ear, her smile tender with pride.

As the night drew on, I remained among the celebration: smiling, bowing, jesting, though the letter burned beneath my clothes, a whisper of parchment and wax I could not ignore. Again and again, my thoughts returned to it. What did it say? Why the secrecy? The revelry around me blurred, voices fading into haze as the question burrowed deeper into my thoughts.

It was as I stood, lost in my musings, that the Master startled me with a bellow and a heavy hand.

"Thomas! A most wondrous evening of entertainment. Young Nathaniel was quite the delight!" He clapped me hard on the back, his grip blurred by drink and cheer. I forced a laugh, stammering my thanks, fighting the urge to recoil from the weight of his touch and the words that followed.

"I am most assured," he continued with a broad grin, "that you shall keep the household safe and properly entertained during my absence."

Before I could respond, a softer voice cut in. Anne.

"I wish you did not have to go away again so soon, Richard."

I had not seen her approach. She stepped to his side and rested a gentle hand on his arm. For a heartbeat, something akin to affection crossed his face as he turned toward her. He raised her hand and kissed her knuckles; an oddly tender gesture from a man like him.

"It will not be for long, my sweet," he said. Then, with a glance at me, his smile curled: tight, jagged. "You'll have Thomas here to keep an eye on you."

The air cooled. That smile said more than his words. A warning. A claim. I bowed slightly, masking the unease blooming behind my ribs. "It shall be my honour, sir."

"But it's not the same as having you here," Anne added, her tone calm and coaxing, carefully rehearsed.

He kissed her hand again, the press of his lips lingering just a moment too long. "I am flattered by your devotion, Anne. Only a week," he said, and there was a weight in those words, a finality that turned my stomach. "Then we shall have the rest of our time together."

A shiver traced down my spine. My hand twitched toward the place over my heart where the letter lay, still sealed.

"Do you require anything arranged for the morning, sir?" I asked, forcing my voice to steady.

"No. All is prepared, Thomas." His eyes locked with mine. "You have your instructions. I trust you've kept them safe."

"I have, sir," I replied, resisting the urge to touch the parchment beneath my tunic.

"Good." He turned back to Anne, her hand still in his grasp. "Come, my sweet. The guests tire. Let us bring this merriment to a close and retire."

His kiss this time was not tender, but possessive, marking her with ownership.

"Indeed, Richard," Anne answered, smiling serenely. Too serenely. Her eyes never reached mine.

Without another glance in my direction, she turned and walked away, and the Master followed at her heels.

"Good evening, Thomas," he called over his shoulder.

"Good evening, sir," I murmured. But they were already gone.

I stood alone in the centre of the hall, candlelight flickering like the last breath of joy. Laughter faded into memory, and the sealed letter in my tunic pulsed like a second heart. I had to read it. But not here. Not yet.

Soon, the guests had withdrawn, the children tucked away, and the servants began clearing dishes and sweeping up pine needles and crumbs. I made my usual rounds of the house, quiet as a ghost, and at last returned to my chamber. There, I withdrew the letter. I laid it on the table by the bed and sat, my heart drumming. I waited, listening to the house settle, waiting for his departure.

Sleep came only in restless patches, broken by shadowed dreams and the echo of that strange finality in the Master's voice. Then, at last, hooves. The clatter of iron on stone. The snap of the harness. He was leaving. I rose, breath tight in my chest, and reached for the letter.

The wax cracked like a whip as I broke the seal; the sound shattered the silence of the room. My hands shook as I unfolded the parchment and began to read. Line by line, the truth struck like iron. Its meaning was clear.
And it was deadly.

Thomas,

Thou hast ever been a faithful and true servant within mine household these many years. For that cause, and none more pressing, do I place in thee my trust regarding a matter most grievous.

Word hath reached mine ears that foul practices of witchcraft have been wrought beneath mine own roof, a most heinous offence, abominable in the eyes of both God and man, and deserving of nought but death. These acts, it is said, concern potions of love and enchantments made to bewitch minds, to bend affections to the will of another. Such malice, I am told, was aimed not only against mine own person, but against the good Mistress as well.

Thus, while I am called to attend the court of Her Most Gracious Majesty, Queen Elizabeth, I do entrust unto thee the charge of uncovering and bringing to account these traitors. Greg, who did first uncover these devilish workings, shall assist thee. He hath my full confidence and command to ensnare the culprits. Together, thou shalt draw them forth upon the eve of the New Year, a most fitting hour, as I now believe their wickedness doth reach even unto the late Mistress Margaret, of blessed memory.

Consult with Greg as thou find needful. He is privy to all manner of detail in this matter. I rely upon thy discretion, thy loyalty, and thy steadfast heart.

Fail me not.

By mine own hand,
R. Stephens

The letter slipped from my hands as I reached the last line. My pulse thundered in my ears, and the world seemed to tilt beneath my feet. I could scarcely believe what I had read. Margaret's death had been the Master's will; his order, his poison, and I had carried it out. Now Greg dared to accuse Wynn? To speak her name in the same breath, as though she had blood on her hands instead of him.

I would have to find Greg. I needed answers, even though the thought of working alongside that snake turned my stomach. I did not trust him. There was something too slick in his words, too quick in his judgments. Still, the Master had given him authority, and I had no choice but to see this through.

As I went about my morning tasks, the letter's contents churned within me like storm-tossed seas. Confusion gave way to dread, and dread to determination. I needed the truth, however foul it might prove. I made for the kitchens, hoping to find Greg.

I stepped within to find Cook in the midst of one of her tempests.

"You'd best not be here to cause any of your messin', Tom," she barked, brandishing a wooden spoon as though it were a cudgel.

"No, Cook, I would not dream of it," I said quickly.

"Hmph."

"I am looking for Greg," I added. "Need his help with something."

Her scowl deepened. "Oh, him. Went to fetch firewood a while ago. Don't know what takes him so long. Might've gone to the far side of the wood."

"Thank you, Cook," I said with a forced smile. "You are far too resplendent."

She muttered darkly as I backed away.

I made my way toward the cottage: Davy and Wynn's home. There was ever a supply of wood stacked there. As I got closer, I noticed a figure at the side wall, hunched, his ear pressed against the timber. Listening.

I slowed, treading softly.

A twig snapped beneath my boot.

The figure turned, startled, then relieved. Greg.

He raised a finger to his lips and gestured for me to halt, then crept toward me with a stealth that unsettled more than it impressed.

Once we had moved far enough from the cottage, he spoke.

"You got the Master's letter?"

"I did," I said. "But there were not many details."

"Ah," Greg murmured, his eyes glancing to my tunic. "What did it say?"

"That witchcraft's suspected, and that it is to be dealt with... appropriately."

"You do not know who?" he pressed.

I shook my head. "No. The Master said you would tell me."

Greg glanced over his shoulder toward the cottage, then inclined his head slightly in its direction.

I stared at him. "No... surely not," I breathed. "You think it is Davy?"

"Not Davy." His smile curled into something sly. "Her."

"Wynn?" The name caught in my throat. "That is absurd."

Greg shrugged, watching me closely. "I have heard her talk."

"That is no proof," I said, my voice rising with disbelief. "What could she possibly have said to make you believe such a thing?"

He hesitated, then spoke with deliberate calm. "You should know, you were the topic of her private talk."

A prickle crept over my skin.

"I do not understand," I said. "I know nothing of witchcraft."

He met my gaze, his eyes flat and cold. "Maybe not. But someone does."

I felt the dagger at my belt; a comfort, and a threat.

"What exactly are you planning?" I asked, bending as if to gather firewood, keeping my voice low.

He crouched beside me. "You know how witches are dealt with," he said, lips curling into a grin. "Fire cleanses everything."

I swallowed hard. My throat burned with bile.

He went on, casual now, as though speaking of the weather. "It will have to be at night, once the house is quiet. You have their trust; you let me in. We give them a draught to keep them still. Then, we fire the place. Nice and quick."

His delight was obscene. I fought the urge to drive my knife through his ribs. Instead, I nodded slowly, my face held still.

"I presume you are thinking New Year's Eve?" I asked.

"The Master wants it seen to before his return."

"So we have a week," I said. "Time to plan properly. No mistakes."

Greg grunted in agreement, his focus now on gathering sticks. I watched him, that creature with ash in his soul, and felt something sour rise in me.

Once I had been like him: quick to condemn, eager to burn. I had worn piety like a shield, using it to justify every horror I committed. But now he spoke of Wynn. Wynn, who tended Anne's bruises; Wynn, who nursed me through more than fever; Wynn, who opened her home and her heart. And now she was marked for death.

We kept gathering wood while Greg muttered plans, tossing out methods. I played along, speaking little and nodding when required. All the while, my thoughts raced, frantic and desperate, as the snare tightened around us all.

18

Echoes of the Past (2018)

Farran climbed into her car, a metallic blue Mazda she had bought a few months earlier from a second-hand garage. It was nothing fancy. It served her well: short trips across town, the occasional grocery run. This, she realised, was the furthest she had ever driven it. Quite pitiful.

She wound her way down the country lanes, hedgerows slipping past in a blur of green. She had deliberately avoided the motorway, wanting to savour the same scenery Richard might once have known. The Shropshire roads curled beneath her, the land slowly rising as the hills gathered around, folding gently like arms trying to hold her within their ancient embrace.

At last, she crested a summit and gasped. A patchwork of fields stretched before her, the greens shifting like the panels of a weathered quilt, stitched with golden seams of sunlit grass. A surge of freedom rose in her chest, quickly followed by anticipation. Whatever she was driving toward, she could feel it waiting. She did not know what exactly she expected to find, only that something was calling her. Somehow.

As she crossed into Gloucestershire, the roads narrowed. Trees arched overhead, parting like theatre curtains to reveal farmland beyond. The fields rolled outward, calm and expansive. A strange sensation washed over her: an uncanny familiarity. She could almost swear she had been here before. She laughed aloud. *Snap out of it*, she told herself, shaking her head. She had been too dreamy lately.

About half an hour later, she turned onto a narrower lane, marked by a solitary chestnut tree, keeping watch at the corner, its roots splayed into the field like fingers. Just ahead, rooftops peeked through the sun-drenched canopy. A small gasp escaped her lips. As she drove on, the house gradually emerged, stately and still. She spotted a discreet sign at the entrance, slowed, and turned in. Then she saw it: fully revealed.

The mansion stood proud, its structure shaped like a capital 'E'. Sunlight caught its many windows, setting them alight with brilliance. Wide stone steps led to an aged wooden door, scarred by time, dignified in its bearing. A fountain danced at the centre of the drive, scattering droplets into a shallow pool where ripples glided across the surface. Lawns stretched out on either side, immaculate and green, bordered by ancient stone walls and neat beds blooming with summer colour.

A sudden horn blasted behind her. She jumped, heart thudding, and waved an embarrassed apology before pulling into the car park. The engine ticked softly in the still morning; Farran did not move.

She stared at the house, and everything stilled. She could not explain it. It was like stepping into a dream she had never known she held. A strange calm settled over her chest, anchoring her in place. It felt like coming home. She blinked, trying to shake the thought. Crazy, she told herself, running a hand through her hair. And yet, the feeling remained.

She stepped from the car and walked toward the entrance, her steps light on the stone rise. The heavy front door now stood open, revealing the dim hall beyond. As she crossed the threshold, her heart seemed to skip a beat.

She paused, letting her eyes adjust from the blaze of sun to the hush of the house. The entrance hall opened around her, steeped in silence, heavy with time. Portraits lined the walls: solemn ancestors peering down from their gilded frames. Some bore faint, knowing smiles; others, eternal scowls of disapproval. She drew in a slow breath. The air was still, touched with polish and old wood.

Ahead, a grand staircase rose with quiet authority. Its bannister gleamed in the half-light. To her right, a corridor stretched into the house, drawing her in. She followed it slowly, taking in the artwork and curated artefacts that adorned the walls.

She turned into the study. Inside, a sideboard stood proudly, cut-crystal glasses and decanters arranged with deliberate care, catching the filtered light. An unlit fireplace sat between two high-backed wing chairs, with a small round table placed neatly between them. Logs were already stacked in readiness.

At the far end of the room, beneath a tall window, stood a large mahogany desk. Farran moved toward it, drawn by something inexplicable. A small plaque noted that many original items had been moved to the exhibition, but still, she could not resist. Her fingertips brushed the surface: smooth, cool, faintly glinting in the low light.

It was just a desk. Yet something about the moment, about touching it, sent a jolt through her chest. Not pain exactly. Recognition, perhaps. A flicker of something half-remembered.

"You know you're not meant to touch the furniture," said a familiar voice behind her.

Farran spun around, startled. "Darnell," she breathed. "You're the last person I expected to see here."

Her chest tightened as he stepped confidently into the room, his bearing that of a man entirely at ease, far too at ease.

"I could say the same about you," he replied with a smile. "I thought you were still recuperating."

By the time he reached her side, the air had shifted, drawn taut around them. His presence felt too familiar, too close.

"I'm feeling much better," she said quickly, unsure why she felt the need to explain. *I'm his manager,* she reminded herself. *Not the other way around.*

"I'm glad to hear that," he said, his smile curling slightly. His eyes gleamed with something too sharp, too knowing. She had only seen him look like that once before, when the artefacts had arrived at the museum.

"It's such a beautiful day," she said, trying to lighten the moment. "And I've become more curious about Richard's life. I thought coming here might be worthwhile."

She took two measured steps back, placing a quiet distance between them. The unease she thought she had left behind crept in again, coiling around her ribs like frost. *Why does he still make me feel like this?*

"Mmm, I know what you mean," Darnell said. His eyes followed her retreat, but he made no move to close the gap.

Farran managed a smile, glancing around the room. "I wonder what sort of dealings went on in here."

"Probably some dodgy ones," Darnell replied, his gaze drifting deliberately across the furniture, though he avoided her gaze.

"What makes you say that?" she asked, brow furrowed. Nothing in her research had suggested anything illicit in the Stephens family's history.

He smiled again, but this one was darker, guarded and unreadable. "Oh, just a hunch. Think about the family seal. I wouldn't be surprised if they had more than a few skeletons tucked away."

"Possibly," Farran said, considering. "Or maybe they wanted people to think that."

Darnell turned his full attention to her then. He really looked. His eyes sharpened; the effect was unsettling.

"I think you're being too kind. Our Mr Stephens strikes me as someone who did what he wanted, when he wanted. A man who lived without regard for anyone but himself. Someone who'd dispose of whatever, or whoever, got in his way."

Farran blinked. His tone was colder than she had expected, more personal. She stared at him, taken aback by his imaginative reinvention of the man she had spent months researching. Until now, Richard Stephens had appeared to be a figure of generosity and duty, a man devoted to his household and the community. But Darnell was casting long shadows across that image, and something in the way he said it chilled her.

"What gives you that impression?" she asked.

Darnell looked away, just briefly. "Okay, I wasn't going to say anything... but I grew up around here," he admitted, offering a sheepish glance in return. "I used to hear all sorts of stories about the Stephens family."

"I knew you were holding something back," Farran said, smiling. "Especially when we were talking about Mr Bromley."

"Guilty," Darnell replied with a grin. "I didn't want to make you feel inferior."

Farran raised her eyebrows, then laughed lightly and said, "Darnell, we are historians. We share stories. Just because you know things I don't, does not mean I would feel inferior, honestly."

She shook her head in mock disbelief, then leaned in slightly. "So? What can you tell me?"

The scent of her perfume caught him off guard for a moment, but without missing a step, he said smoothly, "I'll show you around as we talk."

He smiled, though he trembled inside, and turned to lead her from the room. Farran followed, a flicker of something strange stirring within her. For a moment, she did not see Darnell at all. She saw the Master of the house, his silhouette outlined against the tall windows of the hall, striding the same steps centuries ago. An involuntary shiver rippled down her spine. Was it a memory, or a dream? She could not tell.

They wandered the house, Darnell speaking as they moved. He told inherited tales: fragments of family lore, sorrowful memories, and polished half-truths passed down through generations. Farran listened closely, noting how his voice softened during moments of joy and grew taut when the stories darkened.

"This is the library," Darnell said, pushing open a heavy door.

Farran stepped through and stopped short, her breath catching in her throat. The scent met her first: old paper, leather, woodsmoke, and rosemary. Her eyes swept the tall shelves, the worn volumes, the arched window where a narrow seat nestled beneath the glass. Something shifted within her, a sensation like falling.

"Are you okay?" Darnell asked.

His voice came faintly, muffled by a soft whispering she could not place.

"Yes," she breathed, though the word barely escaped her lips.

She walked forward slowly, trailing her fingers along the book spines. The air thickened around her, with the scent of rosemary. Memories, she thought. Or something like them. Unsung words clung to the corners of the room.

"Mother, you are too generous. How can you forgive him?"

"He has his worries. I am grateful for all he has done."

The voices echoed faintly, not from outside but from within.

"Farran...?"

Darnell's voice. Closer now. She blinked and turned. The sounds faded, like fog dissolving in the sun.

"Are you alright?" he asked again, his brow creased.

She nodded slowly. "Yes. Just... soaking in the atmosphere."

"It is a lovely room," he said, glancing around. His tone had softened. "Richard's third wife, Anne, spent hours in here."

"I can see why," Farran murmured. Her voice had taken on the same dreamlike quality. "It would be my idea of heaven."

Darnell looked at her with something unreadable in his eyes. A glance that seemed out of place.

Farran turned back to the shelves. Her fingers itched to pull down a volume, to sink into the seat and vanish between the pages. A sharp pang of sadness caught her by surprise. She drifted to the window and gazed out. From here, she could see the drive winding through the trees, the fountain scattering sunlight in glittering arcs. The breeze stirred the trees gently, like breath held in wait. In her mind's eye, a figure on horseback emerged. A man paused at the crest of the track, silhouetted in gold. He looked back at the house, nodded once, and rode away into the light.

"She would sit there," Darnell said quietly behind her, "waiting for her husband to return."

Farran turned her head. He had joined her now, his expression contemplative.

"He was often away on business," he added.

"She must have loved him very much," Farran whispered. The vision still clung to her, like smoke in her senses.

"Mmm," Darnell murmured. Then, gently, he said, "Come. Let's carry on."

He stepped back into the corridor.

Farran lingered a moment longer, her eyes roaming the garden paths below. Then she followed, her steps slow, her thoughts caught somewhere between now and then, between the warm present and the ghost of something waiting just beyond reach.

They climbed the portrait-lined staircase, Farran running her fingers along the carved bannister. About halfway up, she paused. A portrait of Richard

Stephens caught her eye. Unlike the one sent to the exhibition, this version seemed gentler. He looked genuinely content, surrounded by his wife and their six children: two boys and four girls. There was a softness in his eyes that tugged at something deep within her.

Darnell noticed she had stopped and returned to stand beside her.

"That was his first wife, Margaret," he said. His voice was different now, quieter, laced with something mournful.

Farran glanced at him. The sadness in his tone tightened something in her chest.

"They were madly in love," he continued, still gazing at the painting. "She died in 1588."

His eyes lingered on Margaret's painted face, and something in him seemed to flicker, like sorrow held just beneath the skin. Without thinking, Farran reached out and gently touched his arm. He glanced down at her hand, then met her gaze. Something unspoken passed between them.

"What happened?" she asked softly. She didn't move. Surprised by her stillness, she allowed the moment to stretch.

Darnell sighed and placed his hand over hers.

"There was an awful accident," he said. "Margaret and her sons, Richard, who was thirteen, and Thomas, fifteen, were travelling to meet Richard in Shrewsbury. He had been there on business with Henry Bromley."

He paused, then added, "Richard had hoped the boys might follow him into law. It was a respected profession then, and well paid."

His eyes clouded, and he turned his head slightly, as if to hide it.

"They were staying at an inn, waiting for him to arrive. He had been delayed; some legal matter dragged on. He didn't get there until after midnight."

Farran saw the shimmer of tears beginning to form, caught in the edge of his lashes. Her grip on his arm tightened instinctively.

Darnell looked away, swallowed hard, and continued.

"By the time he arrived, a fire had broken out. The whole place was engulfed. All three of them, Margaret, Richard, and Thomas, died in the blaze."

His voice trembled. "A young man named Jasper, thought to be related to Bromley and who apparently held a grudge, later confessed to setting the fire."

Farran said nothing. The silence stretched between them.

"Richard never recovered," Darnell murmured. "Losing her, losing the boys, he became bitter. Hard. Some say he was never the same again."

"That's awful," Farran whispered, releasing her breath.

Darnell nodded, solemn. "It was."

She tilted her head. "Why isn't any of this in the records we've seen?"

He gave a faint smile. "The family was private. Reserved. Tragedy seemed to follow them; from that fire to what came after."

"His third wife, Anne," Farran said, her curiosity sharpening. "She vanished in 1593."

Darnell met her gaze, then looked up the stairs. "After Margaret died, he remarried in 1589, another Margaret, oddly enough. Perhaps he hoped to reclaim what he had lost."

He led her a few more steps to the landing and stopped before another portrait. A young woman looked out from the canvas, her expression serene, her hazel eyes bright with warmth.

"They were happy at first, and had two sons," Darnell said quietly. "Edward and Nathaniel. But Edward died young, three months old. Convulsions. Margaret followed him less than a year later."

His voice dropped further.

"She passed on New Year's Day. In her sleep."

Farran's breath caught.

"And then... Anne Kery," Darnell said, voice dropped to a whisper. "The third wife. She disappeared in 1593. Some say she ran off with her lover."

But something in the way he said it made Farran's skin prickle. The story, as he told it, felt practised, like a line repeated too often. She looked again at the portraits. At the smiling faces, long dead. At the silent stories no one had ever written down. A weight was gathering. A thread of unease pulling tight.

"A very good story, sir," said a voice behind them.

Farran turned to see a man standing in the corridor, smiling. The expression lit up his grey-green eyes, softening the angular planes of his face. Dark hair, streaked with silver, fell over his forehead, and his open-necked shirt revealed a glimpse of his chest, dusted with dark hair. Farran shivered. Her body betrayed her with an involuntary reaction, one that left her suddenly uncomfortable in her skin. Beside her, Darnell stiffened. He fixed the man with a glare full of visible hatred.

"Good day to you, sir," Darnell said tightly. The tension between them hung in the air like a thunderclap. "Can I help you?"

"No," the man replied easily, still smiling. "I was simply intrigued by the story you were telling. Fascinating history. Tell me, how do you know so much about the gentleman?"

"I was brought up here," Darnell said curtly, each word sharp and cold.

"Mm." The stranger's eyes gleamed. "I, too, lived here. And I've heard rather different versions of your story."

His words hung in the air, barbed and deliberate.

Darnell shot a glance at Farran. "You go on. I'll catch up."

She hesitated, her eyes still on the stranger. There was something familiar about him, his face, his voice, as though a memory had slipped through her grasp. Before she could pin it down, Darnell was already leading the man downstairs, their voices dropping to harsh whispers.

Left alone, Farran wandered along the landing, drawn to a nearby room, her thoughts buzzing. She stepped inside a richly decorated bedroom. A four-poster bed stood beneath the window, its curtains drawn back and neatly tied. Light filtered in across the embroidered coverlet. As she moved closer, the room seemed to darken. Rosemary filled the air. Pressure built in her head; her vision swam.

She wore a green dress. A hand caught her wrist and yanked her backwards.

"Do not be under any illusion, my dear," hissed a voice. "In public, we are very much in love. In private, you are nothing. How could I love the cousin of a murdering scoundrel?"

He shoved her hard. She stumbled toward the bed.

"No," she whispered. "If my uncle knew about this, he'd have you whipped."

The man leaned in, his breath hot against her cheek. "Your Uncle Henry knows exactly what goes on," he sneered.

He stepped back, studying her with cold disdain. "You are my wife. You do as I want."

A sharp, brutal slap rang out. She gasped and turned to flee. His nails scraped the back of her neck. He dragged her down and threw her onto the bed.

Farran reeled, trembling, but the vision twisted;

Now she lay still, her hands folded over her stomach.

"Do not worry, sir," she whispered. "He has made me understand."

The man joined her. Silent tears streamed down her face as he took her.

Another twist,

"Merry Christmas, husband," she said softly.

"Is it?" he snapped. "Is it a merry time when I discover my wife is seeing another?"

"No, sir. That is not true."

"A jester, no less." His voice broke with loathing.

"No," she pleaded. "Who said such a thing?"

"That is no concern of yours," he said coldly. "Consider yourself lucky it is Christmas, and that I believe this to be the work of witchcraft. Otherwise, you would no longer be walking this earth."

His fist crashed into her cheek. She fell back onto the bed.

"That is just to be going on with," he growled. "When I return from London, we shall see where things truly lie."

Farran could bear no more. She tore from the room and stumbled into the corridor.

"Farran!" Darnell's voice echoed up the stairs. "What is wrong?"

She spun. "You! Keep away from me!" she cried.

She fled down the steps, out through the door and into the gardens, barely aware of the wind whipping at her clothes. She needed distance, from Darnell, from the house, from everything she had just seen.

19

Blood in the Forest (1592)

It had been unbearable ever since speaking with Greg. I had not talked to Davy or Wynn; Anne had shut herself away, refusing to see anyone, and two days had passed. I knew I had to silence Greg and get Anne and Wynn to safety, no matter the cost.

My chance to speak to Davy finally came on a cold, crisp winter morning during a trip to Gloucester to collect supplies for Cook. The usual delivery was suspended over the festivities, and I volunteered to accompany him, offering to help bring the items back.

Before leaving, I sent word to Anne, informing her as Mistress of the house of my departure and requesting Wynn attend to her needs in my absence. Nothing unusual in that; no questions were asked.

We mounted the horses and rode out, our breath forming white clouds in the icy air. The trees and hedgerows blurred past, unnoticed as we focused on the journey. Once safely away from the house,

"How are you and Wynn keeping?" I asked.

"Good," Davy replied. "We're enjoying the time while the Master is away."

"Mm," I murmured, searching for words. How could I tell him what the Master planned?

"And you?" he asked. "You seem otherwise occupied."

"Yes," I said shortly, then drew a deep breath. "I have received troubling information from the Master and Greg."

Davy shot me a sharp glance. "What kind of information?"

"I..." I hesitated. "I have been told that witchcraft is practised in the house. Greg and I are tasked with dealing with it."

Silence fell.

I saw him working to steady himself before asking. "Who has been accused?"

"I think you know."

He kept his eyes on the road, the gentle bobbing of his horse failing to ease the tension in his spine.

"So, how is this to be dealt with?" he asked, his voice even but heavy.

"Death."

A sharp gasp escaped him.

"When?"

"By the end of the week, before the Master returns from London."

His body twitched, shoulders tightening against the reins.

"How?"

"Fire."

A soft, strangled sound slipped from his throat as he bowed his head.

"I swear to you, I will not let it happen."

Davy lifted his gaze slowly. "If it is the Master's order, you know full well it will be carried out." His face was pale, his eyes hollow.

"I have a plan," I urged. "It is only Greg and me. No one else."

"That scoundrel will make sure it happens," he muttered bitterly.

"He will not be able to if he is dead."

A pause.

"That would mean breaking your promise again, Tom," Davy said quietly. "I cannot ask you to do that."

"I am damned either way," I said. He nodded slowly.

"I would rather protect my friends, but I need to know truthfully: is there any truth in the accusations against Wynn?"

He looked at me for a long moment; I knew what was coming.

"Yes, Tom. It is true," he said, pride flashing in his eyes. "She practises witchcraft, but only for good."

"How long has she been doing it?"

"As long as I have known her. Her mother taught her." He paused, his voice softening. "It was always small things: protection charms, healing salves. Nothing serious, not until recently."

He looked down at the horse's neck and sighed.

"I told her to be careful, but she wouldn't stop. She wanted to help the Mistress, help you. *'True love deserves all the help it needs,'* she keeps saying."

I sat in stunned silence. They had put themselves at risk for us. Suddenly, so much made sense.

"Davy," I said quietly, "I don't know what to say. You and Wynn, you are true friends."

A breeze swept across my face, and I straightened in the saddle.

"I have to act quickly; the Master returns at week's end."

Davy lifted his head. "What do you need from me?"

The plan was already beginning to form.

"All I ask is that you invite Greg to dine with us on New Year's Eve."

Davy blinked. "That is all?"

"Yes," I said, gripping his arm. "I will handle the rest."
    The plan was clear; it had to be me.

We rode on toward Gloucester. Davy told stories about Wynn: tales of mischief, quiet acts of magic, how they had built a hidden life within the boundaries of another. When those stories ran out, he spoke of the season's festivities. It all felt surreal, knowing now that Wynn, like me, was living a double life. The difference was that she got to share hers with the one she loved. And I? I found myself wondering if I would ever have that with Anne. Would she ever forgive me? Or were we already doomed? Only time would tell.

* * *

The days passed. Amid my daily routines, I prepared for the task ahead, pushing down the dread that had taken root deep inside me. Greg had been invited to the cottage for New Year's celebrations. He rubbed his hands together gleefully.

"Well done, Tom," he proclaimed upon hearing the news. "Now we can rid the Master of these treacherous beings; they do not deserve to walk upon God's earth."

I laughed with him, feigning delight that the heinous deed was falling into place as planned. His arrogance and lack of regard only strengthened my resolve to fulfil my final murderous duty, this time against the Master's wishes. My stomach tightened, and a wave of nausea rose within me.

New Year's Eve dawned crisp and cold, pale light filtering weakly through the frosted cottage windows. Inside, preparations for the evening's celebration bustled quietly. Davy laughed and joked warmly with his wife, whose bright smile belied the storm of danger gathering around them.

"She doesn't need to know," Davy had insisted earlier, his voice low but firm. I had agreed, adding that Anne must also remain unaware.

Anne hadn't left her room since the Master's departure, retreating into a world of silence and shadows. Wynn was barred from entering; her concerned knock went unanswered. Meals were placed outside Anne's door, half-eaten or sometimes untouched: signs of a spirit breaking under some unseen weight. A knot of unease tightened in my chest whenever I thought of her. Part of me longed to cross the threshold and offer comfort, but I knew any interaction would raise suspicion. So I kept my distance, burying my dread beneath a facade of calm and focusing instead on the grim task ahead: removing Greg.

The thought of what was to come churned in my stomach, a bitter mix of determination and despair. I did not relish the darkness I must wield, but the safety of my friends demanded it. Time was slipping away, and I had to act before it was too late.

The day grew darker, the winter sun slipping behind heavy clouds while a deeper chill crept through the air. With every step toward the cottage, my thoughts twisted and turned like the gathering shadows around us. Greg, who had stuck by my side all day, chattered eagerly; his words were sharp and biting like a knife in the quiet afternoon.

"I'm looking forward to seeing the house freed from that diabolical witchcraft once and for all," Greg said, voice low but fierce, eyes gleaming with dark excitement.

His words scraped something raw inside me. I already knew who he meant and what they planned, but hearing it aloud still felt like a blow to the chest. The way he enjoyed it.

I stared ahead, trying to quiet the rush of panic. Then, as if twisting the knife, he added, "The Mistress has been ordered to stay in her room all week."

The mention of her snapped me out of my thoughts: The Mistress?

"What are you talking about?" I asked, my voice sharper than I intended.

Greg turned to me with a grim smile, something smug in his jaw's set. "The Master insisted it was necessary. He said she shouldn't be involved while we deal with this... situation."

I nodded slowly, a cold weight settling in my chest. Trapped, silenced. No wonder she hadn't been seen. But this wasn't about protecting her; it was about keeping her out of the way.

Greg chuckled darkly. "He made sure she agreed to it and to have absolutely no contact with the witch or her husband." He slapped his palm, then punched the air with cruel finality.

A cold knot tightened in my stomach at the thought of Anne suffering further under the Master's harsh hand. The image of her fragile form, shut away and isolated, pierced me. Yet I forced a smile, careful not to betray the pain clawing within. I slapped Greg lightly on the back. "Well, he certainly made sure," I said with a hollow chuckle, masking the storm beneath.

The desperate urge to rush to Anne's side and soothe invisible wounds gnawed at me, but I clenched my fists and pushed it down. It had to wait until this was over, until it was safe.

We continued toward the cottage, its windows glowing warmly in the encroaching twilight, flickering like watchful eyes in the dark. The crisp winter air carried the rich scent of spices and roasting meat, a stark contrast to the turmoil roiling inside me. Normally, the thought of Wynn's cooking would make my mouth water, but tonight the tightness in my gut would not loosen.

Greg's voice cut sharply through my swirling thoughts. "So, you know what you must do?"

"Yes," I answered, my fingers grazing the cold glass of the bottle tucked securely beneath my coat, the deadly potion Greg had handed me earlier. "I have the bottle with me, ready to slip it into their drinks."

A cruel smile spread across Greg's face. "Good. I cannot wait to see the agony crawl across their faces as the poison takes hold."

I stared straight ahead, careful to hide my scowl from him. I grunted in response, shutting out his gleeful anticipation. My mind raced over the plan I had carefully crafted, the precautions to keep Davy and Wynn safe, the small trinkets hidden and ready to help us escape if things went awry. With renewed determination, I stepped forward, flicked the latch, and knocked, more out of habit than need. The door swung open with a creak. I stepped inside, warmth and light swallowing me as the cottage embraced us.

We were greeted by welcoming heat that pulled us deeper into the cottage's heart, wrapping around us like a protective cloak. The rich aromas that had teased my senses outside now enveloped the room: herbs, roasting meat, and something sweet and earthy simmering in a pot. Despite the comfort of the smells, my stomach knotted tighter with dread.

By the fire stood Davy, his arm firmly wound around Wynn's waist, holding her close. Concern flickered in his eyes, a shadow beneath the hearth's warm glow. Wynn turned slightly, stirring the bubbling pot with a steady hand, humming softly.

"Tom. Greg." Davy nodded in greeting, a stiff smile playing on his lips, as if masking the tension coiled beneath his calm.

Before either of us could reply, Wynn broke free from Davy's hold and approached, her face lighting up with that familiar, cheerful glow. She paused, giving Davy a quick, puzzled glance before turning her attention to us and pulling us into warm, all-encompassing hugs. Her arms were soft and steady, but her body held a subtle stiffness, as if listening for danger.

"It's so good to have company on such a night," she chirped, her voice bright and carefree, but I caught a flicker of something guarded beneath the surface. I wondered if Davy had managed to shield her from the horrors ahead.

Turning to Greg, she beckoned him toward the fire. "Come, have a seat, Greg." She guided him gently to one of the chairs, and he followed with a smirk curling the corner of his lips.

"I hope you're hungry; I fear I may have cooked too much," Wynn added with a nervous laugh, trying to keep the mood light.

Greg threw himself into the chair, eyes gleaming with anticipation. "I could eat a horse; nights like this make me ravenous," he said, giving a knowing wink that made my skin crawl.

I let out a low chuckle and nodded, forcing warmth into my voice. "Your food is always so moreish, Wynn. I can never get enough."

I stepped closer to Davy and lowered my voice slightly. "Thank you for inviting us to your home on such a festive night."

His smile tightened, eyes flickering with unspoken worry. "It's no trouble. We all need a bit of cheer, even in dark times."

The room seemed to hold its breath, the crackling fire the only sound breaking the silence between us. The festive warmth masked the cold threat lurking just beneath the surface.

"Think nothing of it," Davy said with a tight smile, though I caught the faintest tremor in his frame as he turned away. His shudder was barely perceptible, but it spoke volumes, carrying a weight far heavier than the festivities suggested.

"And that we will, Davy," I replied, giving his back a reassuring slap before turning toward the door. "Please excuse me, though; I fear this cold weather has aggravated my stomach." The lie felt bitter in my mouth, but I needed the excuse.

Stepping out into the sharp night air, I drew a deep breath. The chill bit at my lungs as I made my way into the dark woods behind the cottage, the shadows swallowing me whole. The moon cast faint silver patterns on the frosted leaves, guiding my steps to the clearing. My heart thudded hard in my chest as I approached the pit I had painstakingly prepared over the past days.

The clearing lay undisturbed: no footprints, no signs of any lurking threat. Relief washed over me like a balm, though the cold gnawed at my skin. I lingered for a moment, steadying my nerves before turning back toward the cottage, my footsteps crunching on the iced ground.

Re-entering, the warm air hit me like a wave, thick with scents of simmering stew and fresh bread, making my head spin.

"Oh, Tom," Greg's voice rang out just as I closed the door behind me. "Davy here has been keeping me well entertained with stories of your antics. Did you really manage to get your previous Master to sign a deed giving you full control over the household for two whole weeks?"

I thought back to my days at Gravenmarsh Keep, when old Derverall barely kept hold of the reins after the mistress passed. Grief had soured his temper, and the household frayed beneath it: bickering servants, spoiled stores, doors slamming like gunfire at all hours. I slipped a parchment onto his desk amid the accounts: a mock decree, sealed with a smear of wax and bravado, granting me full charge of the house for a fortnight. To my surprise, he signed it without looking, grumbling something about "let the fool sort it out, then."

A smirk tugged at my lips as I nodded, leaning casually against the wall. "That I did, and he was none too pleased. Though once the weeks had passed, he admitted, if reluctantly, that he had enjoyed not having the responsibility."

Greg let out a hearty laugh, already flushed from the ale he'd been nursing. "I could not see Master Stephens being fooled in such a way. He's far too astute for that."

He chuckled again, eyes gleaming with mischief while I recounted more stories; our voices filled the cosy room while Wynn busied herself in the kitchen, finishing the preparations and laying the table. Yet beneath the laughter, a cold shadow lingered in my mind, a silent reminder that the night's true business was far from over.

"Come, sit down, it's ready," Wynn called out, her voice light and musical as she gestured us to the table.

The spread before us was glorious: platters piled with steaming meats, roasted vegetables, freshly baked bread, and spiced puddings. Any other night, I would have tucked in heartily, but now my throat felt as if a rope had tightened around it, squeezing until I could scarcely swallow.

"Are you alright, Tom?" Wynn asked gently, her brow furrowed while she studied me.

"Aye, Wynn," I managed with a smile, although it barely reached my eyes.

"Just the excitement of the night."

Greg grinned across the table while I spoke, the gleam in his eye turning my stomach. I needed this over and done with. Yet I knew that even when the deed was done, the torment would not simply end. I looked at my hands. Some stains could never be washed away.

Davy fetched more ale with every empty cup, yet Greg seemed impervious to its effects. His laughter grew louder, more guttural, but his eyes remained sharp, watching, calculating. Then, finally, as the last bites of the first course were cleared, Greg scraped his chair back and stood.

"Excuse me," he said, swaying slightly while he clapped me on the back. "Alas, the ale must out."

He lurched toward the door, muttering something about the cold air waking him up. I nodded silently as he turned and stepped out into the dark. I heard his boots crunch on the frozen path leading toward the woods. I took a long breath, grounding myself. My fingers slipped into my pocket and closed around the small bottle that had waited for this moment. Davy's eyes locked on mine, wide with fear and disbelief.

"Is that... "

"No," I cut him off firmly, not unkindly. "Do not ask, Davy. Just tell Wynn you are both feeling unwell. You will need to retire early."

With practised care, I uncorked the bottle and poured the contents into Greg's tankard. The liquid vanished seamlessly into the amber ale. No trace remained. My hands did not shake, but a cold sweat broke across my back. This was it. I stood, collected Davy and Wynn's cups, and poured fresh ale for them at the sideboard, setting the small bottle down beside the empty pitcher. Greg's boots crunched on the path, growing nearer.

Thinking quickly, I raised my voice and launched into a tale. "Of course, the master did not know what to do. He had hoped to spend time with the Mistress on his return, but Sir Henry turned up instead."

I let out a bellowing laugh just as the door clicked shut and Greg stepped inside. Davy caught my cue, grinning as he added, "He was furious. He spent the rest of the evening sulking in his study while Sir Henry rambled on about fencing and French wine."

Greg chuckled as he sat down. "What tale of mischief have I missed?"

"Just Tom reminding us of the time Sir Henry turned up uninvited," Davy replied smoothly, lifting his tankard.

Greg glanced toward the bottle on the sideboard. "Let's make a toast," he said, lifting his tankard with a wink in my direction. "To good times ahead, and the Master's health and safety."

We all raised our drinks.

"To the Master," we chorused.

A moment of silence. Then the clink of vessels.

Greg drained his drink in one go, then let out a belly laugh, slamming his tankard onto the table with gusto. We followed, more measured but no less convincing. Laughter resumed. Stories flowed. But beneath the surface, something had shifted. Time dragged on with agonising patience.

Wynn cleared the table, then called softly to Davy. "My love, I do not feel so well," she said, clutching her stomach. "I think I must retire."

Davy stood and rushed to her side, wrapping his arms around her. He looked over at me, concern etched into his face.

"I must apologise, but it appears our evening must end here. It has been a pleasure, Tom, Greg. We'll see you soon."

"Think nothing of it, Davy, Wynn," I said, offering a tired smile. "Thank you for a wonderful evening."

"Thank you," Greg echoed cheerfully. "It's been a pleasure."

Greg turned and headed for the door without a second glance. I moved to the couple still clinging to one another and embraced them quickly. While I held Davy close, I whispered in his ear,

"Wait a short while, then extinguish your light."

I stepped back, gave them each a final nod, and followed Greg out into the bitter cold. The air caught in my throat, raw and sharp. We walked in silence, each step swallowed by the darkness around us, heavy and close. The only sound was the brittle crack of ice in the dark. Greg finally turned to glance back at the cottage. A single flickering light remained in the window.

"Well done," he muttered. "Now we just have to wait. Although I'm a little disappointed we will not witness the traitors' agonising end. That is the best part." He chuckled and dropped onto a nearby stump.

"Aye," I said flatly, sitting down a short distance away, my eyes fixed on that small glowing window.

But doubt crept in like frostbite. Greg showed no signs, a flicker of discomfort. My stomach twisted. Had he known? Had I been outplayed, or had he swapped the potion? No... surely I had played my role well enough. He could not have known.

The light finally went out.

"Come. It is time," Greg whispered, his voice abrupt in the silence.

We rose and retraced our steps toward the cottage. As we neared, Greg groaned and clutched his stomach.

"I think that witch's food is turning on me. All the more reason to rid the world of them," he growled, his teeth clenched.

Greg began gathering dry kindling and placing it by the cottage wall. I followed his lead, each motion buying time. He paused often, groaning louder each time, doubling over in mounting agony. Then, all at once, he screamed, a sharp, inhuman cry, and collapsed to the ground, writhing. Thick, dark liquid burst from his mouth with every rasping cough. His eyes found mine, wide with rage and realisation.

"What have you done, you witch-lover?" he hissed.

I stood over him as a flicker of relief broke through the weight in my chest.

"I could not let you or the Master murder two innocent people," I snapped.

"Innocent?" he choked. "They are far from innocent. And now you will join them. The Master will make sure of it."

His limbs convulsed as the poison claimed him. Blood frothed at his lips.

"The Master will believe," I said coldly, "that his trusted servant betrayed him and fled with his silver and gold."

I turned, crossed to a log and sat down, watching the life drain from Greg's twisted body.

"You'll pay for this, Tom," he wheezed, his breath growing shallow. "The master is not a fool…"

His words dissolved into gurgles. His final breath escaped in a slow hiss. Then, nothing.

I sat frozen on the log, tears of self-loathing tracing burning tracks down my cheeks. They dripped onto the blood-slick earth at my feet. The sight, the mess I had made, was too much. Nausea gripped me. I pitched forward, vomiting hard onto the frozen ground. It was several minutes before I could rise. My legs trembled as I grabbed his feet and began the slow drag toward the pit. Thank God the path was cleared earlier; he was heavy, and each yard dragged like a mile.

At the edge, I let go. His body slumped. With one final push of my boot, he fell with a thud into the hole. I did not rest. I could not. I clawed and flung earth into the pit, my torn hands caked in blood and dirt. It took an age. By the end, my breath came in ragged gasps, my limbs shook, and I could scarcely remain upright. But he was gone.

I stamped down the last of the soil, smoothing it with my boot, then sank to my knees in a breathless prayer.

Forgive me, Lord.

The tears fell freely, and I could no longer name the pain I felt.

At last, I staggered upright and began the long walk back through the woods. The cold gnawed at my skin, stung my eyes. My feet crunched over the ice, the sound loud in the frozen hush, broken only by the distant hoot of owls.

Through a gap in the trees, I caught sight of the dark outline of the cottage. Davy sat on the step, his head in his hands. He looked up as I approached, his gaze catching the moonlight. I stopped in front of him, then slowly lowered myself to sit beside him. The silence between us was heavy, reverent and thick with unspoken fears.

"It is done," I whispered. "Wynn is safe. He shall never torment you again."

But I knew it would not be over for me. Greg's final expression was seared into my mind. Davy exhaled, trembling, his relief barely contained. He placed a shaking hand on my arm.

"Thank you," he said quietly.

I covered his hand with mine and gave it a gentle pat. Then I rose and dragged my weary body back to my room.

In the dark room, I collapsed onto the bed. A wave of emotion struck like a storm: grief and guilt, rage and emptiness, all colliding in my chest. The portrait glared in the gloom, its silence seeming to whisper: Have you truly changed? So I greeted the new year, not with hope, but with blood beneath my nails and a heart in ruin.

20

The Unseen Thread (2018)

Farran ran into the sunshine, heading toward a wooden gate set into the stone wall at the garden's edge. She pulled at the latch and swung it open; the rusty hinges groaned in protest. Hastily, she stepped through and moved toward the nearby woods. A small, derelict cottage stood to one side, its windows dark and empty.

She stumbled along the uneven path, her thoughts tangled in intrusive memories. Reaching the creaking step, she paused. A pull, a whisper of laughter and warmth, drew her closer. Slowly, she reached for the door.

"Hey…"

The voice behind her made her start. She spun around to see the man who had antagonised Darnell earlier running toward her. His chest heaved with breath as he reached the step and stopped.

"Hi…" he said cautiously. "Are you alright? I saw you leave rather quickly… nothing to do with your husband, I hope?"

Farran stared at him. His face, his voice; everything about him felt achingly familiar, safe. The haunting images had faded, replaced by warmer ones that stirred behind her eyes. Yet her head couldn't make sense of them. She kept looking at him, an overwhelming urge to be held in his arms washing over her, drowning all reason.

"Hey, you okay?" He reached out and lightly touched her arm. A sharp jolt of electricity shot through her, and she shuddered, gasping. Quickly, he withdrew his hand.

"Sorry, I didn't mean to startle you."

"Oh... no... You didn't," Farran stammered. "I've just been having a weird day... and Darnell, he's not my husband. We work together... I didn't know he'd be here today. He just kind of... appears."

She flushed, catching herself rambling, unsure why she felt the need to explain anything.

"I see..." He smiled; his eyes lit up, his face glowing. "I just assumed, seeing as you were together."

His smiling face put Farran at ease; she relaxed. She chuckled softly. "To be honest, I'd rather not have that much to do with him; he's always been a bit, I don't know, frosty?" Farran smiled at him. She'd never felt this comfortable with anyone else except Elwyna and Daryll. The sense she somehow knew him grew stronger, sparking a desire to learn more.

"I don't know why, but that actually makes me feel better," he said, his smile widening.

"What does?" Farran asked, puzzled.

"That he's not your husband," he said shyly. She became more aware of an invisible thread between them. Butterflies stirred in her stomach; she didn't want this moment to end. She returned his smile.

"Ah... yes," she replied softly.

They stood silently; a gentle breeze stirred the leaves, and birds sang in the trees. Farran was the first to break the quiet. "You said you used to live around here?"

"Mm, yes, I did," he said. "It was a long time ago now, though."

"I don't suppose you could share some stories about the place? It would really help with my work," she asked.

"Well, yes, anything to help," he replied, clearly pleased she wanted his assistance. "What exactly do you do?"

"I'm the curator at a museum. We're putting together a display in Shrewsbury about the life of Richard Stephens, his wives and children," Farran explained. "Especially as his third wife, Anne Kery, was from Shrewsbury."

Farran thought she saw him flinch at the name Richard Stephens, but quickly dismissed it; what reason could he have to react to a man who died over 400 years ago?

"That sounds interesting," he said, studying her intently. Then, softer, almost to himself, "I'd forgotten Anne's connection to Shrewsbury."

Farran was fascinated by the way he spoke, as if he knew Anne Kery personally, and found herself eager to spend more time with him. She glanced back at the cottage beside them. Its windows were shuttered tight; the door firmly closed, giving it an air of quiet mystery.

"Let's start here," Farran said eagerly. "What do you know about this cottage?"

He studied the cottage with quiet fondness, biting his lip before answering. "Well, the last recorded inhabitants were a couple who worked for Richard Stephens."

Farran felt a surge of excitement deep inside her, rising through her body. She stared at him, eyes wide.

"Davy, a footman in the household, and Wynn, the family nanny," he continued.

"I always thought the nanny lived in the house with the family," Farran said.

"Yes, it was unusual," he replied, "but it was because they were married and the Master regarded them highly; well, that was until talk of witchcraft." He paused, looking around before walking over to a fallen log, looking at it sorrowfully.

"What happened to them?" she asked, a chill prickling her skin as dread eclipsed her curiosity.

He sat on the log's end, shoulders hunched, head bowed. "No one really knows. In 1593, they disappeared, never to be seen again."

Farran watched him sit, unmoving and forlorn. His whole demeanour was as if speaking of dear friends, not a couple who lived centuries ago. A sudden need to comfort stirred within her; on impulse, she moved closer, desperate to console him. Hearing her approach, he looked up. His eyes softened; slowly, he stood and pulled her close. Everything stilled; the world seemed to stop, leaving only the two of them.

"I never thought I would find you again," he whispered, clinging to her.

Though confused by his words, Farran had no wish to move or speak. All she wanted was to stay in his arms and make the moment last forever. She sank against his chest, closing her eyes as he held her tightly and kissed the top of her head. An inaudible whisper brushed his lips as he placed his hands on her shoulders and leaned back to look at her. Gently, he moved a hand to caress her cheek; his touch sent a wave of emotion through her.

How could she feel so much for a stranger, someone she'd met less than an hour ago? Even though it made no sense, Farran knew that this, this was right. She leaned closer, desperate to feel his lips on hers, knowing deep down he was what she had been waiting for as long as she could remember.

"Farran! No!" Darnell's shout came from behind just as their lips were about to meet, and she was pulled away.

"Get off me!" she yelled, shoving him hard to make space.

Darnell stumbled back, desperation clear on his face. "Farran, please, I'm sorry," he pleaded, stepping forward again.

Farran stepped back, firm. "Stay away from me, Darnell."

"You heard her," the man said quietly, appearing at her side.

"Stay out of this," Darnell snapped. "It's because of you we're in this mess."

The man closed the distance, piercing eyes locked on Darnell, fists clenched. "Huh, keep telling yourself that," he spat. "But we all know the truth, don't we?"

Farran stood frozen, watching the men locked in a tense stand-off. Confusion twisted inside her, rooting her to the spot.

"Who do you think you are, speaking to me like that?" Darnell demanded, glare unwavering.

The other man let out a harsh, raucous laugh. "I'm a man, just like you," he spat, every word dripping with hatred.

"Oh, my friend, you're nothing like me," Darnell sneered. "You're a lowly fool."

The man's laugh turned derisive. "In another time, I might have agreed. But now... now we are equals, my friend."

Darnell's voice dropped to a low, dangerous whisper as he leaned closer. "Keep telling yourself that, but we both know the truth. She's mine."

Before Farran could react, the man's fist connected with Darnell's face, sending him staggering back. They crashed into each other, fists flying as the fight escalated.

Unable to watch any longer, Farran shouted, "Stop it, both of you!" Without looking back, she turned and sprinted toward the gate she had come through.

"Farran! Farran, wait!" Darnell called after her, but she didn't stop. She pushed through the stone wall and ran until she reached her car.

Hands trembling, she fumbled for her keys, unlocked the door, and slid inside. Glancing in the rear-view mirror, she saw the two men standing in the car park, watching her as she started the engine and drove away.

* * *

The scenery flew past as Farran mulled over the day's events. So much she didn't understand; so many feelings she couldn't fathom.

Before she knew it, she was racing down familiar roads. Relief wrapped around her; her breath began to steady. The Shropshire hills rose around her, enclosing her in a tight, protective embrace. She welcomed their almost claustrophobic clasp, sinking deeper into the soft upholstery of the seat. The hills swelled like green waves beneath a hazy sky, as if the land itself held its breath.

Her foot eased off the accelerator. Though her thoughts remained tangled, a quiet calm began to spread through her, soothed by the homely, undulating landscape. What had happened? Farran let her mind drift, not just over today but through the past few weeks, so many strange moments since Darnell appeared. Why was he there? She'd grown used to his sudden arrivals, but something about him always left her uneasy. The way he looked at her, possessive, knowing. She shuddered. And yet today, he seemed different.

Amenable.

Almost likeable.

What hold did that place have on him? Had she really seen affection in his eyes for the murdered woman in the painting?

"*I'm going mad*," Farran muttered, turning onto her street and pulling up outside the house.

She sat for a moment, then climbed out and went inside. She made a soothing drink and curled up in the living room. She sipped quietly from her mug, tapping the side absently, her thoughts adrift. She ran her fingers around the rim of the mug, its warmth grounding her, but her mind refused to settle.

Her gaze wandered, then stopped on the painting. She gasped. Surely she was imagining it. But the resemblance to the man she had met earlier was uncanny. Her head spun. What was going on? First Richard's portrait, then Darnell, and now this? This face, these eyes, staring back at her from her wall?

Grey-green eyes.

She stared, drawn in. The eyes seemed different now: sharper, more present. The canvas shimmered, just slightly. Then, in the hush of the room, a whisper stirred her mind:

Anne, I'm here. I'm so sorry it's taken me this long. Don't be afraid. Come to me.

Her head reeled. What was happening to her? Was she losing her grip?

A knock at the door jerked her back. She set the mug down and pushed herself up from the chair. Every movement felt heavy. Farran opened the door to find Elwyna smiling, though her expression quickly shifted to concern.

"Farr, what on earth is the matter?"

Elwyna guided her gently back to the living room, then watched as Farran sank into the seat, shoulders low and eyes clouded. Farran picked up her drink, took a sip, and gave a faint smile before setting it down again. She leaned her head into her hand and sighed.

"I think you were right when you said I was doing too much, going to Coeur House today."

Elwyna settled into the seat beside her and reached across to clasp Farran's hand, giving it a gentle squeeze.

"What's happened?" Her voice was soft, calming.

Farran shook her head. Her thoughts were jumbled, a kaleidoscope of images and feelings with no clear thread to follow.

"I don't even know where to begin..."

"Take your time, honey," Elwyna murmured, giving her hand another squeeze. "Have you eaten?"

Farran shook her head again.

"Let's see what you've got."

Elwyna stood and moved to the kitchen, giving her friend space. The gentle clink of crockery, the splash of pouring liquid, the tap of a spoon against a pot drifted in from the other room. Soon, the warm, familiar scent of stew curled through the house. Farran closed her eyes. An image bloomed behind her lids: a candlelit cottage, the aroma of stew thick in the air, whispers murmuring low, an undercurrent of tension pulsing. Him, sitting, smiling at her. His hand reaching out, touching hers with gentle assurance.

"*Anne,*" he breathed.

"Farran, you okay?" Elwyna's voice pulled her back. Her eyes flickered open.

"Oh, yes," she chuckled lightly. "It's been quite a day."

Her thoughts still drifted at the edges.

"Here's some stew, your favourite," Elwyna said, placing the steaming bowl in her hands. The aroma enveloped her, the heat reaching deep into her chest. Elwyna's stew had always been like a hug, grounding and warm.

Farran smiled, lifting a spoonful and blowing gently before taking a bite.

"Mmm. I don't know how you do it, but your stew…"

She blew a chef's kiss, and they giggled.

"It's that old secret family recipe," Elwyna said with a grin, taking a mouthful herself.

They sat in companionable silence, the occasional chink of cutlery the only sound between them. Eventually, Elwyna spoke again.

"So, what's been happening?" Her voice was soft and caressing, her soulful eyes gently encouraging Farran to sift through the chaos and turmoil.

Farran gave a wry smile. "Where do I start?"

Elwyna stretched over and lightly held her hand. "How about those sleepless nights? They seem like a good place."

Nodding, Farran began to open up, feeling a welcome release.

"It's always the same," she began, a small grimace pulling at her lips. "The dreams: there's always a mirror with a jumbled reflection that slowly assembles into this gentle face."

She paused, glancing at the picture that had hung unobtrusively on her wall all this time. She pointed.

"Him. It's always his face I see."

Elwyna looked at the picture, and something unreadable crossed her face. Turning back to Farran, she smiled.

"Well, I suppose it's your subconscious picking out a face you've seen before bed."

"Mmm, I suppose," Farran said reluctantly, though deep down, she felt it was more than that, a familiarity she couldn't name. She continued,

"We're standing in a beautiful garden outside a mansion. I'm there, I can hear and smell everything. At first, he just beckoned, but more recently, he speaks. He doesn't say my name, though. It's always Anne. He tells me not to be afraid and to 'come home.' Then he's gone. And when I wake… It's always at 3:04."

She hesitated, her brow furrowing. Something about the garden, the architecture, the way the ivy curled up the stone. Her mind scrambled to retrieve a thought, but it drifted out of reach.

She swallowed, her voice lowering. "Just before you arrived, I was looking at the picture, and I could hear his voice again. I'm sure it's the same voice from the radio show I listen to, the one I always play after those dreams. And today, at Coeur House, I saw the most disturbing visions of a woman dressed in green."

Farran stared, unblinking, at Elwyna, who sat in silence, watching her. She sensed a quiet tension building in her friend. Suddenly, Elwyna laughed.

"You have such a vivid imagination, Farr. It's all these history projects you throw yourself into."

Farran joined in the laughter, but deep down, she knew. She knew there was more to it.

"So, when did you say all this began?" Elwyna asked, her gaze lowering to the carpet.

"I suppose... two or three weeks ago," Farran said, searching her memory. "Just after Darnell started working at the museum."

She kept her eyes on Elwyna, noticing something had shifted in her demeanour, her usual warmth replaced by a quiet wariness. Was it concern? Disbelief? Then, just as quickly, Elwyna's jovial humour returned. She glanced at her watch.

"I'd best be going," she said, rising. She gathered the dishes and took them into the kitchen, leaving them to soak in the sink. A moment later, she returned to Farran. "There's a bit of extra stew. I put it in the fridge for tomorrow."

Farran looked at her gratefully. "Thanks."

"Take it easy and try to rest." Elwyna hugged her tightly. "Stay there. I'll let myself out."

Farran settled back and watched her leave the room. Telling someone had helped; she felt lighter, but a deep unease still coiled inside her. And now, after talking with Elwyna, she was starting to wonder... maybe Elwyna knew more than she had admitted.

* * *

Outside, Elwyna was already on the phone as she walked to her car.

"She's fine, but the protection isn't working properly."

"What are we going to do?" came Daryll's voice on the other end, tight with worry.

"We're going to have to remove Darnell," she whispered, her voice trembling.

"No. We can't ask that of him," Daryll snapped, agitation rising.

"Don't be silly," Elwyna muttered. "Not like that. I'll explain more when I get back. Maybe get him over as well, since his presence is causing problems."

She ended the call and climbed into her car, pausing to glance back at the house. Damn. Everything had become so muddled. But she had done what she could, for now. She only had to make sure Farran stayed protected.

21

Shadows and Shields (1593)

"Thomas!"

The Master's voice boomed down the corridor from his study to the library, where Anne and I had stolen a few moments of silence. He had been clattering about for ages, his mood growing darker by the minute.

"Thomas, where are you?"

I hesitated, reluctant to reveal my hiding place. Since that dreadful night outside the cottage, I had awaited the Master's judgment; I feared he believed I was behind Greg's disappearance. Another broken vow weighed heavily on my soul.

I looked at Anne... What if she learned the truth? The blood I had spilt. Could she still love me? Perhaps it was time to end this folly and vanish. With me gone, Davy and Wynn might be safe; the whispers of witchcraft might fade.

"THOMAS!" The Master's agitation rose.

I gave Anne a fleeting smile, then hurried toward the study door.

"Where in blazes have you been?"

The Master did not look at me; his hands tore through the chaos on his desk, rifling through strewn papers.

"Apologies, sir, I... "

"I care not, fool!" he snapped, still rummaging until at last he grasped a crumpled piece of parchment and shoved it roughly into his coat pocket.

"Wentworth has sent word. He calls a meeting to discuss succession. I ride tonight. Can I trust you to watch over the place in my absence?"

His raised eyebrow turned the question into a challenge; the mistrust had not cooled.

"Of course, Sire," I bowed. "You may rely on me."

Relief was short-lived.

"Oh, and to help with general duties, Miles Overton will arrive the day after the morrow. Show him the ropes. Hopefully, he proves more reliable than that useless urchin Greg. Heaven only knows where he went."

He stared at me, directly and deliberately. It took every ounce of restraint not to flinch. Then he turned, sending a flurry of dust into the air; I watched as he vanished through the door. I could breathe again.

Hurrying to the lit library, I was eager to share the news with Anne, a fleeting chance for us to be alone. She sat in her usual place by the window, watching dust swirl in the wake of the Master's departure. At the sound of my footsteps, she turned, her face radiant with joy. Slowly, I walked toward her as she rose.

"You heard?" I asked, a gleeful smile playing upon my lips.

"I did," she breathed, stepping close, close enough for me to pull her into my arms, but I held back.

"I do not know how long he will be gone. And we only have the morrow; another wretched watcher comes to 'help' with the general duties," I murmured.

I studied her face; her beaming smile still held a faint glimmer of despair. How I longed to take her somewhere safe, to protect her, to love her freely. Her smile grew; my heart stuttered.

"Not long now, my Tom," she said softly. And, as though reading my thoughts, she added, "And Wynn will have us away safely... far from here."

I could resist no longer. Though my mind warned me to stop, I drew her close. Her eyes held mine, beauty and love shining within. Our lips met; in that lingering kiss, all my fears fell silent. I wanted the moment to stretch into eternity; reluctantly, we parted.

"Tom," she whispered, "we must wait but a short time longer."

With that, she brushed past me, leaving me alone in the stillness. Her perfume lingered in the air, a gentle caress that clung to me long after she was gone. I was left with my heart full of joy, without a single regret for the kiss and the promise it held.

As Anne walked through the corridor, she smiled. Once, she had believed that marrying Richard would be the end of her life. Now, with Tom, she dared to dream, and from that dream rose a defiant, unshakable hope for the future.

The next day, we savoured the sweet indulgence of freedom. The younger children played gleefully in the garden with Wynn, darting in now and then to check we had not vanished, or to beg for another round of juggling. I obliged when I could, slipping between household duties and stolen moments with Anne. Everything felt peacefully chaotic, joyful.

"The children are in fine spirits today," I said during a lull in the library.

"Yes," Anne replied, laughing as she looked up from her book. "They always are when Richard is away." Her smile wavered briefly. "As are we all."

I joined her at the window seat. From there, the garden spread before us, the fountain's jets dancing in the sun. The gravel path wound around it like a ribbon, bordered by lawns trimmed within an inch of their lives. The children ran in wild loops, shrieking with delight as Wynn tried to catch them in a clumsy game of tag.

Quietly, I reached for her hand and laced my fingers through hers. It was the first time we had been truly alone since the night before.

"I am sorry if I overstepped," I said, eyes fixed on the garden. Doubts pressed in. "It was... a perfect moment,"

"Ssh, Tom," she murmured, tilting my chin until I met her gaze. "It is all right. We need to wait a little longer."

I nodded. Her eyes melted the heaviness from my chest, leaving only hope. I leaned back into the window seat, and Anne shifted so her head rested gently on my shoulder. She sighed, the weight of it sinking into me.

"I could stay like this forever," she whispered.

"Mmm," I breathed, pressing a soft kiss into her hair.

We sat without words, wrapped in the moment, watching as the sun dipped lower and the garden slipped into shadow.

Eventually, I stirred. "I am sorry, my love; I must go. I still have errands, and the Master's new crony arrives tomorrow." I hesitated before standing.

Anne stayed where she was, then said almost absently, "I do wonder what happened to young Greg."

Something in her tone made my breath catch. Did she know?

"He has likely found another household to torment," I said lightly, trying to laugh, but it caught in my throat.

I coughed, awkward and exposed. Anne studied me for a moment. I took her hand and kissed it gently, lingering.

"I will come to bid you goodnight," I said, then turned and left.

As I moved through the corridors, tending to tasks I no longer cared for, my thoughts raced. Would I ever be free of this burden?
   Would I ever truly be happy?

* * *

Outside the little cottage that had become a haven amid the turmoil of my life, Wynn moved through the garden, gathering sprigs of rosemary and rue. She plucked them gently, paused to inhale their bitter-green scent, then tucked them into a rough hessian pouch and drew it tight.

A soft hum escaped her lips as she wandered through the greenery, now cloaked in the lengthening shadows of evening. She seemed lost in her small world, threaded with hope and edged with a quiet ripple of fear beneath the surface.

As she paused to inspect the fruits of her labour, a subtle shift in the air caught her attention. The garden stilled. A breathless hush coiled around her, like silence drawing breath before a storm. She stood still, rosemary crushed between her fingers. A strange gust swept the garden, not cold but wrong, like breath held too long.

"Wynn!"

Davy's voice cut through her drifting thoughts, pulling her back. She turned to see her husband running through the gate and up the path toward her. She smiled; he was her life, her constant. The one who made every hardship bearable. She reached out, her fingers curling around his rough, overworked hand, noting the ever-present strain etched across his tanned face. A ripple of unease stirred within her, subtle at first, like a gentle wave swelling toward shore. It crept slowly, steadily, until it threatened to engulf her, leaving her breathless with dread.

For a moment, he paused and looked at his beautiful wife. He knew she would already sense that trouble was brewing; he could never hide anything from her, and he loved her all the more for it. Leaning forward, he pressed a gentle kiss to her waiting lips, breathing in the familiar, earthy scent that clung to her. He lingered there, drawing comfort, before finally pulling away.

Wynn met his eyes, her heart aching for him. She had carried this weight ever since Tom first arrived, all those years ago. Trouble had followed that man from the moment he stepped into their lives. The swiftness of Mistress Margaret's death had always unsettled her. Deep down, she had suspected Tom's hand in it, though she had never found proof. What stung most was how quickly Davy had taken to him. She understood why. Tom carried a vulnerability and a deep sorrow she, too, could not ignore. She shook her head to rid herself of the irritability she felt, but the unease was still with her.

Her thoughts turned to Anne. She was making these sacrifices to save her, the innocent soul caught in the middle of it all. She despised the Master, with his cruel treatment of both Margaret and Anne. Perhaps if he had been kinder to the latter, she would not have aligned with Tom. The irritation grew within her, but still, she stood quietly, waiting for Davy to unburden his anguish.

He drew a slow, deliberate breath. Wynn watched him patiently, though a growing unease twisted in her chest. His eyes held a tangle of emotions: worry, sorrow, and something darker that chilled her to the bone. At last, he broke the silence. His voice was soft, but the words seemed to thicken the air between them.

"Not here," he said quietly. "Let's talk inside."

Still holding her hand, he turned and walked with purpose toward the cottage. Wynn followed silently as he held the door open for her. She stepped into the dim room where afternoon shadows stretched long across the floor. It was too early to light the candles; some already bore trails of hardened wax like dried tears, while others stood untouched, poised to do their duty when dusk fell.

Wynn laid the pouch on the table and paused. Davy had already sunk into one of the wooden chairs by the hearth. He drew another chair to face him and gestured for her to sit. She did.

"Davy, you are scaring me," Wynn's hushed voice broke through the silence.

Davy rubbed his face, as if trying to scrub the words from his mind. He sat without speaking, minutes ticking past like the fuse of a powder keg. At last, he began, his voice a low stammer.

"As you know, the Master is away, and Tom is running things while he's gone." He coughed, clearing his throat. "Well... tomorrow, another of the Master's agents is due to arrive... Miles Overton." He paused, his eyes on Wynn's face, studying her carefully.

She said nothing, but the tension in her face deepened, and her breath caught. She had heard of Miles Overton, whispers carried on the wind by others like her. A rogue with a taste for cruelty. A man known to hunt their kind with cold efficiency. Just the thought of being in his sights sent a tremor through her soul. The room seemed to darken.

"I will not let him near you," Davy said urgently. "I will protect you, whatever it takes."

He reached for her, pulling her into his arms. Her head rested against his chest, where his heart thundered beneath her ear. His scent, warm and familiar, wrapped around her. She closed her eyes and clung to the moment, willing herself to feel safe, for a breath, for now. Then, gently, she pulled away. Her gaze swept the room and landed on the pouch.

"Come," she said softly, offering a small, brave smile. "You can help me. We have to protect each other."

It was the only way she knew. Davy nodded.

"Where do we begin?" he asked, rubbing his hands together with quiet purpose.

"Get the pots, see if those old rusty nails are still in the shed, and bring in the glass jar I set out with honey to catch the wasps," Wynn said, stepping forward to kiss his cheek before turning her attention to the pouch.

With care, she drew out the sprigs she had gathered and laid them gently on the rustic chopping board she had placed on the table. Nimbly, she chopped and crushed the herbs as Davy bustled about, collecting the items she had asked for.

She dropped the fragrant mix into the pots and poured in sour-smelling vinegar, the scent rising sharply into the air. Soon, the pots bubbled softly on the stove, and yellow steam rose, curling around them, threading a veil of strength and purpose through the cottage.

Turning to the glass jar, Wynn wrapped it tightly in two cloths and reached for the rolling pin. With precise force, she brought it down. The dull thud made Davy jump. He let out a nervous chuckle.

"I shall know not to cross you when that pin is in your hand," he said, laughing heartily; Wynn joined him in that brief moment of levity.

As they worked, the warm interior filled with the scent of vinegar and herbs, laced with intent. It was no longer just a smell: it was the essence of security. They moved in quiet harmony, their hands stirring purpose and protection into every motion. Their hearts swelled with quiet resolve, each beat a silent vow to keep those they loved safe.

Once the mixture was ready, Wynn pulled three crooked jars from the shelf and lined them up on the table. One by one, she filled them: the boiled vinegar steeped with rosemary and rue, a few rusty nails, splinters of broken glass. She sealed each jar tightly.

Then, closing her eyes, she hovered her hands above them. Her lips moved in silent invocation; her breath was steady, her purpose clear. A subtle shimmer passed through her fingers. When she opened her eyes, they glowed with quiet strength. Davy watched, awe rising in his chest. His wife was like no other. His heart surged with pride and with love.

Wynn picked up one jar and held it out to him.

"Take this," she said, her voice soft, yet sure, "and bury it in the ashes of Anne's bedroom hearth. It will keep away those who mean her harm until we can get her away."

Although weariness lined her face, she pressed on.

"I shall bury the other two; one by the gate, and one at our front door. For mercy only knows, we need protection too."

Davy nodded and took the jar, already moving with urgency. Wynn gathered the others and stepped into the fading light.

22

The Mirror and the Flame (2018)

In a small, weathered cottage at the edge of the dark wood, three figures gathered; voices low, urgent, threaded with unease. Soft lighting cast long shadows across the room, wrapping them in the same hush that had once cloaked another time, long ago.

One, clearly the head of the house, carried a twinkle in his eye and a calm in his voice. The woman beside him radiated gentle strength, her presence steady and grounding. The third sat slightly apart, a man with silvery-black hair and grey-green eyes, watchful, still, as though waiting for something he couldn't name.

"Listen, we have to move faster," Daryll said, his eyes locked on Elwyna's, silently pleading for a miracle. "He's already removed the protection bottles from around Farran." His voice rose, tinged with panic.

Elwyna slid her hand over his and gave it a reassuring squeeze, offering a calm smile.

"We've replaced them, my love," she said gently. "I'm going as fast as I can, but it's not the right time yet. If I try to force it... who knows what might happen."

232

The air hung heavy between them.

"Elv is right," the other man said quietly, his voice laced with emotion. "We can't risk anything happening to her. We've come too close."

Silence settled over the room, each of them lost in their thoughts and worries. Finally, Elwyna broke the stillness.

"I have an idea that might work," she said, her voice hesitant but edged with hope. "I can't restore her yet, but I can make it more difficult for Darnell to get close."

The two men turned toward her, expectant.

"I'll need your help," she said, locking eyes with the mystery man and smiling.

"You know I'd do anything for her," he replied, his voice filled with eagerness. "What do you need me to do?"

"Okay. We need the candle."

Daryll rose without hesitation and slipped out of the room. Elwyna crossed to the far end of the room and stood before a small red curtain edged with golden beading. Beneath it sat a plain wooden shelf. She paused, closed her eyes, and began to murmur silently, her lips shaping words the air alone could hear.

Then her eyes snapped open, glowing faintly with a golden gleam. In one swift motion, she pulled the curtain aside, revealing an ornate, gold-rimmed mirror. Its surface shimmered like water held in tension.

Daryll returned, carrying a thick, stark-white candle; unused, untouched.

A virgin candle. He placed it carefully on the shelf below the mirror next to a thick leather-bound book. From his pocket, he drew a match, struck it, and a flame bloomed with a soft, dry rasp. The fire consumed the match tip, flickering to life. He touched it to the candle's wick. It caught. The flame wavered and danced, casting long shadows against the walls. As the wax began to melt, the bitter scent of rosemary and rue filled the air, sharp, earthy, protective.

Elwyna beckoned the man over, pulling a folded piece of paper from the back pocket of her jeans. It crackled faintly as she unfolded it with care.

"You know what to do," she said, her voice quiet but firm. "But this time, I must also join you."

He nodded, his lips set, eyes filled with wonder and urgency.

Turning back to the mirror, she paused again, closed her eyes, and murmured, her lips moving in a rhythm the air seemed to hold its breath to hear. When her eyes opened again, they glowed gold.

"Unveil thy glassed gate to our love, with haste," she whispered, raising her hands.

Sparks flared from her fingertips, trailing through charged air before striking the mirror's surface with a hiss. The glass shimmered and bowed, distorting the reflection it held within.

The man stepped forward, his image now warped and twisting in the bending silver. Slowly, an image began to form within the frame. He saw her, his beloved Anne, her face emerging through the shimmering glass. A familiar ache rose in his chest, tightening with every heartbeat. He fought back the sorrow that never truly left him.

"Come to me, Anne," he whispered, his voice thick with longing, knowing the strength of his love alone could tear through time and bring her home.

* * *

A face blurred in the gold-framed mirror hanging on the plain wall of a long corridor. The air was still, almost expectant, as the image flickered into focus. Grey-green eyes stared intently at her. Dark hair streaked with silver. A softly rounded face. A tender mouth. A slender nose. A hint of stubble. It whispered, soft and rhythmic. She could not make out the words. Her feet moved before her thoughts could catch up, drawing her closer. She reached out, her fingertips trembling. The mirror shimmered at her touch. The face smiled, slow and familiar, then nodded once.

"Come to me, Anne," it said, faint as a breeze.

Her heart thudded; the voice tugged at something buried deep within.

The image began to shift. She searched the glass, desperate not to lose him. Another vision surfaced, rippling through the silver. A voice rose; Elwyna's... or was it? The words wove through like song:

"By fire's light and ember's breath,
I ward against unseen bequeath.
Let all who bear a heart untrue,
Be turned aside from all I do.
By spark and smoke and seal of flame,
Let none approach who cloak their name.
Where secrets lie and hearts deceive,
From her sweet path, I bid them leave."

The mirror fractured, bursting into a silent cascade of colour.

Farran's eyes flew open.

* * *

Elwyna blew out the candle, watching smoke curl upward in thin, silver tendrils. Daryll reached across and gently removed the snuffed-out candle: no longer intact, no longer pure. Without a word, he left the room. She drew the red curtain, veiling the now-dormant reflection, then sank back into the worn cushions beside the man. Their bodies were drained, their hearts heavy with effort and love.

"What was that?" he asked, voice low, the weight in his eyes plain to see.

"A protection spell," Elwyna murmured, closing hers. "To keep Darnell away."

The man slumped deeper into his seat, letting it hold him. Maybe, just maybe, he could sleep now, knowing she was safer.

Daryll returned with a tray bearing three steaming mugs. He set it gently on the table, then sat beside Elwyna and pulled her close.

"Drink your tea. Then bed," he said softly.

She nodded, lifting the mug with both hands.

The three sat in silence, just as they had all those years ago: Wynn, Davy, and Thomas.

23

The Storm Arrives (1593)

The evening came too soon; before I knew it, the day was gone. I was bidding Anne goodnight. By the candlelight softly illuminating our sanctuary, we stood, not wanting to part yet knowing we must. The children had already come to wish Anne goodnight; their laughter echoed through the corridors, bringing a fleeting, welcome joy.

"The morrow will bring new tests, my love," Anne said, her body tightening as she spoke.

"I fear so," I replied. "The arrival of Miles will surely put us under considerable strain."

My stomach churned, haunted by the fear that the past would repeat itself. We stood in silence, wrapped in each other's arms, clinging to a comfort that might soon slip away: the last of its kind. Who knew for how long? A quiet sadness crept over me.

"It will," Anne said after a pause. "But I have every belief and hope this will pass. We will have our time and place."

She looked resolute, certain, and in that certainty, I felt my confidence stir anew. She gazed up at me, a spark burning in her eyes I hadn't seen before. I marvelled at her bravery, at the fierce hope still alive within her. She had endured such brutality, and yet here she stood, carrying a lust for the future, our future.

I smiled softly and was met with the most radiant smile in return, one I would die for. With not a breath between us, I reached out and gently brushed a strand of hair from her cheek.

"Sleep well, my love," I whispered.

"You also," she whispered back.

We lingered a moment longer, as though time itself had slowed for our goodbye, stretching one last moment before the world changed again. Then she turned, her glowing form retreating into the darkness.

The following morning, I awoke with a rising nausea in the pit of my soul. Outside, birds sang a merry chorus, but it did nothing to lift my spirits. Something evil was stirring, intent on descending without mercy. The fight for survival was about to begin.

Miles Overton arrived in a frenzy of dust, his horse rearing sharply before skidding to a halt. He leapt down with a thud and tossed the reins to a nearby stable hand.

"Boy!" he barked, his voice booming with authority and jolting every nerve to attention. "Where do I find Thomas?"

The boy, pale and trembling, raised a quivering finger, pointing toward me as I stepped from the shadowed doorway.

"You must be Miles," I said, striding forward.

I watched his arrival closely: tall, with sharp blonde hair and eyes as dark as pitch.

"That I am," he replied, smiling, but it never reached his eyes.

"You must be tired from your travels," I said evenly. "Davy here will show you to your quarters. We can discuss duties once you've settled."

I glanced toward Davy, who had quietly joined us. His face was ashen, a flicker of fear in his eyes. I gave a subtle nod of understanding. He grimaced in reply.

"Ah, Davy," Miles boomed, his voice louder than before. "Sir Richard has spoken of you often, and your *wife. Wynn*, is it not? The *nanny*."

I saw Davy flinch at the sound of her name, but he held his composure with admirable strength.

"That's right, Sir," he answered, his voice steady. "This way... your quarters are just along here."

I watched them disappear through the doorway. The danger we feared now walked freely among us.

Mid-morning had come before I encountered him again. I heard him first, his heavy steps striking the corridor like warning drums, heading straight for the Master's study. I followed quietly, watching as he marched in without hesitation. He crossed to the sideboard where the Master kept his spirits, poured himself a large beaker of brown liquor, and downed half in one greedy gulp. Without pause, he topped it up again.

Then, as if he owned the place, he made his way to the desk and lowered himself into the Master's chair. Setting the tumbler down with a deliberate thud, he rifled through the carefully arranged items Sir Richard had left behind, inspecting them with the casual arrogance of a man who believed the world already belonged to him. Miles picked up the letter seal and turned it in his fingers, smiling faintly. A metallic tang, like old blood, hung in the air. The room seemed to shrink around him.

A floorboard creaked as I entered the study.

"Ah, Thomas. Good. We can get started," he said without looking, his voice smooth and commanding.

I stepped further into the room. The sharp smell of liquor hung heavy in the air.

"Of course," I replied with an awkward smile. "Shall we begin with the daily rota?"

Miles took another gulp and finally turned his gaze to me, his dark eyes unblinking, sharp. There was a darkness that made my own evil deeds shrink in comparison.

"I think I'd prefer to make the acquaintance of Mistress Anne first." A devilish glint sparkled in his black eyes, a smirk curling his lips. "I imagine she and I will need to work closely to keep Sir Richard's affairs in order."

A vice clamped around my chest. My face remained still, but inside, panic flared like a struck match.

"Of course," I said quietly. "She'll be with the children in the library."

The vice tightened, forcing the breath from my lungs. I fought to keep my tone steady.

"I'll go and fetch her for you," I offered, stalling.

He sipped again, watching me over the rim of the glass.

"No, I'll go to her alone," he said. "I'm sure the nanny can manage the little ones while I get to know her better."

He rose to his feet, draining the last of his drink. "Just show me the way."

I hesitated only for a moment, then turned and led him down the corridor, deliberately raising my voice as we passed paintings and relics. I pointed them out with exaggerated enthusiasm, hoping the warning in my voice would reach them.

As we neared the library, I heard the soft cadence of children's voices. They were reading Aesop's Fables, a favourite. Hester's voice floated through the air:

"Now sit ye still, both of you, and hush your rustling, else I shall read no more. The Lyon and the Mouse, a tale of mercy repaid.

Once, in a hot noonday sun, a great Lyon lay sleeping in the shade of an old oak tree. His breath was steady, his tail still, and the flies did not dare to settle long. But along came a tiny Mouse, light of foot and not half cautious enough. She ran straight o'er his paw, thinking naught of the danger..."

Hester looked up, her face brightening when she saw me, then stiffening when her eyes met Miles'. She drew closer to her brother and sister, who sat at Wynn's feet. Wynn stood, colour draining from her face, her delicate features drawn tight. Anne, seated near the window, turned from the garden at the sudden silence.

"Mistress Anne," Miles boomed. "A pleasure."

Anne gave a polite smile and nodded. "Mr Overton." Her voice was clipped and guarded but courteous.

His gaze shifted to Wynn. "You must be the *nanny*," he drawled, the word stretched just enough to carry disdain. A flicker of menace flashed in his darkened eyes.

"Sir," Wynn replied evenly, her voice calm despite the flicker of dread mirrored in her eyes.

"Would you mind taking the children out while I speak with your Mistress?"

Wynn's eyes never left him.

"Come, children," she said briskly. "Let us get some air before dinner."

She ushered them out quickly, keeping herself between Miles and the little ones, her posture rigid, alert.

I lingered at the threshold, unwilling to let Anne out of my sight. Miles turned, his dark stare landing on me.

"You can go now, Thomas," he said curtly. "The Mistress and I have plenty to discuss."

I didn't move.

"I'm well acquainted with the household business," I began.

He cut me off.

"I said, go."

The tone in his voice sliced clean through the air. Who the hell did he think he was? The fire that had smouldered inside me flared dangerously. Instinct screamed, but I smothered it. For her. For now.

"Of course... Mistress. Miles."

I gave a stiff bow, forcing myself to turn, every fibre of me rebelling as I left *my* Anne alone with that monster.

In the library, Anne remained seated by the window, vexed that her peace, her sanctuary, had been intruded upon by this vile creature. Still, she kept her composure.

"How may I help you, Mr Overton?" she asked, voice calm and cool.

Miles picked up the chair Wynn had been sitting in only moments earlier and placed it beside her, too close. Anne subtly shifted away.

"Well," he said, eyes roaming over her with a leer that made her stomach churn, "before we get into business, I thought we might get to know each other a little better."

She wanted to scream. What is it with these men? Always circling, always consuming. Did they all think her something to be devoured? She steadied her breath and fixed her gaze on him.

"I hardly think that appropriate, Mr Overton. You are here as a servant, are you not? That is what my husband hired you for."

She met his eyes with cold defiance. His own darkened in response, something cruel shifting just below the surface. It made her skin crawl. Miles held her stare, anger curling in his jaw.

"Of course, Mistress Anne," he said, tone clipped and biting. "My apologies for any... misunderstanding."

But he didn't move away.

"So," Anne said briskly, "what instructions did my husband leave for you?"

Miles dropped his gaze to his hands, clenched tightly in his lap, knuckles pale.

"He would have Thomas well supported with the household concerns," he said. He paused, letting the next words land like a curse. "And... the *witchcraft* affair."

The word struck cold. Anne stiffened.

"Witchcraft?"

"Yes," he said, watching her closely. "Your husband believes someone on this estate is dabbling in the forbidden arts."

Anne's brow furrowed. Who could he possibly mean?

"You seem confused, Mistress," he said.

"I am, Mr Overton. I've no idea what you're talking about."

He smiled, slow and smug.

"Don't fret," he said. "I'll uncover the truth soon enough. And their death," he added, standing to full height, "will be a great satisfaction."

He lingered a moment, then strode to the door. At the threshold, he turned.

"For now, Mistress."

Then he was gone, taking the air with him as he went.

Anne sat motionless, her heart thundering like hooves in her chest. Who had he meant? And more urgently, how could she protect them?

* * *

After leaving the library, I went to find Wynn and Davy in the garden. They stood huddled close, voices hushed and urgent.

"Tom," Wynn called as I approached. "Where's Anne?" Her eyes searched behind me.

"He insisted on speaking to her alone," I muttered, raising my hands. "What was I supposed to do?"

Wynn's body tensed, taut with unspoken fury.

"You left her? With him?"

"What choice did I have?" I had already asked myself the same thing.

"Wynn, come now," Davy said gently. "He could not prevent it, Wynn. The matter was out of his hands."

Wynn stared at me, eyes burning with loathing. I flinched.

"There's been nothing but trouble since he arrived," she hissed. "Now we're all in danger."

She turned sharply, calling the children, who had been sitting quietly beneath the tree, to come in for dinner. We watched her go.

Davy turned to me.

"She'll be alright. She's worried about the Mistress... and him." His face darkened.

"I know," I muttered. I couldn't blame her. Her fear echoed my own, curling like rot beneath my ribs.

Anxiety coiled around my chest, each breath tighter than the last, slow and relentless, like a predator. Davy placed a firm hand on my shoulder.

"We need to watch him, Tom. Every moment. If he's truly here to hunt witches, God help us all."

I nodded, but my eyes followed Wynn and the children. I watched her go, her words slicing deeper than I wanted to admit. Perhaps she was right. Perhaps I was the curse. A cold wind stirred the trees. The sky, pale and waiting, held its breath. The storm had already begun.

24

Whispers in the Glass (2018)

Farran's thoughts churned like a storm. That dream, it had been him. The man from Coeur House. The eyes. The voice. And Elwyna. She hadn't seen her face; just a haze, indistinct. But the voice had been clear as day.

"*I'm a flamin' mess,*" she muttered.

She stood in her small kitchen, trying to make breakfast, a simple task, but today it felt like climbing a cliff barefoot. As she gathered what she needed, she noticed a pan out of place. She paused, staring at it. Since her return from the hospital, she had noticed small things like that. Just slightly off. Not wrong exactly, but not how she would have left them. And then there was the smell that had greeted her. She still couldn't place it. Earthy. Familiar.

"*I'm definitely losing it,*" she muttered, sliding the pot back into its usual spot.

Eventually, she pulled together a reasonable breakfast and carried it into the living room. Settling into the chair, she flicked on the radio. A bit of distraction. Something ordinary. Then her eyes landed on the painting. For the first time, she really looked at it.

"*What is going on?*" she whispered, teeth clenched.

The painting was of him. A younger version, perhaps, but without a doubt the same man from her dream. The same man who had made her feel safe. Loved.

She stood, then, striding toward the wall where it hung, she reached up and was hit by that same pain she had felt days earlier, just before she collapsed. Still, she was determined. Clenching her jaw, she pushed through the discomfort, stretching further until her fingers curled around the frame. With effort, she lifted it down. As the painting settled in her hands, her knees gave way, and she dropped into the chair. Her head spun, and her breath caught. She heard him.

"**Come to me, Anne.**"

The whisper slid through her, like a breeze in forgotten halls, pulling her toward something buried deep. His smile. His eyes. They burned into her memory. But why Anne? Why would he call her that? Another voice joined his, soft, familiar: Elwyna.

"**She's protected for now, but...**"

The words faded into silence, veiled from reach. But what?

Farran slowly opened her eyes. She stared at the painting leaning against her chair. Leaning forward, she picked it up and studied the face. The painted eyes were stern, nothing like the ones in her vision. There it was again. That maddening pull. That ache of memory just beyond her reach.

She ran her fingers over the canvas, tracing the curve of his jaw, the line of his brow. Her hand slipped behind the frame. Something dry and sharp caught her finger. Her breath hitched. Slowly, she turned the painting over and found the edge of a folded note, yellowed and brittle with age, wedged behind the backing. Heart pounding, she eased it free. A surge of pressure built behind her eyes.

Pain. No. Stay with it.

She blinked, forced it down.

In the corner of the painting, a name was etched faintly:
Thomas the Jester, 1573

A flicker. A name. A feeling. Recognition hovered just out of reach. Then her eyes dropped to the parchment. The writing curled and flowed across the page in an elegant hand, clearly from another time. She began to read:

My Dearest Anne,
   May this find you safe and protected.
   It won't be long 'til we're reunited.
   Keep the faith.
   My love is yours now and forever.
   Your Tom.

Her heart tightened, and her breath grew shallow.
   Thomas the Jester.

The name repeated in her mind, over and over, a memory drawing near, so very nearly within her grasp. Love and danger, woven tightly together.

Her eyes drifted to the sketched image. She had seen symbols like it before in her studies, a daisy wheel, ancient and purposeful. A charm meant to trap and confuse evil spirits. A mark of protection. She reached out and slowly traced the outline with her fingertips. Faces flashed before her eyes.
   The jester.
   Elwyna.
   Richard... no. Darnell?

Her breath caught as a thick mist rolled in, swallowing each one in turn. Then... another face. Cruel. Twisted. Evil. A shock of blond hair, gleaming like straw in moonlight. It leered at her from the void. Suddenly, she was

falling.
Tumbling through darkness.
So very far.
Until it ended.
A bone-crunching thud.
Then...
Oblivion.

She awoke to a gentle touch on her arm, coaxing her out of sleep.

"Farr... you okay?" Elwyna's voice floated through the fog as Farran blinked against the heaviness.

"Mm..." she murmured, attempting to sit up.

Slowly, her vision cleared. Elwyna was kneeling beside her, concern etched across her face. That scent, Elwyna's scent, curled around her, stirring the visions. The painting. The letter. She recoiled from her friend's touch. Elwyna pulled back, startled.

"What is it, Farr?" she said softly.

Farran looked at her for a moment before answering.

"Another dream..." Her voice was wary, guarded now. Nothing made sense any more.

Elwyna lowered herself into the chair. Silence hung between them.

"Do you want to talk about it?" she asked gently, but her eyes gave her away. Too careful. Too composed.

Farran saw it. The hesitation. The guardedness. The trust between them had frayed under secrets and strain. Elwyna felt it too. Damn it. The men had pushed too hard, interfered too much. Now the walls she had built around her friend, for protection, were crumbling. She would need to move quickly, but delicately. Farran had to believe she could still be trusted. That everything Elwyna had done was to keep her safe.

Silence lingered between them, heavy and fragile, as if it might shatter and unleash some unseen peril. A whisper inside pressed Farran to speak. When she did, her voice came low and hesitant.

"You were there," she said slowly, her eyes wide. "And him... Darnell... or Richard? Whoever the hell he really is."

The words dropped like stones. Sharp. Heavy. Undeniable. Elwyna sat frozen. It was far worse than she had feared. Everything she had tried to protect lay exposed and broken. She drew in a long, steadying breath.

"Farr... I think it's time we talked. All of us."

Her voice was calm, threaded with resolve. No more deflections. No more half-truths. Farran gave a slow, stiff nod. She was done with shadows. It was time to hear the truth and face whatever followed.

25

Reckonings by Firelight (1593)

Several weeks had passed since Miles arrived, and his presence hung over the house, suffocating. The children now played in near silence, subdued and wary. Wynn was always glancing over her shoulder, her shoulders tight. The few glimpses I caught of Anne, reading to the children or passing in the corridor, were brief, and they tormented me. I ached to be near her. It gnawed at me each day.

"Not much longer now," Davy said one evening as we stood in the kitchen.

The table was full, Wynn had prepared a fine meal, but the tension in the room dulled every flavour.

"I know," I said, frustration thick in those two words.

"I know," I repeated, more softly this time, my head full of anguish.

Wynn stopped bustling and looked at me, inhaling deeply before she spoke. Her eyes met mine with urgency and loathing that made me flinch.

"Tom, I know you're yearning to be with Anne... to keep her safe," she said, her voice edged with an irritation that pulled me sharply from my thoughts.

"But it cannot be rushed," she said firmly. "The event will come when it must. If we move too soon, it will fail, and we will all perish. Every one of us. By the Master's hand, or that wretched varlet."

I knew she was right, of course. I did not fully understand the rituals and preparations required, but I trusted her.

"I'm sorry, Wynn," I said, hands open. "You and Davy have always done what's best. I... I just," I faltered, the words vanishing before they formed.

Davy slapped my back.

"We know," he said with a smile. He glanced at Wynn, who had turned back to her task, but not before a sharp glare betrayed her true feelings.

I sighed. "I need some air."

Davy nodded.

I opened the door. A crisp winter breeze rushed in, sharp against my skin. I shivered, pulling my coat tighter.

"He is nothing but a selfish scoundrel," Wynn snapped just as I closed the door behind me.

I walked down the path and stopped to watch the dimming sun shine lazily through a gap in the trees, casting long shadows across the garden. I marvelled at its quiet beauty and its promise. In just a few weeks, it would be our escape, our sanctuary from all of this. If we could hold on until then.

For a while, I stood there before returning to the cottage.

* * *

The Master blustered out the door toward his waiting horse, which let out a soft whicker as it tapped its hoof impatiently on the gravel. He had been away more often than he had been at the house.

"Wentworth has called another meeting in preparation for Parliament," he said, his tone excited but tinged with anxiety. "I am needed to help with the succession suggestions."

"Why not take Miles with you?" I asked casually, eyes fixed on the gravel, hoping he would not catch the quiet plea beneath my words.

The Master paused, one foot in the stirrup, and turned to look at me. Under his scrutiny, my skin burned. He snorted and swung himself onto the waiting beast.

"Miles needs to stay here and continue with his work," he said.

There was something cold in the way he said the word work. What was Miles doing here? I feared for everyone close to me. I bit my lip before daring to ask, "Is there aught I can do to help him?"

He stared again, and for a moment, I thought I saw a flicker of disgust in his eyes.

"No, Tom. There is not."

With a click of his heels, he was off, riding down the long path.

I watched him go, mind slipping back to that stormy day when he had fallen from his horse. Was it wrong to wish it would happen again? This time, with no one there to save him? I shook my head. Yet the thought had already taken root, deep within. And with it came a dangerous hope: that the past might yet repeat itself and finish what it had started.

I returned to the house. It felt colder, stranger, no longer safe. The Master's distrust was sharp and unmistakable. I walked on eggshells; one wrong step would bring the punishments I once handed down. The thought filled me with creeping dread.

Not long past, I would have accepted my fate. I had grown up with nothing and expected nought but the hangman's noose, like my father. I feared not death. But now, there was Anne.

Raised voices pulled me from my thoughts as I neared the library. Anne paced the carpet, wringing her hands as she spoke, her voice steady but fierce.

"I do not believe you. What proof have you to accuse her of such a thing?"

She faced Miles, who stood by the window seat, his mouth curled into the wickedest smile I had ever seen.

"Greg had his suspicions," Miles sneered, flicking at an invisible fly. "Then he vanished, no trace. Just after he was ordered to deal with 'them.'"

He paused, his face taut and unreadable.

"And that fool jester was with him."

His gaze burned into Anne. She froze, her face paling as though she had seen a ghost.

"Greg emptied the Master's safe and ran away," she said quietly.

"And who told you that?" Miles's gaze did not waver.

"Thomas told us," she murmured, barely audible.

"Mm," Miles nodded slowly, picking at a fleck of dust on his sleeve. "Be careful whom you trust, Mistress."

They stood in silence, tension thick between them, before Miles turned and strode from the library, his voice echoing as he called, "Good night."

He vanished into the hallways, leaving a terrible stillness behind.

What should I do? Everything began to unravel, and I knew not how to stop it. I slipped away, unable to face Anne. The truth rose, ugly and inevitable. Soon, she would know who I truly was. For now, I must keep low and pray that no more of my past comes to finish me.

* * *

Anne continued to pace, thoughts racing as long-buried truths began to rise. Of course, she knew what Tom was. She had always known. The stories her uncle told before her marriage to Richard echoed now, half warning, half jest. He laughed as he spoke of the murderous jester who once lived at Coeur House. How poor travellers vanished without a trace while the jester strummed his lute and sang, laughing at their fate.

"A cruel, callous man with no heart, living in Coeur House," her uncle guffawed. "A heartless urchin in the Heart House."

But no. That was not the man she knew. The Tom she knew was kind. Funny. Gentle even. He would not let harm come to her. He was loyal to his friends:

Davy. Wynn. Then the realisation struck her like a blow.

His friends.

His friends who were in danger.

Of course, he protected them.

"Oh, Tom..."

Silent tears slipped down her cheeks as she turned from the room, heart pounding. She needed to breathe. To think. To find solace.

* * *

Wynn stood in the garden with the children, who played a quiet game of tag across the trimmed lawn. She smiled as she watched them, their feet brushing frost-kissed blades of grass. 'Oh, to be so young, untouched by the weight of the world,' she thought, longing for their innocence. She sighed.

"Come along, children," she called, her voice light and singsong.

"Must we?" Johannah asked, pleading.

"Yes, you must," Wynn laughed. "Your father expects it."

The children left their play reluctantly and followed her indoors, padding down the dim corridor toward the schoolroom near the library. As they passed, Wynn glanced into the library, expecting to find Anne in the window seat. Empty.

She led them into the schoolroom and closed the door behind her with a quiet click. It was a sparse chamber: several chairs, a single table, and by the window, an easel bearing yesterday's sums, now faintly smudged. The girls settled into their chairs and reached into their baskets, drawing out samplers already begun. Bright threads danced across the fabric as their needles pricked and poked, adding colour to careful designs.

"Neatly, Johannah," Wynn said, peering over the girl's shoulder with a slight tut.

She turned to Nathaniel, the youngest and most mischievous, though his number work was improving.

"Come now, young Nat. Let us practise your numbers. Here."

She passed him a piece of chalk. He took the task seriously, tongue between his teeth as he shaped each number slowly upon the slate. The girls softly murmured about Christmas, though it had long since passed.

"Thomas was so funny," Hester giggled.

As their chatter continued, Wynn became aware of a presence beyond the door, a shadow, still. She waited, tense, listening for a knock. Instead, a folded slip of parchment slid beneath it. The shadow vanished. She crossed the room, picked up the parchment, and unfolded it. Anne's handwriting. Her stomach tightened.

Wynn,
I must come and see you this night.
I will be there after nightfall.
T is in peril.
A.

Wynn folded the note and tucked it into her pocket. She turned back to the children, smiling gently, but already a chill had settled in her bones.

* * *

"Davy, move the chair closer to the fire. Anne will be here soon, and the night bites with cold," Wynn said, stirring the pot that hung above the flickering flames.

She heard the scrape of wood against the floorboards. Then came a knock at the door. They both stilled. Another knock, followed by Anne's voice, low and muffled through the wood.

"Wynn? Are you there?"

Davy crossed to the door and opened it wide. Cold air swept in, curling about Anne like smoke.

"Come, sit by the fire and warm yourself," he urged. "It is bitter tonight."

Anne smiled faintly and crossed to the chair, the hearth already working to thaw her frozen limbs. She sat with a soft sigh.

"You got my note?" she asked, turning to Wynn.

Wynn nodded, her brow drawn tight.

"Why is Tom in danger?" she asked, her voice measured. She hoped, prayed, that Anne did not yet know everything. But she did. Wynn saw it in her eyes before a word was spoken.

"I know what Tom has done," Anne began cautiously. She looked between them, searching their faces for reassurance.

"What is it you believe he has done?" Davy asked gently.

Anne hesitated, as though speaking it might summon something that could not be undone.

"That Tom... gets rid of Richard's nuisances."

Davy glanced at Wynn. A flicker of understanding passed between them. She knew. But how much? Davy sighed.

"Yes. The Master employed him to do the work he would not. '*Could not soil my own hands,*' he would say."

Anne stared down at her clasped hands, the firelight dancing across her skin.

"The trips to Gloucester?" she asked, lifting her gaze to Davy.

He nodded.

"He did not want to," Davy said, his voice thinning. "He fought it."

Anne's heart twisted. She could feel Tom's torment now; the weight of every order.

"He promised you," Davy added.

Anne blinked, her brow furrowed in confusion. "I do not understand."

Davy smiled faintly, almost wistfully.

"He would dream of you. I heard him call your name, night after night. In those dreams, he promised to stop. Each time the Master gave another order, it broke him a little more."

Anne's breath hitched. Her heart clenched. Grief settled beneath her ribs, sharp as a bruise. She forced down the sob rising in her throat. Then came the question that had haunted her since Miles' last visit.

"What happened to Greg?" she asked, barely above a whisper.

Davy looked to Wynn. She had stopped stirring the pot, her knuckles white around the wooden spoon.

"He ran away," Davy said slowly. "Took the contents of the Master's safe with him."

Anne kept her gaze steady and raised an eyebrow. Davy shifted uncomfortably, his shoulders drawn tight. The truth could be hidden no longer, and it escaped him with a deep sigh.

"The truth is... Greg and Tom were ordered to kill Wynn and me on New Year's Eve."

The room froze. Both women gasped softly. Wynn clutched the edge of the table, her face grey with memory.

"If it had not been for Tom, we would... "

"If it had not been for Tom, none of this would have befallen us," Wynn snapped, turning from the hearth. Her eyes blazed. "His recklessness, his foolishness despite his age, nearly got us killed. And now we have Miles. Witch-finder of great renown."

Her gaze swept across the cottage, their home. The truth settled like a stone in her chest. They would lose it. And it was because of him. She slammed her palm against the table. The dishes rattled. Anne stood and crossed to her, gently taking her hand.

"Wynn, please," she said softly. "That man, the one who did those things, is not the Tom I know. He is kind. Loyal. Yes, he has made mistakes. But he is trying to make amends."

Wynn met her gaze. Anger still simmered beneath the surface, but slowly, she nodded.

"What can we do to protect him?" Anne asked, glancing between them.

"I shall keep him away from you," Davy said firmly. "So that creature cannot twist what he sees."

"Heaven knows I have warned him often enough," Wynn muttered sharply. She lowered her voice and, with a sigh, said. "I shall continue the preparations for the event. The time draws near. Soon, we shall all be safe."

Anne looked tired, her limbs weighted with grief.

"Tell me more about these plans soon," she said, stepping toward the door. "This is too much for one night."

Wynn and Davy nodded. Anne paused, her hand upon the latch.

"What Richard has done..." She shook her head and opened the door. "I shall never forgive him."

She stepped into the night and walked slowly down the path.

Behind a tree, Tom emerged from the shadows, the words still hanging in the air.

"She knows," he whispered, his voice trembling.

His breath rose in the cold, sharp and hollow.

"And she shall never forgive me."

He turned and slipped into the trees. Alone.

* * *

Miles looked out across the garden from the dimly lit study, pausing in his nightly scribblings. There, moving briskly across the lawn from the gate in the far wall. The gate to the witch's cottage. He smiled. Another sympathiser. Perfect. His Master desired to be rid of the wench, and now Miles had the excuse he needed. A wry chuckle escaped his lips as he turned back to his journal, adding the latest finding in slow, deliberate strokes.

Then, movement. Another figure stepped into view, this one solemn, slower. The jester. Another dead man walking. Miles rubbed his hands together in delight and poured himself a drink. He downed it in one long gulp, tucked the journal away, blew out the candle and turned in for the night, laughing.

His mind filled with all the exquisite things he might do. And soon. Very soon.

26

Threads of Memory (2018)

"Hey, Farran!"

Daphne's voice echoed across the gallery.

Farran turned and smiled. "Daphne! You okay?"

"Yes, thanks. How are you now? You gave us a scare," she replied, her face clouding slightly with concern.

"I'm fine," Farran said. "Glad to be back, and desperate to get this exhibition sorted."

"Darnell's been busy," Daphne said as they walked, their shoes tapping rhythmically on the polished floor. "He's made sure everything is ready."

Farran paused. A scent drifted through the air, earthy and familiar. Memories of her recent visit to Coeur House flooded her mind.

"Think about the family seal," Darnell had said. "I wouldn't be surprised if they had more than a few skeletons tucked away."

His raw emotional state when talking about Richard's first wife, and the way he spoke with the man.

"Oh, my friend, you're nothing like me," Darnell had sneered. *"You're a lowly fool."*

She frowned and shook her head, trying to shake the thoughts loose.

"Has anyone else been in here today?" she asked, the scent now filling her senses.

"No," Daphne said, looking puzzled. "Why?"

"Can't you smell that?" Farran glanced around the room, heart racing. She didn't even know what she was expecting to see.

Daphne gave her a concerned look. Farran gave a quick, forced chuckle.

"Never mind; imagination in overdrive."

With each step, the smell grew stronger. By the time they reached the door, it was almost suffocating.

Inside, the office was quiet. Her desk sat just as she had left it. She turned to Darnell's. Papers were everywhere, scattered as if a storm had passed through. It looked like he had left in a hurry. Curious, she stepped around the desk, scanning the chaos. A small piece of parchment peeked out from beneath a stack of files, browned with age, edges ragged. Miles, scrawled across it. Her fingers curled around it, lifting it gently from the pile.

Just as she turned it over, the door burst open. Darnell stood there, eyes narrowing as the scent hit him.

"What is that smell?" he barked, doubling over in a coughing fit.

He smelled it too. Farran remained still, staring as he staggered to the window and flung it open. He gasped for air, face reddening, eyes streaming. Visions flickered across her mind, scenes she didn't want to see again. But she could not stop them. *She saw him reaching for her, terror on his face.*
Hands flailing.
Falling.
Thud.
Her body tensed.

Darnell looked at her through the haze of coughs. His gaze fell to the parchment lying on the desk, disturbed from its hiding place. Something shifted in his expression, a deep sorrow. He knew she had seen something. Something she could never unsee.

Her phone rang, sharp and sudden, from her bag. Startled, she pulled it free.

"Hi, Elv," she said. Her tone was clipped. She glanced back at Darnell, who was still catching his breath.
"Yes... He's here."
Pause.
"Sure."

She held the phone out, confusion flickering across her face.

"She wants to talk to you."

Darnell hesitated, then took it. As he listened, his face darkened.
"Of course," he said at last, and handed it back.

He stormed out without a word, slamming the door behind him. Farran blinked, then raised the phone again.

"Elwyna?"

Elwyna's voice cut through the static, sharp and urgent.

"Farran, are you alright?"

"Mmm," Farran murmured, nodding even though Elwyna could not see her. Her head was pounding. "How do you know Darnell? What did you say to him?"

Her voice came strong now, firm. "You said you were going to explain, but I'm still waiting."
    Silence.
    "Elwyna?"

A long sigh crackled through the line.

"Alright," Elwyna said at last. "We will come to you tonight. It is time to explain everything."

Then the line went dead. Farran stared at the phone. Finally, she thought, the answers might come.

The Stephens exhibition was ready by day's end, but the weight of recent events dimmed the excitement. Farran, determined not to let them spoil it, finished her final checks and faced her team with quiet enthusiasm.

"Well done, everyone. We're ready to open tomorrow, on time," she said, smiling warmly. "You've all been amazing. I couldn't have done it without you."

She glanced around at the cheerful faces, then paused. One face was missing. Darnell had not returned since that morning, and his absence loomed. The painting of Richard caught her eye. A shiver passed through her.

"Let's go to The Wheatsheaf to celebrate!" Simon called out.

"Any excuse for the pub," Daphne laughed, and others joined in the merriment.

"I'll catch up with you," Farran called after them as they began to drift out, chatting and laughing.

Daphne gave her a thumbs-up as she linked arms with Simon and disappeared through the exit.

Farran stood alone, letting the silence settle over the building like a heavy shawl, warm but weighted. She took a slow walk through the gallery, one final sweep before closing. At the cabinet holding the Stephens family seal, she paused. Her thoughts circled back to Darnell, his strange behaviour, the way he had vanished, and the look in his eyes when he handed back the phone. So many questions.

The lights flicked off. Her phone buzzed into life.

"Hey, Elv," she answered, her mind still turning over thoughts of Darnell.

"Hey," came Elwyna's voice, hesitant and subdued.

There was a pause. Farran could hear her breathing on the other end.

"Is it still okay for us to come later?" Elwyna asked.

"Sure," Farran replied, already walking down the corridor and into the amber light of the evening. She needed their visit. "We're just going for a celebratory drink. I'll be home by eight."

"Okay." Elwyna's voice was quiet.

"See you later," Farran said and ended the call.

She slipped into the bustle of the square, letting the chatter and colour of the evening crowd wash over her.

In the shadows, Darnell watched.

* * *

There was a knock at the door.

Farran steadied herself, then walked to open it, taking a deep breath. She had tried to piece the events into something tangible, something she could explain, but it always collapsed into confusion. How could any of this make sense? Dread coiled in her stomach. What would Elwyna say? Excuses, or truths?

She flung the door wide and forced a smile, and froze. Standing behind Daryll was another figure. Dressed in jeans and a grey T-shirt that matched his eyes, he looked exactly as he had in her dreams. A wary smile spread across his lips. Farran stared at him, her thoughts scrambling. The puzzle was shifting again, and this piece did more than fit. It changed everything. Why was he here? How did Elwyna and Daryll know him?

She stepped back automatically, letting them pass, stilling as he walked by. He was still grinning; shy, nervous, as Elwyna led the way into the living room. Farran shut the door, but her hand lingered on the handle, as if releasing it might make it all real. Then she turned and followed.

Tom stood by the painting, now back in its place on the wall.

"Hm. So long ago now," he muttered, emotion crossing his face.

Farran looked at the painting, then at him. The man in the portrait was standing in her living room. Older, but definitely him. A dull throb began behind her eyes.

"I'll go and put the kettle on," she said abruptly, needing distance.

"I'll help," Elwyna offered quickly, following her.

They walked into the kitchen in silence while the murmur of voices faded behind them. Farran moved automatically, the mugs rattling gently as she took them from the cupboard and lined them up on the counter. Then everything spilt out.

"What the hell is going on?"

Elwyna rushed to her side, taking hold of her hand.

"Farr, I'm so sorry for all this," she said, her voice cracking.

Farran looked at her, watching her face twist in distress.

"Sorry for what?" Her voice softened slightly, though turmoil still churned beneath it.

"And who is that?" she continued, her voice rising again. "He was at Coeur House the other day. He fought with Darnell. But I've seen his face, heard his voice, felt his touch... in my dreams, on the radio. And..." She trailed off.

Farran leaned against the counter, resting her throbbing head in her hands and closing her eyes. She wanted the spinning to stop. She wanted sense, logic, a reason. Anything.

Elwyna's arm slipped across her shoulders and pulled her close. Farran leaned into it, willing the chaos to ease. It did not. They stood like that for a while, until Elwyna shifted slightly.

"Come on," she said gently. "Let's get these drinks sorted. Then we can talk."

Farran nodded, her body moving before her thoughts could catch up.

* * *

She had sat quietly, letting them talk, letting the unthinkable words wash over her. Daryll's voice was still soft and low as she tried to make sense of it all.

"So you see, Farr... you are Anne."

Tom gave a nervous smile, hope flickering behind his eyes. Farran sat, her thoughts swirling. Finally, she spoke.

"Let me get this straight." Her voice was sharp, her eyes stormy. "I'm really this Lady Anne Stephens, married to Richard Stephens, the same man whose exhibition I've spent weeks preparing?"

She took a long breath, her eyes locking onto Tom now.

"And he... " she gestured toward Tom, "is the Elizabethan jester who followed his master's orders, including murder. And you're a witch?"

She looked at each of them in turn. Then, suddenly, a burst of laughter escaped her lips. It was thin, close to hysterical. She stood and began to pace the cramped living room. Her footsteps struck the floor hard until she stopped, frozen.

"So I haven't lived here all my life?"

The silence pressed in. Daryll and Elwyna both shook their heads.

"I wove a memory spell," Elwyna said softly. "To help you believe this life was real. And another to help you forget the past until it was time for you to remember." Elwyna drew a shuddering breath, thick with frustration, before continuing. "They couldn't just let things go to plan." Her gaze flicked pointedly to Tom, who shifted slightly under it.

Farran stared at her. Questions surged like a storm, yet the exhaustion weighed more. Thick. Heavy. Dragging her under. She blinked and checked her watch.

"I have to be up early," she said softly, pressing her hands to her sides as she prepared to stand.

Elwyna and Daryll rose, their fingers tightly entwined as they made their way to the door.

"Tom," Elwyna said sharply. "Come on."

But he didn't move.

"May I speak with Anne... sorry, Farran, alone? Just for a moment?"

He looked at her, uncertain. Farran nodded, her movements slow, as she perched on the edge of her seat.

Without a word, Elwyna and Daryll stepped outside, closing the door behind them.

Farran sat in the chair beside Tom. She should have been frightened after everything she had just learned about him. She had every reason to be. Yet somehow, a strange peace had settled over the room now that they were alone.

She glanced at his face. The soft roundness. Those eyes. They were not the sharp, cold ones from the painting. These were warm, searching, glowing with something that looked like love. She felt drawn to him, like that day at Coeur House when they had nearly embraced. It was sheer madness, and yet, it felt so very right.

"Farran." His voice wrapped around her, gentle as silk. "I can get used to calling you that, I think."

He repeated her name, gently, a quiet smile lighting his face.

"I'm willing to wait until you remember me. Until you remember... us." His smile dimmed slightly, a flicker of pain at its edges. "Please, just give me the chance to show you again I am no longer that man."

He nodded toward the painting. Farran studied him. A strange feeling stirred inside her, like warmth rising from deep within. Was it trust? Understanding? Love? She could not say. Yet something unspoken told her, *Do not turn away from him.*

"Yes," she said simply, before she even thought. "I'm willing to trust you. I don't know why, but I feel I must."

She smiled.

Tom reached for her hand, pressing his lips to it with a tenderness that made her skin prickle. His thumb brushed gently across her fingers. Her body responded instantly, excitement blooming through her like spring. He stood, his smile radiant. For a moment, the room seemed to glow. Farran laughed, breathless with hope.

"You have an early start," he said, bowing slightly. "I'll leave you now."

He paused at the doorway.

"I hope to see you again soon."

"I would like that," she whispered.

And then he was gone. Farran sat still as silence returned, but this time it carried something new: a quiet hope she had never felt before.

* * *

Farran had hoped sleep would come easily. She was exhausted after the evening's revelations. Instead, she lay on her back, staring at the ceiling.

Tom's face lingered behind her eyes. A sigh escaped her lips. He had made her happy once. Could he do so again? She was almost certain of it. But her thoughts drifted, pulled back to everything she had learned that night. How could any of it possibly be true?

Lady Anne, married to a monster.

Richard. Darnell. Where had he gone?

Elwyna had mentioned a protection spell. But where was he now? Would he show up at the exhibition tomorrow? The thought sent a shiver through her. Her thoughts twisted and tangled, spiralling through the impossible. No one had explained how she had come to be here, in this time. She knew it must be some kind of witchcraft… but it still sounded too absurd to believe.

And yet…
She had touched the past.
Seen it.
Felt it.
The answers had to come soon.

Eventually, her eyes grew heavy, and she drifted into a fitful, dream-soaked sleep. Yet through the murk of her dreams, one constant remained. Her one solace.
Tom.

* * *

Darnell paced the darkened room, fury simmering just beneath the surface.
They had told her everything.
She knew what he was.
His chance at redemption, stolen.
He clenched his fists.
She had to understand.
She had to see that he was sorry.
That he needed her.
That she was his.

27

Storm Watch (1593)

The rain had poured for days, and the Master was still away at Parliament with Wentworth, with no sign of returning soon. In his absence, Miles lorded over us. He was becoming more unbearable with each passing day.

"That blaggard needs to go," Cook snapped, slamming her rolling pin into the pastry, already flattened within an inch of its life. "I don't know who he thinks he is, barkin' orders like he owns the place."

"Now, now, Cook," I said with a laugh. "That poor pastry deserves better."

I side-stepped a well-aimed swipe of the rolling pin, a rush of air brushing past my ear. Celia giggled in the corner.

"You can hush, girl," Cook snapped, then turned back to the table to inflict more punishment on the dough.

I chuckled at her choice of words. The blaggard. She wasn't wrong. Miles needed to go.

As I considered which task to tackle next, knowing he always chose the worst, I caught sight of Celia still lingering in the shadows. She had started working in the house not long after Anne married the Master. I strolled over and smiled. She returned it with caution, cheeks flushing pink. She was so young, barely eighteen, I'd guess. A slight thing, always keeping to herself, vanishing the moment her duties were done.

"Celia! Get those vegetables washed," Cook bellowed across the humming kitchen.

For a heartbeat, irritation flickered across Celia's face. Her hazel eyes glowed for just a moment; then the light was gone, her features soft and obedient once more.

"Yes, Cook," she said meekly, moving to the sink.

Had I imagined that flash in her eyes?

Before I could think on it further, a loud clatter rang out as the Master's messenger stormed through the kitchen threshold.

"Slow down, yer clutz," Cook huffed, looking up sharply at the commotion that had burst into her domain.

Sam stood in the doorway, breathing heavily, his face red from exertion, rain dripping from his coat and puddling on the tiled floor. Cook shoved a tankard toward him.

" 'Ere, get this down yer, Sam, then out of my kitchen with them wet clothes!"

He took it and drained the contents in one go, setting the empty vessel back on the table with a thunk.

"Tom," he said, eyes locked on mine, his face taut with urgency. "I need to speak with you."

There was something in the way he looked, tense, unreadable. My stomach twisted. Cook muttered curses under her breath as she fetched a cloth, glaring at the trail of water he'd brought in.

"Come," I said, nodding. "We'll talk in your room."

He nodded and squelched away down the corridor, boots sloshing with every step. I followed, unease growing with each echoing footfall.

As soon as we stepped into his room, Sam began peeling off his sodden clothes, flinging them into the corner in damp heaps. I glanced around while he undressed; our rooms were near identical: just a bed, a chair, and a battered sideboard. He dried off with a rag, then slung it on the hook by the door before pulling on a dry tunic. Drenched and weary, he dropped onto the bed, his limbs heavy with fatigue, but urgency burned brighter than exhaustion. I remained standing.

"Come on, Sam," I coaxed gently, though the fear in his eyes twisted something inside me. "Is it the Master?"

He nodded, his wet hair flopping forward with the motion. A flicker of hope sparked. Had my unspoken prayers been answered? Was he dead in a ditch, finally silenced by fate? The thought made me uneasy, but I didn't push it away.

"Sam," I said, my tone sharpening. "What's happened to the Master?"

He looked as though he might cry. His chest rose with a gulp. Then, in a rush, the words came spilling out.

"The Master is seized, Tom. Arrested, along with Master Wentworth and the others who dared raise the matter of Her Majesty's successor in the House. They say it touched the Queen's wrath near enough to burn."

As the words sank in, a strange relief washed over me. Not that he was dead, but that he would not be returning anytime soon. And yet, the realisation struck hard: Miles would remain in charge. The thought settled like lead in my chest. Sam continued.

"They've lodged him in the Tower, but he'll want for nothing, so long as his purse holds out. He's paid for a chamber with fire and board, and he can send letters. I have one here."

He reached into his coat and produced a folded parchment. My stomach turned when I saw the name Miles scrawled across it, unmistakably in the Master's hand. Sam caught my hesitation.

"I cannot give it to that man," he said quietly. "He is the devil. I trust you, Tom."

He pressed the letter closer. Slowly, I reached out and took it. It felt heavier than paper ought to feel. Unable to face its contents then and there, I slipped it into the pocket of my tunic, still feeling its weight.

"Get some rest, Sam," I said quietly. "I'll deal with this."

"Thanks, Tom." He lay back on the bed, eyes closing. Exhaustion engulfed him at last.

I made my way to my room, needing to delay my arrival for a time. When I finally entered, I sat down heavily, sinking into the mattress, listening to the rain hammering against the window panes. I turned the folded parchment over and over in my hands, the name appearing and vanishing with each pass. The uncertainty of what I was about to read kept me frozen. At last, my hands stilled. I could delay it no longer.

Crack. The seal broke, sharp even over the thunderous rain. The sound jolted something in me, as if the act itself were forbidden. I unfolded the parchment, smoothing it with shaking hands to reveal the Master's familiar scrawl.

Miles. I read.

I closed my eyes, swallowing the unease rising in my throat. Then, breathing steadily, I forced myself to continue.

Miles,

Our talk of succession has landed us in the Tower for the foreseeable future, which is most disagreeable, as I am concerned for the goings-on in my household. I thank you for your last correspondence informing me of the after-dark visits my wife and so-called trusted servant have made to the witch's abode. My heart is broken by such disloyalty...

A stifled laugh broke from me. Heartbroken. He had no heart to break. I read on, heat rising in my chest.

I ask, though, that you hold back from carrying out the retributions they so justly deserve until I am released, to bear witness.

My blood ran cold. I had known he would be angry, but this? I kept reading, the words burning.

Send Sam with £6 to secure my holding.

By mine own hand,

R Stephens.

I sat, the letter trembling in my hand, my heart pounding with the rain. My head was in turmoil. I had to see Anne. I had to warn her of the Master's intentions.

Tucking the letter back into my tunic, I bolted from my room and down the empty corridor, the only sound the thunder of my feet. I reached the stairs that led up to her chamber. Just as I began to bound upward,

"Tom!"

Davy. I wanted to keep going. Every instinct screamed for it. But I stopped, turning as he hurried toward me.

"Glad I found you," he said, a little breathless. "I need you to come look at the storeroom roof. Rain's comin' through like a torrent. If we don't move fast, all the grain'll be spoiled."

I sighed inwardly, eyes flicking to the stairs before I turned back to him.

"I've told the Master for months it needed rethatchin'," I muttered.

We made our way to the end of the corridor. As I opened the storeroom door, I could already hear rain pelting every surface.

"Quick, let's get this lot moved into the kitchen to dry," I said, taking charge.

"Cook's gonna have something to say about that," Davy chuckled behind me.

"I couldn't care less about Cook," I snapped, dragging a sack of grain across the threshold. My breath caught as I heaved it into the warmth.

We worked through the day, shifting sacks, barrels, and tools. Finally, we traced the source of the leak.

"It's that old corner again," Davy muttered, squinting up at the steady drip gathering beneath the barley.

I followed the trail with my eyes, watching water slide down a warped beam to the puddle gathering across the floor.

"If we get the ladder and that bundle from the hayloft, we might plug it for now," I said. "Bit of moss, some spar, press it down and bind it with twine. Should hold a week, maybe more."

"A week's enough," Davy replied. "So long as the barrels stay dry."

We ventured out into the grey, sodden yard toward the hayloft. With the letter pressing like a hot coal in my pocket, I took the chance. I glanced around. No soul in sight.

"You heard Sam came?" I asked, voice low beneath the hiss of rain.

Davy nodded. "Aye. Cook's been bellyachin' about him soaking the kitchen, and the grain," he added with a dry chuckle.

I lowered my voice further. "He brought news of the Master," I said, pausing, "and a letter."

Davy stopped mid-step. His expression sharpened.

"What's up?"

Something in my face must have shown too much. His look mirrored the weight pressing on my chest.

"Not here," I said under my breath. "Feels like the walls have ears. I'll come to you tonight, after nightfall."

Davy gave a small nod. We said nothing more, just gathered the bales and finished the job at hand.

After nightfall, I made my way to the cottage. Miles likely saw our trespasses from the study window, so I skirted the edge of the garden, keeping to the shadows. The wind tugged at my cloak, and the smell of wet soil clung to everything. I reached the door and knocked once before letting myself in.

Wynn was, as ever, busy in the kitchen, though tonight the air felt sharper than usual. The scent hit me hard, rosemary and rue; bitter, sharp, and overwhelming. My stomach turned. As she looked up, her eyes caught the candlelight; for a heartbeat, they glowed, just like Celia's had earlier. A wave of nausea swelled in my gut. I stumbled to the nearest chair and dropped into it, dizzy.

"Wynn, stop," Davy snapped, shooting her a warning look.

"He deserves it," she muttered, not looking at me, her movements brisk and sharp.

Davy joined me at the table just as Wynn slammed two goblets down in front of us. The table jumped. He scowled at her, but she only shrugged and turned away, her silence louder than any words.

"Is everything alright?" I asked, glancing toward her.

I thought I heard a low huff escape her lips.

"Yes, Tom," Davy said, smiling, though there it was again, that quiet huff. "It's just been a long day with that leak," he added, taking a long swig from his goblet.

"I'm going to check the garden," Wynn said briskly, already moving toward the door.

"Wynn, it's dark... " Davy began, but the door clapped shut behind her before he could finish.

"She's just worried," he said quietly, his expression bleak.

She wasn't the only one. I shifted uneasily in my chair and reached into my tunic, pulling out the letter I'd kept hidden all day. I placed it on the table between us.

Davy frowned. "It's addressed to Miles. Why have you got it?"

"Sam didn't want to give it to him. Called him evil," I said, a faint smirk tugging at my mouth.

Davy reached out, then hesitated, stopping short of the parchment.

"What's it say?"

I unfolded it and smoothed it flat on the table. The candlelight flickered across the ink as we read in silence. As Davy's eyes moved over the words, the colour drained from his face. He drew in a sharp breath. When he finally looked up, horror swam in his eyes. We sat wordless, the room thick with dread. Then the door slammed again, so hard the cottage shook.

Wynn returned swiftly, her face dark with anger. Davy pushed the letter back toward me without a word. I folded it and tucked it back into the dark hollow of my tunic. Wynn moved sharply around the room, clattering dishes as she avoided our eyes. After a moment, she vanished again into the night, the door clapping shut behind her. Davy buried his face in his hands and groaned low.

"What are we going to do, Tom?"

I stared at the table, empty of answers. Just one truth repeated like a drumbeat in my head.

"I have to warn Anne," I said.

Davy's head snapped up, eyes blazing.

"No. You are not to go near her."

I flinched.

"She's in enough danger already. Your recklessness will only make it worse."

The silence afterwards thundered louder than his warning. My thoughts spun, collapsing once more into the same hopeless conclusion.

"Can Wynn help?"

The words tasted bitter; I hated myself for asking, yet I had nothing left. Davy's gaze drifted to the door his wife had slammed just minutes before. There was something haunted in his eyes, as if he were staring down demons of his own. He sighed.

"I'll speak with her."

I gave a half nod.

"We'll also speak with Anne," he added, voice blunt, heavy with unspoken weight.

I reached for my drink and took a mouthful. It tasted bitter, angry. I pushed the cup aside.

"I think I'd best go."

I stood and walked toward the door. Behind me, Davy had not moved. His face was pale, hollowed by care.

Outside, the cold air wrapped around me like guilt. I crossed the garden in silence, keeping to the edges where shadows clung thick. As I neared the far corner, I paused. A faint glow flickered from Anne's chamber window. Her silhouette passed across it, pausing just for a heartbeat, then vanishing back into the dark. I stood there a moment longer, heart heavy with words I could never speak. Then I turned and continued, the weight growing with every step.

* * *

"Davy, you're asking too much," Wynn sighed, her voice barely above a whisper.

Her hand rested on the table, fingers splayed, tense and unmoving. Davy reached out to soothe her; his touch was feather-light. For a moment, she let him. Then she pulled her hand away, leaving him cold and wanting.

"I know, my love," he said gently. "But what else can we do?" His eyes searched hers; wide, pleading, raw with worry.

She would do anything for him. She always had. And she knew he would do the same for her. But this was different. A task that would drain her and cost her. Perhaps even break her. And still, it might fail. The weight of it pressed hard against her chest, suffocating. She could feel the old power stirring, restless, hungry. As she fought the storm inside, Davy leaned close and pressed a kiss to her cheek, soft and steady. An anchor in the chaos. She closed her eyes, then nodded reluctantly, hoping she would not come to regret it.

28

Shadows at the Exhibition (2018)

Farran awoke and looked at the clock: **6:29**. She had had the most restful night in weeks: no visitations, no visions, only peaceful dreams. Tom had appeared, as though watching over her, keeping her from harm. She still could not remember their original meeting or their days at Coeur House, but it did not matter; he was here now. She hummed and smiled as she dressed, soon walking the streets and marvelling at everything.

Not until she reached the square, with the museum entrance in sight, did her nerves begin to tingle. Unease crept in, and she could not shake the feeling of being watched. Under the old market hall, she glanced around; the unease was growing. Then she saw him.

Darnell. He stood by a stone pillar, eyes fixed on her approach.

Farran felt her whole body tense, but she forced herself forward. He stepped from the shadow, standing directly in her path.

"Farran, we need to talk."

His voice was hoarse, filled with an emotion Farran could not place. She stopped and looked at him. He looked dreadful, not the carefully preened man she had known, but dishevelled, his face pale and his eyes darker than she remembered. His shoulders slumped. Concern stirred in her.

"Darnell, are you all right?"

A flicker of a smile touched his face, then vanished. He shrugged.

"I need to speak with you," he said. "I need to explain."

He took a step forward, and she instinctively backed away.

"We have an exhibition to open. This is not the time," Farran said, longing to put as much distance between them as possible.

"Yes, of course," Darnell muttered. "Later, then?"

He looked at her, eyes searching. Farran nodded, giving him a once-over.

"You should tidy yourself up," she said. "You look awful."

Darnell gave a thin smile.

"We can thank your friend for that."
    Then he was gone.

Farran lingered, gathering her thoughts. She almost felt pity for him. Almost. And yet she could not shake the question: what did he mean? She headed into the building, nerves still tingling from the encounter. She should have known he would not just disappear. Not now. Not after everything.

Inside, she stowed her bag and paused, steadying her breath. The anxiety eased, replaced by a flicker of excitement. Down the corridor, voices carried in cheerful bursts, bouncing off the polished walls. Farran quickened her pace.

"Okay, one last check, then we're ready."

She stood in the centre of the gallery, turning beneath spotlights that gleamed like a hundred watchful eyes. The space shimmered with promise: sleek, precise, ready. Perfect. Almost.

Her gaze landed on the family seal. That same coil of dread struck her chest again. Richard's seal. Darnell's. A symbol of power and deception. She swallowed hard, turned away, and forced a smile just as Daphne approached.

"Hey, Farran, it all looks amazing!" Daphne's eyes sparkled, her excitement fizzing just beneath the surface.

Farran beamed, welcoming the warmth.

"That's thanks to your hard work, too."

A familiar scent wrapped around her: soft, subtle, grounding. The one she had smelled before, the one that felt like protection. Daphne glanced toward the entrance, scanning the quiet foyer.

"Where's Darnell?"

As if summoned, the door swung open with unnecessary force. Darnell walked in: suit pressed, hair combed, but still unmistakably pale. There was a flicker of discomfort in his expression, quickly smoothed into a smile as he strode toward them.

"Morning. Sorry, I'm late," he said, voice light. "Had some business to sort out, but I'm here now."

He winced as he adjusted his sleeve, the smile faltering for half a second.

"Are you sure you should be?" Farran asked, careful to keep her distance. "You look very pale."

He gave a brisk nod.

"Yes, hay fever," he said. His tone was too casual. "I'll be right as rain soon enough."

But something in his voice, that slight strain and the undercurrent of something unspoken, pulled at her. A cold knot began to form in her chest.

The morning passed as the exhibition drew a steady stream of visitors. Farran moved among them, answering questions, guiding curious eyes from one display to the next. People marvelled at the objects: the tapestries, the letters, the delicate embroidery of Anne's gown. Each piece was steeped in centuries of forgotten pain. And yet they smiled, enchanted by the tragic romance of it all.

She watched Darnell speaking with a small group, animated as he shared the family's history. Her history. He gestured to the seal, spinning tales that twisted through the past, but it was not the truth. Not really. Not the truth she now knew. The weight of that thought struck deep. This was her family. Anne's pain. Tom's sacrifice. Wynn's magic. Davy's loyalty. All of it belonged to her now.

And Darnell... Richard had caused so much of it. So much pain. So much fear. Yet here he was, relishing the attention, retelling their suffering with theatrical flair, as if it were some tragic play for the audience to enjoy. There was no shame in him. No remorse. Just smooth charm layered over centuries of cruelty. Farran's chest tightened. She needed air, space, a moment to breathe.

"Daphne," she said, touching her arm, "I'm just stepping out for some water."

Daphne nodded, absorbed in conversation, and Farran slipped away, her pulse thrumming in her ears.

She had not gone far when she heard someone call her name, a voice she recognised instantly.

"Farran! Are you all right?"

She turned. Tom stood at the far end of the corridor, concern etched across his face. The sight of him sent calm through her chest. She smiled, relief washing over her.

"You came," she breathed.

He walked toward her, returning her smile.

"Of course I came."

As he reached her, he pulled her into a warm embrace. She leaned into him, the world narrowing to the warmth of his arms and the rhythm of his breath. She drew back slowly, gazing up at him. His eyes, always so full of light and depth, steadied her. They made her feel strong again.

"Darnell's here," she whispered.

"I thought he would be," Tom replied, his gaze flicking toward the display room at the end of the hall.

"I know you're angry with him..." Farran began, uncertain.

But Tom only smiled.

"I won't start anything," he said softly. "This is your day. I won't spoil it."

Farran let out a breath she had not realised she was holding. Of course, he wouldn't. Tom had never been reckless, not with her. Still, the worry lingered: a faint buzz of unease she could not shake.

Footsteps echoed from the end of the corridor. Familiar voices approached. Farran turned to see Elwyna and Daryll making their way toward them, both smiling. They greeted one another warmly. They exchanged hugs and smiles, though Farran sensed something simmering beneath the surface between Elwyna and Tom. A tension. A conversation left unfinished. She made a mental note to ask about it later.

Together, they made their way back to the gallery doors she had only just passed through. There was laughter, lightness: a sense of reunion, of unity. A moment of peace. Darnell saw them. His face fell. He stood frozen, watching them approach. Pain flared beneath his skin: crawling, burning. His eyes locked on Tom's. The two men stared at one another, unmoving. The air thickened with tension. Farran, sensing its rise, gently touched Tom's arm.

She whispered, "Not now."

Tom turned to her, and the storm in his gaze calmed. He nodded, his expression softening as he reached out and took her hand. Their fingers threaded together with quiet certainty.

Darnell watched.

A surge of jealousy twisted through him, seizing his muscles and tightening his jaw. A low snarl escaped before he could stop it. He began to walk toward them, determined and seething, but a pair of visitors stepped into his path, full of questions and enthusiasm. He stopped abruptly, the mask returning as he turned on the charm. He smiled, nodded, answered, but his eyes flicked once more toward the group at the edge of the room. They could wait.

The day drew to a close. The crowd thinned, the buzz of voices fading to a gentle hum, until only a few stragglers remained; then none.

Left behind were Farran, her team, her friends, and Darnell. They stood together in the quiet aftermath, exchanging congratulations, compliments and tired smiles. On the surface, it was warm: a successful day shared, an exhibition opened with grace and care. But beneath the pleasantries, something darker stirred. Farran could feel it in every glance, every pause in conversation. The loathing. The mistrust. It clung to the air like dust disturbed by motion.

Daphne chatted cheerfully, unaware or unwilling to acknowledge the undercurrents. Farran stood close to Tom, their fingers brushing now and then as if to reassure themselves of each other's presence. Elwyna and Daryll stayed close, their eyes flicking now and then toward Darnell, quiet and guarded. And Darnell, ever the actor, played his part with polished precision. He smiled, he nodded, he praised. But his eyes betrayed him: they burned. Not with celebration, but with something sharper, a hunger, a fury held in check only by circumstance. Farran saw it and knew it was far from over.

"That was a great success," she said, smiling at the small group.

"It was," Daphne agreed. "But I'm exhausted."

Farran nodded.

"It's been a long day. You and Simon get off, I can wait for the cleaners."

The pair smiled, and after a round of brief goodbyes, they walked out hand in hand. Their departure left the space quieter, heavier.

The four who remained stood together, tension still bubbling just beneath the surface. Darnell lingered at the edge of the group, no longer performing, his expression twisted into a scowl now that his audience was gone.

"Is there anything we can help with?" Elwyna asked. Her tone was light, but her eyes never left Darnell. She sensed it; the shift. It was only a matter of time before he tried something.

"No, I just have to wait for them. They should be here in about ten minutes," Farran said.

She glanced around the room, her gaze falling once more on the family seal. For a moment, it seemed to flicker in the light, as though responding to something unseen.

"Look." She tore her eyes away. "I'll wait here, and if you all head back to mine, we can... continue with what we were talking about."

Tom tensed beside her.

"I don't want to leave you alone," he said, eyes fixed on Darnell, still hovering in silence like a storm about to break.

Farran followed his gaze.

"It'll be fine," she said quietly. Then louder, with force, "Darnell was just going. Weren't you?"

Darnell's eyes darkened, clouded with irritation. For a long moment, he said nothing. Then, without a word, he turned and walked out. Everyone exhaled, the pressure lifting slightly. Just then, the doors swung open again and the cleaning crew bustled in, their cheerful voices and clattering buckets breaking the tension. Farran greeted them briefly, giving a few quick instructions, then turned to the others.

"I'll grab my things from the office and meet you outside."

Elwyna hesitated. So did Tom.

"Go on," she insisted gently. "I won't be long."

Still reluctant, they finally nodded and stepped out. Farran turned away, the cleaners' chatter fading behind her as she headed down the corridor toward the office alone. She entered without noticing Darnell already seated silently at his desk, his eyes fixed on the door. She stopped mid-step, frozen. Then, finding her voice, she said,

"I thought you'd gone."

Her voice trembled, and there was something in his face that made her stomach turn, something unfamiliar and unmoored. He let out a long sigh.

"Oh, Farran."

His tone was condescending, cutting through the quiet like a blade.

"I said we needed to talk."

He stood, circling the desk slowly as he came toward her. Farran backed away instinctively until her own desk stopped her retreat. Her heart pounded in her ears. Still, her voice stayed steady.

"Darnell, not now. It has been a long day."

But he did not stop. Step by step, he came closer, and with each step, she saw something ripple across his face: pain. Deep, buried pain that contorted his features, as if something crawled beneath his skin.

"We *need* to talk," he repeated.

It was not a request. It was a command. Farran could not move. She was pinned between the desk and the man she had once pretended to trust; the man she now knew to be dangerous.

"Darnell," she whispered, "this is not acceptable. This is not 1593."

A fire blazed in his eyes. For a moment, she thought he might explode, lash out with all the violence from another life. Instead, he leaned in, his breath sharp against her skin. Then he whispered:

"You are my wife. You're mine."

Then he grabbed her roughly, forcing his mouth to hers. Farran jerked back, fighting him, resisting every inch of the contact. A sudden vision flashed through her: the bedroom at Coeur House, the smell of candle smoke, the chill of the stone floor. The memory surged, filling her with sudden strength. She broke free and slapped him, hard. The sound cracked like a firework in the silence. Darnell staggered back, his eyes narrowing to pinpricks as he glared at her. Farran stepped away from the desk, chest heaving, and held her ground. Through clenched teeth, she hissed,

"I am not your wife. I am not yours. And you will never treat me like that again, do you hear me?"

Her body trembled as adrenaline surged through her, not from fear, but from power. Darnell let out a low, bone-chilling laugh.

"You can believe that, Anne," he sneered, "but we both know the truth."

The sound of her old name, Anne, struck a chord of deep fear inside her. She turned to bolt for the door, but she wasn't fast enough. His hand shot out, gripping her arm, and he shoved her violently to the ground. Farran screamed as his full weight pinned her down. He leaned close, his mouth at her ear.

"You are mine, Anne. I will show you."

Farran struggled and kicked, but he was too strong. She couldn't get free.
 Then, a scent.
 Rosemary.

Its sharp sweetness drifted into the room like mist, curling low across the floor, creeping toward them. Darnell recoiled as though in agony, letting out a whimper as the scent grew stronger. The door flew open. Elwyna burst in, her face pale with fury, eyes burning like fire. Tom was close behind. His gaze turned to steel when he saw Farran pinned beneath Darnell.

Darnell rolled over in agony, tears streaming down his cheeks.

Elwyna rushed to Farran, pulling her from the floor and wrapping her in a fierce embrace as she guided her out to safety. Tom flew across the room. Darnell lay twitching, eyes streaming. Without hesitating, he kicked hard into Darnell's ribs. A harsh grunt escaped him. Then another kick. And another. Daryll caught up, grabbing Tom and pulling him back.

"He's not worth it, Tom!"

Tom roared, shaking with rage.

"He is worse than an animal, a soulless coward!"

Even through pain, Darnell laughed, low and ragged.

"You're nothing but a fool, Tom. She'll be mine. Mark my words."

The threat lingered in the air like smoke. Daryll tightened his grip.

"You'll get what's coming to you," Tom spat, as Daryll finally dragged him from the room.

"Come on," Daryll said gently. "We need to get Farran home."

Grudgingly, Tom followed, still muttering curses under his breath.

Outside, they found Elwyna cradling Farran. She trembled still. Tom rushed to her, wrapping his arms around her carefully. They held each other in silence for a long moment.

"Come on," Elwyna said softly. "We need to get her home."

They walked away from the building, shadows stretching behind them. Upstairs, at the office window, Darnell watched and plotted. She belonged to him. No matter the years, no matter who stood in the way, she would honour the vow her uncle had made. He would make certain of it.

Back home, Farran sat with Tom by her side, his portrait silently guarding the room, the day's events still circling in her mind like a storm that would not break. Around them, silence lingered heavy, each of them struggling to digest the horror they had seen.

"I need to know how we're going to get rid of him," she said at last, breaking the silence. The steel in her voice was unmistakable.

Tom glanced up at the image staring down at them.

"I could think of many ways," he said, his voice taut with the weight of the day.

Farran touched his arm, drawing his gaze back to her, then shook her head.

"You're not him," she whispered.

A wry smile tugged at his lips as he met her eyes and nodded.

Elwyna drew in a slow breath.

"I can send him back, to where he belongs. And I can return your memories. But it will take time."

Farran looked straight at her, eyes sharp, unrelenting.

"Tell me."

Elwyna glanced at Daryll. He gave her a small, encouraging nod, then took her hand in his.

"It is the same way that brought us here," she said softly. "A solar eclipse. It helps draw the power I need."

Farran's brow creased as the pressure of needing answers grew.

"But when? Days? Weeks? Months?" her voice clipped.

Elwyna hesitated; she knew her answer would cause more anguish. Daryll gently squeezed her hand, giving her the strength to speak.

"The next one is on July twenty-eighth."

Farran inhaled sharply.

"That is three months away," she whispered. Her voice cracked beneath the weight of the delay.

Tom squeezed her hand, his quiet earnestness grounding her, yet there was a fire in his gaze that promised he would not let anything harm her.

"We'll be with you," he said, meeting her eyes. His thumb brushed gently across her cheek, then drew her close, just enough to remind her she was safe.

She didn't want to wait. Every instinct screamed for action now. But she looked at the faces around her, and knew: with Tom and the others beside her, she could endure.

29

Spring Preparations (1593)

Spring blossomed again, yet the Master remained locked in the Tower with no sign of release. I remembered how Sam had returned to Miles after that dreadful day, his cheeks pale, his voice shaking. He stammered the lie we had agreed on.

"The Master's letter was ruined in the rain," he said, fearing his legs would buckle beneath him. "But he wants you to wait; he wishes to witness the proceedings himself. He also asked for six pounds for his lodgings and comfort."

Miles stared at him, suspicious. Then, after a pause, he crossed to the safe and pulled out a pouch of coins.

"Take that."

Sam fastened it to his belt, hands unsteady.

"Shall I say anything to the Master?"

Miles shook his head, eyes narrowing on the boy. Sam bolted before he could say another word.

I waited by his already saddled horse. When I saw him approach, I stepped forward.

"Done?"

He nodded, hands still trembling.

"He's the devil, Tom. I was sure he saw through it."

"You did well," I said, trying to ease his torment. "God's speed."

And then, we waited. Time held its breath, and the flowers bloomed while the Master remained confined. Davy still kept me from Anne, though I caught glimpses of her wandering the gardens like a ghost tethered only by sorrow. My need to be near her grew, curling like vines along every stone wall. I knew the distance was for her safety, but knowing did not make it easier.

In the cottage, Wynn was always busy. She prepared spells, gathered herbs, and muttered to herself. I was never privy to her work; her disdain for me grew more evident with each passing day.

"Keep him away from me, Davy," she hissed once as I left the cottage. "He does not need to know what I do."

After that, I busied myself wherever I could: carting grain, mending tools, helping Davy with the orchard. Anything to be away. But the solitude was starting to weigh on me.

One clear morning in late spring, I sat sharpening knives. I worked the blade slowly against the whetstone, back and forth; the rhythm steady, almost soothing. The scrape of metal on stone filled the yard, but my thoughts had long drifted. I had told her I would not kill again. I had meant every word.

And yet…

The steel sang under my hands. Sometimes, when the light caught just so, I still saw the red on my palms. Not fresh: old, dried, sunk into the creases. Impossible to scrub out. His eyes had stared through me that night. Wide. Unbelieving. As though he had only just realised I was more than a fool with bells. I remembered the twitch of his legs after the second blow. And the silence that followed. The loudest thing I had ever heard.

I paused mid-stroke. A promise is only as strong as the man who makes it. And I was no longer certain what kind of man I was, or whether I was strong enough.

"Tom!"

Davy's voice cut across the yard. I blinked. The whetstone slipped in my grip.

"What?"

He trotted over, that welcome smile, the one I had missed, lighting up his face. Was there finally good news? God knew I needed some.

"Hey, you going to be long?" he asked. "Need a hand at the cottage. Floorboards have snapped."

I looked at him, puzzled. When had he ever needed help with that? Then I saw the wink. I tossed the tools into the wooden box at my feet.

"That was the last one," I said. "I can come now. Is Wynn alright? She wasn't hurt, was she?"

"She's fine," Davy assured me. "She wasn't near it. She's nearly done with the preserving, making sure nothing goes to waste." He chuckled.

We kept up the pretence as we walked toward the cottage, two friends on a spring afternoon, nothing out of the ordinary. But as the chimney came into view, its smoke curling into the sky, our voices lowered instinctively.

"So what's this all about?" I asked quietly.

Davy scanned the lane before replying.

"We need to get everything in place. The event is next month; there is still much to do."

Nerves and anticipation flared in my chest.

"Alright. What do you need me to do?"

We reached the door: ajar. A familiar scent met me: thick with memory and magic. It wrapped around me like a cloak. Davy pushed it open wider, and we stepped inside. Wynn bustled around the kitchen. She looked up and gave Davy a tired smile. The glow I had always seen in her was still there, but dimmed now, worn thin at the edges. The table was crowded with jars of coloured liquids. Herbs hung from the rafters. Pots cluttered every surface. The scent hung heavy in the air. Davy crossed to her, catching her hand mid-motion.

"Hey. You can't keep going like this. You're exhausted."

He drew her close for a moment, and she let herself rest in the contact. Then she gently pulled away.

"Not much more now," she said with a small smile. "And help's coming."

She turned back to her work. I stepped forward to assist. She looked as though she might object, then nodded. We worked in quiet rhythm until a knock sounded at the door.

"Come on in," Wynn called.

I turned hopefully. Maybe it was Anne, I held my breath... but it was not her. Celia stepped inside, slight and uncertain. My heart sank, and I knew it showed.

"Celia, I'm so glad you are here," Wynn said quickly, shooting me a glare before embracing the girl.

Celia froze when she saw me, her eyes wide and wary.

"It's all right. He knows about the gift," Wynn said gently, reassuring her.

"Celia." I gave a respectful nod.

A hush fell as Wynn pulled out a chair and gestured for her to sit.

"Tom," Davy said quietly, touching my shoulder, "let's give them space."

I didn't need telling twice. I stepped outside.

The spring air hit me like a balm, but the scent from inside clung to my clothes: rosemary, lavender, and smoke. A promise. A warning. Something ancient waking. We walked the outer path of the cottage.

"What's Celia doing here?" I asked.

Davy led us to a pile of logs that had been left untouched since the New Year. He sat down and gestured for me to do the same. I hesitated. The memory of Greg, writhing, gasping, flashed through me. His face rose like a ghost behind my eyes.

"Tom." Davy's voice pulled me back.

"Yes. Sorry," I muttered, sitting down. The bark scraped roughly against my legs.

"She has the gift, like Wynn," Davy said. "Wynn's helping her learn to control it. She says it'll help the Master."

Davy tugged at a tuft of grass pushing out beneath the logs.

"What help could he possibly need?" I muttered. Let him suffer. He deserved it all.

"I cannot say. Some memory spell, perhaps, or potion. I leave such things to Wynn—she knows her craft."

He shrugged and flicked the grass away.

"In any case," Davy said, half-smiling, "we need to gather some necessities."

"What do you need?"

"We're stowing things beneath the floorboards," he grinned.

I let out a chuckle.

"Under the floorboards?"

He nodded. I laughed louder, the tension releasing in a rush. The breeze caught it and scattered it into the trees.

"Flippin' floorboards," I snorted.

We both laughed, not knowing quite why, only grateful for the lightness it brought.

"We need sealed jars," Davy said as he recovered, "nails, broken glass, wax, silver counters, vinegar and crates to store it all."

A smirk tugged at my lips.

"I don't think I want to know what for."

"Probably best you don't," Davy grinned.

"I'll help gather some of it," I offered.

"Oh, and one more thing," Davy said, snapping his fingers. "Your portrait. The one hanging in your room."

I frowned.

"Why? I'd be happy never to see it again."

"Wynn's orders," he said with a shrug.

We split up; Davy heading around the cottage, me toward the house. A sense of purpose steadied my heart.

* * *

Wynn placed a candle in front of Celia, its flame dancing softly between them. On the table lay a sprig of rosemary, a small white cloth, a salt pot, twine, and a piece of parchment bearing a verse written in careful script.

"This is a simple protection spell," Wynn said gently. "It will help keep you safe."

Celia looked at the items, then up at Wynn.

"Yes, Miss."

"My name is Wynn," she smiled.

Celia nodded, blushing.

"The rosemary is for strength. Always keep some close by; even a small amount can be powerful."

She pointed to the sprig.

"Place it on the cloth."

Celia did so with care.

"Now sprinkle a little salt around it, and read this verse aloud. Read it with intention."

Celia nodded again and took the salt, her hand trembling slightly. Her voice was soft, but steady:
   "Rosemary for strength,
   Salt for purity,
   White cloth for protection,
   I call upon thee,

Keep me safe from harm and fear,
  With this charm, no evil draws near."

As she finished, a small spark bloomed in her eyes. The candle quivered.

"You are doing very well," Wynn encouraged. "Now wrap it and bind it with the twine."

Celia wrapped the bundle carefully and knotted the twine with care.

"Keep it with you at all times. If you feel its power fading, make another. Take this." She handed her the parchment.

"Thank you, Wynn," Celia said with a small smile.

"We must keep the old faith alive. Promise me."

"I promise."

"Right then, let us tidy up before the men return."

Wynn blew out the candle and cleared the table, then sank into the chair by the fire. For a moment, she let her eyes close.

"Are you all right?" Celia asked softly.

"I am fine. Just tired."

Celia sat across from her, fingers twisting in her lap.

"You want to know why Tom is here, do you not?"

Celia nodded.

"I can trust you, can I not?"

Celia bobbed her head.

"All this," Wynn gestured to the jars, "is for Tom and Lady Anne. To help them escape."

Celia's eyes widened as she looked around.

"You know I shall help however I can," she said eagerly.

"I know," Wynn smiled. "But for now, I am going to rest."

A hush settled over the room. The fire crackled low, its light dancing in quiet vigil.

* * *

I hurried to my room and pulled the sideboard from the wall. Kneeling, I drew my small knife and prised up the floorboard beneath. A chuckle quietly escaped me; Davy and Wynn were not the only ones to use such hiding places. Dust rose as the board popped free, revealing a small cavity. I reached in, pulled out a pouch, and carefully opened it to inspect its contents: a modest collection of jewellery and gold coins. Satisfied, I tucked the pouch into my tunic.

I replaced the board and sideboard, setting all back in place, then turned to the painting. I regarded it with distaste; what Wynn wanted with it, I could not fathom. Reaching up, I lifted it from the wall and flipped it over. In the corner, neatly inked: "Thomas the Jester, 1573." I laid it gently on the bed, then fetched parchment, ink, and quill from a drawer. My hand hovered as I thought of her, of her smile, and how I prayed she still bore it. Resting the paper against the painting's back, I began to write:

My Dearest Anne,

May this find you safe and protected.

It won't be long 'til we're reunited.

Keep the faith.

My love is yours now and forever.

Your Tom.

I had seen such protection wheels before and did my best to draw one, whispering words of safekeeping as I worked. I folded the paper and tucked it behind the frame, then wrapped the painting in an old rag hanging by the bed. Grabbing a bag of wax from the kitchen, I dashed into the fading light, heading back to the cottage.

Davy was in the kitchen, with piles of crates of various sizes stacked on the floor, eagerly waiting to be filled.

"Hey, Tom," he said, bending to lift a crate.

"Davy." I set the wax and wrapped painting on the table, then pulled out the pouch.

"What's that?" His curiosity was clear.

I opened it and spread the contents on the table. His eyes widened as he gently touched some of the pieces.

"Where did you get this?"

I shrugged lopsidedly and smirked. "It's what Greg stole."

A nervous laugh escaped me; Davy returned a small smile.

"I'll keep it safe," he said, tucking it into a crate.

I glanced around the kitchen; Wynn was nowhere in sight.

"Where is Wynn?"

Davy's expression grew solemn.

"She is resting. All this is wearing her down. Every night, she chants some spell or another. I hate seeing her like this. I cannot wait for this to end, but..."

He trailed off as a new worry crept in.

"What if it fails? Or if, when we get there, it is just as bad as here?"

I stepped closer and laid an arm across his shoulders.

"Wynn knows what she is doing. I have every faith things will improve."

He gave a faint smile, and I tried to believe it as well.

We set about packing the crates and hiding them from sight, talking and laughing as we worked. The sound of hammering lids echoed through the night. At last, we finished and slumped into chairs, goblets in hand.

"Here is to the future," I said, raising mine.

"The future," Davy echoed, and we drank.

We clinked our goblets; for a moment, hope felt possible.

30

Return to the Cottage (2018)

Spring slipped into summer as nature reclaimed the world. Wildflowers bloomed in full glory, lining the roadside as they drove.

"I can't wait to see the old cottage again," Elwyna said, gazing out from the back seat of Farran's car, watching the landscape roll by. "This will be the first time since we arrived." She turned to Daryll and reached for his hand. He met her with a warm smile and pressed a soft kiss to her knuckles.

As the car moved on, Elwyna's thoughts wandered. She thought back to the day they arrived.

They had woken outside the cottage, disoriented and unsure. Wynn had stood first, scanning the landscape. The air was still, frozen in time. The sky was beginning to brighten. She had wondered if they had truly made it into the future she had worked so long to reach.

Davy groaned beside her, stretched his limbs, and raised his head to look about. A slow smile crept across his face when he saw Wynn.

"Is this the place?" he rasped.

"Aye, I believe it is," Wynn said gently.

The place looked the same, yet it did not. The cottage garden was overgrown, wild and untended, not how she would have kept it.

A soft moan broke the silence.

Anne.

Wynn rushed over, kneeling beside her. "We must fetch aid," she said, her hands moving gently to find some sign of life, listening for breath.

Davy carefully rose, his legs unsteady as he found his footing. "I shall go to the house," he said. "See if any there might render help."

Wynn nodded, then sat beside Anne. She held her hand and whispered quiet words of comfort, words meant to anchor, to protect, to remind her she was safe now.

Davy took the familiar path, noticing subtle differences, but unable to stop in his haste.

People were gathered outside the house. As he approached, they began to point.

"Wow, they really play the part here," someone said, glancing around with a mix of amusement and curiosity.

He gazed briefly around, their strange garments causing puzzlement; women with bare arms and legs, men wearing trousers that clung oddly to their limbs. Peculiar. Immodest. But there was no time to dwell on that now.

Davy called out, "Pray, someone help, she's hurt just beyond the cottage!"

Some people looked up, and a few clapped.

"He's good," one woman murmured to her friend.

Davy's heart pounded. Confusion swirled, yet he forced himself to focus. He strode toward a man standing nearby, clad in a curious short-sleeved doublet and tight breeches.

"Good sir, I pray thee, come quickly. She lies grievously hurt. We require thy aid."

The man blinked, confusion flickering in his eyes. Yet something in Davy's voice stirred him, and without further question, he fell in step beside him. By the time they reached the cottage, Wynn was still kneeling by Anne. The man hurried to her side, pulling out a small, polished slate and tapping quickly on its surface.

"She's breathing," he said swiftly. "I've called an ambulance. They are on the way."

Relief and fear collided in Davy's chest.

Within minutes, the ambulance arrived, its lights flashing silently. The paramedics moved quickly, lifting Farran onto a stretcher. Daryll and Elwyna climbed in beside her, pale with shock. In that moment, past and present folded into one, the echo of another life humming quietly beneath their skin. They shared a glance, knowing that beneath these new names, they were still bound by the same unbreakable thread.

Now, as the car sped down country lanes once more, Elwyna shuddered, sharp, disjointed flashes of that morning replaying in her mind. She drew a steadying breath, comforted that it had all turned out well in the end.

They had not seen the fourth person who travelled with them that day, pinned to the ground where the dark, shimmering grass grew taller. Richard waited until the ambulance left, taking them away. What was he to do? He stood, off balance, as the man called Darnell walked into the woodland shadows.

Farran smiled as she drove. There was still much to organise, many details pulling at the edges of her mind, yet in this moment, she felt content. She cast a sidelong glance at Tom, sitting quietly in the passenger seat. He seemed absorbed in the passing greenery, or perhaps simply lost in thought.

The weeks since she had learned the truth about who they all were had been filled with questions, many still unanswered, yet they had brought her something unexpected: precious time with Tom. Whether alone or in the company of Elwyna and Daryll, their time together had quickly become her favourite part of each day. They shared stories, laughter, and music.

One quiet afternoon, Farran had been listening to a soulful piece when Tom quietly spoke about the song. She turned to him, eyes widening with a dawning realisation.

"You're him," she whispered. "The voice on the radio... the one that soothed me back to sleep when I was having those visions."

Tom gave a sheepish nod.

"Elwyna told me not to push the connection," he admitted. "Each time I saw your face in the mirror, well, my restraint wavered. Music was always so dear to you, so I asked her to help me weave a charm; something gentle, something you might hear late at night when you were alone. Just a voice on the radio."

A small smile tugged at the corners of his mouth.

Farran frowned. "Why that time of night?"

Tom shrugged. "Elwyna said magic is strongest then, at the witching hour."

Farran laughed, exasperated, and shook her head.

"I don't think I'll ever get used to all these weird ideas."

Tom chuckled and pulled her into a gentle hug.

As she nestled into his arms, a hollow ache remained: the space where her memories should have been. She longed for the moments they had shared at Coeur House, though now she felt only their echo. Even happiness felt fragile, as though it might vanish with the mist.

Since Darnell's actions, Elwyna had doubled the protective charms, handing each of them a neatly sewn pouch scented with lavender.

"Carry these with you always," she had urged.

The moment Farran held hers, a gentle calm washed over her: subtle but steady, like a hand at her back. She felt it even now, nestled in her coat pocket, as the car sped along the same country lanes she had travelled just weeks ago.

Beside her, Tom stilled as a familiar sight came into view, and he saw the tree, still standing: tall and resolute, just as it had been when he lay beneath its branches in his carefree days. Visions flickered through his mind: travellers who had passed by, some doomed, some long forgotten. A hand settled on his shoulder; Daryll had reached over, sensing his unrest.

"You're not him any more," he said softly.

Tom managed a small smile and nodded. They continued down the track, the gentle purr of the engine and the quiet strength of companionship carrying them forward.

Eventually, the stately building came into view, and a hush fell over the car. Memories, no more than a whisper away, pressed softly at their souls. Daryll squeezed Elwyna's hand, and she shifted closer along the seat.

He recalled the night they retrieved the hidden items, the tension thick as smoke. Night had already fallen when the three stood at the edge of the wood, torches slicing through the dark.

At the cottage, they prised open the door with a crowbar; the hinges groaned in protest. Inside, the air smelled of time and silence. They crept to the corner where loose floorboards waited and knelt together. One by one, they drew out the bundles still wrapped in salt-stiffened cloth and rosemary, their wards unbroken.

Tom was the one to lift the portrait. He froze, shoulders tense, then shuddered. No one spoke. Some things do not need words.

The moment broke as Farran pulled through the gates, and soft gasps greeted the house as it rose into view.

After they had parked and stepped out, Farran led them toward the front entrance, though Elwyna and Daryll held back. Farran turned to look at them.

"What's wrong?"

They exchanged glances, then giggled nervously.

"We're not used to going in through the front," Daryll said, grinning like a schoolboy caught sneaking into the headmaster's office.

Tom's mouth curled into a roguish smile.

"Well, you're not servants now."

He strode ahead, clutching Farran's hand. Elwyna and Daryll followed, still giggling and whispering.

"He's enjoying this," Daryll muttered, nodding toward Tom with a laugh.

Elwyna smiled. "We all are," she breathed.

A woman welcomed them in and began telling stories of the families who had once owned the place. They listened, but as they walked through the familiar halls and rooms, each drifted into their own recollections: smiles and frowns flickering as old memories stirred. Now and then, they leaned in to whisper to one another, sharing a fragment of some half-forgotten tale.

When they reached the library, Tom's face lit up as he looked toward the window seat. They were no longer allowed to sit there, but he stepped close, Farran's hand nestled in his.

"We spent hours here when... the Master was away," he said softly, voice thick with remembrance, then quickly added, "...Richard, I mean."

Farran gazed out at the garden sprawling beyond the glass, watching the fountain's dancing spray. She longed, achingly, to remember. Even the visions she once had were beginning to fade. She held Tom a little tighter. He responded with a comforting kiss pressed gently to her head. Elwyna came to stand beside them, her expression gentle.

"Soon," she whispered, reading Farran's thoughts with uncanny ease.

The tour ended, and they were free to explore the grounds. They wandered toward the old stone wall and its gate, stepping through as if crossing a threshold between worlds. The cottage came into view at the edge of the wood, and Elwyna gasped as they walked the overgrown garden path. Rosemary and rue pushed up, wild and fragrant. Her hand brushed the plants with reverence, lips moving in silent words only she could hear. They approached the building, dishevelled still, and a tear traced a path down Elwyna's cheek.

"I don't remember it looking like this when we arrived," she whispered.

Daryll wrapped an arm around her.

"We hardly had time to look properly, did we?"

Elwyna shook her head slowly, eyes never leaving the doorway.

They circled the cottage. A padlock secured the door, and windows were boarded up. They peered through gaps, trying to glimpse inside, but all they could see were slivers of shadow. Rounding the back, they found the logs' outlines still visible, the shapes marked by moss and softened by time, untouched in memory if not in form. Tom and Daryll froze; a shiver coursed through them. Their eyes met, and in silence, memory spoke louder than words.

Elwyna rushed to the far corner of the garden, skirts brushing through rosemary and wild thyme. Ivy claimed most of the stonework, draping it in green-veined curtains. She pushed it aside with shaking hands, revealing a crevice worn deep with age.

"It's still here," she breathed, dropping to her knees.

Farran stepped closer, sun warm on her back. Tom hovered just behind, tense and silent. Daryll lingered further off, eyes scanning the tangled garden with the unease of one watching time bend at the edges.

Elwyna reached into the hollow, fingers moving with reverence until they found something nestled deep in the stone's belly. She drew it out with care: a small pouch no bigger than her palm, stiff with age. Its once-rich velvet had faded to sun-bleached brown, the red thread around its neck knotted in a looping seal that shimmered faintly in the light.

"A memory pouch," she murmured, holding it in both hands. She turned it gently, revealing a stitch of red thread coiled like a serpent through the seam. "It was made to keep your memories safe, Farran. Or Anne's. Both, really."

Farran hesitated. Her heart pounded, and the pouch seemed to exhale a scent: bitter rosemary and a faint trace of smoke. Breath from another time.

Elwyna tucked it into her pocket and looked around. Her eyes settled on a familiar break in the wall. Without a word, she slipped through the gap and made her way toward a perfect ring of darkened grass shimmering at her presence.

Tom and Daryll followed, but Farran lingered behind, emotions worn thin by all that had happened. Tom paused, looking back at her, but Daryll called him forward.

"Good," Elwyna said as she examined the spot. "It's still intact. We just need to get Darnell here at the right time and hope Celia has done her part."

They stood in a quiet huddle, making occasional comments as they surveyed the ring. Meanwhile, Farran remained apart, turning slowly.

From where she stood, she saw the chimney of the house in the distance. Overhead, clouds scuttled across the sky, driven by a rising breeze. She leaned against the stone wall. She felt as though she stood between two selves, the woman she was and the one she could not yet remember. A presence stirred beside her. She turned and saw Tom, his face drawn with concern, his gaze locked onto hers. No words were spoken, only a nod. Their arms found each other, wrapping tight in silent acknowledgement of all that had been and all that was still to come.

* * *

Later, back home, Farran sat quietly, listening as the others reminisced. Their laughter and easy memories washed over her like waves she could not catch. She lacked the memories, the history, only the aftermath. They laughed about a world she had only glimpsed in dreams, dreams now fading and leaving an ever-widening darkness. A pang of jealousy flared, sharp and unwelcome. She slammed her drink down on the table. Liquid sloshed over the rim, trailing down the glass and splashing the wood.

"Are you going to tell me how we're going to send him back?" she snapped, the sharpness in her voice surprising even herself.

The room fell silent. They turned to her, as if only now remembering she was there. Tom moved first, shuffling to her side. He took her hand gently and pressed it to his lips.

"Sorry, my love," he murmured.

Elwyna leaned forward, her voice low and soothing. "Farran, we've been so wrapped up in everything... of course."

Farran looked at them, guilt already rising in her chest. She reached for her drink again, her fingers brushing the damp glass where the spill still clung.

She listened as Elwyna began to explain. "The eclipse is on the 28th of July, starting at half past eight in the morning. We must have everything, and Darnell, in place by nine forty-seven, when it reaches its maximum. The power will be at its strongest then."

She looked around the group. Farran noticed a flicker of tension pass between Daryll and Tom, an unspoken message that made her heart skip.

"What... what is it?" she asked, her voice low.

The two men exchanged a glance, and Elwyna sighed softly.

"It's not that straightforward. Things can go wrong."

Farran's stomach clenched. A chill slid down her spine despite the warmth of the room. Her fingers curled tighter around her damp glass.

"The alignment is fragile," Elwyna continued. "If we're off by even a minute, or if someone resists, it could all come undone."

The men looked down, hands twitching with restless energy.

"But we've got this," Elwyna said quickly, her voice steadying. "The spells are ready. I have all the ingredients."

She smiled in reassurance, though her eyes glimmered with weariness. Farran nodded slowly. Part of her wanted to believe every word, to cling to that calm certainty. But outside, the moon and sun raced toward each other, and inside her, hope and fear warred. She hoped Elwyna was right. Because if not, what would become of the future?

31

The Final Days (1593)

We had done everything we could: Wynn's charms, the escape route, the warnings. The sense of safety remained brittle. With Sam's return came news of the Master's release and the return of Miles's ambition.

I had seen little of Miles. Whatever he planned, he kept close. I tried to track his movements: watching from corners, listening behind doors. Yet it was as if he always stayed one step ahead. He moved like a man whose secrets might kill.

"Watch yourselves," I told Davy as we sat by the fire. Its warmth offered little comfort. "That scoundrel is up to something. I have not yet figured out what."

Davy nodded slowly. "Aye. Since Sam brought word of the Master's release, I have noticed him watching us. Mostly Wynn."

Right on cue, Wynn entered the room. Her posture stiffened at the mention of her name. She looked more worn than I had ever seen her. The end could not come soon enough, for any of us, but especially for her.

"Tom was just saying Miles is acting strangely," Davy said with a sigh.

"Mmm." Wynn frowned. "He cornered me the other day, asking about the children: when I taught them, when we played. It were… creepy." She shivered and wrapped her arms around herself.

"Just be careful," I said, uneasiness crawling up my spine like ivy.

"Oh," she added, rummaging in her pocket. "I made one of these for you."

She handed me a small white pouch, tied with twine. It smelled strongly of crushed herbs and something sharp, perhaps rosemary, but the moment I tucked it into my tunic, a strange calm washed over me. Beneath the calming scent was something else: something like woodsmoke and old earth. I wondered what spell she had stitched into its seams.

"It will protect you," she said. "I have made one for each of us, and for Anne."

Her name lodged in my chest. I had seen her in a dream, her voice like smoke, whispering my name from somewhere I could not reach. I blinked it away.

"How is Anne?" I asked, though the question tore at something in me. We had not spoken in weeks: only stolen glances, the ghost of a smile when we passed. I knew why. I understood. Still, it did not stop the ache.

Wynn offered a wry smile. "She is safe. To keep her that way, you must stay away."

Her tone stung more than I expected. I had done what was asked, keeping my distance, loving her from a ghost's length away.

"Yes," I replied curtly. The silence that followed pressed in too thick.

"The Whitsun service is this Sunday," Davy said, trying to cut the tension.

"Think the Master will be back in time for that?"

"Sam could not say, only that it is soon," I answered.

"I will escort Anne and the children there," Wynn murmured, sinking into a chair beside the table. She rested her head in her hands. Her eyes were half-lidded, her movements slow: an exhaustion I had never seen take her before.

I studied her for a long moment. Magic took its toll, even on the strongest, even on Wynn. And now, more than ever, we needed her to stay strong. I bid them goodnight and stepped into the dark. That was when I saw it: a shadow slipping from the house, quiet as breath, gliding across the courtyard. I froze, heart thudding, and watched.

A figure emerged, cloaked in the hush of night. Miles. I hung back and watched as he made his way toward the stables. Careful not to be seen, I followed at a distance. At the stable entrance, a smaller figure stepped out: one of the hands. But he did not lead out a horse. Instead, they stood together, talking in low, urgent tones.

"I 'eard them say something about a warning from the sky, coming soon," the boy said.

"Do you know why they were talking about that?" Miles's voice carried through the stillness.

"Somethin' about it being time to go. I didn't understand the words. Just nonsense." The boy shrugged.

"Good work," Miles said, slipping him a silver coin that caught the moonlight.

The boy snatched it eagerly and darted back inside. I memorised his face. If things went wrong, I would know where to begin. Rage twisted in my gut. I wanted to punish the boy, to strike. But I forced the fury down. My breath hissed between clenched teeth; a growl caught at the edge of my throat.

I followed Miles back to the house. He went to the study, poured himself a drink, and settled into a chair. A low chuckle rumbled from him, dark and satisfied. I had sworn to Anne, to Wynn, to myself, that I would not act out of vengeance. But if I had to break that vow, even once more, to rid us of this monster, I would do it gladly.

* * *

The days rolled on. We sat, just as we had at Christmas, in the little chapel.

"Dear brothers and sisters," the vicar began, his voice gentle yet firm, "on this blessed day of Whitsunday, we gather to celebrate the wondrous gift of the Holy Spirit, that divine light which shineth upon our souls, as surely as the sun riseth in the heavens. Yet even as we speak of light, we must not forget that even the sun, in all its splendour, may be veiled for a season, as when a shadow passeth over it."

My attention caught on the words. We were mere days away from ending our torment at Coeur House. I closed my eyes and let the rhythm of his voice wash over me.

"For when the Spirit cometh upon us, it pierceth through the shadows of doubt, just as the sun breaketh through a clouded sky. Even in the darkest hour, when all light seemeth lost, it is but a passing moment. The Spirit shall return, and with it, the light."

I opened my eyes and looked across the chapel. Anne sat motionless, her gaze fixed on the altar as the vicar prepared the sacrament. There it was, the reminder I needed. The promise. We would be fine. Our future, somehow, would be secured.

"Amen."

I had not meant to say it aloud, but it felt right.

Through veiled eyes, I watched as Anne rose to receive the body and blood. She was smiling. Had she read the same signs I had? Had she, too, found hope in the vicar's words? Her gaze drifted across the pews, calm, searching, and for the briefest moment, our eyes met. Then she turned away and returned to her seat. My heart pounded as I stepped forward, receiving the communion bread and wine with trembling hands. The taste lingered on my lips like a seal: sacred and final.

The countdown had begun.

* * *

Sam had left early the next morning to meet the Master, whose return was now only hours away.

"Is there any way he can be stalled?" Davy asked, pacing across the cottage floor. Each step groaned against the old boards, revealing which ones had been disturbed.

I had prayed for a storm to keep the Master at bay, but the skies offered nothing.

"Barring a miracle," I said, shaking my head.

He cursed under his breath.

"Lover," Wynn chided gently, offering a small smile without pausing her writing. Her quill moved steadily across the weathered pages of a thick book.

"How is Celia doing?" I asked, hoping to shift the mood. The Master's return was my burden to bear.

"She's doing well. A natural," Wynn replied, still writing. "I need to finish a few more spells for her, and then all shall be in readiness."

She laid down her quill, blew softly across the ink, and closed the book with reverence. Her fingers gently soothed the leather cover.

"There's only one task left," she said, turning to Davy. "I need a clean circle of grass near the break in the wall, and these buried beneath it."

She held out two small glass jars. Inside was a strange assortment: a sprig of jasmine, a shard of glass, a raven's feather, salt, and a red liquid as dark as blood.

"Aye," Davy said, taking the jars. He stepped outside, and I followed as he moved through the garden toward the gap in the stone wall.

There was an eerie stillness in the air as we reached the spot. Davy knelt, gently placing the jars on the ground. From his pocket, he pulled out a length of twine.

"Tom, grab a good-sized twig," he said, holding his hands apart to show the length, "and a sharp stone."

I headed toward the trees and found a sturdy, crooked stick, then scoured the ground until I spotted a jagged stone. I brought them back quickly. Davy tied one end of the twine to the stick and hammered it into the ground with the stone. He gave it a firm tug and nodded in approval. Then he tied the stone to the other end of the twine and began to walk the perimeter, dragging it in a slow arc to carve out a circle in the earth. The line was crude but clear. Soon, he lifted a section of grass and dug a hollow with his hands.

"Pass a jar, Tom."

I handed him one. He placed it gently in the hole and pressed the grass back over it, patting the earth down. Then he moved to the opposite edge of the circle and buried the second jar in the same way.

Wynn emerged from the house, her steps slow as she paced along the wall. Her eyes scanned the stonework until they settled on something. She placed a small stone atop the wall and made her way over to us.

"That's perfect, my love," she said, kissing Davy softly. Then she pulled a folded piece of parchment from her pocket, unfurled it, and began to read in silence. Her eyes shimmered faintly, catching the light or something else.

Once completed, we returned to the cottage and sat in quiet contemplation, each lost in thought about what the next three days would bring; the final days of May. Wynn sighed and shuffled to the edge of her chair, bracing herself to rise.

"I had forgotten, I must see Anne," she murmured.

"It can wait until the morrow," Davy said gently but firmly. "You'll be too exhausted when the time comes."

She looked at him, caught in a silent struggle with herself, before finally sinking back down.

"Aye, we have time," she whispered, her eyes already closing.

We left her in peace and stepped outside into the fresh evening air. The sky still held the pale light that heralded summer's approach. As we paced the garden, a stillness settled over everything.

"I cannot restrain her," Davy said, his voice quivering beneath the weight of his fears. "I have bid her take heed, yet she heeds me not."

I placed a hand on his back.

"Come, you need rest too," I said, gently guiding him toward the cottage.

He stopped mid-step. A breeze stirred the trees nearby.

"But what shall we encounter when we arrive?" he asked, gesturing toward the garden and the trees beyond. "It won't be like this."

I followed his gaze, letting it rest on the familiar shapes of our world, one we were preparing to leave behind. His words pricked something sharp and uncertain inside me.

"Why are you saying this, Davy?" I asked, though I feared the answer.

His breath quickened.

"Wynn's told me of her visions," he said. "The future is filled with noise, strange carriages made of metal, people wearing clothes in every colour and style. The noise,"

His voice faltered.

My breath caught. I hadn't truly imagined what lay beyond the spell, only that it was away from here: safer, new.

"But we have to do this," I said quietly. "We have no future here."

He ran a hand through his hair, letting it fall limply by his side. Neither of us spoke again as we returned to the cottage, the weight of silence between us.

My mind reeled. What lay ahead? It was unreal, stranger than anything I could have dreamed. But the moment had come, there was no turning back now.

* * *

The next day dawned, carrying a strange blend of hope and trepidation, a day closer to the end of all they had prepared for. Wynn woke feeling unrested. *When this was over*, she thought, *I'm going to sleep for a week*, as she dragged herself from bed and left Davy gently snoring.

She slipped outside to watch the sunrise, her feet carrying her through the cool morning air to the garden's edge. She paused as the first rays of sunlight crept above the tree line, slowly flooding the garden with golden light. Birds lifted their voices in a bright morning chorus, singing a welcome to the new day.

Wandering among dew-touched flowers, Wynn breathed in the scent of soil and blossom, feeling some small life return to her weary limbs. She yawned and stretched, her bones protesting gently. Behind her, soft footsteps stirred the gravel. She turned to see Davy approaching, hair tousled, face still soft from sleep. She smiled at him. He smiled back.

"Mornin', my lover," she said.

"Mornin'," he echoed, pressing a kiss to her lips. "Why are you up so early?"

"I wanted to see this." She pointed to the sun, now half risen, casting a honeyed glow over the grass and stone walls.

"It is beautiful," he murmured, and they stood side by side, arms wrapped around one another, watching the garden stir to life.

After a moment, Wynn exhaled deeply.

"I must see Anne tonight," she said. "Can you keep Tom away?"

She felt him nod.

"Aye, I'll keep the rapscallion occupied," he chuckled. "I'm heading to the house now. You coming in?"

Wynn shook her head. "Not yet. I want to linger here a little longer."

Davy kissed the top of her head and walked off toward the main house, whistling a cheerful tune.

Once the sun was high in the sky, Wynn returned to the cottage and began checking everything again. She knew it was all prepared, every word, every item, every place set, but still she needed to be certain. It could not go wrong. She had come too far, sacrificed too much, for it to fail now.

The evening rushed toward her. Soon, a gentle knock echoed at the door. Wynn crossed the room to answer, her feet aching for rest. Anne stood at the threshold.

"Come on in," Wynn said, offering a warm smile.

Anne stepped inside, greeted by the soft glow of candlelight and the comforting scent of woodsmoke. She moved to a chair and sank into it, noting the dark rings beneath Wynn's eyes.

"Wynn, you look exhausted. When did you last sleep properly?"

The concern in her voice made Wynn pause.

"I don't recall," she admitted, her voice catching. "There's so much to check. It has to go right."

A rush of guilt swept through Anne. If she and Tom had not fallen in love, had not been careless, none of this would be necessary. Wynn and Davy could have lived out their days in peace.

Wynn spoke softly, as if reading her thoughts. "Our days here were numbered. The Master's dawning realisation of my magic meant it was only a matter of time." Sadness flickered in her eyes, deep and worn. It cut Anne in two. Before she could speak, Wynn rose again. The moment of vulnerability passed, replaced by her familiar resolve.

"Right, we have a few things to do before the evening's end. And I'm sure Tom is eager to get here and see you." She said briskly, laughing. "Davy's promised he won't let him."

Wynn picked up a small knife from the table and walked toward Anne, who leaned back in alarm.

"I just need a lock of your hair," Wynn said with a chuckle.

Anne relaxed as Wynn carefully snipped a small bundle from behind her ear, making sure it would stay hidden from prying eyes. She wound a strand of golden thread around it and laid it beside a sprig of rosemary, bound with red ribbon, and a shard of worn glass. She folded the pieces neatly into a soft pouch and tied it closed with a red ribbon. Anne watched in fascination.

"Your hair is your identity," Wynn said, sensing the unspoken question. "And the gold? Your soul."

How did she always know what Anne was thinking?

"The rosemary is for remembrance and protection. The mirror, worn smooth with time, represents your fractured memory. The ribbon binds life, blood, and memory."

Anne remained silent as Wynn retrieved a slip of paper and beckoned her to follow. They stepped together into the moonlit garden.

Wynn led her to the stone she had placed on the wall earlier in the week, beside the circle Davy had dug. A narrow crevice yawned in the wall. Kneeling, she shifted stone and earth with nimble fingers, placing the pouch deep in the hollow, where it would lie undisturbed for centuries, waiting for Anne to return and be made whole. Then she took the slip of paper and whispered,

"Hold thee fast, soul and name; let no shadow take thy flame."

She folded it carefully and placed it atop the pouch, then covered both with earth. She closed her eyes and knelt in silent prayer. After a long breath, she rose.

"Come, let us go inside."

Before they could move, Davy appeared from the cottage, striding toward them with a wave. Without warning, Wynn collapsed; a soft whimper escaped her lips as she crumpled to the ground.

"Wynn!" Davy shouted as he sprinted toward her.

Anne stood frozen, her heart pounding, uncertain what to do. By the time she gathered her wits, Davy had already lifted Wynn into his arms and was carrying her toward the cottage, murmuring her name. He laid her gently on the bed and pulled the blanket up around her shoulders. In the kitchen, Anne paced in quiet circles. Wynn murmured something incoherent; her breath caught in her throat.

"Rest, my love," Davy whispered, pressing a gentle kiss to her forehead before turning away.

In the kitchen, Anne's voice met him, low and strained.

"Is she all right?"

"She will be," he said, though the words felt hollow with the eclipse only hours away. "She just needs rest."

Anne nodded, though her expression remained troubled.

"I'll go; leave you to take care of her."

She moved toward the door, her footsteps hushed. Davy watched her leave, then returned to Wynn's side. With a sigh, he extinguished the candles, letting the room settle into a hush of shadow, and slipped into sleep beside her.

* * *

Anne returned to the house. Everything was moving too quickly. Celia, who had been watching the children in Anne's absence, greeted her in the library.

"Mistress," she said with a curtsy.

"Celia," Anne smiled. "How have they been?"

"They have behaved well," she replied. "Young Nathaniel has done a bit of teasing, that is all."

"Nat, be kind to your sisters," Anne said, gently chiding.

He ran over and hugged her. She wrapped her arms around him, holding him close. In all the planning and preparation, she had forgotten how little time she had left with them. Her heart ached at the thought of leaving and wished, more than anything, that she could take them with her. The girls, not wanting to be left out, hurried over to join the hug. Anne laughed.

"Oh my, this is lovely," she said, holding them closer.

"Come, let's share a favourite story before bed."

The children began whispering among themselves, debating which tale to choose. Anne and Celia watched, smiling.

"I hear you've been learning from Wynn," Anne said softly, turning to her.

Celia looked momentarily startled, then nodded.

"She's a good woman," Anne added. She hesitated. "May I ask something of you?"

Celia met her gaze, attentive.

"Will you watch over them?" Anne asked, nodding toward the children, who were still squabbling good-naturedly over their choice. Their voices rose in playful protest.

"Of course, Mistress," Celia said with warmth, nodding once.

Anne felt her shoulders ease.

"Thank you," she whispered, emotion catching in her voice.

She crossed to the children and picked up a worn book.

"Come, let us read this together."

She settled into her usual chair while the children gathered around.

"*In the shadowed bounds of Sylvemere,*" she began, her voice low and melodic, "*where the air is ever thick with enchantment, the noble Faerie Queen did charge her true knight...*"

"*Sir Elion!*" the girls squealed in unison.

Anne laughed with them, her face softening.

"That is right, *Sir Elion, who must seek out the fell dragon Virelith, whose fiery breath laid waste to field and fountain.*"

She drew a deep breath and blew out a great huff of pretend fire, sending the girls into fits of shrieking laughter as they ducked and covered their heads. She read in playful voices, laughter rising with every page, their joy tumbling into the quiet corners of the room.

When the story was done, she tucked them into bed one by one, kissing each brow and whispering goodnight. A prayer lingered in her heart as she closed the door.

I pray you keep them safe, Lord.

She drew a steady breath and walked to her room, a hush of calm settling around her.

32

The Bait is Set (2018)

Darnell sulked in his apartment, slouched in a worn armchair. A radio burbled in the background, but he barely registered the sound. Time was drawing close; soon, he'd have to become Richard again. And he was no closer to convincing Farran she belonged with him. He grimaced, replaying the disaster of opening day. Why had he acted like such a fool? He should have shown her how much he needed her, no, loved her. His wife, after all. The fear in her eyes had been real. He shoved it aside. She would come around. She had to. He could make her love him. She was his Anne. His phone rang. He snatched it up.

"Hey," Simon's voice came through, cautious.

"Simon," Darnell replied flatly. "What can I do for you?"

A sigh. "You said to let you know if I heard anything."

"Mmm."

"Well... they went to Coeur House the other day. Did the usual tour, then headed to that old cottage. Dug something up in the garden."

That got his attention. Darnell sat up straighter.

"What did they find?"

Simon hesitated. "Not sure exactly. But they were careful. Secretive. Thought you'd want to know." He added it quickly, eager to prove his worth.

"Appreciate it. And for clearing out those jars from Farran's house, I'll send your payment."

It was soon. She'd be gone if he didn't act now.

He ended the call, slipped the phone back into his pocket, and began pacing. Think. Think. What could he do... The phone buzzed again. He pulled it out and froze. Farran's number lit the screen. He inhaled, smoothed his expression, and answered.

"Farran," he drawled. "It's lovely to hear from you."

"Hi, Darnell." Her voice drifted through the line. He felt the tension in his shoulders ease.

"I'm so glad you rang. I wanted to apologise for my behaviour the other day; it was unforgivable." He smiled, pleased with his own sincerity. She must understand; he couldn't help it. She made him feel that way.

"I appreciate the apology," Farran replied, her skin crawling at the memory.

"What can I do for you?" he asked, keeping his tone light.

She hesitated. Then, steadying her voice, "Would you like to meet up?"

His heart leapt. Finally, an opportunity to show her the truth.

"That would be delightful. Where?"

A pause.

"Coeur House," Farran said, her voice firm. "You spoke so much about it: I want to know more."

Darnell's eyes gleamed. He could end this. Take her home.

"Of course. When?"

"Saturday?" she offered.

The eclipse. Perfect.

"Sounds perfect. I'll meet you there."

"Great. Shall we say nine?"

"Sure," he said smoothly.

The line went dead.

Farran lowered the phone and turned to Elwyna.

"Do you think he believed it?"

Elwyna smirked. "He hasn't a clue."

Back in his apartment, Darnell slipped the phone into his pocket and smiled to himself. This was his chance to show her how things were done and that she belonged to him.

33

The Fall (1593)

I awoke to a commotion, disoriented and unsure of where I was. My eyes drifted to the empty wall where my portrait had once hung. Two days to go, my mind reminded me. I forced myself upright, focusing on whatever had disturbed my sleep. Outside, the thunder of hooves pounded against the gravel. Shouts echoed through the courtyard. Then came the Master's voice, sharp and commanding:

"Where's Miles?"

The question hit hard. Once, it would have been me he called for.

I scrambled from bed, pulling on the clothes I had discarded the night before, and raced out into the courtyard. Chaos churned around me. The stable hand I had seen with Miles was already tending the Master's horse. I clenched my jaw, a growl rising low in my throat. The Master swept into the house. I followed quickly, catching up to him near the study.

"Sir, it is good to have you home," I said.

He turned. His face was pale, drawn, haunted by the Tower.

"Thomas."

I bowed, as I used to when he entertained guests and I served as his amusement.

"Not now," he snapped. "Have you seen Miles?"

"No, sir. But I can go and find him."

"Hmm." He turned and stormed into the study, the door slamming behind him.

Inside, I could hear the clatter of bottles and furious muttering. Not so perfect, your Miles, I thought bitterly, and went in search of the thorn in my side. I found him in quiet conversation with the stable hand. They fell silent as I approached.

"Good job," Miles murmured to the boy, who quickly vanished.

"Thomas," he said, strolling toward me with casual arrogance, hands tucked in his pockets. "What can I do for you?"

"The Master is back. He is asking for you," I replied stiffly.

"My thanks. I shall attend to him now." He sauntered across the courtyard, completely unbothered.

He'll pay, I thought. Somehow, I'll find a way. I went to find Davy. He was in the yard, hammering a broken slat back into a fence panel.

"Davy," I called.

He turned and smiled. "Come and hold this for me."

I stepped forward and held the panel steady.

"The Master is back," I said quietly.

"Mmm. I heard the commotion," Davy replied, his hammer striking true with each blow.

"We need Anne safe," I whispered.

"Mmhm."

We both turned at the sound of movement. The stable hand again: lingering nearby. My blood surged. I was ready to go to him, to finish what I should have done long ago. But Davy reached out and laid a hand on my arm. He shook his head. I growled but turned back to the slat.

"He would deserve it," I muttered.

"He would," Davy agreed, matching my tone. "But he is not important now."

Reluctantly, I nodded. We finished the job in silence, then walked off together toward the garden wall.

* * *

"Now that the Master is home, nothing is stopping Miles from carrying out his retribution," I said, agitation sharpening my voice.

Davy and Wynn sat in silence. Wynn, though still pale, looked better after a full night's rest: her collapse now just a shadow on her face.

"Can we get her away before Thursday?" she asked quietly.

"Where would she go?" Davy replied. "This would be the first place the Master would look."

We were silenced by the conundrum. Then something struck me.

"We could always hold a secret vigil."

They turned to look at me, confusion flickering in their eyes.

"I could hide under her bed," I said, half-grinning despite myself. "Perhaps she could instruct that only Celia be allowed to tend her."

Davy rubbed his chin, considering.

"It could work."

Wynn nodded slowly.

"I can try to speak with her quietly when we are out in the garden with the children."

We exchanged a look, a quiet agreement passing between us.

* * *

I lay in the dark space beneath Anne's bed. She had agreed to the plan without hesitation, eager to be close again, even in silence. Celia entered the room to tend to her.

"*She has learnt so much already,*" Wynn had said earlier, her voice bright with pride. "*She's going to be a great asset to the legacy.*"

I had had my doubts. She seemed so young to bear such responsibility. But Wynn had only smiled.

"She knows what to do. She will soften the Master's heat and ensure he forgets in time."

Her confidence had comforted me. And now, watching Celia move around the bedchamber with steady purpose, fully aware I was there but giving no sign, I knew Wynn had been right to trust her.

Celia blew out the candle and walked towards the door.

"Good night, Miss."

"Thank you, Celia. Good night."

The door closed, and we were alone. I lay on my back, staring up at the underside of the bed. I could see the slight dip in the mattress above me, the soft outline of where Anne lay.

"How do you know the Master will not go into her tonight? He has been away from her for months," Davy had asked earlier.

"If I know the Master, and I do, he will be too busy catching up on what he has missed. I saw what became of Mistress Margaret when he lost interest," I had told him, trying to sound certain, though my voice shook with the memory.

Now, lying here in the hush of the dark, doubt crept in. But I pushed it aside.

"Tom," Anne whispered, her voice a thread of sound in the quiet.

"Shhh," I breathed. I reached up from beneath the bed and found her hand. I held it gently for a moment, just long enough for her to know I was there.

Content, she rolled away, and I listened as her breathing softened into sleep.

* * *

Bang!

The bedroom door slammed open, jolting me from restless slumber. Damn, I had not meant to drift off. I froze, barely breathing. I heard Anne gasp in shock. Feet appeared beside the bed. I lay still, heart pounding, then snapped to my senses. Silently, I rolled to the far side and crawled out just in time to see Miles grab Anne by the arm and yank her from the bed.

"Come on, witch sympathiser," he growled, a twisted smile spreading across his face. "You're going to get what you deserve."

I tried to rise, but my limbs were stiff from the cramped hiding place. A groan escaped me as I lay by the bedside. Miles turned, his eyes narrowing.

"I knew you would be here," he spat. His features contorted, growing more animal with every word.

Before I could think, I launched myself across the bed. I hit the floor with a thud and reached for the dagger tucked at my belt. My fingers found the hilt; I drew it and drove it into his leg. He let out a furious howl, staggering back, releasing his grip on Anne.

"Anne, run!" I shouted, struggling to stand.

Miles regained himself just enough to land a brutal kick into my ribs. The wind exploded from my lungs. Anne bolted from the room. I watched through watering eyes as she vanished into the corridor. Another blow sent stars flashing across my vision. I collapsed, unable to move, gasping for air. Miles limped after her, snarling as he disappeared. I prayed she had made it far enough.

Eventually, I dragged myself to my feet and stumbled to the door. No sign of either of them. I made my way down the stairs and into the blackness outside. My eyes adjusted slowly.

Then...

A scream. From above.

"Anne!" I cried, looking up into the night.

Three figures stood silhouetted on the roof.

"Anne!" I shouted again, my voice hoarse with desperation.

Another scream tore through the air, and panic surged through me. God, please, no. A scuffle, a grunt, then a final, blood-curdling cry. A figure fell from the rooftop, limbs flailing, hair streaming behind her.

"Anne, no!"

The Master's voice rang out from above, raw and broken. He reached out far too late, his hands grasping empty air. She hit the ground with a sickening crack. Her body lay twisted and still beneath the stars. I ran to her, dropping to my knees, hands trembling as I touched her cheek, still warm but smeared with blood. Tears streamed down my face, mixing with the dirt and the dark. Davy appeared beside me, a sheet clutched in his hands.

"Tom, come on. We need to get her to Wynn. She'll know what to do."

Together, we rolled Anne's lifeless form onto the cloth and carried her into the shadows.

* * *

How could this have happened? Wynn steadied herself, her hands trembling as she laid them on Anne's broken limbs. Candlelight flickered around them. The air was thick with the scent of earth and blood. She bent close, voice low and steady as she began to speak:

"Bones may break and blood may flow,

But spirit's light shall ever glow.

By earth's deep strength and water's grace,

I bind thee now in healing's place.

Not whole restored, but safe and still,

'Til time's veil bends to thy will.

Through shadow's gate and fleeting breath,

I guard thy soul from certain death.

Rise not yet in body's might,

But live to see the morrow's light."

When the last word faded, Wynn stood still, looking down at Anne. Then the tears she had been holding back began to fall quietly, steadily, and unstoppable. She wrapped Anne tightly in the sheet, binding broken limbs with care and hope.

I looked up as Wynn entered the kitchen.

"She's resting," she said, her voice raw. "But we'll have to move her somewhere safe. They'll come looking for the body."

I shuddered, unable to form a single coherent thought.

Davy spoke first. "There's the crypt in the chapel. They won't look for her there."

I nodded, though I hated the thought of her being alone in that cold place.

"Come on," I said, rising stiffly. My ribs still ached from Miles' boot.

We moved silently, carrying Anne through the shadows as the house behind us erupted into frantic motion.

Miles' voice cut through the night: "Search everywhere!"

We pressed ourselves into the dark, watching as a small figure, one of the younger servants, scurried toward the woods. When it was clear, we continued. The chapel door creaked open. A musty dampness clung to the air, the scent of stone and death. At the back of the chapel, we found an empty casket. We gently laid Anne inside. It was a snug fit.

"I'll stay with her for a while," I said quietly. I couldn't bear to leave her yet.

Davy nodded. He was already anxious to return to Wynn.

I sat alone beside her.
    And I prayed.

I hadn't prayed since I was a boy, back when I went to mass with my mother more from duty than faith. Raised Catholic under Henry's reign, I had long seen religion as a dangerous idea, too tangled in power and punishment to offer peace. But now, as I looked at her still form in the flickering candlelight, I didn't care about politics or fear or history.
    If God was listening, I needed him now.

* * *

They stood on the rooftop, wind whispering in their ears, Richard unable to tear his eyes away from Anne's broken body below. His breath came ragged, panicked. He hadn't caught her.

Her face.

The scream.

That god-awful crack as she hit the ground.

It played over and over.

She still hadn't moved.

"Good riddance to the witch sympathiser," Miles cackled. "That's one less in the world, hey?"

Richard turned slowly. A red mist clouded his vision.

"You've killed her," he hissed through clenched teeth.

He rose to his full height and strode toward Miles, face contorted with rage and grief. Miles blinked, confused.

"I thought that was what you wanted," he said, voice rising. "She was a witch lover, filth. That's what you said."

"I wasn't ready," Richard stammered. "I could have convinced her."

He broke off, hiding his face in his hands. A low cry escaped him.

"The children, they adore her."

I adore her, he admitted to himself, too late. He stood there, grief and guilt wrapped tight around him, suffocating.

After a long silence, he whispered, "Go. Lay her in her room." Then, sharper, "Find that fool and his cronies. They'll pay for this."

He turned and stumbled down the stairs, dragging himself to the study. There, he grabbed a decanter, poured a glass, and downed it in one savage gulp. He poured another and slumped into the chair behind his desk. Grief and hatred warred inside him. Darkness rose to meet them. And Richard let it in.

***

The scream shattered the silence, deafening and ear-piercing.

For a moment, Anne didn't know where it had come from. Then the horrifying truth struck: it was her own voice. Darkness pressed in, thick and suffocating. She was not alone. A steady breath sounded beside her. Warm fingers gently closed around her own.

Tom's voice emerged from the shadows, soft but urgent.

"It's alright. Not long now."

Pain throbbed through her legs, sharp, deep, unbearable. She tried to move but found herself wedged tightly in a narrow space.

"You can't move," Tom said gently, though his tone was firm. "Your legs... they're too badly damaged."

Panic surged, squeezing the breath from her lungs like a vice.

"We're going to help, but you have to keep still," he coaxed. "Trust me. Please."

Something in his voice, that steady urgency, steadied her. What had happened? Her memory was fractured, drifting... an attack from behind, a sudden shove, and then the fall. So far. So fast.

"I have to leave you for a while," Tom whispered close to her ear. "But I'll be back. I promise."

A soft kiss touched her forehead.

"I love you."

Then came footsteps on stone, echoing, fading into silence. The darkness returned. Heavy. Alone. Panic clawed at her again, rising like a tide. But those last words, whispered and tender, gave her something to hold on to.
   "I love you too," she breathed. Barely audible.

The pain crescendoed, swelling beyond reason, until the world slipped away into quiet oblivion.

* * *

In the weathered cottage nestled at the edge of the dark wood, we gathered in tense discussion, voices low but urgent.

"Anne can't take much more," I said, my voice edged with desperation. "The longer we delay, the slimmer her chances."

Wynn stood still, her brown woollen dress falling from neck to toe like a cloak of gravity.

"It won't be long now," she said, her eyes flickering with cautious hope. "The spell will hold. The Master will believe she's dead. Then we can move her safely to the ring."

Davy placed a hand on my shoulder, offering a faint, grounding smile.

"She'll make it," he said with quiet conviction. "But the timing must be exact."

My expression twisted with anguish, but I nodded.

"I know. I just... I want this nightmare to end. None of us is safe until it's done. He'll hunt us down. I should know."

"Come, sit by the fire," Davy urged gently. "You're exhausted."

"I have to get back to her," I said, eyes darting toward the door.

"You need to conserve your strength," Wynn said firmly, though her tone held warmth. "The journey ahead will be treacherous. You'll need every ounce of your wits to see it through."

She guided me to a sturdy wooden chair by the open hearth. I sank, the heat of the fire crackling around me. A rich aroma drifted from the pot of vegetables bubbling gently above the flames. Closing my eyes, I let the sounds and scents settle around me. The hush before the storm.

34

The Eclipse (2018 & 1593)

Tom had wished to be closer.

"*No,*" she had told him, catching the flicker of panic in his eyes. "*He needs to think I am alone.*"

She reached into her pocket, fingers brushing the memory pouch.

"*I have this. And Elwyna has protected me, too.*"

His face, still taut with worry, softened into a small smile. He nodded. She stepped forward and kissed him: a kiss that lingered, warm and steady, grounding them both in the fragile hope that, soon, the future they had once dreamed of might finally begin. He watched her as she turned and walked back toward the house.

Left in the quiet garden beside the old cottage, Tom stood in stillness. Elwyna and Daryll waited silently at his side.

"She will be fine," Elwyna said gently, her certainty offering him the thinnest thread of comfort.

She checked her watch, then looked to the sky.

"It is starting. We will not have much longer now."

Together, they turned and walked toward the shimmering ring of grass: the place where past and future would meet one last time.

Farran reached the fountain and stood alone, her eyes fixed on the gate. Somewhere beyond the hedgerow, the eclipse had already begun. And soon, he would come.

Darnell saw her standing alone by the fountain and let out a long, relieved sigh. He had half-expected to see that fool lurking nearby, protective and possessive.

But she was alone.

Her back was to him, and when she heard his footsteps, she turned. A smile hovered on her lips. She looked radiant. He smiled back. The tension melted from his shoulders, replaced by a smug, self-satisfied warmth that settled in his gut. He reached out and gently lifted her hand to his lips. Farran resisted the urge to recoil. Instead, her smile held steady, composed.

"I did think you wouldn't come," he drawled. The sound of his voice made her stomach flip.

He was still holding her hand. She let him. She needed him to believe Anne intended to return with him.

"Of course I'm here," she said. "We have so much to talk about."

"Shall we walk the grounds while we talk?" he offered, gesturing ahead with his free arm.

Farran nodded, her other hand brushing the pouch tucked in her coat pocket. They walked in silence, hand in hand. Few people were out this early, and the world around them was quiet: too quiet. Above them, the sky had begun to change. A shadow crept slowly across the sun.

"We're going to have a happy life together," Darnell said, his gaze sweeping the grounds. "I promise I will look after you. It will not be like before."

He smiled again, a warm, wistful thing that made her skin crawl. Did he really believe what he was saying? A monster like that could never change. Farran smiled, measured and calm.

"Let's head to the old cottage," she said casually. "The garden is lovely."

Darnell nodded without hesitation. Farran's heartbeat quickened. This was too easy. She had expected resistance.

Still hand in hand, they walked the familiar path. The cottage came into view, its crooked charm unchanged. They moved around to the back garden. Darnell was still talking, promising an impossible life. He seemed to know exactly where she wanted him to go.

Above them, the sky continued to darken. Birdsong fell quiet. The air stilled. And the eclipse deepened.

Tom saw them, hand in hand, walking toward the gap in the wall where he and the others lay hidden. He flinched. Daryll reached out and steadied him, placing a hand on his arm.

"He can't know we're here, remember," he whispered.

Tom stilled, though every muscle was a coil ready to spring.

The sun was vanishing faster now, consumed by the moon as Darnell and Farran approached the ring of darkened grass. Finally, they stepped through the gap. Farran's glance flicked downward, catching the eyes of her hidden friends. Darnell didn't notice. His focus was fixed on the ring. On the thought of home.

Farran's steps faltered. Darnell sensed it instantly.

"My darling, what is it?"

His voice softened, but there was fear in it. He had feared this: her sudden hesitation, her reluctance to leave this life behind. But surely she must see... he could offer so much more. He looked up. The sun was seconds from full eclipse.

"No," Farran whispered, almost imperceptibly.

He gripped her hand tighter. "We have to go."

And then, Tom struck.

A flash of movement, and Darnell was thrown to the ground. His arms and legs flailed in surprise as Tom crashed into him, fists striking. Farran fell too, scrambling backwards on the grass, away from the struggle. She watched, wide-eyed, as Tom straddled Darnell, striking him with the weight of lost years.

Daryll's voice rang out from the stillness.

"Tom! Get out of there!"

Tom looked back, and in that instant, Darnell landed a heavy punch, knocking Tom farther into the ring. Farran screamed as a hand grasped her ankle. Darnell's fingers, sticky with blood, dragged her toward the centre of the circle. She writhed, kicking, struggling, but the grip was relentless. Then Daryll was there; he seized her arms and yanked her away with all his strength. They tumbled backwards, gasping for breath.

Elwyna stepped forward. Her voice rose into the gathering dark:
"By starlight cast and candle's gleam,
I call thee out from borrowed dream.
Thou who wear'st another age;
Be gone, return, unbind thy cage."

"No!" Farran cried, twisting in Daryll's grip. "Elwyna, stop!"

But she didn't. She couldn't. The spell had begun. If Darnell stayed, all would be lost. And if Tom was caught in the ring... Then so be it.
"With rue and rosemary I trace
Thy steps across both time and place.
Thy name I speak, thy power I break,
No longer shall the present quake.

As sun is swallowed by the shade,
The time is ripe, the price is paid.
Thy shadow cast, thy truth revealed,
The sky's dark eye becomes unsealed.

Return, return through waning light,
Be gone before the sun burns bright."

Tom and Darnell still struggled, twisting in the glowing grass. Farran screamed again, Daryll holding her back with all his strength.

Elwyna's voice soared. The final lines roared against the wind.
"In earth and air, in flame and flood,

I wash thee from the living blood.
Thy path unwinds, the veil now thin;
Let old world take thee back within.

Turn, turn, O shadowed man,
Walk backward now from where began.
Be bound to thine own time and tide,
Where no false face nor form may hide.

Yet mercy stays my guiding hand;
I bless thee too, as fate hath planned.
May truth unmask thee, dark undone,
And cleanse thy soul 'fore day is won.

So I do seal with silvered breath,
This charm of life, not spell of death.
By elder craft and heart held true;
Depart, and let the light renew.
So mote it be."

Sparks flew from Elwyna's fingertips, arcing outward in every direction. The darkness lit with sudden flashes, searing bright. A low rumble shook the ground.

Then louder.

Louder.

CRACK!

A blinding flash exploded across the ring.

Thunder shattered the silence.

Farran and Daryll turned away, shielding their eyes from the blaze.

Then...

silence.

∗ ∗ ∗

We had kept ourselves out of sight since that awful night, hiding in a derelict barn, near enough to the chapel to tend to Anne, but far enough from the cottage that we would not be found.

"Only one more night," Wynn murmured to herself as she bustled about, her voice heavy. "We shall be free by then."

Davy walked over, intending to comfort her, but she gently pushed him away, lost in her thoughts and tasks. He retreated to the corner of the barn and settled himself on a bale of straw, picking up a flat slab and began scraping away at it. I entered, feeling the tension coil in the air.

"How is she?" Wynn asked without looking up.

"Sleeping. The lotion for the pain you gave me seems to be working," I replied, lowering myself onto another bale and watching Davy's work.

"What have you got there?" I asked.

Davy paused, lifting the slab so I might see the letters carved into the stone:
'Anne, Wynn, Thomas, Davy — 1593'

"Something to remember us by when we are gone," he said simply, then returned to his work, making our names stand proud and immortalised.

I nodded, a lump rising in my throat.

"That is a great idea. Perhaps we might even find it in the future."

A wry smile played at the corners of his lips.

Just then, Celia appeared in the doorway, her silhouette haloed by the evening light. Wynn looked up at once and welcomed her inside.

"How are things?" Wynn asked, concern softening her voice.

"There is such melancholy in the house," Celia said, stepping inside. "The Master sits in the study, drinking and muttering, while Miles is still searching; he is looking for her body, and for you." Her voice dropped to a hush, filled with sorrow.

"I cannot believe it is nearly here," she whispered, her voice catching. "I do not know what I will do when you are all gone."

"You will be fine," Wynn said, drawing her into a quick but heartfelt hug.

Celia held her close for a moment longer.

"You have taught me more than anyone ever has. I will carry it on: everything - the garden, the learning, the care. I promise."

Wynn nodded, brushing a hand gently down Celia's arm before releasing her.

Davy stood abruptly, lifting the slab.

"I am going to place this by the cottage."

"Davy, it is too dangerous," Wynn warned, her heart thudding in her ears.

"I am going," he said firmly, already moving.

"I will go after him," I said, hurrying out into the crisp evening.

I caught sight of Davy striding purposefully toward the woods and jogged to catch up.

We walked in silence to the gap in the wall. He took out his penknife and knelt to cut away a patch of grass just large enough to cradle the slab. He pressed it into the soil with the flat of his foot, grounding it. Then he sat beside it, elbows on his knees, his head resting in his hands. I sank next to him, watching the moonlight filter through the leaves.

Somewhere far above, the sky was beginning to change. The moon's slow dance was already underway.

"We will never forget," I said softly.

We did not speak again for some time. We just sat, the weight of tomorrow pressing down around us. Then it was time to make our way back to the shed, keeping to the shadow of the trees. The air was heavy, the night quiet, too quiet. Suddenly, a sharp crack echoed behind us. We froze.

I turned, heart pounding, and saw him. Miles stood barely ten feet away, dagger in hand. He grinned, feral and cruel.

"I'm glad we could do this face to face," he said, his voice low and mocking. "Stabbing you in the back would have been such a coward's way to be rid of you."

He lunged. The blade sliced clean through Davy's tunic sleeve, grazing the skin beneath. Davy reacted quickly, lashing out with a swift kick to Miles's shin. The blow knocked him off balance, halting his advance, but not for long. Miles came at him again with renewed fury, but Davy dodged, sidestepping with just enough precision to wrong-foot him. Miles stumbled.

I took the opening. Sliding between them, I raised the silver blade. Miles surged forward again, too blind with rage to see what I held. The blade met flesh with a sickening tear. He screamed, sharp and ragged.

Davy stepped in and, without hesitation, shoved his torn sleeve into Miles's open mouth to muffle the sound. I twisted the blade deeper. Hot blood spilt over my hand, soaking my grip. His eyes widened in disbelief.

With a final thrust, I drove the dagger home, the hilt pressing into his gut. His body writhed, then slumped forward, twitching. We let him drop. The earth beneath him drank the blood as life fled from his limbs.

Davy collapsed beside me, shaking. Blood splattered his arm, thankfully not his own.

"Come on," I said hoarsely. "The body must be hidden."

He nodded, still pale, still stunned.

We dragged Miles into the woods, barely speaking. A narrow ditch provided what we needed. We shoved his body in, covering it with soil, branches and leaves until nothing remained but the churned scent of disturbed earth. Then we ran.

Breathless, we hurled ourselves through the shed door. Wynn looked up, alone and wide-eyed.

"What has happened?" she cried, taking in the blood on Davy's sleeve.

"It is not mine," he said quickly, moving to calm her. "Miles followed us.

He sought to waylay us."

Wynn's face crumpled as tears spilt over.

"I fare well," Davy whispered, wrapping her tightly in his arms. "I fare well."

We sat in silence after that, shaken, grim and waiting. Waiting for tomorrow. Hoping it would come quickly. Hoping it would be enough.

* * *

The time had arrived. As the skies darkened, we carefully carried Anne, still drifting in and out of consciousness, towards the ring of grass. It shimmered faintly before my eyes, and I wondered at Wynn's gift. Privileged that she cared for us all. We laid Anne gently in the centre. The three of us formed a circle around her, our hearts pounding in silent prayer. Wynn unrolled a small piece of parchment, her hands trembling only slightly.

Then we waited.
   The air stilled.
   The birds fell silent.

* * *

Richard stood among the trees, cloaked in shadow. His eyes fixed on the small group gathered in the ring.

"Anne," he breathed. His chest constricted. "She's alive."

He crept closer, lowering himself into the tall grass, heart hammering, not daring to blink.

The air shifted. Wynn lifted the parchment and began to speak, her voice strong and clear.

"By jasmine dark, I seek thy grace,
from 1593 to future's place.
Beneath the grass, beneath the earth,
I call forth, from time of birth.

Veiled of sun, and moon so gay,
Let shadow's veil take flight this day.
Glass of 1593, through time I peer,
Blood of past, I draw thee near.

From raven's wing and silver mist,
Show me the future, by time's twist.
Salt from the seas, coin of fate,
Guide me to 2017's gate.

Let the veiled shadow fall,
And carry us through time's great hall.
Not to change, but to see and learn,
The world of 2017, I yearn.

Grass of old, I call thee near,
Let thy magic last through year to year.
For if the time of shadow ends,
Bring us back, through temporal bends."

Sparks flew. Thunder cracked. The ground beneath them glowed. Richard flinched but held his position, pressed low against the grass, eyes wide.

When the lightning ceased and the thunder stilled, the ring was empty. The sun broke free once more. Birds resumed their song, sweet and serene.

The cottage stood still and waiting, silent as breath held in a chest... alone.

35

Home

Farran fell to the ground, sobbing, heartbroken and breathless, clinging to Daryll like a lifeline. A voice whispered inside her head.

"It's okay. I'm here."

New arms wrapped around her, warm and steady. She looked up into grey-green eyes: Tom. He was safe. Relief surged through her, so overwhelming it stole her breath. He held her close, his hand gently brushing her hair back, grounding her in the now.

"Come," Elwyna said urgently, her voice cutting through the moment. "The power is fading. If you want your memories, we need to act now."

Farran nodded faintly, her body still trembling. Elwyna reached into her pocket and withdrew the small pouch tied with red ribbon, along with a crumpled piece of parchment worn from time and use. She closed her eyes.

Her voice rang clear in the dimming light:
"Thread by thread, the veil I tear,
Name and soul laid true and bare.
Let time uncoil, let shadows part,

Return her name, restore her heart.
By moon's light and blood once shed,
Awake what once was thought long dead."

Sparks crackled from Elwyna's hands, leaping like fireflies toward Farran. She gasped, clutching her chest as if her heart itself had been struck. Her body bowed, breath fleeing her lungs. Tom tightened his grip, anchoring her in his arms.

Visions burst behind her eyes - thick, fast, unstoppable. Snatches of laughter, the scent of herbs, candlelight flickering in shadowed rooms...
A cottage in spring...
Anne. She was Anne.

Tom looked at Elwyna, fear edging into his expression.

"She will return," Elwyna said softly, her eyes never leaving Farran. "Be still and calm. She will return."

$* * *$

Farran slept deeply. The dream stretched on, endless and shifting.

One moment, she was at Coeur House, laughing in the garden with the children and Tom, sunlight dancing through the leaves.

Then...

Richard appeared. Fear coiled around her like smoke.
Wynn, smiling, sparkling, her eyes alive with magic.
Davy's laughter. Tom's grin.

Then...

A face twisted with malice: Miles.
Pain lanced through her body. Bright lights flashed above her.
Unfamiliar voices echoed.
"She's broken several bones... But how?"
A man in a white coat, his brow furrowed in confusion.
Wynn, no, Elwyna, stood at her side. Daryll paced behind.
Darnell leered from the shadows.
More flashes. Darkness. A bright light, searing.

Then...

She woke with a gasp, air rushing into her lungs. She was still lying on the grass, and Tom wrapped protectively around her. Elwyna was beside them, checking her pulse, brushing hair from her face with careful hands.

"How do you feel?" she asked softly.

Farran blinked, then gave the smallest of nods.

"I remember it all," she whispered. Tears spilt over her lashes, trailing down her cheeks. Tom brushed them away with the pad of his thumb, then bent to kiss her, memory and future colliding, making her whole.

No hesitation. No restraint. Only love reclaimed.

* * *

Richard awoke to the brush of a cool breeze upon his face. His head throbbed sharply as he struggled to open his eyes.

At last, he prised them open, only to be blinded by bright daylight flooding his vision. Blinking, he winced as the pain intensified. A low groan escaped him as he clutched his hair.

He realised he lay upon soft earth. The woody scent rose to his nostrils. He tried to sit, but pain forced him back down. He lay there, confused, listening to birds sing their merry greeting, utterly unaware he was the broken man on the ground.

"Master!" a soft voice called through the air.

He turned his head, the movement sending a wave of nausea through him. Through blurred sight, he made out a woman running toward him. She knelt beside him, placing a gentle hand upon his arm. No longer the timid girl who once flinched beneath his gaze, Celia's hand was steady now.

"Anne?" he whispered.

"No, Sir. It's Celia," she said, concern etched upon her delicate features.

Richard tried again to sit. His body protested with bruises and swelling, small gasps escaping cracked lips.

"Take your time, Sir," Celia said kindly.

"How did I come to be here?" he asked, looking about. The familiar woods at the edge of his estate stretched before him, ancient trees hiding secrets now beyond his reach. Behind them stood the small caretaker's cottage, still now and no longer a home. The wind whispered past, tousling his hair and easing the ache in his bones.

"How did you know I was here?"

Celia hesitated, biting her lip.

"Girl! Tell me!" he snapped, instantly regretting the flare as fresh pain coursed through him.

Celia flinched and edged back, fear growing. Richard stilled, aware of her reaction. No... this was not right. Too many times, he had seen that look. Anne, his lost wife, had carried the same fear, the same reluctance to be near him. It flashed before him: the horror of her fall, the thud of her body striking the unyielding ground. Motionless. Gone.

A sound escaped him, a groan twisting into a primal, guttural scream.

"Anne!"

Tears fell unchecked, regret and self-hate pouring from him in waves.

"Anne," he whispered again, her name fading into the breeze.

'Come, Sir," Celia said gently, her voice drawing him back. "Let us get you back to the 'ouse."

He rose slowly, unsteady. Celia steadied him, and together they walked toward the estate, leaving Darnell behind.

* * *

That evening, Richard lay on his bed, restless, alone, and guilt-ridden, as past and future memories tormented him.

Behind the dressing screen, Celia moved with quiet purpose. She had prepared for this. The window stood open beside her. From one pocket, she withdrew the crumpled parchment Wynn had given her and carefully unfurled it. A candle flickered in the corner, its flame dancing to some silent rhythm. From the other pocket came a pouch. She pulled out sprigs of rosemary, lavender, and thyme, their scents rising to meet the candle's glow and wrapping the space in a shroud of peace. A shimmering bowl of clear water rested on the sill.

Remember Wynn's words, she reminded herself: his peace is in God's hands if I get this wrong. Her hands trembled. She closed her eyes, lips moving soundlessly. When she opened them, they glowed, sparkling with hidden light.

In a low, steady voice, she read aloud:
"Ye winds that pass o'er hill and glen,
Take hence the grief that dwells within.
Let not the heart remember pain,
But find, in dreams, sweet peace again.
O gentle night, thy mercy lend,
And teach the soul its wounds to mend.
Let every sigh be tuned to sleep,
And none but quiet thoughts to keep.
As dew doth cleanse the weary leaf,
So cleanse this breast of heavy grief.
As shadows fade with morning's light,
So let these sorrows take their flight.
Be still, my soul, and trouble cease;
I summon now the gift of peace.
By moon above and earth below,
Let calm within the spirit grow.
So I do speak, with heart made free;
Let it be done. So mote it be."

As the final words left her lips, she lit the parchment. After a moment's burn, she dropped it into the water. It hissed softly, smoke spiralling through the open window. A faint glow passed from Celia across the room, settling on Richard's sleeping form. His body stilled into a restful slumber.

Silence.

* * *

In the quiet crypt beneath Coeur House, a family reunited. Stone tombs and metal plaques lined the cool, shadowed room. Names from the past lingered in silence, keepers of secrets, love, and tragedy alike.

The Stephens Family Vault

Coeur House Chapel | Est. 1471

Here lie the honoured dead of the House of Stephens.

Richard Stephens, Master of Coeur House
b. 1540 – d. 1605, aged 65 years
Margaret Audley, his first wife
b. 1551 – d. 1588, aged 37

Their children:
Richard Stephens b. 1570 – d. 1588, aged 18
Thomas Richards b. 1575 – d. 1588, aged 13
Sarah Stephens b. 1571 – d. 1626, aged 55
Abigail Stephens b. 1571 – d. 1627, aged 56
Hester Stephens b. 1580 – d. 1628, aged 48
Johannah Stephens b. 1583 – d. 1643, aged 60

Margaret St. Loe, second wife to Richard Stephens
b. 1548 – d. 1590, aged 42

Their sons:
Edward Stephens b. 1588 – d. 1588, aged 3 months
Nathaniel Stephens b. 1589 – d. 1660, aged 71

"From dust they came; to dust return'd.
May the Lord receive them in mercy."

The house stood above, alive with voices once more. Beneath, at last, all was still.

* * *

He watched them approach, their footsteps crunching on uneven gravel, and ran to greet them. It felt like ages since they had all been together.

"Thanks for coming. I know it's been a difficult time," Tom said, his voice a little nervous.

"Tom, it's great to see you," Daryll replied, his broad smile lighting up his face. He had missed his friend, though he understood. Elwyna had needed time. That day had changed them all.

"Tom," Elwyna said softly, holding onto Daryll's arm. Her voice was cautious.

Tom accepted her lingering distrust quietly, determined to earn her trust again.

"Come with me," he said, nodding toward the woods at the edge of the estate. They followed him through the gate and along the familiar winding path.

The caretaker's cottage stood ahead; not the old wooden frame she remembered, but a beautifully crafted brick home. Sunlight gleamed on its windows, and the garden brimmed with life. They walked between bushes of rosemary and rue, the familiar scents guiding them like old friends. Bees and butterflies flitted between blooms, the air warm with the hum of summer.

"It's beautiful," Elwyna sighed, her longing to stay growing with each step. Daryll felt it too and tightened his arm around her waist.

Something caught Daryll's eye, a stone slab set into the wall near the crevice.

'Anne, Wynn, Thomas, Davy – 1593,' the inscription read.

His heart swelled.

"They're remembered," he whispered.

Tom nodded, smiling.

"Come on, I want to show you inside."

His excitement was barely contained. He stepped forward toward the door.

"Are you sure we can go in?" Daryll asked, uncertainty flickering across his face.

Tom turned with an impish grin.

"I've spoken with the new owners. They're fine with it," he said, laughing as he knocked once, then turned the handle and pushed the door open.

Elwyna and Daryll exchanged puzzled glances and then stepped inside. The scent of fresh paint greeted them. Everything looked clean, bright and new.

A wooden table with four chairs stood in the centre of the kitchen. Two rocking chairs flanked the fireplace, recalling a time long gone.

"It's beautiful," Elwyna said, taking in the warm colours and gentle light. "It's like the old cottage... but not."

Daryll nodded. "Whoever the owners are, they've done a grand job."

Tom's face nearly split with joy. He reached into his pocket and pulled out a set of keys. A silver charm engraved with a crescent moon dangled from the ring. He held them out to Elwyna.

"It's yours... if you want it."

She froze, hardly daring to believe it.

"What do you mean?" Daryll asked, his brow furrowing.

"You can live here," Tom said simply.

"I don't understand." Daryll's confusion deepened.

"The owners want someone to look after it. I suggested you two. I know how happy you were here. It's your home."

Elwyna moved slowly through the cottage, her fingertips grazing the smooth wooden surfaces. A forgotten happiness bloomed in her chest.

"Is this real?" she whispered, eyes shining with tears.

Tom nodded. "It's yours."

She turned to Daryll. He nodded, his eyes full.

"Then yes," she laughed. "We'd love to."

Daryll swept her into his arms as Tom beamed.

"Welcome home."

They hugged, laughed, and stood there together - friends then, now, and always.

* * *

A group of visitors stood at the entrance to Coeur House, gravel crunching softly beneath their feet. It was a beautiful day. Birds filled the air with joyful song, their melodies rising in celebration before cascading down like a blessing over the gathering below. On the wide stone step stood a woman, her radiant smile casting a warm light over the expectant faces before her. She raised her hands to catch their attention. As the crowd hushed, she took a steadying breath.

"Hi, everyone. It's so lovely to see you all on this beautiful day. I'm Farran, and I have the honour of being the curator here at Coeur House and your guide for the day."

A ripple of applause passed through the group.

"This house is steeped in mystery, drama, and romance," she added with a wistful smile, memories brushing the edges of her thoughts, memories from another time, another life.

"Follow me."

She turned and led them inside, pausing at the base of the grand staircase. The scent of beeswax and age clung to the air, wrapping them in history. The house breathed with memory.

A man with silver-threaded hair and grey-green eyes passed through the foyer, carefully carrying a weathered pot filled with rust-coloured fragments. As he brushed past Farran, he reached for her hand and gave it a quiet squeeze. She laughed, light and effortless, a sound that lit his world.

"This is Tom Gester," she said, beaming. "The owner of this beautiful house and my wonderful husband."

Tom offered a wave, his eyes gleaming with contentment. Farran turned back to the guests and gestured up the staircase.

"And if you look to the top, you'll see a remarkable portrait. A family painting of the house's former owner from the late 1500s, Richard Stephens."

Gasps and murmurs of awe rippled through the group as they craned their necks.

Tom stepped closer beside her and murmured, "I hope he's found peace."

Farran squeezed his hand.

"I think he has," she whispered.

Their eyes met. He remembered the first time he saw her, those sorrowful eyes already calling him to follow. Now, the past and present would live side by side in peace.

They had made it.

Home.

The End

My journey now is at its end,
Time and love did help to mend,
This *jester's* heart, once dead and cold,
Until the fates brought tales untold.

Whispered spells in shadows cast
Healed the lonely, troubled past.
Memories torn, deeds unforgiven...
Yet when truth, love, and courage driven,

Hope and friendship brought me... *home.*

Fool's Thread

Prologue

My life began the moment the last Plantagenet's ended. The axeman's blow was faltering, clumsy, a shambles. Her death dragged on beneath a grey sky, torn from her by men of faith. A *martyr* in the making.

In the North, rebellion simmered. Men whispered treason behind stable doors and prayed to saints in secret. The old world was burning.

And me? I was born in blood and smoke, in the shadow of power undone. What am I, then? A symbol? A ghost of rebellion?

Or *fate's joke*, doomed to stir trouble until trouble ends me?

* * *

There, in a dirty Richmond street behind an old tanner's, amid the cries of traders hawking wares and the clang of bells tolling for a life cruelly taken, I entered this God-forsaken world. My Mother, widowed by the hangman's noose, screamed as the midwife scrambled, muttering and cursing the lateness of the hour.

"She was the last of the true," my Mother gasped, delirious on a straw-filled pallet in the corner of a room that stank of vinegar and blood. "What will become of us now?"

"None of that treasonous talk, Brenna," croaked the old woman, wrapped in sackcloth and soot. Her hands did not pause, fetching water, straightening invisible folds, clattering pewter bowls into place as though order might keep death from stepping through the door.

"They'll come for us too," my Mother whimpered. "We're not safe. No one is, not now."

A gust of wind howled through the broken window, as if it agreed.

"You hush now," the midwife snapped. "Bring that child forth before your tongue gets us all hanged."

And so I came, feet first, fists clenched. A birth fit for a thief or traitor. The last scream had not yet faded from Tower Green, and still the blood ran here. Hers. Mine. The old woman's rag soaked in it.

They say the axeman botched it. Took five strokes to finish her. Margaret Pole. Noble by name, stubborn to the end. That is how my story begins: one death above the law, one birth below it.

A martyr for a crown, and a bastard for a gutter.

* * *

Every thread tells a story. Discover the truth of Tom's life before Anne in *Fool's Threads*, coming soon.

The Coeur Legacy Series

The Coeur Legacy is a series of interwoven novels and novellas exploring memory, magic, and the weight of inheritance across time.

Follow the tales of Tom, Anne, Richard, Davy and Wynn as they weave their stories through time, uncovering the lives they lived before Coeur House and the shadows that shaped them.

From a jester's fatal vow to a girl erased by history; from spells hidden in herbs to secrets buried beneath Coeur House, and entwined in its very heart, each story follows those caught in the web of a legacy too powerful to die.

Bound by love and betrayal, shaped by silence and sacrifice, their lives are threaded through two eclipses, one in the age of witch hunts, one in the modern world, when the veil between past and present thins, and forgotten truths demand to be heard.

Each book can be read alone, but together they reveal a haunting, defiant tapestry of resilience, resistance, and the quiet magic of those who remember.

Acknowledgements

My heartfelt thanks go to my wonderful ARC readers, whose encouragement and insights meant so much in the final stages of this book.

Annabelle and DTF, your early enthusiasm reminded me why these stories matter.

And to my sister, Pauline Proctor, your thoughtful eye and patient editing helped shape these pages in ways I'll always be grateful for.

About the Author

Hope Bytheway is the pen name of **Lorraine Watson**, an English teacher, writer, and editor with a deep love for stories that weave together history, emotion, and quiet magic. She has spent over twenty years helping others find their voice through language, and now brings that same passion to her own fiction.

Wandering Strong is her debut novel, inspired by a fascination with forgotten voices, dual timelines, and the threads that connect past and present. When she is not writing or editing, she can be found playing the saxophone, singing, or sharing her home with four cats, one loyal dog, and far too many books (if that's even possible).

Her mother was given the name *Hope* after her father died a month before she was born on Christmas Day. *Bytheway* was her grandmother's maiden name, a quiet tribute to the women who shaped her, whose strength lives on in every story she tells.

You can connect with me on:

- http://jesterpublications.co.uk
- http://tiktok.com/@hope.bytheway.aut
- http://facebook.com/farran.293796
- https://www.youtube.com/channel/UC5rUGaGNEa8DspsNvqZ9Pew
- https://hopebytheway.my.canva.site/writer-author

Subscribe to my newsletter:

- https://substack.com/@musicandmirrors?utm_source=user-menu